*What's a bride-to-be to do when
she loses her heart to another...?*

Say Yes to the Marquess

"You have it wrong," he forced himself to say. "I don't dislike you."

"Oh, truly?" She turned to face him. "Look me in the eyes and tell me, honestly, just how eager you are to call me your sister-in-law."

Bloody hell.

Outside, the rain beat down like a rebuke. His blood thundered in his ears.

"You can't say it," she whispered. "Can you?"

"Honestly? No, I can't."

Hurt flickered over her features. He wanted to punch a hole straight through the wall.

"Well, then." She hugged herself. "Good. Now that we know where we stand with each other, we can stop pret—"

Damn him and his impulsive, reckless soul.

His hands were out before he could stop them. Reaching for her, pulling her close, turning her face to his. Skimming a touch over her soft, trembling lips.

And holding her still for his kiss.

By Tessa Dare

Tessa Dare

Say Yes to the Marquess

Castles Ever After

WITHDRAWN

AVON

An Imprint of HarperCollinsPublishers

This is a work of fiction. Names, characters, places, and incidents are products of the author's imagination or are used fictitiously and are not to be construed as real. Any resemblance to actual events, locales, organizations, or persons, living or dead, is entirely coincidental.

AVON BOOKS
An Imprint of HarperCollins*Publishers*
195 Broadway
New York, New York 10007

Copyright © 2015 by Eve Ortega
ISBN 978-0-06-224020-0
www.avonromance.com

First Avon Books mass market printing: January 2015

Avon Trademark Reg. U.S. Pat. Off. and in Other Countries, Marca Registrada, Hecho en U.S.A.
HarperCollins® is a registered trademark of HarperCollins Publishers.

Printed in the U.S.A.

10 9 8 7 6 5 4 3 2 1

For the big brown dog, in loving memory.
You've been such a good boy.

Acknowledgments

So many smart and talented people had a hand in making this book happen. I owe much gratitude to my brilliant editor, Tessa Woodward; my fantastic agent, Steve Axelrod; all the wonderful people at Avon Books/Harper-Collins, and copyeditor extraordinaire, Martha Trachtenberg.

Thank you to Courtney, Carey, Leigh, Bren, Bree, Susan, Laura, Karen, and all on The Unnamed Loop for your invaluable friendship, hugs, and support. I'm indebted to the following friends for sharing their experience and subject expertise: Brenna Aubrey, Jeri Smith-Ready, and Greg Nagel. Thank you to Diana and Carrie for the badger (bruiser) balm, and many thanks to Larimar for loaning her irreplaceable ring.

To my wonderful family, who put up with so much artistic angst and takeout—I love you.

And as always, thank you to my readers. I wish I could give you all some cake.

Chapter One

"Oh, Miss Whitmore. Just look at this horrid place."

As she alighted from the coach, Clio took in the narrow, cobbled passage between two rows of warehouses. "It looks like an alleyway, Anna."

"It smells of blood. Lord preserve us. We'll be *murdered*."

Clio bit back a smile. Her lady's maid was a marvel with curling tongs, but her capacity for morbid imagination was truly unmatched.

"We will not be murdered." After a moment's thought, she added, "At least, not today."

Miss Clio Whitmore had been raised by good parents, with the benefits of education and close attention to propriety, and she was engaged to marry England's most promising young diplomat. She was not the sort of foolhardy young woman to go skulking about dodgy alleyways at midnight with an un-loaded pistol in her pocket, in search of London's most infamous scoundrel.

No, that would not do.

When Clio struck out in search of London's most infamous scoundrel, she waited until midday. She entered the dodgy alleyway with a footman, her lady's maid, and a minimum of skulking. And she didn't carry any weapons at all.

Really, what could be the purpose? When the man you sought was a six-foot, sixteen-stone prizefighter, an unloaded pistol wouldn't be any help. The lethal weapons in the mix were his fists, and a girl could only hope they were on her side.

Rafe, please be on my side. Just this once.

She led the way down the dank, narrow alley, hiking her lace-edged hem and taking care that her half boots didn't catch on the uneven pavement.

Anna skipped from one to another of the cleaner cobblestones. "How does the second son of a marquess end up here?"

"On purpose. You may depend on it. Lord Rafe spurned good society years ago. He delights in anything brutish or coarse."

Inwardly, Clio wondered. The last time she'd seen Rafe Brandon, the man who was to be her brother-in-law, he'd been nursing grave wounds. Not only the physical aftermath of the worst—more aptly, the *only*—defeat of his prizefighting career, but the blow of his father's sudden death.

He'd looked low. Very low. But not so low as *this*.

"Here we are." She rapped on the door and lifted her voice. "Lord Rafe? Are you there? It's Miss . . ."

She bit off the name. Perhaps it wasn't wise to announce herself in a place like this. "I need only a few minutes of your time."

That, and his signature. She clutched the sheaf of papers in her hand.

There was no answer.

"He's not at home," Anna said. "Please, Miss Whitmore. We need to be on our way if we're to reach Twill Castle by nightfall."

"Not just yet."

Clio leaned close to the door. She heard sounds coming from within. The screech of chair legs across a floor. The occasional hollow thud.

Oh, he was in there. And he was ignoring her.

Clio was painfully accustomed to being ignored. Her engagement had given her years of practice.

When she was seventeen, Lord Piers Brandon, the handsome, dashing heir to the Marquess of Granville, had obeyed the wishes of their families and proposed marriage. He'd gone on bended knee in the Whitmore drawing room, sliding a gold-and-ruby ring on her third finger. To Clio, it had felt like a dream.

A dream with one snag. Piers had a new but promising career in foreign diplomacy, and Clio was rather young to assume the duties of managing a household. They had all the time in the world, he pointed out. She didn't mind a long engagement, did she?

"Of course not," she'd said.

Looking back, perhaps she should have given a different answer. Such as, "Define 'long.' "

Eight years—and no weddings—later, Clio was still waiting.

By now, her situation was a public joke. The scandal sheets called her "Miss Wait-More." The gossip trailed her everywhere. Just what could be keeping his lordship from England and the altar, they all wondered? Was it ambition, distraction . . . devotion to his duty?

Or devotion to a foreign mistress, perhaps?

No one could say. Least of all Clio herself. Oh, she tried to laugh away the rumors and smile at the jokes, but inside . . .

Inside, she was hurting. And utterly alone.

Well, that all ended today. Starting this moment, she was Miss Wait-No-Longer.

The brass door handle turned in her gloved grip, and the door swung open.

"Stay here," she told the servants.

"But Miss Whitmore, it isn't—"

"I will be fine. Yes, his reputation is scandalous, but we were friends in our childhood. I spent summers at his family home, and I'm engaged to marry his brother."

"Even so, Miss Whitmore . . . We should have a signal."

"A signal?"

"A word to shout if you're in distress. Like 'Tangiers,' or . . . or perhaps 'muscadine.'"

Clio gave her an amused look. "Is something wrong with the word 'help'?"

"I . . . well, I suppose not."

"Very well." She smiled, unable to bear Anna's look of disappointment. "'Muscadine' it is."

She passed through the door, walked down a dim corridor, and emerged into a soaring, empty space. What she found made her blood turn cold.

Oh, muscadine.

She blinked and forced herself to look again. Perhaps it wasn't him.

But there was no mistaking his profile. That rugged slope of a nose healed from multiple breaks. Add in the thick, dark hair, the strong jaw, the impressive breadth of his shoulders . . . That was Lord Rafe Brandon himself, perched on a crossbeam some dozen feet above the bricked floor. He had a rope in his hands, and he was knotting it securely to the beam. At the end of the rope was a loop.

A noose.

Apparently, his spirits hadn't fallen as low as she'd feared.

They'd sunk lower.

And she'd arrived not a moment too soon.

Her heartbeat went into a panicked stutter, *whomp-whomp-whomp*-ing in her chest. "My lord, don't. Don't do this."

He glanced up. "Miss Whitmore?"

"Yes. Yes, it's me." She advanced in small steps, lifting an open palm in a gesture of peace. "It's Miss Whitmore. It's Clio. I know we've had our differences. I'm not sure if we have anything *but* differences. But I'm here for you. And I beg of you, please reconsider."

"Reconsider." He gave her a hard look. "You mean to stop me from . . ."

"Yes. Don't do something you'll regret. You have so much to live for."

He paused. "I've no wife, no children. Both my parents are dead. My brother and I haven't been on speaking terms for nearly a decade."

"But you have friends, surely. And many fine qualities."

"What would those be?"

Drat. Clio should have known that was coming. She mentally ran through everything she knew of his life in recent years. Most of it came from the newspapers, and nearly all of it was horrid. Rafe Brandon had earned a reputation for being ruthless in a boxing match and shameless everywhere else. His endurance in the bedroom was almost as legendary as his quickness in the ring. They called him the Devil's Own.

"Strength," Clio offered. "That's a fine quality."

He cinched a knot tight. "Oxen are strong. Doesn't save them from slaughter when they can't pull anymore."

"Don't speak that way. Perhaps you're no longer the champion, but that doesn't mean you're worthless." Her mind groped for something, anything else. "I recall that you gave some of your winnings to a war widows' fund. Isn't that true?"

"Probably."

"Well, then. There's that. Charity is the best of virtues."

He finished tying off his knot and pulled on it to test the strength. "It's no use. A stray good deed or two could never balance my sins. What of all those women I've seduced?"

"I . . ." Oh, heavens. How did one speak of such things aloud? "I . . . I'm sure a few of them enjoyed it."

At that, he laughed. It was a dry, low chuckle—but a laugh, nonetheless.

Laughter was a good sign, wasn't it? Laughing

men didn't hang themselves. It shouldn't bother Clio that he was laughing at *her*.

"I assure you, Miss Whitmore. They all enjoyed it."

He let the length of rope dangle from the beam, then made his way down it, hand over hand, until he dropped directly before her. He was barefoot, dressed in gray trousers and an open-necked linen shirt. His green eyes dared her to break with propriety in a dozen unthinkable ways.

And that smug quirk of his lips?

It said he already knew she wouldn't.

"Breathe," he told her. "You haven't walked in on a tragedy."

She took his suggestion. Air flooded her lungs, and relief filled her everywhere else. "But what was I to think? You up there on the beam, the rope, the noose . . ." She gestured at the evidence. "What else could you be doing?"

Wordlessly, he walked to the edge of the room. There, he retrieved a straw-stuffed canvas bag with a hook affixed at the top. He walked back and hung the sack from the loop of rope, sliding the noose to make it tight.

"It's called training." He gave the bag a single, demonstrative punch. "See?"

She saw. And now she felt unbearably foolish. In their youth, Rafe had always teased her, but of all the mischief he'd pulled over the years . . .

"Sorry to ruin your fun," he said.

"My fun?"

"It's a popular enough female pastime. Trying to save me from myself." He threw her a knowing look as he sauntered past.

Clio blushed in response. But that was the wrong word. A "blush" was a whisper of color, and right now her cheeks must be screaming. Just ridiculously pink, like a flamingo or something.

Wretched, teasing man.

Once, when Clio had been a small girl, she'd seen a fistfight in the local village. A man buying hazels challenged a merchant over the honesty of his scales. The two argued, shouted . . . a scuffle broke out. She'd never forgotten the way the atmosphere changed in an instant. Everyone in the vicinity felt it. The air prickled with danger.

She'd never witnessed another bout of fisticuffs. But she felt the same prickle in the air whenever Rafe Brandon was near. He seemed to carry things with him, the way other men carried portmanteaux or walking sticks. Things like intensity. Brute power, held in check—but only just. That sense of danger mingled with anticipation. And the promise that at any moment, the rules that governed society could be rendered meaningless.

Were his rakish exploits any mystery? Really, the corsets must unlace themselves.

"I thought you'd given up prizefighting," she said.

"Everyone thinks I've given up prizefighting. Which is what will make my return to the sport so very exciting. And lucrative."

That followed a strange sort of logic, she supposed.

"Now explain yourself." He crossed his arms. His large, massive, all-the-words-for-big arms. "What the devil are you doing? You should know better than to come to a neighborhood like this alone."

"I do know better, and I didn't come alone. I have

two servants waiting outside." On a stupid impulse, she added, "And we have a signal."

One dark eyebrow lifted. "A signal."

"Yes. A signal." She forged on before he could inquire further. "I would not have needed to come here at all if you'd left some other way of reaching you. I tried calling at the Harrington."

"I no longer have rooms at the Harrington."

"So they informed me. They gave this as your forwarding address." She followed him toward what seemed to be the living quarters. "Do you truly *live* here?"

"When I'm training, I do. No distractions."

Clio looked around. She hadn't been in many bachelor apartments, but she'd always imagined them to be cluttered and smelling of unwashed things—dishes, linens, bodies.

Lord Rafe's warehouse didn't smell of anything unpleasant. Just sawdust, coffee, and the faint aroma of . . . oil of wintergreen, perhaps? But the place was spartan in its furnishings. In one corner, she glimpsed a simple cot, a cupboard and a few shelves, and a small table with two stools.

He removed two tumblers from the cupboard and placed them on the table. Into one, he poured a few inches of sherry. Into the other, he emptied the remaining contents of a coffeepot, added a touch of pungent syrup from a mysterious brown bottle, then into it all he cracked three raw eggs.

She watched with queasy fascination as he stirred the slimy mess with a fork. "Surely you're not going to—"

"Drink that?" He lifted the tumbler, drained it one long swallow, and pounded the glass to the tabletop. "Three times a day."

"Oh."

He pushed the sherry toward her. "That's yours. You look like you could use it."

Clio stared at the glass as waves of nausea pitched her stomach to and fro. "Thank you."

"It's the best I can do. As you can see, I'm not set up to receive social calls."

"I won't take much of your time, I promise. I only stopped by to—"

"Extend a wedding invitation. I'll send my regrets."

"What? No. I mean . . . I gather you've heard that Lord Granville is finally returning from Vienna."

"I heard. And Piers has given you permission to plan the most lavish wedding imaginable. I signed off on the accounts myself."

"Yes, well. About those signatures . . ." Clio twisted the papers rolled in her hand.

He walked away from the table. "This will have to be quick. I can't be wasting time on chatter."

He stopped beneath a bar hanging parallel to the floor some three feet over his head. In a burst of quickness, he jumped to grab it. Then he began to lift himself by means of flexing his arms.

Again, then again.

"Go on," he said, clearing the bar with his chin for the fourth time. "I can talk while I do this."

Perhaps *he* could, but Clio was finding it difficult. She wasn't accustomed to carrying on a conversation with a barely dressed man engaged in such . . . muscular exercise. Awareness hummed in her veins.

She picked up the tumbler of sherry and took a cautious swallow.

It helped.

"I wouldn't expect you to have heard, but my Uncle Humphrey died a few months ago." She waved off the condolences before he could offer them. "It wasn't a shock. He was very old. But the dear old thing left me a bequest in his will. A castle."

"A castle?" He grunted as he cleared the bar again. Then he paused there, muscles tensed with effort. "Some crumbling pile on the moors with a mountain of unpaid taxes, I suspect."

"No, actually. It's situated in Kent and quite lovely. It was one of his personal properties. He was the Earl of Lynforth, if you recall."

Good heavens, she was babbling. *Pull yourself together, Clio.*

"Ideal for a wedding, then." His voice tightened with exertion.

"I suppose it could be. For someone. But I'm on my way there today, and I stopped by to—"

"Inform me." *Lift.*

"Yes, and also—"

"To ask for money." *Lift.* "I just told you, you're free to spend as much on the wedding as you wish. Send the bills to my brother's men of business."

Clio squeezed her eyes shut, then opened them. "Lord Rafe, please. Would you kindly stop—"

"Finishing your sentences?"

She suppressed a little growl.

He paused midlift. "Don't try to tell me I got that one wrong."

She couldn't tell him that. Not honestly. That was the most galling part.

He went on, "As I said . . . I'm training." Each phrase was punctuated by another lift. "It's what prizefighters do. We concentrate." *Lift*. "Anticipate." *Lift*. "React. If it bothers you, try being less predictable."

"I'm calling it off," she blurted out. "The wedding, the engagement. Everything. I'm calling it all off."

He dropped to the floor.

The air prickled around them.

And his dark expression told Clio, in no uncertain terms, he hadn't predicted *that*.

Rafe stared at her.

This was *not* how his month was supposed to be going. He'd holed himself away in this storehouse to train for his comeback. When he met Jack Dubose for the second time, it would be the biggest bout of his life and the largest purse ever offered in English history. To prepare, he needed intensive physical conditioning, undisturbed sleep, nourishing food . . .

And absolutely no distractions.

Then who should walk through the door? None other than Miss Clio Whitmore, his most persistent and personal distraction. Of course.

He'd always been at odds with her, ever since they were children. He'd been an impulsive, rough-mannered devil. And she'd been the picture of an English rose, with her fair hair, blue eyes, and delicate complexion. Genteel and hospitable and well-mannered, too.

Just so irritatingly *sweet*.

In sum, Clio Whitmore was the embodiment of polite society. Everything Rafe had spurned at the age of twenty-one. Everything he'd vowed to dismantle.

And that had to be what made it so damned tempting to dismantle her.

Whenever Clio was near, he couldn't resist shocking her proper sensibilities with a flex or two of brute strength. He liked to devil her until he turned her cheeks some new, exotic shade of pink. And he'd wondered, many times, how she'd look with that slick knot of golden hair undone, tangled from lovemaking and damp with sweat.

She was his brother's intended. It was wrong to think of her that way. But outside a boxing ring, Rafe had never done much of anything right.

He pulled his gaze from the frothy white fichu edging her neckline. "I think I misheard you."

"Oh, I'm certain you heard me correctly. I have the papers right here." She unrolled a sheaf of papers in her gloved hand. "My solicitors drew them up. Would you like me to summarize?"

Annoyed, he reached for the papers. "I can read."
Somewhat.

Like all the legal documents shoved in front of him since the old marquess's death, the papers were written in hen scratches so tight and close as to be indecipherable. Just glancing at it gave him a headache.

But that one glance told him enough.

This was serious.

"These aren't valid," he said. "Piers would have to sign them first."

"Yes, well. There is someone with the power to sign for Piers in his absence." Her blue gaze met his.
No.

Rafe couldn't believe this. "That's why you're here. You want me to sign this?"

"Yes."

"Not going to happen." He thrust the papers back

at her, then walked over to the punching bag and gave it a booming right cross. "Piers is on his way home from Vienna. And you are meant to be planning the wedding as we speak."

"Exactly why I hoped to have these papers signed before he arrives. It seems the best way. I'd hate to make an unpleasant scene, and . . ."

"And unpleasant scenes are my specialty."

She shrugged. "Quite."

Rafe lowered his head and threw a barrage of jabs at the punching bag. This time, he wasn't putting on a display. His brain worked better when his body was in motion. Fighting brought him to his sharpest focus, and he needed that now.

Why the hell would Clio want to break this engagement? She was a society debutante, raised for advantageous marriage the way thoroughbred horses were bred to race. A lavish wedding to a wealthy, handsome marquess should be her fondest dream.

"You won't find a better prospect," he said.

"I know."

"And you must *want* to get married. What else could you hope to do with your life?"

She laughed into her sherry. "What else, indeed. It's not as though we ladies are allowed to have interests or pursuits of our own."

"Exactly. Unless . . ." He held his punch. "Unless there's someone else."

She was quiet for a moment. "There's no one else."

"Then it's the anticipation getting to you. Just a case of cold feet."

"It's not that I'm a nervous bride, either. I simply

don't wish to marry a man who doesn't want to marry me."

"Why would you think he doesn't want to marry you?" He threw a right hook at the bag, then followed it with a left.

"Because I've looked at the *calendar*. Eight years have passed since he proposed. If you truly wanted a woman, would you wait that long to make her your own?"

He let his fists fall to his sides and turned to her, breathing hard. His lungs filled with the scent of violets. Damn, she even *smelled* sweet.

"No," he said. "*I* wouldn't."

"I didn't think so."

"But," he continued, "I'm an impulsive bastard. This is about Piers. He's the loyal, honorable son."

Her eyebrow made the slightest quirk. "If you believe the scandal sheets, he has a mistress and four children tucked away somewhere."

"I don't read the scandal sheets."

"Perhaps you should. You're often in them."

He didn't doubt it. Rafe knew the vile things that were said about him, and he took every opportunity to encourage the gossip. Reputation didn't win fights, but it drew crowds and lined pockets.

"It's not as though Piers hasn't had *reasons* for delaying. He's an important man." Rafe fought to keep a straight face. Listen to him, singing his brother's praises. That didn't happen often. It didn't happen ever. "There was that post in India. Then the one in Antigua. He came home between assignments, but then there was some delay."

She looked down. "I was ill."

"Right. Then there was a war to settle, and another after that. Now that all these treaties in Vienna are hammered out, he's on his way home."

"It's not that I begrudge his sense of duty," she said. "Nor how essential he's made himself to the Crown. But it's become abundantly clear that I'm not essential to *him*."

Rafe rubbed his face with both hands and growled into them.

"My solicitors told me I'd have a case for a breach of promise suit. But I didn't want to embarrass him. Now that I have Twill Castle, I don't require the security of marriage. A quiet dissolution is best for all concerned."

"No. It's not best. Not at all."

Not best for Piers, not best for Clio.

And definitely not best for Rafe.

He'd put his prizefighting career on hold after his father's death. He didn't have a choice. With Piers out of the country, Rafe found himself, however unwillingly, at the helm of the Granville fortune.

He belonged in a boxing ring, not an office. He knew it, and so did the solicitors and stewards, who barely managed to veil their disdain. They came armed with folios and ledgers and a dozen matters for his attention, and before Rafe sorted his way through one issue, they were on to the next. Each meeting left him restless and simmering with resentment—as though he'd been sent down from Eton all over again.

Rafe could all but hear his father twisting in his grave, spitting worms and grinding out those same, familiar words.

No son of mine will remain an uneducated brute. No son of mine will disgrace this family's legacy.

Rafe had always been a disappointment. He'd never been the son his father wanted. But he'd made his own life, earned his own title—not "lord," but "champion." As soon as Piers returned to England and married, he would be free to fight again and get that title back.

If Clio called off the wedding, however . . . ?

His globe-wandering brother might turn around and disappear for another eight years.

"Piers has likely been hoping for this outcome all along," Clio said. "He wanted out of the engagement, but his honor wouldn't permit him to ask. When he learns the dissolution is already done, I expect he'll be relieved."

"Piers will *not* be relieved. And I'm not going to let you do this."

"I don't wish to quarrel." She rolled the papers and tapped the cylinder on its edge. "You have my apologies for the intrusion. I'll take my leave now. And I'll bring these papers with me to Kent. If you change your mind about signing them, I'll be at Twill Castle. It's near the village of Charingwood."

"I won't sign. And mark my words, you won't ask him to sign it, either. When he comes back, you'll know at once that the gossip was baseless. You'll be reminded of the reasons why you consented to be his bride in the first place. And you *will* marry him."

"No. I won't."

"Think of it. You'll be a marchioness."

"No," she said. "I truly *won't.*"

Her quiet, solemn tone unnerved him more than

he cared to admit. Hell, his palms were even growing damp. It was as though he could feel his career—
everything he'd worked for, and the only thing that
made his life worth a damn—slipping from his grasp.

She moved to leave, and he lunged to catch her by
the arm. "Clio, wait."

"He doesn't *want* me." Her voice broke. "Can't
you understand that? Everyone knows. It took me
too many years to see the truth. But I'm done waiting. He doesn't want me, and I no longer want him.
I have to protect my heart."

Damn it all. So that's what this was. He should
have guessed. The reason for her sudden reluctance
was as plain as the lion on the Granville crest.

Rafe was the rebel of the family, but Piers had
been chipped straight from their father's stone. Up-
right, proud, unyielding. And most of all, unwilling
to show emotion.

Rafe didn't have a damned thing in common
with a society debutante, but he knew that it hurt to
feel unwanted by the Marquess of Granville. He'd
spent his own youth starved for the slightest sign of
his father's affection or approval—and he'd loathed
himself when those signs never came.

"Piers wants you." He silenced her objection, rubbing his thumb up and down her arm. God, she was
soft there. "He *will*. Make those wedding plans, Clio.
Because when he sees you again for the first time, it's
going to come as a blow to the ribs, that wanting. He's
going to want to see you in that grand, lacy gown,
with little blossoms strewn in your hair. He's going
to want to watch you walk down that aisle, feeling
his chest swell closer to bursting from pride with

every step you take. And most of all, he'll want to stand before God, your friends and family, and all of London society—just to tell them you're his. His, and no one else's."

She didn't respond.

"You're going to want that, too." He released her arm with a squeeze, then chucked her under the chin. "Mark my words. I'll see you married to my brother within the month—even if I have to plan the damn wedding myself."

"What?" She shook herself. "You, plan the wedding?"

A little smile played about her lips as she looked to the exposed ceiling rafters, the barren brick walls, the rough-hewn furniture . . . then back to him. The most crude, inelegant thing in the room.

"Now I'm almost sorry it's not going to happen," she said, pulling away. "Because *that* would be amusing."

Chapter Two

"Which room do you think Daphne and Sir Teddy will prefer?"

Clio stood in the corridor, at the center point between two doorways. She smoothed fretful hands over her new emerald green silk.

"Should we put them in the Blue Room, with the windows looking over the park? Or should I give them the larger chamber, even if it faces the shaded side of the property?"

Anna fussed and clucked, pulling loose one last curling paper from Clio's hair. "Miss Whitmore, if you want my opinion, I think you shouldn't fret over it. Whichever one you choose, she's certain to find fault."

Clio sighed. It was true. If there was a door to shut and a candle to read by, Phoebe was content. But Daphne took after their mother—impossible to impress.

"Let's put them in this one," she said, crossing into the first bedchamber. "It truly is the best."

The Blue Room boasted four soaring windows and an expansive view of Twill's lovely gardens. Plump hedges like sugarplums. Rosebushes in endless varieties. Arbors lush with flowering vines. And beyond it all, the rolling expanse of Kent in late summertime. The fields were the same brilliant jade as her new frock, and the air smelled of blossoms and crushed grass—as though the sun were a magnet hung in the sky, extracting life from the earth. Drawing out everything green and fresh.

If anything could impress her sister, surely it would be this room. This view.

This *marvelous* castle. Which was, thanks to some whim of her uncle's, now Clio's.

Twill Castle was her chance at . . . well, at everything. Independence. Freedom. Security. A future that would have been hers already if only Rafe had cooperated.

She should have known better than to ask. Rafe Brandon simply didn't cooperate, in the same way lions didn't cuddle with zebras. It wasn't in his nature. Every explosive, muscled inch of him was formed for rebellion and defiance . . . interspersed with heavy lifting.

A thin plume of white in the distance caught her eye. Two coaches, approaching on the gravel drive.

"They're here!" she called out. "Oh, dear. They're here."

She rushed down the corridor toward the front stairs, pausing to peer into each room on her way.

Good. Good. Perfect.

Not perfect.

Reeling to a stop on her way down the grand staircase, Clio paused to nudge a hanging portrait square. Then she took the remaining steps at the fastest clip she dared, hurrying across the entrance hall to the open front door.

Two carriages rolled to a halt in the drive.

Servants began piling out of the second coach, unloading valises and trunks. A footman hastened to open the door of the family carriage.

Daphne emerged first, dressed in a lavender traveling habit and a spencer with matching piping—both the height of this summer's fashion.

Clio moved forward, arms outstretched. "Daphne, dear. How was your journ—"

Daphne shot a meaningful look at the servants. "Really, Clio. Don't be common. I have a title now."

After nearly a year of marriage, Daphne was still . . . Daphne.

Thanks to all the effort their mother had invested in Clio's education and breeding, Mama had been too distracted to mold her second daughter into anything but a fashion-mad, rake-chasing chit. It had been a sort of relief when Daphne eloped with Sir Teddy Cambourne last year, only two months after her debut. He was a shallow, preening sort of gentleman, but at least he had an income and a baronetcy. Her sister could have done much worse.

"Lady Cambourne." Clio made a formal curtsy. "Welcome to Twill Castle. I'm so delighted you and Sir Teddy have come."

"Hullo, dumpling." Her brother-in-law gave her a familiar nudge on the arm.

"But of course we would come," Daphne said. "We couldn't let you stay here all alone while you wait for Lord Granville's return. And once he does return, we'll have a wedding to plan."

Fortunately, their youngest sister emerged from the carriage at that moment—saving Clio from inventing a reply.

"Phoebe, darling. It's so good to see you."

Clio wanted to catch the girl in a hug, but Phoebe didn't like hugs. Already, she had a thick book positioned as a shield.

"You've grown so tall this summer," she said instead. "And so pretty."

At sixteen, Phoebe was willowy and dark-haired, with soft features and bold blue eyes. Well on her way to becoming a beauty. Based on looks alone, she would be a grand success in her first season. But there was something . . . *different* . . . about Phoebe. There always had been. It seemed as though there was so much happening within her own remarkable mind, she struggled to connect with the people around her.

"We would have been here hours ago if not for the dreadful crush at Charing Cross," Teddy said. "And then two hours to cross the dashed bridge. Two *hours*."

"I thought the smell would make me sick," Daphne said.

Phoebe consulted her pocket watch. "We misjudged the time of departure. If we'd left twenty minutes earlier, we would have arrived fifty minutes ago."

"I'm just happy you're here now," Clio said, leading the way toward the arched entrance. "Please do come in, all of you."

Daphne held her back. "I come first, you know. Perhaps you will be a marchioness within the month, and perhaps I am your younger sister. But since I am married and a lady, I take precedence. For a least a few more weeks."

Clio stepped aside. "Yes, of course."

The gawping mouth of Twill Castle swallowed them in, and an awed hush seized their tongues.

Even four hundred years ago, stonemasons knew how to build to impress. The castle's entrance hall soared the full height of the building. A grand staircase wrapped around the space, drawing the eye upward. And then upward yet some more. Gilt-framed paintings and portraits—not small ones—climbed every inch of available wall, stacking four or five high in places.

After several moments, Teddy whistled low.

"It is nice, isn't it?" Daphne said. "Quite grand. Only I think it would be better if it weren't so . . . so old."

"It's a castle," Phoebe said. "How can it not be old?"

Daphne pinched Clio's arm in a gesture that seemed half affection, half spite. "But a home is a reflection of its mistress. You shouldn't let the place *show* that it's getting on in age. For instance, you could cover all these ugly stone walls with new paneling. Or French toile. And then we'll drape some fresh silk on *you*."

Her sister swept Clio with a look that made her new frock feel frowsy and tattered. Then she clucked her tongue in a frighteningly accurate impression of Mama.

"Not to worry," she said, patting Clio's shoulders. "We do have a few weeks yet to improve. Isn't that right, Teddy?"

"Oh, yes," he agreed. "We'll make certain his lordship doesn't bolt again."

Clio smiled and turned away. Partly because "smile and look elsewhere" was the only way to cope with her brother-in-law, but mostly because her attention was drawn toward the gravel drive.

A lone rider approached on a dark horse, churning up great clouds of dust as he thundered down the lane.

"Did someone else come from London with you?"

"No one," Teddy said.

"Could that . . ." Daphne joined her in the arched entryway and squinted. "Oh, no. Could that be Rafe Brandon?"

Yes.

That could *only* be Rafe Brandon.

He'd always been a magnificent rider. They seemed to have a sort of animal understanding, he and horses. A communion of beastly natures.

As if to demonstrate, he brought his mount to a halt in the circular drive without any shouting or hauling on the reins, but merely using a firm nudge of his knee to steer the beast into a tight circle.

With a calming word to the horse, Rafe dismounted in one smooth motion. Massive boots punched the ground. His riding breeches were buckskin. All men's riding breeches were buckskin. But she would wager anything that *this* buckskin was stretched over *this* man's thighs more tightly than it had stretched over the original buck.

Billowing greatcoat. Black riding gloves. No hat. Just waves of dark, heavy hair. A gust of wind gave it a rakish tousle.

He was sin in human form. No wonder they called him the Devil's Own. Lucifer probably paid him to advertise.

"Good heavens," Daphne said. "Do you think he *tries* at that?"

Clio was glad to know it wasn't only her. "I can't imagine why he'd try for our benefit. I think it's just how he is."

"Surely you weren't expecting him."

"No." But perhaps she should have been.

"Oh, no. It looks as though he means to stay."

As the dust settled, they could see that a coach had followed Rafe down the drive. The castle's stables would be full to overflowing tonight.

"Can't you make him go away?" Daphne asked. "He's so brutish and common."

"He's still the son of a marquess."

"You know what I mean. He doesn't behave like one anymore. If he ever did."

"Yes, well. Every family has its idiosyncrasies." Clio patted her sister on the shoulder. "I'll go greet him. Anna and the housekeeper will show you and Phoebe to your chambers, so you can settle in."

As Clio went out to greet him, Rafe's silhouette grew larger and larger in her vision. And she felt herself growing pinker in response.

He nodded in greeting.

"This is a surprise," she said. "And I see you've brought friends."

A man alighted from the carriage—a slender fellow who wore a dark greatcoat and the sort of genial, unruffled manner one would need to possess if one were friends with Rafe. And from the coach's interior, he lifted the squattest, oldest, ugliest bulldog Clio had ever seen. Goodness. The poor, aged thing. Even its wrinkles had wrinkles.

Once placed on the ground, the dog promptly made a puddle in the drive.

"That's Ellingworth," Rafe said, removing his riding gloves.

Clio curtsied. "Good day, Mr. Ellingworth."

Rafe shook his head. "Ellingworth is the dog."

"You have a dog?"

"No. Piers has a dog." He looked at her as though she should know this.

But she didn't know this. How curious. Clio couldn't recall Piers ever mentioning a dog. Not aside from the hunting hounds his groundskeeper kept at Oakhaven.

"Some souvenir from his Oxford days," Rafe explained. "There's a story behind it. A mascot or a prank . . . maybe both. Anyhow, the dog's been living with me. He's fourteen years old. He requires a special diet and round-the-clock care. I had the veterinarian write it all out."

He reached into his pocket and handed Clio some notes.

Three full pages of them.

"Well," she said. "Now that I know Ellingworth is the dog, might I be introduced to your friend?"

"This is Bru—"

"Bruno Aberforth Montague," the man interrupted. "Esquire." He bowed over Clio's hand and brought it to his lips. "At your service."

"Charmed, I'm sure."

In reality, she wasn't entirely sure. Not about this Mr. Montague, and not about Rafe.

While Mr. Montague put the dog on a lead and walked him to the grassy edge of the drive, she went after some answers. "Dare I hope you've merely dropped by to sign the papers?"

"Absolutely not. It's like we discussed. I'm here to plan the wedding."

She froze. "Oh, no."

"Oh, yes."

Don't panic, she told herself. *Not yet.*

"I thought you were in training. No distractions."

"I can train here in Kent. The country air is beneficial for the constitution. And you can keep the distractions to a minimum by cooperating with the wedding plans. Piers wants you to have everything you ever dreamed of on the grand day."

"So I'm to believe this is Piers's idea?"

He shrugged. "It might as well have been. Until he returns, I have the full weight of his fortune and title at my disposal."

Now, she told herself. *Panic now.*

"Rafe, I can't play your little game. Not this week. My sisters and brother-in-law just arrived."

"Excellent. That's three wedding guests we won't need to invite."

She rolled the papers in her hands. "You know very well there won't be any wedding."

He glanced at the castle. "And you've told your family this news?"

"No," she was forced to admit. "Not yet."

"Ah. So you're not truly decided."

"I *am* truly decided. And you are truly vexing. Rolling in like a storm cloud on your black horse, all dark and dramatic and unexpected. Demanding to plan weddings and bringing me lists."

"I'm all kinds of trouble, and you know it. But I know you, too."

Her breath caught. Then she reminded herself that what sounded like flirting was often just male presumption. "You don't know me nearly as well as you think you do, Rafe Brandon."

"I know this much. You won't turn me away."

* * *

Rafe watched her carefully.

It wasn't any hardship, to watch her carefully. But he had extra reason today.

Clio might not have made her final decision on marriage, but it was clear she didn't want another pair of houseguests right now.

Another trio of houseguests, if one counted Ellingworth.

He took the lead from Bruiser and crouched beside the dog. He was so old, he was completely deaf, but Clio didn't know that.

"Not to worry, Ellingworth." He scratched the dog behind the ear. "Miss Whitmore is a model of etiquette and generosity. She wouldn't turn an old, defenseless dog out into the cold." He slid a glance at Clio. "Now would she?"

"Hmmph. I thought champions are supposed to fight fair."

"We're not in a boxing ring. Not that I can see." After a moment's thought, he decided to take a chance. "Is that a new frock?"

"I . . ." She crossed her arms, then uncrossed them. "I don't see that it matters."

Oh, it mattered. He knew these things mattered.

Rafe might not know a damn thing about planning weddings, but he knew a thing or two—or twelve—about women.

This was all Clio needed. A bit of attention. Appreciation. She'd been left waiting for so many years, she was feeling unwanted. Well, that was bollocks. Just look at her. Any man who didn't want this woman would be a damned fool.

Piers wasn't a fool.

Unfortunately, neither was Rafe.

"The color suits you," he said.

And it did. The green played well with the gold of her hair, and the silk fit her generous curves like a dream. The kind of dream he shouldn't be having.

He rose to his feet, letting his gaze sweep her one last time, from toes to crown.

By the time their eyes met, the flush on her cheeks had deepened to a ripe-berry hue. He smiled a little. Clio Whitmore's complexion had more shades of pink than a draper's warehouse. Every time Rafe thought he'd seen them all, he managed to tease out one more.

Just imagine teasing her in bed.

No, you idiot. Don't. Don't imagine it.

But as usual, his thoughts were three paces ahead of his judgment. The image erupted in his mind's eye, as unbidden as it was vivid. Clio, breathless. Naked. Under him. Stripped of all her good manners and inhibitions. Begging him to learn her every secret shade of pink.

Rafe blinked hard. Then he took that mental image and filed it away under Pleasant-Sounding Impossibilities. Right between "flying carriage" and "beer fountain."

He looked nowhere but her eyes. "We'll send in our things, then."

"I haven't said yes."

"You haven't said no."

And she wouldn't. They both knew it. No matter how much she disliked Rafe, no matter how much she wanted him gone . . . Her conscience wouldn't let her turn him out.

Her little sigh of surrender stirred him more than

it ought. "I'll have the maids prepare two more rooms."

He nodded. "We'll be in once I've put up my gelding."

"We have grooms to do that," she said. "I was fortunate that all my uncle's housestaff stayed on."

"I always put up my own horse."

Rafe walked his gelding toward the carriage house for a good brushing down. Whenever he came in from a hard ride—or a hard run, a hard bout—he needed a task like this to calm him. All that energy didn't just dissipate into the air.

And tonight, he needed a private word with a certain someone. A certain someone who'd just up and declared that his name was *Montague.*

"What the devil was all that about?" he asked, as soon as Clio was out of earshot. "Who's this Montague person? We agreed you'd act as my valet."

"Well, that was before I saw this place! Cor, look at it."

"I've looked at it."

The castle was impressive, Rafe had to admit. But he'd seen finer. He'd been raised in finer.

"I want a proper room in that thing," Bruiser said, gesturing at the stone edifice. "No, I want my own tower. I certainly don't want to be your valet. Stuck below stairs, eating my meals in the servants' hall with the housemaids. Not that I can't appreciate a fresh-faced housemaid on occasion. Or, for that matter, a well-turned footman."

That was Bruiser. He'd tup anything. "How egalitarian of you, Mr. Bruno Aberforth Montague."

"Esquire. Don't forget the esquire."

Oh, Rafe was trying very hard to forget the esquire. "Miss Whitmore's sister is here. That's Lady Cambourne. Along with her husband, Sir Teddy Cambourne."

"So?" Bruiser said. "I know you try hard to forget it, but you're Lord Rafe Brandon. I have no problem speaking with you."

"That's different. I don't answer to that title anymore. I walked away from all this years ago."

"And now you're walking back. How difficult can it be?"

More difficult than you could imagine.

Hell, Rafe was worried about feeling like an imposter, and he'd been raised on these grand estates.

"Listen," he said. "You're the son of a washerwoman and a tavernkeeper, who makes his living organizing illegal prizefights. And you've just inserted yourself with a class of people so far above your usual world they might as well be wearing clouds. Just how do you plan to pull this off?"

"Relax. You know me, I get on with everyone. And I have a new hat."

Rafe looked at the felted beaver twirling on Bruiser's finger. "That's my hat."

"At dinner and suchlike, I'll just watch what you do."

Wonderful plan, that. Rafe scarcely remembered proper etiquette anymore.

"And then there's my secret weapon." With a glance in either direction, he pulled a small brass object from his pocket. "Picked up this little beauty in a pawnbroker's."

Rafe looked at it. "A quizzing glass. Really."

"I'm telling you, these things scream upper crust. You should get one, Rafe. No, I mean it. Someone talks over your head? Quizzing glass. Someone asks a question you can't answer? Quizzing glass."

"You honestly think a stupid monocle is all you need to blend in with the aristocracy?"

Bruiser raised the quizzing glass and peered at Rafe through the lens. Solemnly.

The idiot might be onto something.

"Just don't cock this up," he warned.

"Oh, I'm not going to cock this up. Remember, I'm your second. I'm always in your corner."

But this wasn't a prizefight. It was something much more dangerous.

As a visitor to Twill Castle, Rafe would be out of his element. When he was out of his element, he grew restless. And when he grew restless, his impulsive, reckless nature came to the fore. People got hurt.

He would need to be careful here.

"So when is the wedding planner arriving?" he asked.

Bruiser went curiously silent.

"You did engage the services of a wedding planner?"

"Certainly I did. His name is Bruno Aberforth Montague, Esquire."

Rafe cursed. "I can't believe this."

Bruiser lifted his hands in defense. "Where was I supposed to find a wedding planner? I'm not even certain such people exist. But it doesn't matter. This is going to be perfect. You'll see."

"I doubt that. You know less about planning weddings than I do."

"No, no. That's not true."

Bruiser's eyes took on that bright, excited glint that Rafe had learned to recognize over the years. And dread.

"Think about it, Rafe. I'm a trainer and promoter. It's what I do all the time. I find two people, evenly matched. Send out the word. Draw crowds desperate to see them in the same place. And most of all, I know how to get a fighter's head"—he poked a single finger into the center of Rafe's forehead—"into the ring, long before fight day."

"Bruiser."

"Aye?"

"Take your finger off my head, or I will break it."

He complied, patting Rafe's shoulders. "There's that fighting spirit."

Rafe brushed down the horse with vigorous strokes. "This will never work. It's going to be a disaster."

"It will work. I promise you. We're going to drape her in silks. Drown her in flowers and fancy cakes, until she's giddy with bridal excitement. Until she already sees herself walking down that aisle, clear as day in her mind. I'm your man, Rafe. No one knows how to drum up anticipation and spectacle better than me."

"Better than I," Rafe corrected.

Bruiser arched one eyebrow and lifted the quizzing glass.

Rafe finished hanging his tack on the hooks. "Let's just go inside." Together, they walked out of the stables and toward the castle. A few paces from the door, he stopped. "One more thing. You don't kiss her hand."

"She didn't seem to mind it."

Rafe wheeled on his boot and grabbed him by the shirtfront. "You don't kiss her hand."

Bruiser lifted his own hands in a gesture of surrender. "Very well. I don't kiss her hand."

"Ever. At all." When he thought his message had sunk in, Rafe released him.

Bruiser pulled on his waistcoat. "Do you fancy this girl?"

"She's not a girl. She's a gentlewoman. One who will soon be a lady. And no, I don't fancy her."

"Good," Bruiser said, "because that could become awkward. Seeing as how she's engaged to your brother and all."

"Believe me. I haven't forgotten it. That's the reason we're here."

"I know you have a liking for those fair-haired, buxom types. But you usually don't like them quite so wholesome," Bruiser said. "Nor so . . . What's the word?"

"*Taken.* She's taken."

Piers would marry Clio. It was a truth they'd all grown up knowing. The match just made sense. It was what their parents had wanted. It was what Piers wanted. It was what Clio wanted, even if she'd forgotten it temporarily.

And it was what Rafe wanted, too. What he *needed*.

"It's not a concern," he said. "To her, I'm a coarse, barely literate brute with few redeeming qualities. As for her . . . She's so innocent and tightly laced, she probably bathes in her shift and dresses in the dark. What would I do with a woman like that?"

Everything.

He'd do everything with a woman like that. Twice.

"I'm not going to touch her," he said. "She's not mine. She never will be."

"Indeed." Bruiser rolled his eyes and dusted off his hat. "Definitely no years of pent-up lusting there. Glad we have that sorted."

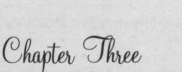

Chapter Three

For once, Clio was grateful for her sister's choosy nature.

As Anna had predicted, Daphne and Teddy didn't care for either the Blue Room *or* the larger chamber across the corridor. Instead, they preferred an apartment in the recently modernized West Tower.

Clio couldn't understand how papered walls could ever trump ancient character and a superior view, but at least she had two available rooms for her unexpected guests.

She showed Mr. Montague into the north-facing room. "I hope you will be comfortable here."

The man pulled a quizzing glass from his pocket, lifted it to his eye, and made a great show of surveying the space—from the tapestry wall hangings to the Louis XIV armchair rescued from a French château.

"It will suffice," he said.

"Very good. If you need anything at all, you've only to ring for the maids." Closing the door behind them, Clio directed Rafe across the corridor to the Blue Room. "I trust this will—"

"Wheeee!"

The faint cry came from behind the closed door of Mr. Montague's room. It was promptly followed by a springy sort of thud. The kind of sound that one might expect to result when a man leapt into the air and dropped his weight onto a mattress.

Followed by more bouncy noises. And something that sounded like a chortle of glee.

Clio tilted her head and looked at Rafe. "Where did you say Mr. Montague hails from?"

"I didn't."

She paused, listening to new sounds. The sharp reports of cupboards opening and closing.

"Look at all this storage." The muffled words were followed by an appreciative whistle. "Good Christ, there's a *bar*."

She raised her eyebrows at Rafe.

He gave a defensive shrug. "He's one of Piers's diplomatic associates. Probably last stationed in some remote, godforsaken outpost. You know how it is."

Declining to question it further, she showed him into the bedchamber. "This is the Blue Room. I trust it will suit you and your dog."

"I told you, he's not my dog."

The dog that wasn't his tottered all of three feet forward before dropping flat to the carpet. A thick puddle of drool spread from his jowls.

Rafe was more thorough in his appraisal of the space. He prowled the chamber, pinging from one piece of furniture to the next. His gaze skipped over every surface, never lingering.

"There's a lovely view of the gardens and countryside, if you'd care to have a . . ." Clio watched as he ducked and peered under a wardrobe. "My lord, is something wrong?"

"Yes." He'd stopped beside the carved rosewood bed, frowning. "There are twenty pillows on this bed."

"I don't think there are *twenty*."

"One." He plucked a tasseled, roll-shaped cushion from the bed. Then he cast it aside. It bounced onto the floor and rolled to a stop just short of Ellingworth's drool.

"Two." He reached for another and flicked it aside. "Three." Another. "Four."

One by one, he tossed the pillows from the head of the bed toward the foot of the mattress, where they mounted in a haphazard heap.

"Fourteen . . . fifteen . . ." Finally, he held the last pillow in his hand and shook it at her. "Sixteen."

"I told you there weren't twenty."

"Who the devil needs sixteen pillows? A man only has one head."

"But he has two eyes."

"Which are shut when he sleeps."

Clio sighed. "Perhaps you've been residing in a storehouse, but I know you weren't raised in a barn."

Crossing to the opposite side of the bed, she began replacing the cushions in their proper order. "The pillows," she said, "serve a decorative purpose. The symmetry is pleasing."

"Right. Everyone knows that's what a gentleman finds most *pleasing* in a bed. Symmetrical pillows."

She felt her cheeks going from pink to scarlet. "Lord Rafe—"

"That's another thing." He'd moved on to the washstand now. No doubt to find fault with the basin, or question why there were two—heaven forfend, two!—cakes of soap. "I don't answer to that title anymore. There will be no 'my lord'-ing. Not from you, not from the servants."

"Lord *Rafe*." Her voice frayed at the edges as she reached for another cushion. "I am trying to be accommodating. But this is my home, not a Southwark warehouse. And I am—for the moment, anyhow—still engaged to Lord Granville. Unless you mean to dissolve the engagement by signing those papers tonight—"

"I don't."

"Then I suggest that for once, you comport yourself in a manner that honors the family name. The very name you are urging me to take."

"That's what I'm doing." He turned his head, checking the closeness of his shave in the small mirror. "The best honor I can do the family name is to distance myself from it."

Clio paused.

Surely he didn't think *that*. Prizefighting might be illegal and scandalous, but it was a sport revered by every Englishman. He would no doubt cause an uproar at Almack's, but any evening he wished, Rafe might stroll into London's most exclusive gentlemen's clubs and walk among the members as a demigod.

And yet . . .

There was a hard, jaded quality to his baritone.

"Don't worry," he said. "Once you've married my brother, I'll keep my distance from you, too."

"Lord Rafe . . ."

He snapped his fingers, drifting on to the closet. "Just Rafe. Or Brandon, if you prefer. Since I turned twenty-one, I only use the titles I've earned."

The titles he'd *earned*?

Right now, in Clio's estimation, he was earning the title Lord Pain-upon-Arse. Goodness, the man was exhausting.

"I suppose you mean the title of champion," she said, feeling peevish as she resettled a pillow in its row. "But that's Jack Dubose's title now. Isn't it?"

He turned to face her, and for the first time since he'd entered the castle, there were no restless motions. His gaze ceased wandering and focused, dark and intent, on her.

She squared her shoulders, refusing to look cowed.

Meanwhile, the back of her neck prickled like mad. And her heart skipped around her chest.

He spoke three simple, solemn words. "Not for long."

The room vibrated with an unbearable tension.

Desperate to resolve it somehow, Clio tucked the last pillow back in its place. "There."

He looked at the pillow. Then at her. "You are so perfect for my brother."

The words did something strange to her.

Perfect, he said.

Perfect for *Piers*.

Rafe could have no idea how that statement affected her. All those years of language tutors and etiquette lessons and . . . and worse. Much worse. Her mother's efforts to mold her to the role of Lady Granville had made Clio sick, quite literally.

But she'd endured it all without complaint, desperate to be deemed satisfactory, let alone perfect. When she had been seventeen—or nineteen, or even twenty-three—Clio would have given *anything* to hear those words.

And now, when she'd made up her mind to stop chasing perfection . . . Here came Rafe and all his trunks full of dangerous, arrogant nerve.

You are so perfect for my brother.

Witty responses eluded her. All she could say was, "Don't."

"Rafe." A breathless Montague burst into the room, carrying something in his hands. He didn't seem to notice Clio where she stood at the head of the bed. "Rafe, these rooms are unbelievable. You have to see this chamber pot. I've eaten from plates that weren't this clean."

"Montague . . ."

"I'm in earnest. I'd lick this." He turned the glazed pot over in his hands. "Dare me to?"

"No."

"Because I'll do it."

"*Don't.*"

Rafe and Clio spoke the word in unison. A mutual, primal cry of desperation.

Montague froze—tongue out, eyebrows up— finally taking note of Clio's presence. He spoke without retracting his tongue. "Ah. Mih Wih-muh."

"Mr. Montague."

Montague thrust the chamber pot behind his back. "I was . . . just remarking to Lord Rafe on the exceptional thoroughness of your housekeeping."

"Quite."

Clio didn't know what was going on with this

Montague character, but she sensed that it gave her an edge with Rafe. And she needed any advantage she could get.

"I'll leave you both to settle in," she said, plumping the final pillow. "Dinner is at seven."

Dinner was . . . long.

The first course *started* well, Rafe thought.

Which was to say, both he and Bruiser managed to use the proper spoon for the soup and didn't overturn any tureens.

Then came that awkward moment when Rafe looked up from his empty bowl to realize everyone else at the table was only on the second or third spoonful.

Clio looked at him, amused. "Did you enjoy the soup?"

He peered at the empty bowl. "Pea soup, was it?"

"Jerusalem artichoke. With rosemary croutons, lemon oil, and a dollop of fresh cream."

"Right. That's what I meant."

Rafe cracked his knuckles under the table. He'd always hated these formal dinners, from the time he was old enough to be allowed at the dining table. Food was fuel to him, not a reason for hours of ceremony. One would think a rack of lamb had graduated Cambridge or made naval lieutenant, for all the pomp it received.

"How many courses are you serving?" he asked, when the servants removed the soup and brought out platters of fish.

"It's just a simple family dinner." She lifted her wineglass. "Only four."

Bloody hell. He'd rather fight forty rounds.

He could feel himself growing restless, and that never boded well.

Somehow he made it through the fish course, and then it was on to the joints and meats. At least the carving gave him something to do.

"So Mr. Montague." Lady Cambourne eyed Bruiser keenly over a carved leg of lamb. "I assume you're a barrister?"

"A barrister? God, no." Bruiser forced down a swallow of wine. "Er . . . What would make you think that?"

"Well, the 'esquire,' naturally. It must be for something. So if you're not a barrister . . . Either your grandfather was a peer, or your father was knighted. Which is it?"

"I . . . ahem . . ." He hooked one finger under his cravat and tugged at it, throwing Rafe a *help-me-out-mate* glance.

In return, Rafe gave him a *you're-on-your-own-jackass* smile.

"Oh, don't tell us." Daphne sawed away at her beef. "We'll guess. I suppose there are other ways of meriting the honor. There's proving oneself of special service to the Crown. But aren't you a bit young for that, Montague?"

He lifted that damned quizzing glass to his eye and peered at her. "Why, yes. Yes, I am."

"Ah." Her lips curled with satisfaction. "So I see."

"I thought you would."

For the love of God. Rafe couldn't believe that thing was actually working. Had Daphne Whitmore always been this dim? He couldn't recall. The last time he'd seen her, she'd been little more than a girl.

He cleared his throat. "Mr. Montague's origins aren't important. My brother dispatched him to Twill Castle for a reason. To assist with the preparations for the wedding."

"The wedding." Daphne looked sharply from Bruiser to Rafe. "You're here to plan the wedding? My sister and Lord Granville's wedding?"

"The very one," Bruiser said. "Lord Granville wishes for everything to be readied in advance of his return. So he can marry Miss Whitmore without delay."

"But he's due to return within a few weeks," Daphne replied. "That's not enough time to plan a wedding. Not a wedding fit for a marquess, at any rate. You'll need invitations, flowers, décor, the wedding breakfast. A gown."

"I think you're right," Clio said. "It can't be done. Better to wait until Piers—"

Daphne held up a fork, gesturing for silence. "Improbable. But not impossible. You'll need a great deal of help with the planning. It's a good thing Teddy and I are staying on here at the castle. We should be glad to offer our assistance."

"That's kind of you," Clio said. "But unnecessary."

Damn right it was unnecessary, Rafe thought.

Clio didn't need her sister's help pulling together events on short notice. Clio had planned the old marquess's funeral earlier that year, when he was injured and in no condition to help. Now she was managing this castle all on her own.

Hell, there were sixteen pillows on his bed, arranged like a Druid monument to her powers of organization.

Besides, these wedding plans were supposed to make her enthusiastic about the prospect of marrying Piers and becoming the Marchioness of Granville. That would be a great deal less likely with Sir Cox-comb and Lady Featherbrain meddling in everything.

"Miss Whitmore may have anything she wishes," he said. "Anything at all. No expense will be spared."

"Of course," Daphne said. "Fortunately, I keep abreast of all the latest fashions, both in London and on the Continent. This wedding will be the finest England has seen in a decade. After dinner, we'll start on a list of tasks."

"I can start the list now." Phoebe pushed aside the berries and custard a servant had just placed before her, withdrawing a pencil and small notebook from her pocket.

"We'll need a location," Daphne said. "Does the castle have a chapel?"

"Yes," Clio said. "A lovely one. I'd been hoping to give you all a proper tour after dinner. The architecture of the place is—"

Daphne waved her off. "More boring stones and cobwebs. If they've been here for four hundred years, they can wait. The wedding plans cannot. I suppose there's a curate or vicar in the neighborhood. Then there's only the matter of a license . . . Someone will need to procure a special license from Canterbury."

"I'll do that." Rafe would be needing excuses to leave the castle anyhow. What was the distance, some twenty miles? A good length for a run. Then he'd hire a horse for the return journey.

"We already have the wedding party in atten-dance," Phoebe said, making a note, then imme-diately striking it through. "Daphne will stand up with Clio, and Lord Rafe will be the best man."

At those words, his thoughts reeled to a halt somewhere on the outskirts of Canterbury.

The best man?

Out of the question. Rafe would be the worst man for that duty.

Abandoning her untouched custard, Clio rose from the table. "Shall we adjourn to the drawing room, ladies? We can leave the gentlemen to their port."

A glass of port would have been welcome. As a rule, Rafe didn't take strong spirits while training. He might reconsider that rule this week.

Then he caught Clio's gaze, pleading with him over a sea of cut crystal.

On second thought, he decided against the port. There would be no reconsidering the rules. This was a week for the rules to be unbendable. No spirits stronger than wine. No indulgent foods.

No women.

"Yes, let's go to the drawing room," Daphne said. "We'll start on the guest list."

"This is all happening too fast," Clio said. "I don't see any reason to make plans until Piers returns."

"I see a reason, dear sister. I see eight years' worth of reasons."

"Don't argue it, dumpling." Cambourne motioned for the footman to bring port. "Best to have the mousetrap all baited and set, considering how many times he's escaped it already. Clap that ball and chain on him before he has a chance to run. Isn't that right, Brandon?"

The man laughed heartily at his own joke.

Rafe wasn't laughing. He could feel that familiar,

reckless anger rising in his chest. "My brother is looking forward to the wedding."

"Believe me. We're all looking forward to this wedding." Cambourne leaned forward. "Word to the wise. Ball and chain. Look into it."

Slam.

Rafe's palms met the tabletop with a violent crash. China rattled. Crystal shivered.

People stared.

He pushed back from the table and rose to his feet. "If you'll excuse me."

Rafe needed to look into something other than Sir Teddy Cambourne's smirking face, or he was going to overturn this dining table—china, crystal, silver, and all.

Chapter Four

*B*y the time Rafe had charged upstairs, gathered the dog, carried him downstairs for a quick turn out of doors, then carried him *back* up three flights of stone steps and deposited him by the hearth in his bedchamber, he'd lost the volatile edge of his anger.

Now he was just . . . lost.

He stopped a footman in the corridor. "Miss Whitmore and her guests?"

"In the drawing room, my lord."

"Very good." He took two paces, then stopped and turned on his heel. "And the drawing room would be . . . ?"

"In the east wing. To the end of the corridor, turn right, down the stairs, and through the entrance hall to the left, my lord."

"Right."

Or was it left?

Rafe stalked down the passageway before he could forget that litany of directions. He was navigating his way through the maze of passages and corridors, picking up speed as he rounded a corner—

When he collided, bodily, with someone coming the other way.

Clio.

"Oof."

She recoiled with the force of the impact, like a grasshopper bouncing off the flank of a galloping horse.

He caught her by the wrist, steadying her. "Sorry."

"I'm fine."

She might be fine, but Rafe needed a moment. In just the brief instant of their collision, he felt like he'd been branded with her body. The impression of lush, curvy warmth lingered in inconvenient places.

A few sprints up the staircase weren't enough. He needed to run tomorrow. Far, and hard. He needed to hit and lift things, too. Many times.

"I was just dashing down to the drawing room," he said.

"Then you were dashing in the wrong direction."

Rafe shrugged. "This place is a maze. And you're supposed to be downstairs with your sisters, making the guest list."

"I slipped away. You seemed . . . agitated when you left dinner. I wanted to make certain you were well."

He couldn't believe it. After all her brother-in-law's snide remarks at the dinner table, she was concerned about *Rafe's* feelings?

She touched his arm. "You seemed uneasy through the whole meal, actually. Is there anything you need?"

God. There were a great many things he needed, and a full half of them were squeezed in that gesture alone. He told himself not to make too much of her kindness. She'd been groomed to be the consummate hostess, always thinking of her guests' comfort.

"Get married," he said. "Then I'll feel fine."

They turned and began walking down the corridor together.

She sighed. "This wedding-planning nonsense. Can't you see that it's just wasted time? Not to mention, trifling with my sisters' feelings."

"Strange, then, how you don't simply tell your family you plan to call the wedding off."

"Before the papers are signed? I don't dare. Then I'd have all four of you bent on changing my mind. No, thank you." She shook her head. "I don't know how I'll forgive you for showing up like this."

"You've forgiven me worse."

"If you're speaking of the way you reserved the third dance at my debut ball, then failed to attend?" Her clipped footsteps accelerated. "I'm still vexed over that."

"*That* was doing you a favor." He matched her pace as they turned to traverse a long, narrow gallery. "I was thinking of the birthday party where I dipped your gloves in the punch."

"Ah, yes. And then there was the time when I was eight and you were eleven, and you scorched my frock with an ember." She slanted him a look. "But that was nothing compared to when you humiliated me at indoor tennis that rainy week at Oakhaven. Winning four times in a row? The height of ungentlemanly behavior."

"Should I have let you win just because you were a girl? I wanted the silver cup."

"It was an old copper blancmange mold," she said. "Anyhow, I had my revenge when I bested you at footracing."

He frowned. "You never bested me at footracing."

"Yes, I did."

"When?"

"Well, let's see." She halted in the center of the gallery, pondering. "That would have been right about . . . Now."

She kicked off her slippers. Hiking her skirts, she took off in a dash, sprinting down the length of the gallery. When she neared the end, she stopped running. The momentum carried her forward, and she coasted on stocking feet, skating over the polished hardwood until the doors at the other end caught her.

"There." She turned to regard him, breathless and smiling. "You lose."

Rafe stared at her, struck immobile.

If this was losing, he never wanted to win.

Good Lord, look at her. Her hair coming loose from its pins, her throat flushed the shade of china roses . . . and that labored breathing doing magic—a dark, wicked kind of magic—on her abundant bosom.

Most alluring of all, that glint of laughter in her eyes.

The girl needs finishing.

That had been the common wisdom, back when the engagement was first announced. While Piers sailed for India to launch his diplomatic career, Clio was meant to remain in London for "finishing." Rafe didn't know what the devil "finishing" meant, but he knew he didn't like it. Within a few years, she'd been finished indeed. Everything remotely unique or spirited about her had been scrubbed off, pinned back, or drilled straight out of her demeanor.

So he'd thought.

But apparently, the old Clio was still in there somewhere—the Clio he'd rather liked, before the dragons had taken her in their clutches and stifled her with ten coats of lacquer.

The Clio he had no right to be admiring now.

Damn. He had to bring himself under control. He wasn't here to ogle her. He was here to make certain that in a few weeks' time she walked down the aisle and married another man.

Not just "another man." His own brother.

"We did have fun in those days," she said. "Before the engagement was settled and everything grew . . . complicated. Well, at least the two of us had fun. Phoebe and Daphne were just babies then, and even in my earliest memories, Piers had grown too old for such games."

"Piers was *born* too old for such games."

"And it would seem I haven't outgrown them. Another sign he and I are poorly matched." She tucked a wisp of hair behind her ear and shrugged. "I've been a very good girl for a very long time. I'm ready to have fun again."

Don't. Don't say that.

"Do you know what's great fun? Weddings." Good God. The things that came out of his mouth this week. "Just give this a chance. You'll have every indulgence you could ever dream. Doves released into the air. Swans in the pond. Peacocks wandering the gardens if you want them."

"That's a great many birds."

"Never mind the birds."

."I mean, there would be feathers everywhere. Not to mention their droppings."

"No birds. Forget I said anything about birds." He scrubbed a hand over his face. "What I'm attempting to say is this. You shall have everything you want, and nothing you don't. We'll spare no expense."

It was just as Bruiser said. A wedding was like a championship bout, and Clio's head wasn't yet in the ring. She needed to step into some gowns, plan a menu or two, start envisioning herself as the admired and envied bride on Piers's arm. Triumphant. Victorious.

This would work. It *had* to work. He could not let her dissolve this engagement.

"It's no use, Rafe." She went to retrieve her slippers.

He tried not to watch as she lifted her skirts to slip her toes inside.

Tried, and failed.

"Even if I *were* so easily persuaded . . . It's not as if my Uncle Humphrey left me a seaside cottage or a string of matched pearls." She bounced up and down, wriggling her foot into the slipper.

Other parts of her wriggled, too.

Really, she was just torturing him now.

"I have a castle," she said. "My very own *castle*. How can a wedding—even a lavish one with dozens of birds—possibly compete with this?"

"So it's a castle. There are castles all over England. I'm certain the Granville title comes with one or two. If it's a great, fancy house you're after, you'll be mistress of Oakhaven."

"It's not just a great, fancy house I'm after. It's . . ."

She looked to the corner and sighed. "You don't understand."

"What don't I understand?" His pride was piqued, the way it always was when someone questioned his intelligence. He might not have graduated Oxford with top honors the way Piers had done, but he wasn't a lummox.

"It's hard to explain in words. Come along. I'll try to show you."

He shook his head. "Downstairs. The guest list."

"Not yet." She came to his side. "You want to understand why this place is different? Why I'm different now, too? Give me a chance to show you, and I promise I'll join my sisters in the drawing room for the rest of the evening."

He stood unmoved. "The week."

"What?"

"I want a full week of bridal compliance. You'll make lists and menus. You'll choose flowers. You'll be fitted for gowns. No grousing, no evading."

"Let's say I agree to this plan. I allow you to stay for a week. I keep an open mind about marriage. You promise to keep an open mind about me. If at the end of the week, I still wish to break the engagement . . . what then? Will you sign the dissolution papers?"

He inhaled slowly. He was putting a lot of faith in the power of lace, silk, and Bruiser's competence, but he didn't seem to have a choice. The preparations couldn't sway her if she didn't take part.

"Very well," he said. "It's a bargain."

"Shake hands on it?"

He clasped her small hand in his and pumped it once.

She squeezed his fingers tight and didn't let go. "Excellent. Now come along. I've been dying to show *someone* around this castle. We'll see how much trouble we can find on our way downstairs."

As she led him through the opposite end of the gallery, a sense of foreboding gathered in Rafe's chest. Above all things, he had a talent for finding trouble.

And a week suddenly seemed like a dangerously long time.

Clio swelled with a modest amount of confidence as she tugged him out of the gallery and down the spiraling flights of stairs.

A quarter hour would be more than enough time to prove this place wasn't just another heap of stones littering the English countryside.

Of course, then came the trickier part—making Rafe see what Twill Castle meant to *her*.

"Quickly," she whispered, peeking into the corridor to make certain no one observed them. "This way."

"But—"

"*Hurry*."

As they ducked into a smaller, darker stairwell, Clio clutched his hand tight and tried to ignore the stupid thrill that ran through her every time her skin met his.

Ridiculous, really. Yes, he was an infamous rake. But they'd known each other since childhood, and she'd been engaged to his brother for almost a decade. There wasn't anything forbidden about taking the man's hand.

Nevertheless, her heartbeat drummed in her chest

as she drew him down the stairs. At the bottom, they were greeted by cold, clammy darkness. The only illumination was the last lingering bit of twilight struggling through a ceiling grate.

"See?" She lowered her voice as they crept through the cavernous space. "This castle has dungeons."

"These aren't dungeons."

"They are so dungeons."

"They're far too big for dungeons. These were clearly cellars."

She went to a hook where a lamp was hung and gathered a flint from the nearby tinderbox.

"Stop ruining the fun." She struck the flint. Nothing. "Battles were fought in this place. It's over four hundred years old. The very air is thick with history. For centuries, people have lived and loved and died here. Just think of it."

"Here's what I think. You've been reading too many of those knights-and-ladies stories in the *Gentleman's Review*. People have lived and loved and died everywhere. And for every crusading knight who won a tournament for his lady in this castle, I promise you—there were a hundred men who spent a solid decade scratching themselves and having pissing contests from the ramparts."

She cringed and tried the flint again. "Men are disgusting."

"Yes," he said proudly. "We are. But we're useful, on occasion. Give that here."

He took the flint from her hands and struck it. The sparks didn't dare disobey. Holding that warm, nascent glow cupped in his powerful hands, he could have been Prometheus, as painted by a Florentine master. The reddish gold light flashed over the strong planes of his brow and jaw, then lingered on the rugged slope of his oft-broken nose.

"Well, I'm not a man," Clio said, feeling keenly aware of her womanliness. "I'm not going to spend a decade pissing from the ramparts. I'm going to *do* something with this castle."

"Let me guess." He lit the lamp, then whipped the straw, putting out the flame. "You want to open a school for foundlings."

"That's a lovely thought. But no. If I'm to maintain this place, it needs to generate income. No offense to the poor dears, but there isn't much money in orphans."

Clio took the lamp, went to the far wall, and counted off the stones.

One, two, three, four . . .

"Here's what I brought you down to see."

If *this* didn't impress him, she didn't know what could.

She pushed hard on the fifth stone. An entire section of the wall swung outward.

"Behold," she declared. "A secret passage."

He took the lamp from her and thrust it into the darkened tunnel, peering hard into the gloom. When he whistled, the whistle echoed back.

"Very well," he said. "One point to you. That's capital."

At last. Clio warmed with satisfaction. She wanted him to appreciate the history and see the potential of this place, but there was more to it than that. She wanted him to *enjoy* this castle, the way she enjoyed it.

She thought of his spartan warehouse, with its humble cot and sawdust floor. All those slimy raw eggs.

He needed more enjoyment in his life. A home and warm comforts and amusements that didn't end in bloodshed. To live like a human rather than a beast bred for fighting.

"So where does this secret passage lead?" he asked.

"Go through it and find out." She arched a brow. "Unless you're frightened."

He pulled himself to full height. "I defended the title of Britain's heavyweight champion for four years. If there's anything living in that passage, *it* should be frightened."

"Ah, yes. I suppose even the spiders will scatter at their first sight of the Devil's Own."

He looked at her, surprised. "Where'd you hear that name?"

"Oh, I know all the things they call you. Brawlin' Brandon. Lord of Ruin. The Devil's Own."

"You've been following my career," he said. "What business does a proper, well-bred young lady have, following the world of illegal prizefighting?"

She was suddenly, unaccountably nervous. "It's not that I follow *you*. I follow the newspapers. You're often in them."

Clio had always paid close attention to current events. And to world history, geography, languages, and more. Her mother had insisted. A diplomat's wife needed to be apprised of all the world's happenings.

Strictly speaking, a diplomat's wife probably didn't need to be apprised of all the happenings in underworld boxing, but Clio hadn't been able to resist.

Rafe had always been such a source of fascination to her. In the middle of their polite, manicured garden square of a society, there had grown this wild, rebellious vine that refused to be tamed. She wanted to understand him. She wanted to know why he'd walked away from that world, and where he'd gone, and whether he was happy there.

Caring about Rafe Brandon seemed a dangerous habit, but it was one she couldn't seem to quit.

"Speaking of names," he said, "since when do you go by 'dumpling'?"

She winced. "Since Daphne married, and her husband decided to give his new sisters-in-law pet names. Phoebe is kitten, and I'm dumpling."

"Stupid name."

"I can't disagree. But I don't know how to tell him to cease using it, either."

"I'll tell you how. Just say, 'Don't call me dumpling.'"

It wasn't so easy. Not for her. She moved to enter the passageway. "Are we going to follow this tunnel or not?"

He held her back. "This time, I'll lead the way."

She handed him the lamp. They ducked and entered the tunnel. The way was narrow, and the ceiling was low. Rafe had to hunch and twist to thread himself through the smallest spots.

"Why do you do it?" The question tumbled out of her. She asked because he was here, and they were alone—and she could. "Why do you fight?"

His answer was matter-of-fact. "I was cut off with no funds or inheritance. I needed a career."

"I know that. But surely there are other ways to earn a living. Less violent ways."

"Ah." He paused. "I see where this is going. You want to know my secret pain."

"Secret pain?"

"Oh, yes. My inner demons. The dark current of torment washing away little grains of my soul. That's what you're after. You think that if you keep me here in your pretty castle and cosset me with sixteen pillows, I'll learn to love myself and cease submitting my body to such horrific abuse."

Clio bit her lip, grateful it was too dark for him to see her blush. If she'd been flamingo pink the other day, she must be fuchsia now. "I don't know where you get these ideas."

He chuckled. "From every woman I've ever met, that's where. You're not the first to try it, and you won't be the last."

"How disappointing. Can I at least be the best?"

"Perhaps." He stopped and twisted around in the tunnel, so that he faced her. "Do you want to know my deep, dark secret, Clio? If I were to unburden my soul to you, could you truly bear it?"

She must have quivered, or shuddered, or something—and he mistook it for a nod of assent.

"Here it is."

She held her breath as he leaned close to whisper in her ear. The back of her neck prickled. His deep voice resonated in her bones.

"I fight," he said, "because I'm good at it. And because it makes me money." He turned away. "That's the truth."

Clio wasn't convinced.

Oh, she didn't doubt that he spoke some of the truth—but she suspected it wasn't *all* of the truth. There was something more, something he wasn't willing to admit. Not to her, and perhaps not even to himself.

Soon the passageway curved and began to slope upward.

They opened a panel and emerged into a narrow alcove.

"Where the devil are we?" He was so broad and tall, he filled almost the entire space.

"Near the front entryway." Clio squeezed herself into a corner. "This is my favorite part of the castle."

"This." He plucked a bit of moss from a jutting stone. "This is your favorite part."

She tilted her gaze upward. "See that lever up there?"

"Aye."

"Can you reach it?"

He reached up and grabbed the ancient iron handle. His giant hand fit around the lever as if it were made for him.

"Go on, then. Give it a pull."

Uncertainty drew his brows together. "What happens when I pull it?"

"You don't want to ruin the surprise."

"If the surprise is a spike through the chest, I do."

"Trust me. You're going to like this." Clio went up on tiptoe and put both her hands over his one, pulling down with all her weight.

The centuries-old mechanism groaned and creaked.

"Now come see. Hurry!"

She waved him out of the alcove just in time to watch. From a slot above the archway, an iron grate began to descend. Like a massive, sharp-toothed jaw biting through stone.

"Get back."

Rafe's arm whipped around her waist. With a gruff curse, he yanked her backward, well away from the gate as it crashed into place.

The echo reverberated through them both. Exhilaration pulsed through her veins. Clio loved that sound. That sound declared this wasn't just a house.

It was a stronghold.

"Well?" she asked. "Isn't that something?"

"Oh, it's . . . something."

"You sound displeased." She turned to face him. "I thought you'd like it. Do you know how many castles in England still have a functioning portcullis?"

"No."

"Neither do I," she admitted. "But it can't be a great number."

He still hadn't let her go. His arm remained lashed about her waist, protective and crushing. And his heartbeat pounded in his chest, sparring with hers.

Goodness. He'd truly been frightened. Coming to chest to chest with the proof of it . . . Well, it made her feel safe in some ways and utterly defenseless in others.

"Rafe," she whispered. "It wasn't going to hit me."

"*I* wasn't going to take chances."

"You needn't worry so much. You do realize, if I end the engagement—or if something ends me— Piers will find another bride. The ladies will queue up by the score. I assure you, I'm very replaceable."

He shook his head.

"No, truly. I know our fathers desired a connection between the two families. But they're both gone now, and I don't think they'd—"

He put his thumb to her lips, shushing her. "That's absurd. You are not replaceable."

"I'm not?" The words were muffled by his thumb.

"Hell, no." His thumb slid over her lips, and his gaze seemed to hover there, too. His voice dropped to a low, impatient growl that simmered in her knees. "I swear to you, Clio. Somehow, I'm going to make you see—"

Footsteps clattered from the direction of the corridor. Oh, drat.

At once, Rafe stepped back, releasing her.

No. No!

Somehow, I'm going to make you see . . .

What, precisely? What was he going to make her see? His point of view? The error of her ways? His collection of seashells and sealing wax?

Now she'd lie awake all night, wondering.

And thinking of his arm lashed about her waist. His touch on her lips.

"Good heavens." Daphne's high, unmistakable voice rang down the corridor. "What was that unholy racket?"

"Just the portcullis." Clio fluttered one hand in the direction of the gate. "Lord Rafe wanted a demonstration."

"Yes. And Miss Whitmore was good enough to oblige me. Despite how eager she is to begin on the wedding preparations." He gave her a pointed look. "For the remainder of the week."

Clio had no choice now. She would suffer through a few days of wedding plans. What else was there to do? She couldn't announce she'd broken the engagement unless the dissolution papers were signed. And the days had to be passed in one fashion or another.

In fact, as she succumbed to the inexorable pull of the drawing room, Clio began to worry this task wouldn't take a full week. Surely a simple country wedding could be planned in a day or two.

How difficult could it be?

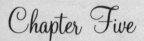

Chapter Five

"*I*'ve drawn up a list of seventeen tasks. And a schedule."

Rafe would say one thing for Phoebe Whitmore. She was startlingly efficient. She presented this list at breakfast the next morning before he'd even touched his coffee.

How old was the girl now? Sixteen or so? If Rafe had drawn up a list of tasks at Phoebe's age, he could only imagine it would have looked thusly:

1. *Skip lessons.*
2. *Chase girls.*
3. *Any excuse for a fistfight.*
4. *Is that a squirrel?*

End of list.

As he sat down to the table, a servant placed a

bowl containing three speckled eggs beside his plate. "For your coffee, my lord."

He tugged his ear, bemused. Clio didn't miss anything, did she? He didn't know how to take it, that she'd been thinking of him that morning. Doing him this small kindness. He'd woken thinking of her, too.

But his thoughts were anything but nice.

In his imagination, she was flushed and breathless with laughter, and they'd been . . . racing, in a fashion.

A horizontal fashion.

His blood stirred, just at the memory.

Damn it. Ten miles, he had run that morning. Ten miles through the misty Kentish countryside should have left him too sapped of energy to contemplate carnality.

He wasn't quite sapped enough.

No, he could do with a touch more sapping.

Daphne snatched the list from her sister. "We'll need to send to London for many of these items on the list. Sample gowns for fitting. Bunting and ribbons for the décor. For the invitations, fine paper and ink."

Clio looked up. "I have ink."

"You don't have the *right* ink. But while we're waiting on supplies, there are some things we can tackle."

"Toast?"

Daphne kept her gaze on her list. "No, no. The toasts and speeches can wait. Though we should start testing the punch recipe."

"I meant this kind." With a smile, Clio passed a plate of white and brown toast points.

"Oh." Daphne took a point of white and immediately leveled it at Rafe, like a buttered weapon. "But come to think of it, my lord, you should start writing a draft."

"A draft of what?"

"The toast. You *are* the best man."

Then she turned away, giving some direction to her husband, who was moving down the sideboard and loading two plates as he went.

Not this again. Rafe had no intention of performing any best-man duties at his brother's wedding. They'd scarcely spoken in a decade, and Rafe didn't expect they'd be mixing much in years to come, either. The only thing more uncomfortable and inappropriate than harboring lust for his brother's intended bride would be harboring lust for his brother's wife.

No, he was only here to make certain the wedding took place. Then he'd hand over the marquessate duties and get back to *his* life. *His* career. *His* title.

His women.

Not that there'd been many women of late. No doubt that was part of his sapping problem.

"Today, we'll meet with the vicar to start planning the ceremony," Daphne announced. "After that, the menus."

"Must we do all that today?" Clio asked. "You've only just arrived, and I never had the chance to show you about. I'd love for you to see the castle grounds."

Cambourne glanced to the window, dismayed. "It looks like rain. And these are new boots."

"We don't have time for these things," Daphne said. "There are seventeen items on Phoebe's list. Seventeen."

"Are you sure there aren't sixteen, my lady?" a new voice inquired. "Or perhaps it's eighteen." Bruiser leaned over her shoulder, examining the list with the aid of his quizzing glass.

If that quizzing glass survived the week without meeting the heel of Rafe's boot, it would be a miracle.

"Seventeen," he pronounced at length. "I ought to never have doubted you, Miss Phoebe. Where would we be without your sterling accomplishment in counting?"

"What about flowers?" Clio asked. "Are flowers one of the seventeen items?"

"But of course they are."

"Then we can compromise. We'll all take a stroll in the castle gardens, and I can decide which blooms I like for the bouquet."

Rafe supposed flowers were as good a start as anything.

As they made their way toward the summer garden, Cambourne approached him. The man dug an elbow into Rafe's side in a manner that Rafe guessed was meant to be chummy.

He didn't want to be chums.

"Say, Brandon. I was a few years behind your brother at Eton. But I don't recall crossing paths with you there."

"I wasn't there. Not for long, anyway." Rafe hadn't lasted one term with the snobbish prigs at Eton. "Sent down for fighting."

"Right-o. 'Course you were."

It was mostly the truth.

Rafe had never taken to book learning. He preferred to be out of doors, riding his horse or chasing clouds of starlings from the fields.

He'd struggled through those early years with tutors

at home, but by Eton he'd fallen behind other boys his age. He'd been embarrassed to sit in lecture, not having completed his work for the day, unable to focus on what went on around him. He was an undisciplined, unruly scamp, his masters agreed. So Rafe played the role they assigned him. He started fights, and he won them. He'd rather be sent down for fighting than stupidity.

That elbow again. "Do you know," Cambourne said, "I dabbled in a bit of pugilism myself, in my day."

"You don't say."

"Champion at the club, two years running." He thrust his tongue in his cheek. "I say, how about it, Brandon? Fancy a few rounds of sparring? I wouldn't mind testing myself against you."

Rafe sized up the man. A solidly built fellow, with a florid complexion, scarlet waistcoat to match, and a smug grin. What with his comments to Clio at dinner last night, the man had all but painted a target on his jaw.

Rafe would have enjoyed punching that face. Immensely.

"I don't think so," he said.

"Oh-ho-ho." The man boxed Rafe's biceps with a clumsy jab that might as well have been a fleabite. "Not in top form anymore? Afraid of embarrassing yourself in front of the ladies?"

No. I'm afraid of killing you in front of the ladies, you idiot.

Rafe would never spar with an untutored amateur—and especially not with a man he personally disliked. The danger for his opponent would be too great. He enjoyed cultivating a dangerous, brutish reputation, but he stopped well short of maiming.

Anger might have made him a fighter, but discipline had made him a champion. The best thing boxing had done for him was teaching him when *not* to punch. Without the sport, Rafe probably would have landed in prison by now. If not a grave.

"This isn't the time or place for sparring," he said. "We're here so Miss Whitmore can choose her flowers."

No sooner had Rafe spoken the words than Clio lifted a clutch of blossoms.

"Well, that's done," she declared. "Now we can take a wander over the meadows. There are deer in the park."

He crossed to her. "You can't be finished already."

"It appears that I am. Mr. Montague was kind enough to cut these for me."

He stared at the floral hodgepodge in her hands. A few of the buds weren't even open yet, and others had shed half their petals. He saw roses and ... some white flowers and some yellow, clumpy things. He didn't know the names.

"You promised to cooperate with the wedding plans," he said.

"And I am cooperating."

Before he could argue back, Daphne joined them.

She took the flowers from Clio's hand and tutted. "This won't do. Horrid. Hideous. And wrong, all wrong. Montague, do you know nothing of the language of flowers?"

There was a language of flowers? Ye gods. Rafe didn't even know what to call them in English.

"Each blossom imparts a different message. And this dreadful posy is saying all the wrong things."

One by one, Daphne plucked the flowers from the bunch and cast them to the ground. "Yellow roses are for envy." Away went the roses. "Primrose? That's inconstancy." The primroses dropped to the grass. "And tansy . . ." She scowled. "A declaration of war."

"There's a flower to serve as a declaration of war?" Clio plucked one of the yellow, puffy flowers from the ground and turned to Rafe. "How very interesting. I wonder if we sent a bouquet of these to Napoleon. Or maybe it's like calling a man out with a slap of the glove?"

"If a man slapped me with a tansy," Rafe said, "I wouldn't take kindly to it."

"What if a woman did?"

"Well, then I'd pay her double."

She turned away, but not before he saw the corner of her lips curl up and her cheeks go pink. An absurd swell of triumph rose in his chest.

What was it about those blushes of hers? He never could resist provoking them. When he saw that color bloom on her cheek, it made him feel he'd done something right. Like a little banner hoisted with the words writ, *Well Done, You.*

"Now wait, wait." Bruiser angled his way into their group, retrieving the rest of the discarded blooms from the ground. "I am, in actuality, well versed in the language of flowers." He stood tall and tugged his waistcoat straight. "The Viennese dialect."

Good God. Rafe couldn't wait for this.

Daphne looked skeptical. "The Viennese dialect?"

"Let us not forget, my lady, Lord Granville has been living for several years on the Continent." Bruiser held a yellow rose aloft. "In Austria, these roses speak not of envy, but of devotion." He added the primrose to the bunch. "These, tenderness of spirit."

Daphne crossed her arms. "And the tansy?"

"Ah. The tansy. The tansy says—"

"I wish to sexually reproduce."

This interjection came from Phoebe, who had heretofore been silent.

She had everyone's attention now.

Bruiser didn't miss a beat. "Well, yes. In the low country, perhaps. In the high country, it's an invitation to yodel."

"I wish to sexually reproduce," Phoebe repeated. "That's what the tansy says. That's what all blossoms say. Any plant that produces a flower is seeking to procreate."

"Oh, kitten," Daphne said. "Really."

She and Bruiser moved on, discussing the merits of hydrangea and nasturtiums.

Rafe drew Clio aside, tugging her in the opposite direction. "Forget all of this. We need to order hothouse blooms. Orchids or lilies or . . ." He churned the air with one hand. "Whatever else is finest."

"What's wrong with these?" She lifted her pathetic bouquet. "I think they're cheerful."

"There's nothing exactly wrong with them."

"Well, then. They'll do."

"No. They won't." He plucked the posy from her hand. "That's my point. These might be good enough for a vase on the windowsill, but this is your wedding day."

"Perhaps I'm satisfied with 'good enough.'" She took the flowers.

He took them back. "*I'm* not satisfied with 'good enough.'"

"You said it's my wedding. You said I could have whatever I wanted."

"I want you to want something better." She reached to take back the posy, but he refused to let go. He flexed his arm, drawing her close. "You should have the best. Always."

He held her firm. She didn't pull away.

And the world shrank around them, to something the size of two stubborn heartbeats and a wilted bouquet.

It must have been the arguing, because Rafe rarely felt this way outside a fight. Sharp. Intent. Powerful. Aware of everything at once. The petal pink flush of her skin against her white frock. The sleekness of her wrist contrasted with the clinging flower stems. The breeze that caught a stray curl of her hair and twirled it in a dance. The tender sweetness of violets.

Only there weren't any violets in the bouquet. Which meant he was breathing in the tender sweetness of Clio herself. The scent of the French-milled soap she used in the bath, or maybe the pomanders she tucked between her folded underthings.

He shouldn't be thinking of her underthings. Much less envisioning those crisp, white underthings on her otherwise-naked body.

Or worst of all, picturing them as a heap on the floor.

Eyes. He kept his gaze stubbornly locked with hers. But that wasn't safe, either. Her eyes were the clear, brilliant blue of mountain lakes. Water that came pure and sweet and deep, and could drown a man in seconds.

Already, he felt himself leaning forward. As if to bend his head and drink.

Gods save me.

And for the first time in his life, some deity actually answered his prayer.

His deliverance came in the form of a piercing shriek.

At the sound of her sister screaming, Clio wrenched her gaze from Rafe's. A strange, smarting pain accompanied the motion. As if she'd pulled her tongue from a block of ice too swiftly, leaving a small piece of herself behind.

She wheeled in place, looking for the crisis.

In the center of the summer garden, Daphne stood pale and utterly immobile, like a piece of garden statuary that had begun shrieking in outrage. "No. *No!* Stop, I say!"

Clio started toward her sister, searching for the source of danger. "Is it a wasp? A snake?"

Rafe said, "It's the dog."

"Oh." She clapped a hand to her mouth. "Oh, dear."

Evidently she wasn't the only one who'd mistaken Daphne for statuary.

Ellingworth was urinating on her foot.

"No!" her sister shrieked. "Stop! Stop it this instant, you odious beast."

Having finished his task, Ellingworth shuffled off and disappeared under a hedge. An agitated Sir Teddy gathered his wife, and together they began walking back to the castle. Phoebe and Bruiser followed.

Clio fought back laughter. "I really shouldn't find this amusing, should I?"

"No, that's good," Rafe said. "If you're amused, I don't have to be sorry."

"We'd better find the dog, poor old dear. It's going to rain."

Distant thunder rumbled in agreement.

Together they searched the garden, peering into hedges and parting dense clusters of mums to search the ground.

At last they found Ellingworth, lying flat on his belly beneath a rosebush.

The bulldog seemed too fatigued to go anywhere.

"I'll have to carry him in," Rafe said.

"Wrap him in this first." She slipped the shawl from her shoulders. "Or you'll be covered in mud."

"I don't want to ruin your shawl."

"It's only an everyday shawl. Nothing special."

Without entertaining further argument, Clio draped the length of printed cotton over the sleeping bulldog. Rafe scooped him up.

The distant thunder rumbled again. Only this time, the thunder wasn't so distant, and the castle was even farther away.

"We'll never beat the rain," she said. "Come this way."

She led him toward an old stone tower standing sentinel on the castle's northeastern border.

The storm broke just before they reached the structure. Rain spattered the ground in heavy drops. They ducked inside the tower, breathless.

"What is this place?" Rafe asked. Despite the muting force of the rain, his voice rang through the gutted stone silo.

"A watchtower, once," she managed. "It's been used to store hops for the past hundred years. I thought this would be helpful for Ellingworth."

She tugged an old hopcart out from the shadows. The wooden, hand-pulled wagon was just the perfect size for the bulldog. "There. Won't that suit him? We'll pull him back to the castle once it stops raining, then store this in the carriage house. This way, the servants can take him on walks."

"Not bad, but it's lacking in pillows," he said gravely. "It needs at least a dozen."

She ignored his teasing. Mostly.

Once he'd deposited the dog in the cart, and she'd arranged her shawl as a blanket, Rafe stood and surveyed her appearance. "You're wet."

"Just a little." She hugged herself.

He shrugged out of his coat and draped its weight about her shoulders.

"Thank you," she said, looking out at the rain. "I suppose we should stay here until it stops."

Clio gathered the lapels and pulled the coat tight about her. The thing must have weighed ten pounds, at least. The wool was still warm with the heat of his body. But the best part was how it smelled—intensely wonderful and intensely Rafe. She inhaled deep, surreptitiously breathing in the scents of coffee, leather, oil of wintergreen. And that faint musk that was uniquely his. She'd never been so thoroughly enveloped by another person's scent before. It felt intimate somehow.

Almost like an embrace.

She laughed at herself.

Says the girl who's never once been embraced.

She said, "I've been conferring with the land agent ever since the property came to me. We're planning to convert this tower into an oast."

"An oast."

"You do know what an oast is, don't you?"

"Of course *I* know what an oast is." He crossed his arms and regarded her. "You tell me what *you* think an oast is, and I'll judge if you're correct."

She shook her head. Even to a relative innocent like Clio, sometimes men could be so transparent. At a moment like this, it was comforting.

"An oast is a tall, round building for drying hops and malt," she said. "To convert this tower, we'll need to build a great kiln here on the ground floor. Upstairs, there'd be a flat platform for drying. Then a vent at the top to draw the heat upward. There, now. How was that definition?"

"Acceptable."

"And that's just the beginning. Not only is the soil in this region ideal for hopfields, but we've a river with clear, crisp water that runs straight through the property. Once we complete the oast, we'll start building the brewery."

His head jerked in surprise. "Wait, wait. A brewery?"

"It's as I told you last night. I mean to do something with the place."

"You want to run a brewery." His gazed raked her. "You."

"Yes. Twill Castle is a touch far from London, but just here in Kent we can sell our product to countless public houses. There's ample storage space under the castle."

"Ah. So you agree. Those are cellars."

"Fine." She rolled her eyes. "Have it your way. They're cellars. And they're perfect. The entire scheme is perfect. Even you must admit it."

"I'm not admitting anything." He shoved a damp swoop of hair from his brow. "It's a terrible idea. What could you know about beer?"

"More than you know about weddings."

Over the past eight years, she'd studied not only foreign etiquette and world events, but agricultural news and land management, too. Her mother claimed it was all in service of becoming the perfect bride. She must be prepared to converse with her husband on any topic that might interest or concern him.

Clio hadn't minded, truly. Reading all those newspapers and books helped pass the time while she was . . . waiting, on one thing and another. Chaperoning Phoebe with her tutors. Sitting through Daphne's dressmaker fittings. Keeping vigil by Mama's sickbed, after the doctors declared there was nothing more to be done. Clio read through it all.

Then came the day she learned that this castle belonged to her. And she realized that something else belonged to her, too. All that knowledge she'd accumulated . . . It was hers.

She was as prepared to manage an estate as Piers could have been, what with his incessant traveling. There was only one significant difference that set them apart.

Unfortunately, it was the one difference everyone—including Rafe—couldn't seem to see past.

"You're a woman." He pronounced this statement as though it were the beginning, end, and sum of any argument.

"And you think a woman can't run a brewery? Or is it just that you don't believe in me?"

"It doesn't matter what *I* think. It matters what all the farmers, brewers, and tavernkeepers think."

"Until a few centuries ago, all brewing was women's work. Even today, any sizeable estate brews its own small beer. It's where we get yeast for the bread."

"There's a difference between making small beer for the servants' hall and brewing ale for distribution."

"I know there is. This is why I wanted you to sign the dissolution papers. If we're to start brewing next year, we need to start building now. That means I need my dowry unencumbered, and the sooner the better. The architect won't begin the drawings without payment."

"Listen, if you've set your heart on opening a brewery on this property, all the more reason to marry Piers. His men of business could oversee everything."

"I'm not marrying Piers. And I can hire my own men of business. Can't you see? I want something that's *mine*. A challenge."

"*When* you marry Piers, you'll have the title of marchioness. A house in London and a vast estate to manage. He'll have diplomatic duties. There will be children. If that's not enough, there are any number of worthy charitable ventures to which you could lend your time and your name. You won't lack for challenges."

"But this is different."

"How so?"

She gestured with frustration. "This is a challenge where I have some chance to succeed."

"What? That's absurd. You'll make the perfect Lady Granville."

There it was. That bold, ridiculous word again. *Perfect.*

"I mean what I'm saying." He put his hands on her shoulders, turning her to face him. "Look at me."

She looked at him. It wasn't easy. He was so close and so large. She had to tip her head back, exposing the vulnerable length of her throat to the cool, damp air. Her pulse beat like an indecisive rabbit's.

"I know it's been a long wait," he said. "I know there's gossip."

"Those are under—"

"Understatements. I know that, too."

There he went again, finishing her sentences. Oh, he was in fighting form now. But this time, Clio wouldn't back down. There was more to her than he believed. More than anyone suspected.

"Most of all," he said, "I know what it's like to be the dark horse. To have everyone betting against you, counting you out. And I know the vindication you'll feel when you finally win. When you walk down the aisle in your big flouncy gown, on the arm of one of England's great men, and all those gossips' wagging tongues turn to ash. Believe me . . ." His big hands squeezed her shoulders. "Triumph is sweet. It's so damned sweet."

His green eyes were nearly black, and his voice was so earnest. And a deep, lonely part of her wanted to believe him.

"This was a mistake," she said, backing away. "I don't know why I try to explain anything to you."

"I know. I'm a stupid, uneducated brute. Next time, speak slowly and use smaller words."

"That's not what I meant. You are far too clever, and I've always known it. I just wish you'd give me the same credit."

"Me? I don't think you're stupid."

"You *must.* You think a pretty gown and a big party will be enough to change my mind about something so important as marriage. How can that not be insulting to my intelligence?"

"Now, Clio . . ."

"Don't 'Now, Clio' me." She turned and started up the winding steps. Thanks to the downpour, she couldn't flounce and leave the tower. This was the next best thing. "Maybe I am a fool. You arrived unannounced, with all your lists."

He mounted the stairs behind her. "There was only one list."

" . . . and your ridiculous 'esquire' of a friend . . ."

"I can explain him."

" . . . and your dog . . ."

"He's not my dog."

" . . . and I was fool enough to let you stay. I welcomed you into my home because I hoped you'd see that Twill Castle is just that. My *home.* But you're so stubborn." She trod hard on the steps as she spiraled toward the top. "You're just like Piers, caring only for your career and nothing for me. I wish I'd shown you the door."

As she took the next step, her ankle twisted. Her slipper skidded on the damp stone.

Rafe's hand shot out to steady her.

"I have you." He flexed his arm, pulling her flush with his chest. "I have you."

Clio clutched his shirtfront. She would have caught herself, even without his help. But for this one fleeting moment, she would let him play the hero.

She was growing dangerously used to this. The way it felt to be held in his arms. Protected. Valued, to whatever small degree.

"Still wishing you'd shown me the door?" He cocked his head at the unforgiving stone floor, some twenty feet below. "It's a long way down. We could have landed there in a heap of broken bones, waiting days for someone to find us."

"Hah." She released him, turned, and resumed climbing. "If we were found here together, we would be better off dead. You can well imagine what people would conclude."

"What would they conclude?"

"That we were lovers, of course."

Chapter Six

L overs?" Rafe asked.

The round, echoing walls threw the word back at him, like a teasing chant.

Lovers . . . Lovers . . . Lovers. . .

He cleared his throat and dropped his voice to a quiet, commanding timbre. "Why would anyone think that?"

"It's all around us," she said, climbing the remaining few steps to the second floor. "Just look."

What with the rain and the paucity of windows, it was difficult to make out anything at first. But as his eyes adjusted to the dimness, Rafe began to understand what she meant. The stone walls surrounding them were carved and etched with letters. Letters in pairs. Some of them enclosed in hearts.

The initials of lovers.

This must have been the local trysting place for decades now. Perhaps for centuries.

"It's rather charming, isn't it?" She traced a heart with her fingertip. "So many couples over the years. I wonder who they all were."

Rafe decided this was a welcome development. Anything that churned up thoughts of romance and couples in her imagination had to aid his cause.

"What about you?" She turned to him. "Are your initials carved in a wall somewhere in Somerset? Or . . . many somewheres?"

"Me?" He shook his head. "No. When it comes to women, I don't car—"

"You don't carve anything in stone." She shook her head. "Of course not."

He looked at her, annoyed.

"What? Fighters aren't the only ones who can concentrate, anticipate, react." She held up weak little fists and mimed boxing his shoulder. "If you don't like me finishing your sentences, try being less predictable."

He chuckled to himself. Damn. She was clever, this one. And perhaps not quite so innocent as her looks would suggest. Still, she could never predict what kind of thoughts were churning in his mind right now.

During her almost fall, she'd dropped the overcoat he'd lent her. The cursed thing was probably to blame for pulling her off-balance in the first place.

But now she was left in just her thin, wet, nearly transparent muslin frock—and shivering, either from cold or from the lingering fear of falling.

He couldn't look at her without wanting to warm her.

Hold her.

Guard her.

More.

"Piers," he said. "Piers would be the sort to carve your initials in the wall, right alongside his."

She settled on the floor. "I doubt it. He's spent years declining to write his name beside mine in a wedding register."

"That's different." He sat beside her.

"Rafe, I wish you'd stop denying the obvious. He doesn't love me."

"Of course he does. Or he will. Love has a way of creeping up on a man. I'd venture to say love *has* to creep up on a man. If men ever saw it coming, we'd only run away."

"Love's never caught you."

"Well, that's me." He gave her shoulder a teasing nudge. "I've spent years honing these reflexes. Love can take all the swings it likes, but I've always managed to dodge the blow."

"So far," she added meaningfully.

"So far."

They listened to the rain for a moment.

The truth was, Rafe doubted love would ever catch him. He lost interest in things too easily. He'd always been this way. His studies, tasks, clubs . . . friends and lovers, too. Fighting kept his body and wits engaged because the challenge changed with every bout. It was the one pursuit that had managed to capture and hold his fascination.

He glimpsed a faint wash of pink on Clio's cheek.

Well, perhaps it was one of two.

"What if it's the opposite?" Clio asked. "What if Piers returns, sees me, and what hits him isn't love but the realization that he feels nothing for me? That he never has and never will."

"Impossible."

"It's not impossible. He must have changed in his time away. I've changed, too. I've grown older, and I've grown . . . Well, I've just *grown*." Her voice went quiet. "I've gained a full stone since he saw me last."

In all the best places, he wanted to say.

But he couldn't say that. He considered it rather heroic that he only dropped his gaze to her breasts for a moment and not ten.

"Clio, you're still—" Damn. "Still" was not the word he wanted there. "You've always been—"

"Just stop. Please don't try to flatter me. It's so unconvincing. Especially when it's clear you don't like me."

That's right, he didn't like her. He didn't like her *so much*, he'd just risked plummeting to his doom to catch her when she stumbled.

"In eight years, you haven't answered one of my notes," she said. "You've never repaid any of my calls. Until you showed up here, you hadn't accepted a single one of my invitations. And I made several."

He exhaled slowly. Goddamn him. Yes, she had.

Rafe had assumed she made the effort out of duty. Why else would a gentlewoman treat her betrothed's estranged, disreputable brother in such fashion? All those holiday greetings, birthday wishes, invitations to family dinners . . . They had to be mere obligation, he'd reasoned. At best, they came from an essential sweetness in her character. Troubling her with unwanted replies seemed a poor way to repay the gesture.

But the gesture *had* meant something. He'd saved those notes and calling cards. Every last one. He didn't pull them out and fondle them, or sniff them, or anything so stupid. But he'd kept them.

She made him feel more a part of the Brandon family than his own family ever had.

He didn't know how to put that in words. Much less pen it in a note. When it came to feelings this strong, he only dealt in actions.

"You have it wrong," he forced himself to say. "I don't dislike you."

"Oh, truly?"

"Truly."

"Then do me a favor, Rafe."

"Anything."

God, yes. Please. Enough with this trial by prattle. Give me something to do.

She turned to face him. "Look me in the eyes and tell me, honestly, just how eager you are to call me your sister-in-law."

Bloody hell.

He cast a wistful glance at the stone floor below. Was it too late to plummet to his doom and make it look like an accident?

He could manage the first of her requests. He looked her in the eyes—her lovely eyes, the same blue as a cloudless sky—for a very long time. Without saying anything.

Outside, the rain beat down like a rebuke. His blood thundered in his ears.

"You can't say it," she whispered. "Can you?"

"Honestly? No, I can't."

Hurt flickered over her features. He wanted to punch a hole straight through the wall.

"Well, then. Good. Now that we know where we stand with each other, we can stop pret—"

Damn him. *Damn* him and his impulsive, reckless soul.

His hands were out before he could stop them. Reaching for her, pulling her close, turning her face to his.

Skimming a touch over her soft, trembling lips.

And holding her still for his kiss.

When his lips first touched hers, Clio was certain there'd been some mistake.

That could be the only explanation.

Obviously, Rafe had meant to put his wide, sensuous lips somewhere else—and she, being clumsy, had gotten her face in the way. How very embarrassing. How very *her*.

But . . . Then again, his big, warm hands did seem to be *holding* her face.

And those wide, sensuous lips were moving over hers, again and again, with something that felt suspiciously like purpose.

Good heavens. Rafe was kissing her.

And what was more shocking by half? By the time her brain put it all together, the rest of her was kissing him back.

Oh, Rafe. Yes.

She scarcely knew how, but it didn't matter. He taught her the way of it, in much the same way he'd once taught her to angle trout in the stream. With practiced skill and gentle teasing, and a patience that belied his hunger.

They kissed tenderly. They kissed deeply.

They kissed as though it were *right*.

As though it made perfect sense. As if all the talking and not-talking and arguing and ignoring they'd done over the past eight years—no, so much longer than that—had all been entries on one long list of "Things We Do to Avoid Kissing." And now that they'd reached the end of it, they had a great deal of lost time to make up.

They kissed and kissed, as the rain fell around them.

It was so absurdly romantic, Clio thought her heart would burst.

And sweet. So sweet. His mouth brushed over hers again and again, each kiss lingering a bit longer than the last. A cloud of breath and longing formed between them. Their own small, secret storm.

His hand cradled the back of her head, tilting her face to his. He drew her close to his chest and deepened the kiss, exploring her mouth with bold sweeps of his tongue. All Clio could do was cling tight.

Her senses opened wide to take in everything. The firm beat of his heart. The faster pulse of her own. His sweet taste, and the spicy wintergreen scent of his skin.

It intrigued her, that scent. Some kind of aromatic shaving soap, perhaps? It wasn't cologne.

Curious now, she slid one hand to touch his jaw. Though it was barely afternoon, and yes—he had shaved that morning—the faint beginnings of whiskers rasped against her fingertips. She found the texture wildly exciting. So foreign to her, and so masculine.

So *real*.

To her surprise, he didn't press her for more than

kisses. Didn't stroke or grope in any of the ways good girls were warned that wicked men would try to do. Oh, she could feel the power pulsing through his body, the need coiling hot and tense in his muscles. He wanted more. He wanted everything.

But he only kissed her. As though this were enough.

As though it *must* be enough, and God help them both if it wasn't.

"The rain stopped," he said, sometime later.

She nodded drowsily. So had the kisses.

His hands slid from her face. He turned his back to the wall and let his head fall against the stone with a soft *thunk*. "I'm a bastard."

"If you're a bastard, I don't know what that makes me."

"It's nothing to do with you."

Her chin ducked. "It isn't?"

"Well, it is, of course. It's a great deal to do with you. If I try to explain, I'll make a hash of it."

"Try anyway." She waited, still cocooned in his scent and the warm, lingering glow of his embrace.

"I should have outgrown this by now," he said. "I thought I had, curse it."

"Kissing?"

"Envy. I always envied my brother. His playthings, his accomplishments. The praise he earned. From the earliest time I can remember, I wanted whatever was his." His jaw tensed. "You were his."

"Oh."

He rubbed his face with both hands. "What the hell am I saying? You *are* his."

Clio didn't know quite how to take this. Rafe wanted

her. He'd wanted her for ages, but not because he found her especially desirable or attractive. He wanted her because she belonged to Piers. Apparently, she could be a hideous, troll-faced lump, and it wouldn't matter. He would still want to kiss her for hours in the rain.

That warm, lingering glow began to fade. Rapidly.

"This won't happen again," he said. "Ever."

And . . . there it went. Glow extinguished.

"Well," she managed, after an uncomfortable moment spent piecing together what little remained of her pride, "I see why you're so popular with the ladies now, Rafe. You truly know how to make a girl feel exceptional."

She tried to untangle her sodden skirts.

He put a hand under her elbow, scooping her off the stone and setting her on her feet.

The nerve of him, acting so chivalrous less than a minute after rejecting her, and *that* less than a minute after kissing her with abandon. Was he dizzy from all these about-face maneuvers?

"At least this means I win," she said.

"You win what?"

"You'll have to sign those dissolution papers now. They're in my dressing table. Now that it's stopped raining, we can go back at once."

"Wait, wait. You do not win. I'm not signing those papers."

"How can you refuse after . . . ?" She gestured lamely at the spot of floor where they'd kissed. " . . . after that? You're still going to encourage me to marry your brother?"

"Of course I am."

"You *kissed* me."

"Don't make so much of it. A kiss is nothing."

Nothing? To him, perhaps. But that kiss hadn't felt like nothing to her.

"I've kissed a great many women who moved along and married other men," he said. "Sometimes the same day."

"You can't be serious."

"And as for you," he plowed on, denying her an explanation. "If you'd had the experience of a proper season, you wouldn't make anything of this, either. You'd have been kissed by a dozen randy scapegraces on verandahs and in follies, and you'd have realized on your own that marrying a man like Piers is for the best."

Clio knew better than that. There was a reason she'd been known as the luckiest debutante of her season. Because not only had she become engaged to the most eligible bachelor of the *ton*, but everyone knew she would have had no chance at him, had their fathers not arranged it years ago. If she'd had a normal season, she might not have been kissed at all.

"But this is your own brother you want me to marry. How do you see this working, exactly?" She started down the stairs. "Every Christmas and Easter, we'd sit down across the table from one another and try not to think about that time we kissed like lovers in the rain?"

"You needn't worry about making polite conversation. I'm not coming around on Christmas or Easter."

Clio paused on the steps. She knew that Rafe and his father had conducted their own at-home reenactment of the Hundred Years' War. But surely now that the marquess was dead, the two brothers needn't continue it.

"You wouldn't come?" she asked. "Even now, when your father's gone?"

"I don't see a reason."

What a liar. His kiss had been full to bursting with reasons. There was emotion in that embrace they'd shared. Perhaps it wasn't attraction or affection or love—but it was yearning. He might have rebuffed all her invitations over the years, but it was plain to her now that he hadn't ignored them completely.

They reached the bottom of the stairs. Ellingworth had fallen asleep in the hopcart.

Or *was* he asleep? He was so still, she worried for a moment. But she touched her fingers to his coat and found it warm. She massaged his neck a few strokes. The old dog scrunched his already-scrunched face and snuffled contentedly.

Clio gathered her courage. "I know it's only been a matter of months since he died, Rafe. And you've been alone. When my own mother passed, I would have been lost without my sisters." She stood tall. "Did you want to talk at all?"

He pulled a face. "No."

"Are you certain? Sometimes it helps."

"There's nothing to help. I stopped thinking of the marquess as my father years ago, and the man never looked on me as a beloved son. I was always the mistake." He took the cart handle and tipped a glance toward the tower's upper level. "I still am, apparently. But despite what happened up there, I'm not going to sign your papers. If you mean to show me the door, I—"

"No," she interrupted. "No, I want you to stay."

"Don't be polite. Courtesy's wasted on me."

"I'm not being polite." To prove it, she added, "Drat you."

Oh, this man. He tried to seem disbelieving. Indifferent. But just a look at him gave everything away. His eyes were daring her to cast him out, begging her to let him stay. Two thin green boundaries of wariness encircling deep, dark wells of . . .

Secret pain.

He tried to deny it, but he was hungry for connection, a sense of belonging in his life. Family. Acceptance. Home. A reason to come around on Christmas and Easter.

Clio could see it. And maybe—just maybe—if she kept him here a bit longer, he'd start to admit that to himself.

"I want you to stay, Rafe. Because we made a bargain. One round doesn't decide the bout. I need those papers signed, and I'm not giving up."

Not on herself, and not on him.

"As for the kiss . . ." She hugged herself tight, trying to preserve the last bit of that tender warmth. "You're right. It was just a kiss. Let's forget it ever happened."

Chapter Seven

Let's forget it ever happened.

Easy enough to say. Damn difficult to accomplish. Thus far, Rafe was finding it impossible.

By the time he, Bruiser, and the three Whitmore sisters had gathered in the castle's jewel box of a chapel the next afternoon, some twenty-two hours had passed. Rafe had thought about, dreamed of, or berated himself for kissing Clio approximately . . . twenty-one-and-a-half of them.

He'd run twelve miles that morning, then taken an ice-cold plunge in the pond.

Hadn't helped.

He couldn't cease looking at her. And he had far too much opportunity to stare because she refused to so much as turn his direction today.

She was angry with him. For good reason.

The worst of it was, he rather liked angry Clio.

She stood a little taller, hiked her chin a bit higher. Her eyes had fire in them. If he'd been coaching her toward a prizefight, he would have been feeling confident.

Talking her into a wedding, however . . . ?

"Dearly beloved," Bruiser announced from the front of the chapel, "we are gathered here today to set the scene for this most joyous of occasions." He rubbed his hands together. "Are you prepared to be dazzled, Miss Whitmore?"

"I . . . don't rightly know."

"Miss Whitmore is ready to be dazzled," Rafe said, glancing in her direction. "She told me so. The other day."

She looked at him then.

He sent a message with his eyes. *We have a bargain, remember?*

"Very well," she said, sounding resigned. "I'm ready to be dazzled."

"Excellent." Bruiser spread his arms wide, hands lifted. "Picture this. We'll drape the entire chapel in white bunting."

"Oh, I do love bunting," Daphne said. "My own wedding suffered from such a dearth of it."

"You eloped," Clio pointed out.

Rafe opened his mouth to question this plan. Then he caught himself. Instead, he took a seat in the benches and stared numbly forward, trying to understand how he, the infamous Devil's Own, had arrived at this moment in his life: sitting in a chapel, in a storybook castle near Charming-Something, Kent, possessing opinions on *bunting*.

Good God.

Word of this could never escape these walls.

Daphne charged ahead, sweeping down the center aisle in a flounce of ribbons. "Let's see. We'll place fabric bows to festoon the end of each bench. That's one, two . . ."

"Twelve," Phoebe said.

The youngest of the Whitmore sisters had seated herself in the pew in front of Rafe's and pulled a loop of string from her pocket. While the plans went on around her, she worked her fingers through the string and began to make figures with it. Like a game of cat's cradle, only more elaborate.

"Twelve rows," she said. "Four-and-twenty benches." She stretched her fingers wide to reveal a lattice of string shaped like a row of diamonds.

Rafe slid closer and stacked his arms on the back of her pew. "You're good at that, aren't you?"

"The string or the counting?"

"Both."

"Yes," she said.

Rafe watched her, intrigued. Of the three Whitmore sisters, Phoebe was the one he'd never had much chance to know. She'd been a small child when he and the marquess had their falling-out, and he'd avoided family gatherings ever since. He guessed this string fancy of hers must explain her pet name.

"So four-and-twenty bows," Daphne said. "And then a swag for each window. How many windows, Phoebe?"

"Fourteen. With thirty-two panes in each."

Rafe said quietly, "You didn't even look up."

"I didn't need to." Phoebe peered at her string through a fringe of dark hair. "With numbers, counting, shapes, chances . . . It's always like that. I just know."

Now there was a sensation he couldn't identify with. Learning had never come easily to him.

"What's that like?" he asked. "To just . . . know things, without trying."

She looped her fingers through the string. "What's it like to have the power to knock a full-grown man to the ground?"

"It means I have to be careful how I carry myself. Especially around new acquaintances, or people I don't like. But it's useful in certain situations. And sometimes, highly satisfying."

For the first time, her glance flitted in his direction. "Then I don't need to explain it."

As Rafe watched, she stretched her fingers wide to reveal a new figure. The arched opening in the center matched, precisely, the proportions of the stained-glass window before them.

Then she let her fingers slip from the string, and it was gone.

Daphne came to stand before them, making calculations. "So if we need two yards of bunting per swag and three-quarters per bow . . . Come along, kitten. Don't force me to find a pencil and paper."

"Forty-six yards," Phoebe said.

Clio laughed. "You mean to order *forty-six* yards of fabric? Are we decorating a chapel or swaddling an elephant? What with the carvings and the stained glass, it's a lovely setting as it is."

"Anything lovely can be made lovel*ier*," Daphne said. "Don't you recall what Mother always said?"

From the look on Clio's face, she did recall whatever it was their mother always said—but not with any particular fondness.

Bruiser cleared his throat for attention. "Right, then. Carrying on. The chapel will be lovelier. And Miss Whitmore will be the most lovelier part of all."

"'Lovel*iest*,' Montague," Daphne corrected.

"Yes, of course. Loveliest."

Clio looked doubtful. If not miserable. And Rafe knew he was to blame. He'd been an idiot yesterday, kissing her, then telling her it was nothing. Hardly the way to increase a woman's confidence.

He pulled Bruiser aside. "This isn't working. You said you could make her excited about the wedding. You promised dazzle."

"She'll be dazzled, Rafe."

He took another glance at Clio. "I'm not seeing it yet."

"Give it a moment, will you?" Bruiser went to Clio's side and gently steered her to stand at the end of the aisle. "Just imagine, Miss Whitmore. The rows filled with your family and closest friends. Even better, your vilest enemies. All of them waiting, in breathless anticipation, for you to make your grand appearance."

"My grand appearance?"

"Yes. In a flowing gown with an exquisite lace veil."

In the chapel's small vestibule, there was a narrow table with a lace runner and a small vase of flowers. Bruiser whisked the lace runner from the table and tucked it into Clio's upswept hair, creating a makeshift veil to cover her face.

Rafe could see her smiling behind it. Smiling at the absurdity, no doubt—but any smile was better than the morose expression she'd been wearing all morning.

"And a bouquet." Bruiser plucked the flowers from the vase and put them into her hands. "There now."

She held them away from her body. "They're dripping."

"Never mind that. Imagine a velvet carpet spread out before you, strewn with rose petals. And your sisters will precede you as you walk down the aisle." Bruiser moved first Daphne, then Phoebe into place in front of Clio. "Go stand at the other end, Rafe. Just to the side of the altar. That's where your place will be."

Good God. Not this "best man" nonsense again. If there'd been any doubt about Rafe's unsuitability for that post, his behavior in the tower yesterday should have erased it.

Nonetheless, Rafe did as he was asked, moving to stand just to the side of the altar. For once, Clio seemed to be enjoying the wedding idea. He wasn't going to ruin that.

"A vicar," Bruiser muttered to himself. "We need a vicar. Someone solemn, dignified, wearing a collar . . . Aha."

He plucked Ellingworth from the carpet and lugged him up to the altar, depositing the old, wrinkled bulldog in the place where a vicar would stand. With a wheeze, the dog sank to rest on his belly, head between his two front paws. His wrinkled jowls pooled around his black nose.

Daphne said, "Now all we're missing is a groom."

"A sadly familiar sensation," Clio replied.

"Not to worry. We can remedy that, Miss Whit-more." Bruiser dashed behind Rafe and prodded him forward, toward the center. "Rafe will stand in for Lord Granville. I'll be best man."

"What?" Rafe muttered under his breath. "No. I'm not playing the groom."

"You're his brother," Bruiser whispered back. "You're the logical choice. I can't very well send her down the aisle to kiss Ellingworth, can I?"

Rafe cast a glance around the chapel. What the devil had happened to Sir Teddy Cambourne? The man was always where he wasn't wanted and never around when he might be useful.

"Next," Bruiser said, "the orchestra will strike up the processional."

"I don't know where you mean to fit an orchestra in this chapel," Clio said from somewhere beneath her tablecloth.

"They'll squeeze in somewhere."

"Really, the organ would be good enough."

"No," Rafe interjected. "Nothing 'good enough' is good enough. Not for this wedding. An orchestra it is."

"Ready, then? Bridesmaids first." Bruiser began humming a processional.

Daphne joined in the humming, leading Phoebe down the aisle.

"Now the bride." When Clio hesitated, Bruiser nudged Rafe. "Hum along, will you?"

"I'm not humming. I don't hum."

His trainer jabbed him in the kidney. "Do you want to sell her on this wedding or not?"

Damnation.

Rafe started to hum, too.

Clio gave in, walking down the aisle of the chapel—toward a bulldog, in time with the strains of tuneless humming, draped in a tablecloth and clutching a handful of wilting, dripping flowers. Halfway down, she started to giggle. By the time she reached Rafe at the altar, she was laughing aloud.

"I'm telling you, Miss Whitmore," Bruiser said. "The guests will rise to their feet in awe."

"Oh, yes." She was still laughing as she lifted the tablecloth from her face. "I'm sure they will. With a bride like this before them, how could they not?"

Curse it, Rafe should have known this wouldn't work. She wasn't dazzled. She was only amused. It had gone all wrong.

Except, in a strange way, it felt rather right. If he were ever to be married, this was just how he'd want his bride to look as she walked down the aisle to meet him.

Happy. Joyful. Even laughing. Having the time of her life.

But Rafe wasn't getting married.

And Clio was *not* going to be his bride.

"What time is it?" Phoebe asked. "Mr. Montague, will you check your pocket watch?"

"I . . . er . , '"

Bruiser looked down at the flashy watch fob where it disappeared into his pocket. Rafe would wager it wasn't attached to a timepiece of any sort.

Rafe pulled out his own watch and opened it. "It's seventeen minutes past two."

Phoebe nodded. "You should have the wedding at eighteen minutes past two."

"Don't be ridiculous, kitten." Daphne gave her younger sister a pinch. "No one has a wedding at two o'clock, much less eighteen minutes past. Whyever would they do that?"

"Wait a minute," Phoebe replied. "You'll see."

No sooner had she said this than a shaft of light pierced the stained-glass window above the altar. A column of luminous, breathtaking gold enveloped Clio in its warmth. Her fair hair gleamed. Her skin glowed. Her blue eyes had the depth and richness of lapis. Even the stupid lace tablecloth was transformed into a thing of delicate beauty.

"Cor," Bruiser said, forgetting his Montague role completely. "I did promise dazzle, didn't I?"

Rafe didn't know about Clio, but he was dazzled.

He was dazzled to his bones.

"What is it?" Clio looked around at them. "You're all staring. Have I grown a second head?"

"No," Daphne said, sounding uncharacteristically genuine and kind. "Not at all. Oh, Clio, you're lovely."

"Lovelier," Bruiser corrected.

"Loveliest." The word was out before Rafe had time to consider it.

He wouldn't take it back if he could. She was, quite simply, the loveliest thing he'd seen in years. Perhaps in all his life.

"Me?" She laughed and touched her tablecloth veil. "In this?"

Everyone hastened to assure her it was the truth.

"You should see yourself," Rafe said. "You're . . ."

He couldn't find any words to describe it. He hoped the look in his eyes would convey the message. When a man admired a woman this intensely . . . surely it must be palpable.

Her eyes warmed. One corner of her lips lifted. And then, as if he'd called it into being, a wash of pink touched her cheeks.

Thank God. He hadn't seen that blush since yesterday. He'd missed it.

"Really?" she whispered.

"Found it!" Cambourne came jogging into the chapel, breathless and looking smug. As always. "I knew there had to be one in this place somewhere. Took me all morning searching, and even straight through luncheon, but I finally found one."

"One what, Teddy?" his wife asked.

The man held up a finger in a signal to wait, then disappeared for a moment. When he returned, he did so slowly. And with a great deal of scraping, clanking racket.

"It's a ball and chain, see?" He laughed, demonstrating the clamshell shackle and rattling the iron links. "Now that's what this wedding's missing."

And there—in the space of a moment—any small progress they'd made toward dazzling the bride disappeared.

"Have no fear, dumpling," Cambourne said. "We won't let him get away."

Thank you, Sir Teddy Cambourne. You obnoxious prig.

"A ball and chain," Clio said. "How amusing."

She was forcing a laugh to be polite. Because she was kind, and she wouldn't want anyone to feel slighted. Even the man who'd just slighted her.

The earth had turned, and the shaft of sunlight had moved on, leaving her looking pale and small, draped in a tablecloth and clutching a soggy bouquet.

Rafe was furious. The brute in him was rising. He wanted to shake Bruiser, punch that smirking fop Cambourne in the jaw, throw Clio over his shoulder, and carry her somewhere else. Somewhere far away from all these fools who paid more attention to malicious gossips and scandal sheets than to the obvious loveliness—inside and out—of their own sister.

But none of that would help his cause.

She'd only given him a week to convince her. He couldn't risk changing the subject. But if there was going to be any bridal excitement generated, it wasn't going to happen like this.

His only alternative was clear.

"I have to leave." With a curt bow to the ladies, he turned to make his exit. "Mind the dog while I'm gone," he told Bruiser.

"You're going?" Clio called after him. "Will we see you at dinner?"

He didn't turn around. "No. I have business in London. I'll be leaving at once."

Chapter Eight

"Where did Lord Rafe say he was off to again?"

"London." Clio reached for the crock of currant jam. "That's all I know."

True to his word, Rafe had left Twill Castle in as little time as it had taken to saddle his gelding. Clio had watched his retreating figure from the window of her bedchamber.

And now, sitting at breakfast two days later, she hadn't seen him since. She told herself not to worry. He was a grown man—an overgrown man, more accurately, and a champion fighter. He could handle himself in any situation. It would have been silly to spend hours sitting at the same window, scanning the horizon for any sign of him.

But she had done that, just the same.

She couldn't help but feel a little disappointed,

really. This wedding battle of theirs had begun to grow amusing, and mostly because the advantage was all hers. So far all of the wedding planning had been disastrous. Did he mean to forfeit?

If so, she hoped he would be decent enough to honor the terms of their original bargain. One week was what they'd agreed. If nothing else, he needed to return to sign those dissolution papers in a few days.

"We could work on the invitations this morning," Daphne said, stirring sugar into her tea. "Then they'll be ready to post the moment Lord Granville returns."

Of course the rest of her family had no idea these wedding preparations were about to become irrelevant. Clio felt increasingly uneasy about the deception, but she didn't dare mention breaking the engagement until those papers were signed. They wouldn't understand. And by "they," she mostly meant "Daphne."

"We can't start on the invitations," Clio said. "We don't even know the date Piers will return."

Daphne dismissed this with a wave of her spoon. "We'll just have everything else written out and leave a space for the date."

Clio would have argued the point, but she was interrupted by a rattling commotion in the drive.

"Are you expecting a delivery?" Teddy asked.

"I ordered in more coal," Clio said. "That must be what's arrived. This castle is so drafty, even in the summer."

"Imagine what it would be like in winter." Daphne shuddered. "Freezing."

"Expensive," Teddy amended, lifting a forkful of kippers and eggs.

Her brother-in-law was right, and Clio knew it. Given enough wood or coal to burn, any space could be heated, but fuel required income. Her dowry, once unencumbered, could support her for some years. But if she meant to live in Twill Castle indefinitely, she would need to make the brewery profitable.

The operations were just a matter of time and investment. Winning over the farmers would take some work. Earning the custom of the tavernkeepers, however? That required more strategy. She would need to cultivate a reputation for quality, a consistent production schedule. And most of all, a memorable name.

Castle Ale?

Twill Brewhouse?

None of the alternatives she'd dreamed up so far were inspiring.

Phoebe spoke up. "Since Lord Rafe is out, I was thinking that we ought to use this morning for the eighteenth item on my list."

"Eighteenth item? Even including the ice sculptures, I thought there were only seventeen."

"We need to discuss the wedding night."

All around the table, forks, spoons, and teacups paused in midair.

Clio swallowed her mouthful of chocolate with difficulty. "What, dear?"

"Item number eighteen on the list of wedding preparations. Education in your marital duties."

Clio exchanged a desperate glance with Daphne, who showed no indication of having known of this beforehand. *"Don't look at me,"* she mouthed.

"Our mother is dead," Phoebe said, in the same tone she would have used to explain simple arithmetic. "By rights, she would have been the one to give Clio this talk. Since she is unable, the duty must fall to us, her sisters." From beneath the table, she produced a few curled slips of paper. "I took the liberty of doing some reading. I have notes."

Oh, dear.

"Phoebe, darling. That's so kind of you, but I'm sure it isn't necessary."

Daphne quickly agreed. "If Clio has any questions, she can come to me. I am a married lady now."

"Yes, but you are married to an Englishman. And as Mr. Montague reminded us in the gardens, Lord Granville has been living on the Continent for some years. If she is going to keep her husband satisfied, Clio will need to be well versed in the ways of Continental women, too. I was able to locate a few books in French. They were illustrated."

Bad manners or no, Clio put her elbow on the table. Then she buried her laughter in her palm. "Truly."

"Yes, but they weren't very helpful. And the words they use are ridiculous. All this talk of folds and rods and buttons. Are we copulating or sewing draperies?"

At that, Clio was glad for an excuse to laugh aloud.

"In the end, I had to cross-reference my flora and fauna compendiums."

"Oh, kitten. You didn't," Daphne said. "Clio, whatever will we do with this sister of ours?"

Her face blank, Phoebe turned from Clio to Daphne and back again. "Did I do something wrong?"

"No," Clio assured her. "You are frighteningly brilliant and adorably well-intentioned, and I hope you will never change in either respect."

Each of her sisters could be absurd at times, and irritating at others. But Clio was protective of even their foibles and faults. Perhaps Daphne and Phoebe weren't always perfect sisters. But they were *her* sisters, and that was much better.

"I don't see what's frightening or adorable about it." Her youngest sister sat a bit taller and sifted through the papers in hand. "But I should hate for all this work to be for nothing. I've made a thorough survey of the mechanics and prepared some diagrams. Such as I could define them, I created a taxonomy of terms such as 'lust,' 'desire,' 'arousal,' 'climax.' For the emotions and sensations attached, we shall have to rely on Daphne's reports."

Clio's brother-in-law had been chewing the same bite of toast for several moments now. And with Phoebe's last comment, he choked on it.

"Oh." Phoebe looked at him. "I didn't mean to exclude you, Teddy. Did you wish to contribute something helpful from the male point of view?"

A red-faced Teddy promptly pushed back from his place and stood, abandoning a full plate of food. "I have a pressing letter to write. Upstairs." He swallowed. "Just remembered it. If you'll excuse me."

After a curt bow, the poor man was gone from the room so quickly, Clio could have sworn she heard a whooshing sound.

"That's for the best," Phoebe said. "Better if it's only females."

Daphne, who had buried her face in both hands

for much of the conversation thus far, finally lifted her head. "We're not going to have this conversation, kitten. Clio's husband will be the best person to instruct her on the . . . er . . ."

"Mechanics?" Clio suggested.

"Yes. And as for the sensations . . . There's really no use in describing them. What feels nice to one person might leave another cold. It's best if she makes the discoveries herself. With the assistance of her husband, of course."

In truth, Clio had made a *few* discoveries without the assistance of any husband. She was twenty-five years old, and she had been in the possession of a mature body for some eight or nine of those years. She understood her body's responses to touch, and . . .

"Good morning." The deep voice rang through the breakfast room.

. . . and thanks to the man filling the doorway, she was now well acquainted with the meaning of desire.

"Why, Lord Rafe," Clio said. Because it seemed something must be said, and he'd left her at a loss. "You've returned."

"I've returned."

"Yes. You are. I mean, you have." *Stupid, stupid.* As Clio rose from the table, she glared at Phoebe, sending a silent big-sister message.

Stash those papers away. Now.

Rafe must have noticed the three of them looking guiltily from one to the other. "Am I interrupting something?"

"No," Clio said, much too hastily. "No, you didn't

interrupt anything important. We were just discussing . . ." She felt her face go pink. " . . . draperies."

At the other end of the table, Daphne burst into giggles.

"Well, I'm glad I'm not interrupting anything important. Because I need a word with you, Miss Whitmore. If you'll come with me."

Bewildered, Clio followed him into the corridor.

He was so big, he nearly took up the entire passageway, and sheer virility filled any leftover space.

Her heartbeat quickened. "What is it? What's happened?"

"I've something to show you," he said.

"What is it?"

"You don't want to ruin the surprise." A boyish grin tugged at the corner of his lips.

Her body's reaction was immediate and intensely feminine. Had someone attached a thread to one corner of his mouth, then secured the other end to her nipple, the effect of that smile could not have been more direct.

"Shouldn't we wait for my sisters and Mr. Montague?" she asked.

His voice didn't drop, or sink. It *plummeted* down a mine shaft of manliness. "No."

Her giddy heart skipped a beat. Then two.

Oh, this grew worse and worse.

"Trust me. You're going to like this."

He tucked her arm through his and led her down the corridor. Clio sensed she would only embarrass herself by resisting, so she didn't.

And truly, how many times in her life would she have the chance to be on the arm of a man with . . .

well, a man with these *arms*? Her fingers lay on his wrist, making no more dent than fallen leaves made on a rock. She could have believed him to be carved from stone if his heat weren't palpable through the layers of linen and wool.

Her senses exploded with memories of that kiss in the tower.

Perhaps they'd agreed to set it aside and never speak of it.

But that didn't mean Clio had stopped thinking of it. Dreaming of it. Wishing, against all logic or sense, that it could happen again. It was like this wanting had been inside her all along, just years of it building and growing . . . and now she felt the force of it hitting her all at once.

This was lust, and she understood the power of it now. Every part of her body thrummed with desire.

She knew nothing more could come of it, and yet somehow that knowledge did little to quell her imaginings. Quite the reverse.

"I can't imagine what your great secret could be. We've already decided on the venue, met with the vicar, and planned the breakfast for this imaginary wedding that's never going to take place. We've discussed bunting, bagpipes, peacocks in the garden . . ."

"Precisely. We've been wasting time on inanity. I decided to take matters into my own hands. This morning, we're going to have this done. The two of us. Alone."

"Alone?"

Oh, Lord.

He threw open the doors to the music room. Clio

was relieved to see at a glance that it was full of people. They weren't too terribly alone.

"Pianoforte," he announced, indicating the grand instrument lodged in one corner of the room. The pianist seated at it poured out a stream of flawless, sparkling Handel.

"Harp," he said, pivoting them both.

In the center of the room, a serene-looking woman set her fingers to the harp strings, skipping up and down them in an intricate melody and finishing with a majestic glissande.

"String quartet."

In the far corner, a violinist nodded to his associates. The rich, warm harmonies of Haydn soon filled the room, delivered to her ears with unparalleled skill and in perfect tune. It felt like sipping chocolate through the eardrum, if one could do such a thing.

When final chord ended, Clio blinked, overwhelmed. Then she applauded them. "That was lovely. Thank you."

"So?" Rafe turned to her. "Choose one for the wedding. Or take all three."

"I . . ."

"Think on it," he said. "We can have them play more selections afterward."

"After what?"

He said, "There's more."

He led her through the connecting door, into the next chamber—the morning room. A heady perfume engulfed her at once.

"Oh, my."

Orchids. Lilies. Irises. Hydrangea. Roses in every color she knew, and some she didn't know could exist. Not only cut flowers, but aromatic herbs and potted bulbs that would bloom just this one day, then wilt. They covered every available surface.

Her morning room had been transformed into a hothouse conservatory.

"Oh, Rafe."

"I just told them to send everything best," Rafe said. "I don't know a damn thing about that language of flowers."

"It doesn't matter."

Clio didn't care about Daphne's floral ciphers, either. Nor Phoebe's botanical explanations. As far as Clio was concerned, flowers of any sort had just one message to convey.

They said, *I care.*

And this room was screaming it.

I care, I care, I care. Bouquets of consideration over here, pots of solicitousness over there. Thoughtfulness, blooming in every color of Nature's rainbow.

No wonder he'd been flashing that boyish, hand-in-the-biscuit-tin smile. Rafe had put so much effort into this display.

And it would be the best thing anyone ever did for her—if indeed it *was* done for her. But was it Clio he cared for, or merely his career?

Whatever it was, she was afraid it might be working. For the first time since the idea of wedding planning had been hatched, she found herself feeling a touch of bridal excitement. To walk down the chapel aisle before all her friends and family, floating on a glistening cloud of harp strings and clutching two dozen perfect hothouse blooms . . . ?

That would be something.

"Surely there must be a flower or two here that appeals to you," he said.

Was it her imagination, or did he sound anxious?

"I'm overwhelmed. They're all so beautiful." She walked through the room, touching petals here and there.

"Well, you can think on these, too." He caught her arm again. "What's in the next room can't wait."

"Did you say the *next* room? You can't mean there's more."

"Come see."

He led her to the connecting door on the opposite side of the room and opened it. They emerged into the formal dining room, and Clio was stopped cold by the sight that awaited them.

Cakes.

Cakes *everywhere*.

"You didn't," she breathed.

"I did," he replied, shutting the door behind them.

The entire length of the dining table—and the castle's dining table stretched to an impressive length—was laden with cakes. Of every conceivable variety.

Cakes iced with peaks of whipped cream and garnished with wild strawberries; cakes covered in rolled-gum icing and clever marzipan violets. Cakes cocooned in spun-sugar floss.

On closer inspection, Clio could see that a narrow slice was already cut from each, so that the flavor and filling were visible. As she walked the length of the table, she saw layers she suspected to be chocolate, spice, toffee . . . and various shades of light yellow that would no doubt prove to be vanilla, almond, lemon, pineapple, rosewater, and who could know what else.

"You brought these from Town? All of them?"

"I just went to Gunter's and asked for one of everything."

She shook her head. "They'll go to waste."

"Don't worry, we'll distribute the surplus to local cottagers or something. First, have a taste and choose your favorite for the wedding cake. Hell, choose three. Or ten. You can be the bride with a twelve-tiered cake, with cupids bursting from it the moment it's sliced, and all London will talk of it for years to come." He caught her gaze. "I know you've waited a long time, and you've had every right to feel impatient. But this wedding is going to be your day, Clio."

He stood tall and made a magnanimous sweep of his hand, as if he were a king ruling over Cakelandia. *Just imagine*, that gesture said. *All this could be yours.*

She understood his strategy now. He meant to overwhelm her with luxury, lavish choices upon her. If he piled on enough fantasy and spectacle, surely Clio would give in. A little cake waved under her nose, and she would give up all her dreams and plans to walk down the aisle instead.

She couldn't decide whether he failed to understand her, or didn't respect her. After their talk in the tower, she had hoped he might afford her a touch more credit.

Apparently not. All her plans for this place—and her own independence . . . Rafe thought she would trade it all for a twelve-tiered cake with cupids bursting out the top.

He took a slice of chocolate cake and dug into it with a fork. "Try this one first."

He extended the plate to her.

She looked at it. "No, thank you."

"Did you want to start with another?" He set the plate down and prodded an orange-colored slice with the tines of the fork. "I think this one's filled with apricot cream."

"I don't care to taste any of them."

"Come along. You have to choose one."

"Do I?"

"Yes. We had a bargain."

"Then let Daphne and Phoebe and Teddy choose for me. Or you do it. Cake is for the guests, not the bride."

He gave her an annoyed look. "I didn't go to all this trouble and expense just so someone else could select your wedding cake." He jabbed a fork into a lemon yellow slice and pressed the plate on her. "Taste it."

"I don't care for cake."

"Liar. You love cake."

"Who told you that?"

"You did."

"*I* did?" She didn't recall that conversation.

"Yes, you did. Years ago. The summers you spent at Oakhaven. I remember it clearly."

He was very near her now. Near enough that when he dug his fork into the slice of cake, she could smell the fragrance of lemon and hear the tiny *ping* of silver tines striking china.

He gathered a forkful and held it just inches from her lips.

"You," he said, "make cake sounds."

"Cake sounds?" she echoed. "What on earth are 'cake sounds'?"

"Just what they're described to be. When you eat cake, you make sounds."

No, she didn't. Did she?

He nodded. "Oh, yes. Sighs. Gasps. Breathy little moans. You . . . *love* . . . cake. Or at least you did, once. I know they've forced you to spend the past decade all pinned and buttoned and corseted and restrained. But I know"—he waved the fork before her—"you want this."

A flush crept up her throat. "Even if I do make 'cake sounds'—and I am not admitting that I do—it is most ungentlemanly of you to take notice of them."

"I'm sure it is. But I'm not known for my gentlemanly behavior."

No, he wasn't. Rafe Brandon was a black sheep. A hotheaded rebel. The Devil's Own. He was known throughout England for being quick, crude, strong, dangerous.

And tempting. Devilishly, irresistibly tempting.

She swallowed. Not audibly, she hoped. "I don't make cake sounds. Not anymore."

"Then have a bite and prove me wrong." He lifted the fork again. When she hesitated, he said, "It's just one tiny little bite of cake. What are you afraid of?"

You. Me. Cake. Piers. Marriage. Spiders.
Everything.

"Nothing," she lied.

There was no use in explaining it. He had no idea what he was asking of her. He couldn't possibly understand.

"Then have a piece."

"You won't give up on this, will you?"

He shook his head no.

"Very well." She took the fork from his hand and stuffed the bite of cake in her mouth.

Chew, she told herself. *It's only one bite. Chew, swallow, be done with it.*

But . . .

But the man was right, drat him. She did love cake. And this wasn't mere cake, it was . . . bliss. Like a wisp of sugary, velvety cloud on her tongue, melting into a lemon mist that teased and delighted.

She couldn't help it. As she swallowed, a helpless moan of pleasure rose in the back of her throat. "Mmm."

"What did I tell you? You make cake sounds."

Clearing the sweetness from her throat, she shook her head in protest. "That's not fair! That's not mere cake, it's . . . It's sin on a plate. Whoever baked it has surely bargained with the Devil."

Rafe chuckled.

"I mean it. No one could taste this cake and fail to make cake sounds. *You* try it. You'll see."

"No rich foods or sweetmeats for me. Not when I'm training." He set the slice aside and surveyed the others. "Which next?"

Oh, no. He wouldn't get out of it so easily. She picked up the lemon cake and gathered a bite with the fork, determined to avenge herself. "Taste the cake."

She moved closer, and he took a step in retreat. At last, she had *him* on the defensive.

She held out the fork and lowered her voice to a

sultry whisper, doing her best imitation of Eve in the garden of Eden. Offering Adam not an apple, but a slice of sinful lemon cake.

"It's just one . . . tiny . . . little . . . bite of cake." She pursed her lips in a pout. "What are you afraid of, Rafe?"

His green eyes locked with hers.

She pushed the fork toward his mouth, trying to sneak the bite between his lips. He ducked his head. When she tried again, he spun away, laughing.

"Oh, you."

She lunged a third time, but his reflexes were too quick for her—as always. He not only dodged the forkful of cake, but he caught her wrist, forbidding her to strike again.

"You truly think you can land a blow?" he asked. "On me? Impossible. I was the heavyweight champion of England, sweetheart."

"And I was the terror of the schoolroom." Clio reached wildly toward the table with her left hand. She couldn't manage to grasp a fork, so she dug her bare fingers into the nearest cake—a chocolate one—and gathered a handful. "Eat the *cake*, drat you!"

He dodged her swipe, then released her and dashed to the other side of the table. They were both breathless and laughing now, facing off from opposite sides of the cake buffet. If she sprang to the right, he countered with a move to the left.

He grinned at her frustrated efforts to catch him. "It's like I told you. Concentrate. Anticipate. React."

"React to this." She flung her handful of cake at him.

Curse the man, he ducked. Then he turned to regard the splattered fireworks of icing on the wall and whistled low, amused. "Why, Miss Whitmore. I can't believe you did that."

"Watch me do it again." She dove for an almond torte. It glanced off his shoulder, and she gave a cheer. "Aha! First blood."

"That's it," he said, reaching into a strawberry-studded cake for some ammunition of his own. "This is happening. This is real now."

She dove to the side, but he was too quick for her. Icing splattered her hair and face, like sugary shrapnel.

Time to reload.

Clio's eye landed on a dense, bomb-shaped plum cake in the center of the table. Now *that* would make an excellent projectile. No coming apart in the air. There was only one problem.

Rafe had his eye on it, too.

His gaze lifted from the plum cake and locked with hers. He smiled. "It's mine."

Not if I get there first.

They lunged for it at the same time. Rafe was first to grab the plate, but Clio thrust her hand straight into the center of the cake. She flexed her fingers and pulled, as if to lift the cake itself from the plate.

Instead, she doubled over and cried out in pain.

The plate clattered to the floor.

Chapter Nine

When Clio doubled over, Rafe's heart kicked him in the ribs.

"Jesus." He slammed what remained of the plum cake to the floor and vaulted over the table. "Clio, what is it? Are you injured?"

She nodded, clutching her right hand. "It's . . . It's my hand. I think my finger . . . Oh, it hurts."

Goddamn it. Goddamn him.

What could have been in that cake? A fork? A knife?

"Did you cut yourself? Let me see it. Don't worry. I'm here. I'll take care of you. I'll take care of everything." He reached for her hand, drawing it toward him.

He had just enough to time to wipe away the crumbs and icing and confirm that her hand was unmarred by blood or bruises. It was delicate, lovely, perfect.

And soft. So unbearably soft.

"I don't see any—"

Wham.

She used her other hand to give him a faceful of cake.

He stood sputtering, temporarily blinded by marzipan. Her laughter rang dimly through the icing in his ears. And, as he wiped his face clean, he was caught off guard again—this time by a sense of admiration.

It took a sharp opponent to land a blow on him. Well done, her.

"You cunning little minx. Now you're in for it." He wrapped his arm around her waist, lifting her off her feet. His boot caught the hem of her frock, and she gave a shriek of laughter as together they tumbled to the ground.

They landed in a heap. One of his legs covered both of hers.

"I win," he said.

She began to object. His hand was still coated with strawberry cake. Using his thumb, he pushed a morsel of it into her mouth.

That was a mistake.

Her lips and tongue wrapped around his thumb, sending a jolt of arousal straight to his cock.

Worse yet, she moaned as his thumb slid free. The gentle vibration slid down his spine, making him wild.

She fed him the hunk of plum cake she still clutched, pushing it into his mouth with her delicate fingertips. He caught her wrist and sucked her fingers clean, one by one, groaning softly. The tastes of spice and chocolate and ripe berries mingled on his tongue.

"There," she breathed. "See? I win. You make cake sounds, too."

"Those aren't cake sounds."

They were Clio sounds.

It wasn't cakes he craved. It was this. This closeness. This softness. This sweetness that came not from spun sugar and candy floss, but from her.

Just her.

Every shred of his conscience shouted at him to remember his career. Think of his brother. For the love of God, get the hell *off* her.

But she was so lovely and fresh—and not only sweet, but the perfect amount of tart. Her chest quaked with laughter, and her breasts danced under his chest. Damn, he hadn't laughed like this with anyone in years. Perhaps he never had.

He didn't know how to pull away.

Women liked him. He'd never had difficulty finding female company. But his lovers wanted the scoundrel and prizefighter. A big, hotheaded brute to toss them around the bed and pump them until they screamed. As a younger man, he'd been happy—hell, ecstatic—to oblige. But over the years, he'd come to crave more in the bedchamber than a bit of sweaty exertion.

Things like tenderness. Understanding. Laughter.

Moments just like this.

"Rafe . . ."

He shushed her, swiping the mussed hair from her brow. "You have icing on your forehead."

"Oh, dear." She reached to dab her left temple. "Here?"

"No. Here." He licked the smear of vanilla from the right side of her brow.

She trembled, but she didn't shy from him.

"There's some here, too," he lied. He ran his tongue over her cheekbone. She was more delicious than any icing. More tempting than any cake.

"Is that all of it?"

"No." He touched his tongue to the corner of her lips.

And then they were kissing again, and her lips parted beneath his. Her arms went around his neck, and his legs tangled in her skirts. He rolled atop her lush body, shameless. Letting her abundant curves cradle all his hard, aching need. Sweeping his tongue between her lips. Again and again.

As if he kissed her deeply enough, he could claim her for his own.

She's not yours, a voice inside him said.

He ignored it. He kissed down her neck and he slid one arm beneath her, gathering her by the waist and drawing her body tight against his. Until he held her so close she could have been a part of him.

She's not.

She's not yours.

He lifted his head abruptly. They were both breathing hard.

"I—"

"Don't," she said. "Don't explain or make excuses. Please. If I have to hear again how this is just a bit of impersonal lust, or to settle a score from your adolescence . . . you'll crush me."

"I won't tell you that." He would be lying if he did. This was more dangerous than lust or envy.

Rafe rolled to the side, staring up at the ceiling. He didn't know what the hell to call this feeling in his chest. But labels didn't matter. He wasn't free to explore it.

"You're. Engaged. To. My. Brother." Maybe if he spoke the words aloud, and slowly enough, they might sink into his conscience.

"I don't have to be." She struggled to a sitting position. "I could be not-engaged with a stroke of the pen."

"It's not that simple." He sat up, too.

"It truly is." She reached to wipe a bit of cake from his face. "Emotionally, he and I have no attachment. It's just a matter of legalities. The moment you signed those dissolution papers, I'd be free. *We'd* be free."

"To do what? Something you'd immediately regret?" He flicked a morsel of cake from his trouser leg.

"Why would I regr . . ." Her voice trailed off, and she frowned. "Oh, God. Oh, no."

"What is it?"

"My engagement ring." She flashed her naked, sticky hand at him. "It's gone."

He swore.

"We have to find it. It's worth a fortune." She rose from the carpet, looking high and low in her search. "It must have come off when I was sticking my hand in one of the cakes. I think I remember having it after the chocolate. And the almond. That would mean it got stuck in the . . ."

"Plum cake. Which I threw to the floor when you cried out." He looked to the far corner. "Over there."

Together they dashed around the table.

"Oh, drat."

Well. The plum cake *had* been there, on the floor.

It would now appear that the entirety of it—and Clio's ring, as well—were currently inside Ellingworth's stomach.

At first, Clio struggled not to laugh.

The picture was so comical—the ugly old bulldog's flattened face snuffling over the empty platter.

Rafe, however, didn't seem to find it amusing.

"Ellingworth, no." As he ran to the dog, he let loose a string of curses, many of which Clio had never heard before and couldn't have dreamed existed. "How did he get in here?"

"I don't know. Perhaps he waddled in and fell asleep in the corner hours ago."

"No. No, no, no." He lay flat on the floor and pressed his ear to the dog's stomach. "It's gurgling."

"Isn't that normal?"

"I don't know." He sat up and speared his hands through his hair. "It could be. I've never listened to it before."

"The poor thing." She knelt on the bulldog's other side. "But he'll probably be fine."

"What should we do? Should we make him puke? Turn him over and give him a shake?"

She stroked the dog's ear. "I don't think so."

"He feels warm." Rafe pounded his fist against the carpet. Then he punched to his feet, stripped off his coat, and began waving it up and down to fan the bulldog.

Clio was starting to feel a little less touched at the protective care Rafe had displayed toward her. Whisking her away from the falling portcullis, catching her misstep in the tower—those acts had seemed dashing at the time, but it was nothing compared to this effort. And to her, the dog didn't even appear to be ill. If anything, he looked rather fat and content.

If he died now, he'd go happily.

"It's just a plum cake," she said.

"No. It's not just a plum cake. It's a plum cake and an enormous gold-and-ruby ring."

This was true. "At least it's a cabochon setting. No sharp edges. Give him a bit of cod liver oil, and it ought to go right through."

"It had better." Rafe only fanned harder. "Do you hear me, you deaf old thing? Damn you, dog. Don't you die on me now."

In response, Ellingworth belched.

Clio tried not to giggle.

"We need a veterinarian," Rafe said, throwing the coat aside. "A proper surgeon if you have one near. An apothecary, if not. Send for whoever is in the neighborhood."

"Of course."

Good Lord, she'd never seen him this way. She wasn't overly concerned about Ellingworth's health, but she was starting to worry for Rafe.

"Rafe, look at me."

And when he did, the fierceness in those bold green eyes nearly knocked her over.

"We're in this together," she said. "We'll do everything we can. We'll send to London for specialists, if need be. I promise you." She reached out and squeezed his big hand in both of hers. "This dog isn't going to die today."

* * *

Twelve hours, three veterinarians, two doctors, and one apothecary later, Clio sat on a chair outside the room dedicated as an infirmary, working a bit of embroidery by the light of a single candle.

The hour was late, and everyone else had gone to bed hours ago. But Rafe remained closed in the room with Ellingworth, and so Clio was still sitting here.

During the course of the day, she'd found a spare hour to bathe and change out of her cake-smeared clothing. At least the chaos of Ellingworth's accident had saved her from making explanations for that. All she'd needed to do was raise her hands, and say, "The dog," and everyone had seemed satisfied.

At last, the door opened. "You're still here?"

Clio crammed her needlework into the drawer of a nearby table and stood.

Rafe looked so solemn. Unlike Clio, he hadn't changed—other than removing his coat, waistcoat, and cravat, then rolling his sleeves to the elbow. His hair stood at wild angles.

She began to fear the worst.

"Well?" she prompted.

"They say he'll live."

"Oh." She released the breath she'd been holding. "That's good to hear. I'm so relieved. You must be, too."

"He seems to be sleeping soundly now. The veterinarian will stay with him, so I'm going up to bed." He turned his head in both directions, then glanced upward, too. "Which way is my bedchamber, again?"

She picked up the candle from the table. "I'll walk you there."

He hooked his coat on one finger and slung it

over his shoulder. They ambled down the corridor, side by side.

"The good news is, they've given him a dose of some purgative. The ring should"—he cleared his throat—"appear within a few days."

Clio shuddered. "I'll never put that ring on my finger again."

"Yes, you will. I just told you, the veterinarian says it will only take a few days. That's good news. You'll have it back before Piers returns."

She turned and blinked at him. "Be that as it may, Rafe. I'll never put that ring on my finger again."

"We'll *wash* it."

"Not because of where it's been," she said. "Well, partly because of where it's been, but mostly because I'm not going to marry Piers."

He sighed. "This would never have happened if you'd just tasted the cakes."

"It would never have happened if you'd respected my wishes and signed the dissolution papers days ago." Clio took a moment to compose herself. "But let's not quarrel now. The important thing is, the dog is well."

"Yes."

They mounted a flight of stairs. When they reached the top, Rafe spoke to her again, more gently. As if he'd left his impatience and hard feelings at the bottom of the staircase.

"I should thank you for keeping watch with me. Again."

"Again?"

"I never told you what it meant. Never properly thanked you at all, and that's my fault. When the marquess died, you were a true help."

"I didn't do anything, really."

"You were *there*. You made the arrangements for the funeral and answered the calls. You brought that little basket of . . . biscuits or something."

"Muffins. They were muffins. Your father died, and I brought muffins." She closed her eyes and pinched the bridge of her nose. "I *am* a muffin. Warm and bland and nice enough, but nothing to get excited about."

"Nothing to get excited about. Right. That's you, Clio. Do me a favor, will you? Tell that to my—"

Her pulse stuttered. She could imagine too many endings to that sentence, some of them lewd and others heart-wrenching. "To your what?"

"Nothing. Never mind."

Drat.

"I'm just glad Ellingworth will be well in the end," she said. "I didn't realize how much you cared for the poor old dear."

"I don't, really. It's just . . . he's not mine. He's Piers's dog. I can't let something go wrong on my watch. I've had no choice but to take responsibility for the marquessate in his absence. But when my brother comes home, I mean to hand over everything in the same condition I received it. Then I'm done."

Clio slowed to a halt in the center of the corridor. She pressed a hand to her heart. "Oh my Lord."

Rafe stopped, too. "What? What is it?"

"I'm the dog."

"What?"

"That's it." She turned to him. "I'm the dog. That's why you've gone to all this trouble. It's why you're so bent on keeping me engaged. In your mind, I'm like the dog. I belong to Piers, and you're not too attached to me—but you don't want something to go wrong on your watch. You need to hand me over in the condition you received me."

He opened his mouth to reply—then hesitated, seemingly at a loss for words.

Clio didn't need any words. That moment's pause told her everything she needed to know.

She'd pegged it absolutely right.

She was the dog.

She stormed ahead, not caring if she left him alone in the dark. He was welcome to wander these corridors all night.

He caught up to her, whipping her around by the arm. "Clio, wait."

She clenched her free hand into a fist. How she despised those words. They were the sum of her life, those two words: *Clio, wait.*

"You're misunderstanding me," he said.

"I don't think I'm misunderstanding anything."

"You are not the dog."

"I might as well be. I'm a faithful, drooling little thing you want to keep alive, so Piers can come home and pat me on the head. Toss me a biscuit, perhaps."

She started to growl in frustration, but held herself back. Considering the circumstances.

"Clio, Clio. You are so . . . so much more."

"So much more than a dog. A high compliment. Thank you."

"Will you stop going on about the dog?" He covered his eyes with one hand. "It's late, and I'm not saying things right. But if you've somehow formed the impression that I don't see you as a beautiful, intelligent, remarkable woman, we need to clear that up immed—"

She hooted with laughter. "Please. Just stop. We both know your brother could have had dozens of ladies more elegant, more accomplished. And as for you . . . well, you've *actually* had them."

"My history is irrelevant. Yes, perhaps Piers could have married a lady more elegant or more accomplished. But he could never find one better. You don't know, Clio. People toss around the words 'loyal' and 'kindhearted' as though they're common qualities. But they aren't. They're so rare. A man could search the world and not find another you."

She shook her head, refusing to look him in the eye. "I can't listen to this anymore. You're unbelievably selfish. You don't admire me. You would marry me to a man I don't love, and who doesn't love me, just to satisfy your own convenience."

"My *convenience*?"

He stepped back and took a glance down the corridor in either direction before steering her into his bedchamber and closing the door behind them. Then he removed the candlestick from her hand, placed it on a narrow side table, and braced his hands on her shoulders, holding her still.

His voice lowered to a raw whisper. "You think this is convenient for me? Planning your wedding to another man, then preparing to walk away forever? Do you think I'm not going to be tortured, thinking of you in all the years and decades to come? Imagining you bearing his children, hosting his parties, sharing those countless little moments happy couples never think to catalog, but the rest of us notice and envy like mad?"

Good heavens. What was he saying?

"It's not going to be convenient for me," he said. "It's going to be hell."

"But if you feel that way, then why . . . ?"

"I'm the Devil's Own, remember? I've earned my place in hell. You deserve better." His hands soothed up and down her arms. "You should have the best. Not only the best flowers, the best cake, the best gown, the best wedding . . . but the best possible life, with the best possible man. You deserve all those things. And just for the way I'm touching you now, I deserve to face a pistol at dawn."

She shook her head. Who was this perfect, virtuous woman he was describing? Not Clio, surely. Every time he'd kissed her, she'd kissed him back. And she'd spent hours dreaming of just this moment. Being alone with him, at night. In his bedchamber. With his big, capable hands all over her body.

Perhaps he didn't understand that.

Well, there was no better time to let him know.

She stepped toward him, placing her hands flat against the broad expanse of his chest.

He sucked in his breath. "What are you doing?"

"Touching you." She stroked her palms over the softened linen of his shirt and the hard, sculpted wonder of his torso beneath.

"Clio . . ." His voice was strangled. "I can't do this."

"You're not. You're not doing anything. This time, I'm doing it all."

"For the love of God, why?"

"Because this is something I've wanted for the longest time."

She stretched her arms around him, placing her hands flat on his back, and leaned forward until her cheek settled against his galloping heartbeat. And then she squeezed him tight.

"Relax, Rafe. It's only a hug." She nuzzled into his shirtfront, settling in. "When's the last time you had a proper one?"

"I . . ." He exhaled from somewhere deep in his chest. "I can't even recall."

Neither could Clio. She'd been born into a loving family, but it was the wrong family for hugs. Daphne was a perfunctory hugger—loose embrace, a few brisk pats on the back, and done. Phoebe didn't like to be hugged at all.

But there were few things Clio loved more in life than a tight, affectionate embrace. She was good at them, too. She smoothed her palms up and down his back, coaxing the tension from his muscles.

"You could hug me back," she said.

At last, he surrendered to it, wreathing his strong arms about her waist and resting his chin on her head. His thumb traced comforting circles on her back, and he swayed her gently back and forth.

Oh, sweet mercy. He was an excellent hugger. A true champion.

She didn't want to ever let go.

"I'm sorry for earlier," she whispered. "You worked hard to bring all those lovely things from London, and I ruined it."

"You didn't ruin it."

"Then all that excitement with the dog. I know you were concerned. It's been a long, difficult day."

It had been a long, difficult year for him. He'd lost his father and his championship, both within the space of a week.

He could pretend all he liked that he wasn't grieving. Clio knew better. She remembered the way he'd looked when she called at Granville House shortly after the marquess's death. His face had worn the marks of a brutal beating, but his eyes showed that his true pain was deep inside. She wished she'd had the courage to hug him then.

Tonight, she was making up for the oversight.

"Why would you think you don't deserve to be happy, Rafe?"

He paused before answering. "It wouldn't be in you to understand. I'm bad at being good, and only good at being bad. You don't know who I am, what I've done. You don't know the half."

"Perhaps not. But I know what you deserve for your actions today." Stretching up on her toes, she pressed her lips to his cheek. "That's for the music."

Ducking her head, she kissed the underside of his jaw, where his pulse beat hard and fast. A day's growth of whiskers scraped against her skin. "That's for the flowers."

"Stop."

"This is for the cake."

She pressed her lips to the notch at the base of his throat. Then she held the kiss for long moments, breathing in the scent and heat of him.

A tortured growl rose in his chest. He probably

meant it as a warning, but Clio was emboldened by the sound.

She loved knowing she had this effect on him. This was Rafe Brandon, one of the fiercest, strongest, most fearsome men in England. And she, Miss Clio Whitmore, had him weak in the knees.

When she lifted her head, she found him staring down at her. His eyes were hazy with desire. "You need to leave this room. At once."

Clio didn't try to argue with him.

But neither did she move to leave.

She sensed a battle going on within him—desire and the simple need for closeness, warring with his ambition and loyalty. It was a true struggle, and as a spectator, she was breathless. Riveted. Tense with anticipation, waiting to see which side would win.

His hands lay flat on the small of her back.

And then . . . slowly . . . she felt his fingers gathering the fabric of her frock, drawing it into tight fists. He flexed his arms and pulled her close, sweeping her heels off the floor. Her breasts crushed against the solid wall of his chest, and a ridge of pure male heat pulsed against her belly.

His breathing was rough. His lips, so close to hers.

Yes.

Lord, yes. This was how it felt to want, and be wanted.

And now that she'd known the sensation, he couldn't expect her to settle for anything less. She didn't want a marriage that was tame and polite. She wanted wild. She wanted wrong.

She wanted *him.*

Clio reached for fistfuls of his shirt, forbidding him to let her go. *"Rafe."*

The bedchamber door swung inward.

"Hullo."

Rafe, to his credit, only clutched her tighter. "Who's there? Declare yourself."

Oh, no.

Sir Teddy Cambourne stood in the doorway.

And he did not look pleased.

Chapter Ten

allelujah.

That was Rafe's first, instinctive reaction when the door opened to reveal the stern countenance of Sir Teddy Cambourne.

Excellent. Perfect. Thank God.

The struggle was over. The jig was up. He'd been caught with his fists twisted in the back of Clio's frock, pulling his brother's intended bride tight against the rudeness of his hardening cock . . . and that was that.

Now he'd be called out for the villain he was. He could give up the entire wedding–planning charade. He'd allow Sir Teddy to take a shot at him in the first mists of dawn . . . and whether he was killed, maimed, or merely disgraced, he'd slink away. Disappear from Clio and Piers's future happiness, forever.

Good.

But Cambourne didn't seem to have read the script. He didn't shout or rage, didn't denounce him as a villain or a blackguard. He didn't demand Rafe unhand his sister-in-law and name his second for a duel.

He merely stood there, wearing only his nightshirt and a blank expression, clutching a pair of black Hessians in his hands.

He held the boots out to Rafe. "Take these."

Rafe just stared at the man. Was this some part of the dueling code he'd never learned? He thought the slap of a glove was the usual way of calling a man out, but perhaps there was a new fashion: handing him boots.

Then, from down the hall, he heard Daphne calling, "Teddy? Teddy where have you got to now?"

The man didn't even turn at the sound of his wife's voice. He just pressed the boots toward Rafe again. "They need to be polished by tomorrow morning. Mummy's taking me to see a menagerie."

"Just take them," Clio whispered. "He's walking in his sleep. He does this sometimes."

Rafe took the boots.

Clio put her hands on Teddy's shoulders and turned him back toward the doorway. "There now. That's done. You can go back to bed."

"I hope they have tigers. Mummy says there will be tigers."

"Well, now. Won't that be fine."

He shuffled numbly toward the doorway. "Tigers are stripey. They say grrrrrowr."

Rafe choked back a laugh.

Down the corridor, Daphne's cries were growing increasingly frantic. "Teddy! Teddy, where are you?"

"He's here!" Clio called. "He's fine." To Rafe, she whispered, "Don't tell my sister about the menagerie. She'll be embarrassed enough as it is."

They met with Daphne in the corridor. "Oh, thank heaven." She flung her arms around her husband's neck and kissed his cheek.

Cambourne didn't seem to notice.

Phoebe had come out of her room, too, wrapped in a dressing gown and holding a book in one hand. "It's not surprising. We should have expected it. He's in a new place."

Clio nodded. "But we must find some way to keep him in his room. As big and ranging as this castle is, it could be dangerous for him to go wandering."

"I did turn the key in the door, but I left it in the lock," Daphne said. "I've learned my lesson. After tonight, the key sleeps under my pillow. Or perhaps around my neck."

Rafe resisted the urge to suggest clapping good Sir Teddy in a ball and chain.

"I'll station a footman in the corridor, just in case," Clio said.

"Thank you." Daphne turned to Rafe. "I'm so sorry. He hasn't done this in ages."

"There's no need to apologize," Rafe said.

On the contrary, he should be thanking the man. Stripey tigers notwithstanding, Cambourne had single-handedly yanked Clio from the brink of ruination.

Rafe pushed a hand through his hair. What the hell was wrong with him? The reasons he should leave Clio alone were stacked so high, he'd need Phoebe to count them. Nevertheless, he couldn't keep his hands—or lips—off her.

A better man would have managed it.

But a better man wouldn't have been so desperate for her touch.

"Can I help at all?" Rafe asked.

"No, no. We'll be fine now." Daphne herded her husband back toward their bedchamber. "Come along, dear. Back to bed."

Phoebe yawned and returned to her room, as well.

"What shall I do with these?" Rafe still clutched the boots in his hands.

"I'll see that they're given to his valet." Clio took them. "And you needn't worry that he saw us. He never remembers anything of these episodes in the morning."

"Has he seen doctors?"

She nodded. "There's nothing to be done, short of dosing him with opiates every night. In that case, the cure would be worse than the condition. He truly has improved over the past year. It was more severe when they first wed."

"It must be difficult for your sister."

"Yes." Her gaze slanted to the side. "But oddly enough, I envy her that difficulty."

"Why?"

"Because it shows that theirs is a true marriage. This is what you've been failing to see all this time, Rafe. A wedding is more than staging the perfect event, or having everything that's best. It's two people vowing to stand by each other through everything that's worst. It's compromise and unconditional love."

"That isn't how marriage works in most Mayfair town houses. And I doubt Piers is expecting it, either.

We all know that at this level of society, love is a luxury. Marriage is a contract. You agreed to your part."

"That's unfair."

He knew it was unfair. She'd been far too young and raised to believe she had no other choice. Then Piers had left her dangling for years. And Rafe was hardly the one to talk about social obligation when he'd walked away from everything.

"Speaking of contracts . . . You struck a bargain with me, Rafe. And in two days, it's done. You gave me your word, and I expect you'll honor it."

She turned from him and walked away, and there was nothing he could think to say.

A door creaked open, and Bruiser's head popped into the hall, quizzing glass and all. "I say. Is there some commotion, what-what?"

"You can drop the act, Montague. Cambourne was walking in his sleep. It's over now."

Bruiser snapped his fingers. "Damn. I'd been hoping to show off in these."

He stepped into the hallway, wearing a banyan of patterned silk and a nightcap with a peak that fell all the way to his knees. A gold tassel dangled from the tip.

"Got them at the same place I found my quizzing glass." Bruiser tugged the fringed sash tight. "I'd been hoping for something to go bump in the night, so I could rush into the corridor and look high-class."

"Then why didn't you?

"Took me too long to put the dashed things on. I can't sleep unless I'm naked as a newborn."

Rafe scratched his head, as though he could scrub the image from his brain. "I didn't need to know that."

"That's right, get angry. Stay angry. I can see it

coming back." Bruiser clapped him on the shoulder. "That hunger, that envy, that drive to prove yourself . . . It's in your eyes. We'll be champions again in no time. Just be certain to save it for the ring."

"I'd be able to focus on my job if you were doing better with yours." Rafe flicked the stupid tassel on the stupid nightcap. "What-what."

"Oh, yes. About that. I didn't have a chance to tell you earlier. You were with the doctors and the dog. But tomorrow's the day we win her over."

"I doubt that."

If today's efforts didn't impress her, he was running out of ideas.

Clio wanted compromise and love, and someone who'd vow to stand by her always. Rafe knew she deserved all that, and more. When he'd held her in his arms, he'd wanted to promise her anything.

But he could not sign those papers. He simply couldn't.

"Two words, Rafe. Italian silk. Belgian lace. French modistes. Seed pearls, brilliants, flounces . . ."

"I'm no mathematician, but I'm fairly certain that was more than two words."

"The *gowns*." Bruiser gave him a punch on the arm. "There's your two words. The gowns. They've arrived. And they're magnificent."

"I don't know that gowns will be enough. Miss Whitmore is a gentlewoman of means. She's donned her share of pretty frocks."

"Not like these. I'm telling you, she won't be able to resist. Cor, I'm tempted to wear them myself."

Rafe opened the door to his room. "In case it needs saying: Don't."

"I won't. Again." He held up his hands. "Joking, joking."

The next day, Clio woke early. It might be more accurate to say she scarcely slept.

She knew Rafe would be awake early, too. He always was.

She didn't know how to face him so she took the coward's way out. She washed and dressed, took breakfast in her room, then scrawled a few lines to a friend in Herefordshire and sealed the envelope, just to have an excuse to walk into the village.

At the last moment, Phoebe joined her. "I'll go along. I need to buy string."

"Of course."

Clio knew her sister had an entire trunkful of string upstairs, but she grew anxious if she went more than a few days without purchasing more. Somewhere in Yorkshire, there was a string factory that thrived on Phoebe's custom alone.

They hadn't reached the end of the castle drive before Phoebe asked, "So what happened last night?"

"You know already. Teddy went walking in his sleep and caused a commotion. It's happened before, and it's sure to happen again."

"I do know all that. I was wondering what happened before it."

"What do you mean?"

"I saw you coming out of Lord Rafe's room."

Drat.

Clio had feared that might be the case, and here was confirmation. She tried her best to remain calm.

"Yes, so I did. We'd stayed up late with the dog to be certain he didn't suffer any ill effects from the cake. Afterward, we were talking."

"I see."

"We had important matters to discuss," she went on. "But the others might form the wrong impression if they knew, so please keep that between us."

And please don't ask for further explanations.

Her sister shrugged. "Very well. I won't tell anyone. Although I don't understand why any of the others should care about the two of you talking."

No, Phoebe wouldn't understand.

For all her intelligence, Phoebe was blind to human subtleties. She took every person at his or her word, as though she couldn't conceive of a reason why anyone would bother to prevaricate.

Clio was terrified of what would happen when it came time to introduce her youngest sister to society. She could delay another few years . . . but they were granddaughters of an earl. Eventually, Phoebe must be presented. And unless Clio was vigilant in protecting her, the dragons of the *ton* would devour the poor thing alive.

But for this morning, she needn't think of it yet.

The day was fine. The rain had ceased, for once. Yes, the ground was muddy underfoot, but the sun was steadily climbing in the sky. Clio threw back the hood of her cloak to bask in its warmth.

She loved this bit of Kentish countryside. It suited her. There weren't any dramatic peaks or valleys. Just well-tended fields bordered by stone fences and hedgerows, with the occasional pocket of woods. From the turrets of Twill Castle, it looked like a quilt pieced in a dozen shades of green. Cozy. Comfortable.

Safe.

She led her sister toward a narrow, two-plank footbridge crossing a rain-swollen rill. They crossed it one at a time, holding their arms stretched to either side for balance.

"In time, I should replace this with a proper bridge," Clio said. "But I rather like the charm of this one."

She took the last bit of distance in a leap, then held out a hand to help Phoebe across.

Clio kept that hand in hers as they walked down a footpath between two fields—barley on one side, clover on the other. "What do you think of the place?"

"I like it as well as I like any place."

"Would you like to live at Twill Castle?"

"Permanently?" Phoebe frowned. "Why would I do that?"

"Because I'd invite you to."

"Won't Lord Granville want to remove to Oakhaven?"

"Perhaps I can convince him to stay here. It's closer to London."

Her sister shook her head. "You'll be newly married. He wouldn't like having me underfoot."

"What makes you say that?"

"Because Teddy and Daphne are newly married, and *they* don't want me underfoot. Daphne told me so. Aside from dinners, I'm not allowed to trouble them unless the house is afire."

Clio gave Phoebe's hand a squeeze, but she knew her sister preferred to be reassured with facts.

"I would always want you underfoot," she said. "And as for Piers . . . well, he's a powerful man, but even he can't decide who stays in the castle. Twill Castle is mine."

"Only until you're married," Phoebe pointed out. "Then the castle becomes his."

"Perhaps I won't marry him."

Her sister halted in the middle of the path, and Clio stopped, too. The words had just erupted from her. She hadn't planned them. But now she would find out how her family—at least one member of it—would react.

Phoebe stared hard into the distance.

"Well?" Clio prompted. Her heart pounded in her chest, and a bee droned nearby.

Her sister lifted one hand to shade her brow. "Is that Lord Rafe? Over there, by the fence."

Clio shook herself, surprised by this sudden change in topic. Had Phoebe even heard her confession? There was no telling with her youngest sister. Sometimes she would make no note of something, then remark on it a day or a week later.

Clio peered hard in the same direction. "That's Mr. Kimball's farmland."

On the other side of the clover field, a group of laborers were stacking flat rocks to repair a dry-stone field border. Except one of the laborers was nearly twice the size of the rest. When he turned to the side, she could recognize his profile across the field—but by then, her pulse was already pounding.

Her body knew his.

"That is Lord Rafe," she said. "Yes."

He saw them and lifted one hand.

"What on earth is he doing?"

"Mending a fence, it would seem." Phoebe tugged

her by the arm. "Come on, then. We ought to greet him since he waved to us."

"He didn't wave."

"Yes he did."

"He lifted a hand. He didn't move it to and fro. That's not waving."

Nonetheless, they were halfway to the stone border and committed now. As they approached, Rafe slipped his linen-clad arms back into his coat sleeves and ran both hands through his hair.

He looked instantly marvelous.

"I should have worn a different frock," Clio muttered.

"Why?" Phoebe asked.

"No reason."

And there truly was no reason. It didn't matter how she looked. Whatever it was between them . . . It wouldn't come to anything.

It *couldn't* come to anything.

And on some level, enjoying the attraction had to be wrong. Until he signed those papers, she was still—on paper, if not in her mind or heart—engaged to Piers. But she'd been waiting so long to feel even the slightest glimmer of this exhilaration. Who could tell when she would feel this way again?

Rafe bid the laborers good-bye and started walking toward them. They met in the center of the field, knee deep in clover.

"Are you helping mend a fence?" Phoebe asked.

"Been working on it a few hours." He looked over his shoulder. "Mostly finished, I think."

"That's good of you," Clio said. "I'm sure Mr. Kimball appreciates the help."

He gave a modest shrug. "I'm in training. I need the exertion."

Oh, and did it ever look well on him. His skin was bronzed from the sun, and he wore that aura of exertion like a golden fleece, radiating health and power. She got rather lost in the dazzle for a moment or two.

"We're going to the village," Phoebe said. "I'm buying string."

"I have a letter to post," Clio added lamely.

"I'll join you, if I may."

So they walked into the village. Clio posted her letter. Phoebe purchased her string. Rafe was hungry from his morning's work, and he suggested they take luncheon at the pub.

It was a simple, unfussy establishment. A dozen or so tables, a small bar. The day's meal choices— all two of them—were chalked on a slate. The pub was crowded with customers, and as they entered, everyone in the place turned to gawk.

Clio nodded and smiled, noticing a few familiar faces. She'd made her best efforts to visit the homes of her tenants and become acquainted with the local merchants.

But it wasn't her appearance that had the caught their fascination—it was Rafe's. His reputation sailed ahead of them, cutting through the room and leaving quite a wake.

As they moved through the pub, she could hear the whispers.

"That's Rafe Brandon, isn't it?"

"The Devil's Own. I'd heard he was here on holiday."

"I saw him fight once, you know. At Brighton. He did an exhibition for the regiment just before we shipped to the Peninsula."

If Rafe heard the gossip, he didn't acknowledge it. He guided Clio and Phoebe to the last free table in the pub, one tucked in a corner behind a group of men playing cards. When the tavern girl came, he ordered shepherd's pie for the ladies, and a ploughman's luncheon of cheese, sliced ham, and buttered bread for himself.

While they waited for their meal, Phoebe pulled out a length of string, cut it off with her teeth, knotted the ends, and began to weave string figures.

"I've been working on something new, but I can't get it right." She shook her head, frustrated. Then she slipped the string loose and began over again. "Perhaps this through that loop . . . There. Lord Rafe, do you see that bit of string in the middle? Third one down. Pinch it tight, please."

He did as Phoebe asked, and she pulled her hands downward, widening her fingers to reveal a web of string in the shape of a castle. The bit of string Rafe held had become a soaring spire in the middle, and there were turrets on either side.

"Oh, well done." Clio applauded.

Rafe whistled in appreciation. "That's the best yet."

"It's a useless accomplishment," Phoebe said, letting the string drop. "I don't suppose I can stand up and make string figures when I have my debut."

"Speaking as someone who attended a few debuts," Rafe said, "I'd far rather watch a girl make string figures than endure another unfortunate performance at the pianoforte."

Phoebe looked to Clio. "What did you exhibit at your come-out ball?"

"I played the pianoforte." Clio gave a wry smile. "Most unfortunately. But Rafe was spared the pain of listening since he didn't attend."

He took a draught of ale.

Perhaps she shouldn't poke at him for it, but his absence had hurt. In childhood, Rafe had always teased her, but she'd thought they were friends, of a sort. And then he'd abandoned her, on the one night when she needed a friend the most.

"It's just a shame that we can't preserve the figures somehow," Clio said. "I wish I could hang them on the wall for everyone to see."

"Better this way," Rafe said. "On the wall, it would just be string. Phoebe is what makes it special."

His praise didn't seem to have much effect on Phoebe, but it caught Clio by surprise. A tender spot throbbed in her heart. Like a toothache, only somewhat lower down.

He had so many decent qualities. Why did he insist on maintaining such a reputation for devilry? She supposed it must do with his career. "The Dog-Coddling Demon" or "The Fierce Fence-Mender" probably wouldn't draw many spectators to a fight.

The serving girl brought their food from the kitchen. Phoebe ate quickly, then picked up her string and turned her chair to watch the men playing cards. Clio poked at her serving of pie.

Rafe moved closer to Clio's corner, where they could speak in relative privacy. "Mr. Kimball was telling me about your land agent and his meeting with the farmers. He shared your ideas for the hopfields and brewery."

"Oh?"

"He's not convinced. Neither am I."

"Why not? Hopfields might require an initial investment, but the farmers will have a ready market for their harvest."

"Assuming the crop doesn't fail." He pushed a wedge of cheese into his mouth.

Clio tried not to stare, but she was quietly fascinated by the unapologetic, masculine manner with which he ate. He didn't pay any special attention to etiquette. He didn't make a show of flouting it, either. He just . . . ate.

She found this appealing in a strange, visceral way.

Perhaps she envied him.

"We'll be keeping coopers, cartwrights, and woodmen furnished with custom," she said, taking a dainty bite of her own food. "The brewery itself will employ dozens. It's good for the entire parish. The plans are sound."

"Be that as it may," he said, scratching the light growth of whiskers he hadn't shaved. "Starting a brewery requires a tremendous investment. Hops are a delicate crop. You could lose your entire dowry, and the castle with it. Where will the farmers and coopers be then?"

"I know there's risk. But it's not as though I'm chasing some fickle fashion." She nodded at the crowded pub. "Englishmen aren't going to cease drinking beer anytime soon."

"But you're not an English*man*. You're an unmarried gentle*woman* with no experience in agriculture or trade."

"Of course I lack experience. Where would I have acquired it? At finishing school?" She poked at a chunk of beef. "It's so unfair. Women are allowed to do one-tenth of what men may do, and yet we are scrutinized for it ten times as closely. If I'm going to be found wanting, at least this time it will be different. I would rather be judged for my failures at estate management than for my failures at the pianoforte. It might be a rough start, but I have the funds and determination to make it a success. I'll be the first to admit there's much I don't know. But I'm willing and able to learn."

When she looked up, Rafe wasn't at the table. She looked on as he walked to the bar and returned with three pewter tankards, brimming with beer.

"Brown ale," he said, pushing the first tankard toward her. "Bitter. Porter."

"All three? You're very thirsty from your work."

"They're for you," he said. "You said you were willing and able to learn. Let's see you prove it."

Ah, so he meant to give her a lesson. That was rather sweet. Ridiculous and unnecessary, but sweet.

Conscious of people watching them, she lowered her voice to a whisper. "Thank you. But I know. I would not propose to open a brewery without first understanding brown ale, bitter, and porter."

"Then let's see if you can tell the difference." He slid the tankards around on the tabletop, jumbling them like walnut shells with a pea underneath. "Taste, and tell me which is which."

"I can tell you which is which by sight. This is the brown ale." She nodded at each in turn. "This is the porter, and the bitter. But I'm not going to drink any today."

Clio could hear Mama's ghost hitting the floor in a swoon at the mere suggestion. Well-bred ladies drank lemonade or barley water. Perhaps a touch of cordial or a glass of claret. Small beer, at home. They didn't drink ale. Much less porter. Not in public.

"So you want to produce beer, but you don't want to be seen drinking it. That makes no sense."

"It makes perfect sense in a nonsensical world."

He was a man; he had no idea. Ladies were encouraged to produce all manner of things—beauty, dinner, and children, most commonly. But those productions must appear to be effortless. Drawn from feminine mystery and ether. Woe to the lady who plucked her chin hairs in public, or welcomed callers with flour on her hands. Much less dared to admit desire.

"This isn't the place," she said.

"This is a public house. It is, by definition, *the* place for drinking." He nudged the brown ale toward her.

Her pride won out over propriety. With a cautious glance about the pub, Clio lifted and sipped from each heavy tankard in turn. "There. I've tasted them."

"And . . . ?" he prompted.

"And . . . they're fine."

"Wrong," he said. "Two are fine. One is swill. How can you go asking farmers to risk their harvests on the prospect of your brewery if you can't tell good ale from bad?"

She sighed. There seemed no getting around it. "The brown ale is quite good. Freshly brewed with local water. Sweet, nutty. There's a touch of honey in it, too. Someone had clover growing next to his barley. The porter is decent. The coffee flavors would be richer if they'd used dark malt, not just burnt sugar for coloring. But everyone's using the light malt these days. Now, the bitter . . ." She sipped it again and tilted her head. "I wouldn't call it swill. It had potential, but the yeast didn't dissolve properly. What might have been crisp sky and grassy fields is just . . . swamped in fog. Pity. A waste of good Kentish hops."

She raised her gaze to find him staring at her.

"Where did all that come from?" he asked. But his eyes phrased the question slightly differently. *Where did* you *come from?* they asked.

Oh, Rafe. I've been here all along.

Just waiting.

"A girl needs a hobby." She felt a bit cheeky. No doubt the work of the ale. Or perhaps the expression on his face.

He regarded her with those intense green eyes of his, and even though he was violently attractive and oh-so-close, Clio tried not to do something silly and girlish. Such as touch her hair. Or wet her lips. Or recall the feeling of his aroused manhood pressing against her tender flesh.

Naturally, she did all three.

Vexed with herself, she lowered her gaze. "Are you going to keep staring at me like that?"

"Yes."

"Why?"

"I've a bet with myself. To see if I can make you turn ten shades of pink."

Well, in that moment he must have counted off yet another. Some muted crimson hue, most likely.

"A man needs a hobby, too." With a sudden, lethal flash of charm, he pushed back in his chair and stood. "I'll settle our bill."

Phoebe leaned toward the neighboring table, where the men were playing cards. "Don't wait on the king," she told the man nearest to her, peering over his shoulder at the cards in his hand.

"Phoebe," Clio whispered sharply. "Don't. It's rude to interrupt."

"But he needs to know." She tapped the man on the shoulder. "Don't wait on the king of diamonds. It's not in the deck."

"What?" The man looked over his shoulder at her.

"I've been watching for fourteen hands now. Every other card in the deck has appeared at least once. With an average of twenty-one cards revealed per hand, the chances of the king of diamonds remaining unplayed would be less than one in . . ." She paused. "One million, three hundred thousand."

The man brayed with laughter. "There's no numbers that big."

"What the devil's wrong with her?" a man across the table said. "She some kind of half-wit?"

"She's got more wits than you." The dealer turned over the remainder of the deck and riffled through it. "She's right. No king of diamonds. If it isn't in the deck, where is it?"

Phoebe shrugged. "I'd ask your quiet friend."

Across the table, a burly, ginger-haired man scowled. "Keep your nose out of men's business, girl."

Clio tried to distract her sister, to no avail. When Phoebe latched on to a fact, she could be like a dog with a bone.

"There." She nodded toward the man with ginger hair. "It's in his left sleeve. I see the edge of it."

Now the man rose from the table, looming over them all. "Are you calling me a cheat, you little wench? Because if you are, I won't stand for it."

He grabbed the tabletop's edge with both hands and flipped the entire table, cards and beers and all.

Clio gathered her sister into her arms. Phoebe stiffened at the contact, but it couldn't be helped. She would not let this man hurt her sister.

"Lying, unnatural witch," he snarled. "I tell you, I'll—"

Rafe stepped in, confronting the man chest to chest. His voice was a low, controlled threat. "You'll stop. That's what you'll do. Because if you touch or threaten either one of these ladies again, I swear on everything holy, I will kill you."

Chapter Eleven

O h, yes. Rafe could kill him. He could demolish this vile, reeking piece of scum. Easily. With one hand.

Which meant he had to be very careful now.

"Do you know who these ladies are?" he said, both to inform the scum and to remind himself to keep some hold on civility. "They're both nieces of the Earl of Lynforth. Miss Whitmore is the local landowner and soon to be married to my brother, Lord Granville."

Rafe still held his tankard of beer in his right hand. With his left forearm, he nudged the man in the chest. Repeatedly.

"You don't touch them." He strode forward, backing the man toward the edge of the room. "You don't speak to them. You don't look at them." He pushed the man against the timber-and-plaster wall. "You don't breathe in their general vicinity, ever again. And in exchange, I let you leave this pub with the same number of teeth you brought in. Miss Whitmore's intended groom might be a diplomat, but he's not here right now. I am. And I don't do anything the nice way."

In his youth, he'd lived with anger at a constant simmer. Smaller insults than these had sent him boiling over with violence. Ten years ago, he would have punched first and thought later, leaving blood on the walls and no apologies.

He was older now. Wiser, he hoped. But when it came to scum like this? No less angry.

He was closer to losing control than he had been in years.

Easy, Rafe.

The card cheat chuckled. "Oh, I know who you are, Brandon. You had a good run in your day. But that's all over now, isn't it?"

"Not for long. I'll be reclaiming my title soon."

"That so? Let's see what you have, then." The man cracked his neck and shook out his fists. "I've been in a brawl or two myself. I'll take you on."

Rafe rolled his eyes. Damnation.

This ginger-haired jackass couldn't be a compliant, fearful, reeking piece of scum. No, the idiot was just drunk enough to make this difficult.

"I don't spar with amateurs, as a rule."

"So the gossip's true," the drunk taunted. "You're washed up. Running scared."

"I said, I don't spar with amateurs as a rule. But every rule has its exceptions."

Behind him, someone in the growing throng of onlookers crowed. "It's a fight, boys!"

"No fighting is necessary," Clio said, speaking from somewhere behind him.

Rafe heard her.

His eyes never left the card cheat, but he heard her. And though he couldn't reassure her, she needn't worry. He knew very well what was at stake in this situation—for her and for him.

"This was all our fault for interrupting the card game," she said bravely. "Sirs, you have our sincere apologies. Isn't that right, Phoebe?"

"I see no reason to apologize," Phoebe said. "He was cheating. I was right."

"Neither of you owes this man a damn thing," Rafe growled, taking a handful of the scum's shirt-front and twisting it in his grip until he'd hauled the man up on his toes. "I'm going to give him what he's got coming."

The man's face paled in a most satisfying fashion.

All around them, the tavern customers' excitement reached a new pitch. Men cleared the tables and chairs to the edges of the room. Wagers were being made. And the reeking filth he held dangling in his grip . . . well, he had to be hearing how few of those bettors liked his chances.

Rafe was getting hungry. And he didn't mind who saw it. He had earned this brutish reputation, and it was his to use as he pleased.

A soft touch landed on his shoulder. Clio's voice broke as she whispered, "Rafe, please. Don't do this."

"Oh, I'm doing this. And I'm going to enjoy it. Just as soon as I set down my drink."

With that, he drove his right hand forward, crash-ing his tankard into the limewashed plaster of the tavern wall, just six inches from the man's blanched, ugly face. Beer sloshed the floor.

When he withdrew his hand, the tankard stayed there, embedded in the plaster. As though he'd made it its own little shelf.

"Still eager to fight me?" Rafe asked.

The man flicked a glance toward the tankard stuck in the wall, no doubt picturing it embedded in his teeth. "I . . . That . . ."

"Didn't think so." Rafe released the man, and he dropped to the floor and lay there. Just like the scum he was.

Before the onlookers could catch their breath, Rafe had both Clio and Phoebe under one protective arm.

"Sorry to disappoint," he told the crowd. "No fight today." To Clio, he murmured, "Let's be on our way. *Now.*"

Rafe didn't have to ask her twice.

Clio was only too happy to leave the place.

The three of them walked out of the village without stopping or speaking, all the way until they reached the country path.

When they came to a stile, Rafe stopped and turned to them. He swept them both with a concerned glance. "Are you both well? Not harmed at all?"

Clio shook her head. "We're not harmed. Just rattled a bit."

"That was my fault, wasn't it?" Phoebe's delicate dark brows knitted in a frown. "I made him angry."

"No," Clio said. "He was a drunkard and a cheat, and you did nothing wrong."

"But I did. I did." She tugged at her hair. "I'm always doing or saying the wrong thing. I know I'm odd."

"Phoebe, darling. You're not odd. You're special."

"Why make the distinction, as if they aren't the same thing?"

Clio moved to comfort her with a pat on the shoulder.

Her sister brushed the touch aside. "If you're worried I'm going to weep or go into hysterics, don't. I never do either. That's what makes me odd. Or at least, it's part of it. You can't think I haven't noticed. I don't think or behave the way others do. There are things that are important to me that no one else seems to give a fig about. And then there are things everyone else seems to prize, and try as I might, I can't understand the fuss. Daphne teases me. Clio, you're too polite, but I know you're worried. I've heard you discussing it."

"We both love you," Clio said.

"And I don't understand that, either." Phoebe clambered over the stile and strode away.

Clio moved to rush after her, but Rafe held her back.

"Let her go," he said. "She knows the way home."

"But she's upset and hurting. I can't abide it."

"You don't have a choice. Because she's got it right. She's not like other girls." He silenced her objections with a touch to the arm. "I may not be brilliant with numbers like Phoebe, but I know something about being troubled at sixteen. Trust me on this. From time to time, she'll need the space to sort things through. It's all right to let her walk away. Just make certain she knows she can always come back."

Clio suspected he was right, but that didn't make it any easier.

To distract herself, she tilted her head and looked at his hand. What she saw made her wince. "You're bleeding. You must have scraped your knuckles on the plaster."

"It's nothing."

"Let me see to it anyway." She pulled a handkerchief from her pocket and lifted his hand into the sunlight for closer examination. "If I'm letting Phoebe walk away, I need to fuss over someone."

He relented, leaning against the stile while she dabbed at his wounds.

With his free hand, he reached into his pocket. "Here. Use this. It's good for all manner of aches and pains." He withdrew a small, disc-shaped tin, smaller than a snuffbox. "Bruiser swears by it."

"Bruiser," she repeated, taking the tin and tracing its circumference with her thumb. "So he *is* your trainer. I thought as much. Wherever did you find that man?"

"I don't recall. It's been years now. And I'd taken some strong blows to the head that week."

She smiled.

"I can make him drop the Montague act if you like. Believe me, it wasn't my idea."

"No, don't bother. It's amusing to watch Daphne fawn over him. And he's enjoying himself. It's nice to know at least one of my guests is appreciating the castle."

With a flick of her thumbnail, Clio opened the lid

of the salve. A wave of rich, pungent scent reached her. She recognized it instantly.

Oil of wintergreen.

She stood motionless for a moment, reckoning with its effect on her.

He stretched his fingers. "If you're trying to tell my fortune, you're staring at the wrong side of my hand."

She gave herself a brisk shake, breaking the spell. With the tip of her middle finger, she gathered a small amount of the salve and dabbed it on his scraped knuckles.

No, she hadn't been trying to tell his fortune. But that moment had given her painful insight into her own.

Sometimes, she believed, it *was* possible to see the future. No need to cross a palm with silver; no crystal ball required. All it took was the courage to look inside your own heart and be honest about what you found there.

What she saw today was this: For the rest of her life, even if she lived to see a hundred summers, anytime she smelled wintergreen, she would think of Rafe Brandon. The warmth of his coat, and the devilish tip of his grin, and the sweet way he'd kissed her in the rain.

She soothed her fingertip over his abraded flesh. Gently, as if his hand were a damp-feathered hatchling instead of an instrument of violence. "He never made you feel welcome to come back, did he? The late marquess, I mean. When you were a troubled youth and needed time to walk away, sort things out . . . He was too stubborn to welcome you home."

"Can't blame the man." He shrugged. "I wasn't like Phoebe. I was a true hellion. Too far gone."

"Yours was the calmer head today." She stroked his hand. "Thank you for coming to our rescue."

"I know how you hate an unpleasant scene."

"Sometimes an unpleasant scene is warranted."

In truth, Rafe had dealt with the situation perfectly. He'd punished the cheater, defended Clio and Phoebe . . . And he'd given the crowd what they craved, as well. An impressive display of strength and danger. A story to tell, retell, and embellish in months and years to come. All of that with no blood spilled, no part of his pugilistic reputation compromised.

"Tomorrow I'll go back to smooth things over," he said. "And I'll pay the tavernkeeper for the damage."

She laughed a little. "You mean the plaster? They're not going to patch that hole. They'll probably make a frame around that tankard and display it with pride. 'Rafe Brandon Drank Here.'"

As soon as the words came out of her, an idea took hold. Her mind began turning faster than a waterwheel.

"That's it," she said, closing the tin with a snap. "That's what I need to make this brewery successful. A business associate."

"An associate?"

"Yes. Someone who has a good rapport with the farmers and tradesmen. Someone with a name known in pubs and taverns all throughout England." Excitement rose in her chest, and she looked him in the eye. "I don't suppose you know anyone like that?"

His jaw was steely. "No."

"Come along, Rafe. This could be perfect. We could . . . We could call it the Devil's Own Ale. To advertise, you could go about England, punching tankards into tavern walls. I'd give you a share of the profits."

"You want to *hire* me?"

She shrugged. "Why not? At some point, you have to take up a career."

"I have a career. I'm a fighter."

"But—"

"It won't happen, Clio." He cut off her objection by lifting her over the stile. Then he vaulted the wooden fence himself and resumed walking along the path.

End of conversation.

Clio walked a step behind him, sighing to herself. How could the idea of a brewery compete with the glory of a prizefighting career? How could anything?

She had to admit, the prospect of imminent fisticuffs *had* been rather exciting. When she'd thought Rafe was preparing to fight that cheating blackguard, chills had raced over her skin. Not merely because Rafe was *a* champion, but because he was acting as *hers.*

But even that rare, heady thrill was nothing—absolutely nothing—compared to the relief she felt when he punched the wall instead.

She'd followed the sport for years now, and she knew how these fighters too often ended. Forgotten. Impoverished. Sometimes imprisoned. Broken, in body and mind.

It would kill her to see that happen to Rafe.

Between the relative privacy and the lingering courage imparted by the beer, Clio felt brave enough to tell him so. She jogged to his side. "I think you lied to me when I came to your warehouse in Southwark."

"How's that?"

"You told me I hadn't walked in on a suicide. Now I'm not so sure. I know you weren't planning to hang yourself, but going back to fighting . . . ? Isn't it a slower route to the same end?"

He shook his head. "Not at all."

"I read the accounts of your fights, Rafe. And not just because I read the papers, and you happened to be in them. I sought them out. I read about all thirty-four rounds of your bout with Dubose. The magazines recounted it in such breathless detail. Every blow and bruise."

"The reporters make it sound more dangerous than it is. It's how they sell magazines. And it helps generate interest for the next fight."

Clio's concerns weren't soothed. "I hate the way people speak about you. Even in that pub today, the way they all leapt to clear space and place wagers. As if you were an inhuman creature meant to bleed and suffer for their amusement, no better than a fighting cock or a baited bear. Doesn't it bother you?"

"No. I don't fight for them. I fight for me."

"For God's sake, why?"

"Because I'm good at it," he said, sounding agitated now. "I am bloody great at it. And I was never good at anything. Because it's the one place where I know that my success is mine, and my failure, too. In the ring, I might be facing an Irish dock laborer or an English tanner or an American freedman. When the bell rings, none of it matters worth a damn. It's only me. My strength, my heart, my wits, my fists. Nothing I was given, nothing I took. I fight because it tells me who I am."

"If you're looking for someone to tell you who you are, I can do that."

He shrugged her off.

"No, truly."

She dashed in front of him and put a hand to his chest, holding him in place.

His heartbeat throbbed against her palm. Every beat pushed excitement through her veins.

"I can start by telling you you're stubborn and impulsive and prideful. And generous and protective and passionate. In public, you ride like the devil and fill out a pair of buckskin breeches like pure liquid sin, but in private, you behave as though you've joined a monastic order. You're kind to ugly dogs, and you're patient with awkward sisters. Your kisses are sweet. And your life is worth something." She fought back the emotion rising in her throat. "I'll tell you who you are, Rafe. Anytime you find yourself in doubt. And I won't even leave you bleeding."

He glanced at the horizon. "Not outwardly, perhaps. There are places inside me you're beating to a pulp."

"Good."

It was only fair. He was cutting her heart to ribbons, too.

"We should be going," he said. "They'll be waiting on us. You're to be fitted for wedding gowns this afternoon."

He still meant to put her through that? "I wish I'd drunk more beer."

"Are you begging off?"

"Oh, no." Clio smoothed the front of her frock. "I'm not giving you any excuse to back out of our agreement. Today, I'll step into a few frilly gowns. Tomorrow, you let me off the leash."

"For the last time," he said, "you're not the dog."

She muttered under her breath, *"Woof."*

Chapter Twelve

"Come out already," Daphne called. "It's been ages."

Rafe was impatient, too. He, Daphne, Teddy, Phoebe, Bruiser, and Ellingworth all sat in the drawing room. Waiting.

Clio was with the dressmakers in the adjoining chamber. Dressing.

That was the idea, anyhow. Supposedly, they were going to be treated to a viewing of three or four gowns, so that Clio might choose her favorite.

A half hour had passed, and she hadn't appeared in even one. Had something gone wrong?'

He tapped one finger on the arm of his chair. Then he began to jostle his knee. Sitting like this was torture for him. Always had been. He didn't know how "gentlemen of leisure" like Cambourne could stand passing whole days and months and years this way.

He stared at those doors hard enough to bore a hole through the oak.

Come out, damn it.

Eventually, Rafe couldn't sit waiting anymore. He excused himself and went into the corridor, where he prowled the full length of the Savonnerie carpet. Back and forth, like a tethered beast.

This had to work. The gown fitting was the best chance of salvaging the engagement. The *last* chance, to wit.

Even an ill-mannered brute like Rafe knew that the gown was the most crucial part of this enterprise. He just hoped his trainer was right about the quality of the materials and workmanship. This would need to be a gown with silk so fine and lace so intricate that when Clio saw her reflection in the looking glass, she would want to never take it off.

And then she'd *have* to get married.

That, or become a batty old spinster who roamed her castle in a decaying wedding gown. Rafe didn't think the latter would suit Clio, but he wasn't going to mention the possibility, just in case.

Thump.

The sound drew him to a halt.

Strange. Perhaps the servants were moving things.

Or maybe the place was haunted. Any castle worth its parapets ought to have at least one ghost.

Then it happened again.

Thump.

Followed by a stifled cry of pain.

Both sounds were coming from behind a set of double doors. If he wasn't mistaken, that would be the chamber designated as Clio's dressing room.

He was at the door in seconds. "Miss Whitmore?" He pounded on the door. "Clio. Are you well?"

After endless moments, the door opened a fraction. He spied an inch-wide slice of Clio's face through the gap. One blue eye and a quirk of pink lips.

"Can I help you, Rafe?"

"Yes, you can bloody well help me. You can tell me what the devil's going on. What's been taking so long, and what was that sound? Is someone moving the furnishings?"

"No, I . . ." He could tell she was struggling for breath, composing her words.

Then it *was* Clio's shriek he'd heard. Her cheek was red, and her eyes—well, the one eye he could see—looked teary. Damn it.

He lowered his voice. "Tell me what's happened. Now."

"It's nothing. I promise you."

"Then open the door so I can see for myself."

"Rafe, I'm fine. Please don't mind me."

"I mind you. You've been in there for ages. I heard you cry out. Your face is red. You're scarcely able to speak. And there were thumps."

"Thumps?"

"Maybe clunks."

Her mouth quirked. "Clunks."

"*Noises.*" His hand balled in a fist. "I heard noises. You're visibly overset. Something's going on in there. Either you open the door, or I break it down."

That single blue eye widened. "You'd truly break down the door?"

"You saw me today in the tavern. If I thought you were in danger, I'd break through the wall."

That single blue eye blinked.

She must know this about him by now. He enjoyed a bit of witty banter as much as the next man, but when his blood started pumping, he couldn't bother with words. What came out of him was action.

"Very well. Since you insist." She stepped back, opening the door. "See?"

Oh, he saw.

He saw a lot of her that he probably shouldn't be seeing.

She was dressed in a gown of delicate ivory lace. However, the lace was fitted so tightly that it was stretched to the point of transparency. Her breasts overflowed the bodice in twin fleshy scoops, and . . .

And his gaze got rather stuck in the dark, mysterious valley between them. The rest of the gown could have been more lace . . . or tweed or crimson velvet. Or on fire, for all he knew.

"I . . . That's . . ." He had no words. None that he could utter aloud.

"Is this some sort of joke?" she asked. "This is your idea of a wedding gown?"

"Not particularly. Or generally."

That gown was entirely unsuitable for walking down the aisle of a church. However, when it came to the wedding night . . .

Damnation. His thoughts could not stray there. His gaze needed tethering, too.

Eyes, Rafe.

The other pair.

She said, "And here I worried you might succeed in overwhelming me with elegance and finery."

"It's not . . . bad."

She leveled a gaze at him. "I look like I've been cast as an angel in the bawdy-house nativity play."

He couldn't help but laugh. "Someone has to get us sinners to church."

"I can't even move." She took three stuttering steps in demonstration, waddling into the corridor like an arthritic duck. "The *thump* you heard was me falling over."

"Twice?"

"Yes, twice." She grimaced. "Thank you for rubbing salt in the wound."

"Try another gown, then."

"I did. I tried them all. They're all too small."

"But I thought Bruiser specially requested them based on your measurements."

"I didn't give him my measurements. And surely Anna would have . . ." Confusion drew little furrows in her brow. Then some sudden realization ironed them flat. "Daphne. Of course. This would be just the sort of trick she'd pull."

"Why would she pull any tricks? I thought she was all aflutter about planning the wedding."

"Oh, she is. This is just her way of reminding me that I . . ."

"That you what?"

"Never mind. It doesn't matter."

"It matters. I can tell it matters."

A hint of sadness had crept into her eyes. It made Rafe want to break things. Then arrange the pieces in a barricade around her.

"There you are." Daphne appeared in the corridor. "Oh, Clio. You do look lovely."

Clio spoke through clenched teeth. "I look ridiculous. You gave Mr. Montague the wrong measurements."

"No, I didn't. I gave him just the *right* measurements."

"But the gown doesn't fit her," Rafe said.

"It *will*." Daphne patted her older sister on the cheek. "You'll see. What with the bridal nerves and all the work to be done, this will be a perfect fit by your wedding day. And if that's not quite enough . . . ? I'm here to help. We'll bring back Mother's game."

Mother's game? What the devil was this about?

"I . . ." Clio's voice broke. "Excuse me, I . . . I need to go upstairs."

"But you've only tried one gown," Daphne said.

"It's more than enough for today." She turned and shuffled down the corridor, heading for the entrance hall.

"You're not peevish, are you?" Daphne called after her. "I meant to help, you know." She looked to Rafe, then shrugged and smiled. "She'll thank me later. You'll see. From time to time, we all need a little motivation."

Motivation.

Rafe was feeling motivated. To do just what, he didn't know. But he was highly motivated to do . . . something. Anything. His blood thundered through his veins.

And then, all the way from the entrance hall, Clio gave him a purpose.

Thunk.

* * *

"Curse this wretched gown."

Clio had suffered a great many mortifications in the past eight years. Smiling through the weeks following Daphne's elopement, knowing that everyone was whispering about whether it would *ever* be Clio's turn. Then there was the first time she'd seen herself called "Miss Wait-More" in the *Prattler.* That had been miserable, too—surpassed only by the day she'd seen the list of wagers from the betting book at White's. Dozens of England's most influential gentlemen, making her elusive wedding date a matter for their sport.

But this? This went beyond everything.

She'd never been more humiliated in her life. Embarrassed by her own sister, desperate to make her escape, hampered by this diabolical gown, and reduced to waddling down the corridor.

Until the hem tripped her, of course.

Then she took tumble number three.

Clio blinked away a scalding tear. Truly, could this be any worse?

"Don't get up. I'm here."

Rafe's voice.

Yes. It could be worse. The most attractive, compelling man of her acquaintance, and the only man to ever look at her with desire in his eyes, could be present to witness it all.

Now her humiliation was complete.

He knelt at her side. "Are you hurt anywhere?"

"Only my pride." She tried to regain her feet.

"So this is why you wouldn't eat the cake yesterday." He took her elbow, steadying her. "You can't be worried Piers will judge you on your measurements?"

"I'm a woman. *Everyone* judges us on our measurements."

And Clio's mother, God rest her, had never missed an opportunity to remind her of it. Her mother was the daughter of an earl, expected to make an excellent match; yet she'd condescended to marry a naval officer of common birth. If only she'd been a little less stout, she'd once told Clio in confidence . . . she thought she might have married a peer.

Mama was determined her daughters would not fall victim to the same mistake. Daphne and Phoebe were naturally svelte, but Clio's figure had always tended toward curves.

"My mother had this . . . Well, she called it a game. We started playing it just as soon as I'd been engaged to Piers. She would have my dinner sent up to the room on a tray. Each course on a separate plate. And then she would drill me on whatever we'd studied that afternoon. French grammar, Bavarian etiquette, the correct forms of address for Hanoverian royalty. She'd ask me question after question, and for each mistake I made, she took one dish from my tray, starting with dessert. Some nights, I made so many mistakes that I had no dinner at all. Only broth. Other nights, I had three or four courses. But I never managed to keep my dessert."

"That 'game' doesn't strike me as amusing."

"There was one dinner I particularly remember. On the tray was a slice of toffee-nut cake. My favorite. I remember staring at it so intently, I could taste the browned sugar and the buttery walnuts. I was so careful as she quizzed me. I answered every question perfectly. No mistakes. I was giddy with victory. At last. And then, while I was sitting there simmering with triumph, she took that slice of cake from my tray."

"Why would she do that, if you didn't make any mistakes?"

"Because I was the mistake," Clio said, not bothering to hide her emotions any longer. "I was wrong, just for being me. I was growing too heavy."

Rafe cursed. "Your mother was a fool. Your sister, too."

"My mother wanted the best for me. And I know Daphne means well. We're family."

"Just because they're family doesn't mean they won't hurt you. It means they know how to cut deep."

She didn't answer.

"What's more," he said, "they've lied to you. Because you're not heavy."

"You don't need to say that to preserve my feelings."

"I'm saying it because it's the truth."

"But I—"

He sighed gruffly. "You asked for this."

He braced one hand on her back, then slipped the other under her legs. And with one effortless motion, he swept Clio straight off her feet.

Into his arms.

His large, massive, all-the-words-for-big arms.

"What are you doing?"

"Proving a point." He bounced her in his arms, and her stomach took a brief flight. "You're not heavy. Not to me."

Oh. Oh, mercy.

He took her breath away, the rogue. And for long, dizzying moments, he refused to give it back.

Clio was certain she'd never beheld a more hand-some man in her life. She'd always known Rafe to be attractive, virile, dangerous, desirable. But from this close vantage, in the light of day . . . Her gaze skipped from the strong angle of his jaw, to the proud cut of his cheekbone, to the vibrant green of his eyes, framed by lashes dark as ink.

He was beautiful. Utterly, masculinely beautiful. She didn't know how she'd never seen it before. She supposed he hadn't let her close enough to see.

"Very well," she managed. "Now that you've made your point, you can set me down."

"Not a chance." He adjusted her weight in his arms and began carrying her up the staircase, taking two steps at a time. "You'll never get up all these stairs in that gown."

"I'm not going to treat you like a beast of burden."

"I might be a beast," he said, pausing on the land-ing, "but you could never be a burden. Just tell me where to go."

She relented when they reached the top of the stairs. "That way." Then, as they reached a bend in the corridor, "Turn here."

Rafe wheeled on his right boot, following her di-rection.

"My chamber is almost at the end. A little far-ther." By now, she was enjoying this so much, she rather wished it were miles away. "There. The one on the right. Mind the doorjamb."

He tucked her head to his chest and nudged the door open with his boot.

They burst into the room, and Rafe suddenly stopped.

Clio wondered if the image had struck him the way it had done her. How this must appear: Him, carrying her into the bedchamber. Her, dressed in an ivory lace gown.

They looked like newlyweds.

And there, looming before them like a raft of in-evitability, was Clio's four-post bed.

Chapter Thirteen

oly God, that bed.

Rafe marveled at it. Four soaring, carved wooden posts. A canopy of emerald velvet. And pillows. Of course, there'd be pillows.

Row after row of them, in every shade of green.

They took up half the bed, all neatly ordered by size and shape. They made Rafe want to muss them. Send them tumbling to the floor, one thrust at a time.

He set Clio down at once.

"This is not how it was supposed to go," he said. "We'll order more gowns. Ones that fit properly. I'll see to it myself."

"That won't be necessary." She turned her back to him and lifted her hair from her neck. "Just let me out of this one."

"You . . ." Rafe tugged at his neckcloth and cleared his throat. "You want me to remove your gown."

Not just any gown, but a *wedding* gown. With that bed nearby.

"Undo the buttons, that's all. I can't breathe in it. I've learned to survive without a lot of things—cake, weddings, the respect of my peers—but I haven't yet learned how to live without air."

He hesitated, staring at the milky softness of her exposed nape and the row of tiny, silk-covered buttons that couldn't possibly look any more innocent—and would cheerfully lead him straight into hell.

She braced herself against the bedpost with her free hand. "Please, Rafe. I'm starting to feel faint."

With a silent curse, he reached for the top button. What choice did he have? He couldn't allow her to suffocate. And as for him, he'd made his name on profligacy and bare-knuckle violence. He was already damned.

He struggled to grasp the tiny button between his thumb and forefinger without bracing his knuckles against her bare neck.

"Can you manage it?"

"I can manage it." He gritted his teeth and willed his trembling fingers to be still. "It's just that I broke this hand once, a few years ago."

"I'm sorry."

"You needn't be sorry. Just be patient."

She laughed a little, making him lose his grip again. "That's the story of my life."

At last, the first button slipped through its hole. His thumb slid beneath the fabric, brushing across the soft skin of her back.

There. Now they were under way. One button down, and . . .

He cast a glance downward.

. . . what seemed like several thousand to go. Good Lord. Did dressmakers earn wages by the button these days?

He focused his attention and concentrated on the task.

A few buttons more, and he was exposing her corset. Really, he was well acquainted with women's undergarments. How many laced corsets had he seen in his life? Dozens, surely. Perhaps scores.

None had affected him like this one.

The band of linen and whalebone was cinched so tightly around the thin, white lawn of her shift. The fragrance of violets was everywhere. Not overwhelming. Violets weren't the kind of flower to overwhelm. Their scent teased him. Cosseted his senses. Made him feel warm and safe.

And this wasn't safe at all.

If she were any other woman in the world, he could have had her half-naked by now.

But if she were any other woman in the world, he wouldn't have ached for it half so much.

He'd always had a taste for the forbidden. He'd always had a liking for her. Add in the thrill of innocent white lace against the delicate blush of her skin? His heart was thumping in his chest. Blood was rushing everywhere it shouldn't.

With every button he loosed, his depravity grew. He wanted to spread his hands, smooth his palms over the small of her back. Lay claim to her. Press his lips to the hollow at the base of her neck. Hook his finger beneath those knotted laces and pull her tight against his swelling cock.

Damn it, Rafe.

He grabbed the edges and ripped the last few buttons free.

"There. Finished." And not a moment too soon.

"My corset, too," she begged.

Oh, God.

He stood back a pace, examined the knot, and found the end of the laces. When he caught the grommet between his finger and thumb, he felt like he held the loose thread of his sanity. One tug, and he'd be completely unraveled.

He pulled it anyway. He'd come too far to do anything else.

"Breathe," he told her.

She obeyed, and her sharp intake of breath made him wild. Suddenly, this wasn't just a thousand buttons and the most enticing corset he'd ever unlaced. It was the soft heat of her lips under his. The sweetness of her kiss. Her fingers in his hair. The rain spinning a cocoon around them. Laughter and warmth.

"That's better. Thank you." She turned to face him, arms crossed over the bodice of her loosened gown. "Until this week, I hadn't tasted cake in years. It's so curious, isn't it? How if you're denied something again and again, eventually you start telling yourself you didn't want it in the first place."

He swept a lock of hair from her neck. "I think I might be familiar with that."

"When Piers was coming back from Antigua, my mother starved me for months in advance of his return. I was allowed nothing but watercress soup and beef tea, she was so determined to cinch in my waist. In the end, the malnourishment made me ill. I was so weak, I couldn't lift a pen, much less stand through a wedding ceremony. We had to postpone everything again."

The rage was enough to choke him. "She was wrong. Wrong to deny you. Wrong to make you feel anything less than perfect."

"But I'm not perfect. Not for this. If Piers thought I was perfect at seventeen, he would have married me then. The same with nineteen, and twenty-one, and twenty-three. The last time he saw me was almost two years ago, when he was here for that brief sojourn before leaving for Vienna. We could have exchanged our vows that very week, and I could have gone with him to the Continent. But he didn't want me there. I would have embarrassed him, perhaps."

"You would *not* have embarrassed him." Goddamn. Any man who would feel anything less than proud to have this woman at his side was a man Rafe wanted to pound into mince. Brother or no.

"My mother always said the same thing. I was a good girl. But for a marchioness, that wasn't good enough."

Rafe was beginning to understand why she'd been resisting him all this week. Time and again, she'd been saying she just wanted "good enough," and time and again he'd told her to want better.

"Clio, you are . . ." *Sensual, alluring, voluptuous.* "Beautiful."

Somehow he had to make her believe this. If his sordid past and plainspoken nature would ever come in useful, this was the time.

"Believe me," he said. "There are a great many men who *prefer* women with something to them."

"Are you saying Piers is one of those men?"

"There's a solid chance of it. I'm his brother, and I'm one of those men."

God, the feel of her under him in the dining room yesterday. He could still sense her lushness embossed on his body. Every curve.

"Then that means there's no chance at all," she said. "You and Piers are nothing alike."

"You're right," he said. "My brother and I are different in many ways. In almost every way. He's a diplomat. I'm a fighter. He's driven by duty. I'm a rebel. He spent eight years neglecting to tell you just how goddamn attractive you are." He walked to the door, shut it, and turned the key. "I'm not going to wait another minute."

At the click of the lock, a shiver raced down Clio's spine. She crossed her arms over the bodice of her unbuttoned gown and hugged herself tight.

"I'm not going to touch you," Rafe said. "I'm just going to talk."

She shivered again. Did he mean that as some sort of comfort? His voice was the most dangerous thing about him.

"Unlike my brother, I don't have any difficulty saying what needs to be said. No matter how rude or impolitic." He paced back and forth in front of the door. "Listen to me. You . . . you didn't have brothers. You don't know the adolescent male mind. We can't get enough of female bodies. Breasts, hips, legs. Hell, even a glimpse of ankle will get our blood pumping. We spy on the maids when they're bathing, we trade lewd sketches . . ."

"Why are we speaking of this?"

"Because every man has one woman who was his first proper fantasy. The first he thought about, day and night. The first he woke from dreams of, hard and aching." He met her gaze. "You were that woman for me."

"I . . ." Clio was breathless. "I was?"

"You were." He stepped toward her. "Hell, you still are. I've wanted you since I was a randy youth. This body made me wild. Every lush, round, maddeningly erotic curve. There are a thousand carnal things I've dreamed about doing to, with, on, or inside you."

Clio didn't know how to reply to that. So, naturally, she came out with the most pedantic, silly reply possible. "A thousand? That's a rather incredible number."

"An exaggeration, perhaps. But not by much. Do you want to hear a list?

She nodded. If it saved her from speaking, she would love nothing more.

"Let's see." His gaze roamed her body. "I can start with your breasts. They take up the first fifty places on the list alone. One, fondling. Two, nuzzling. Then kissing, licking, sucking in that order. Five, biting gently. Six, biting harder. Seven, pressing your breasts together, holding them tight around my thrusting cock."

She blinked at him. "Really?"

"You said it yourself. Men are disgusting."

"I suppose I wouldn't call that disgusting. Just . . . surprising."

In fact the mere picture of it—if she could trust

her imagination to picture it properly—was drawing her nipples to tight points and making her warm between her thighs.

"And I'm not even to ten yet," he said. "I'm just getting started. There are things on that list even *I* can't say aloud."

He took a step back and began to circle her in slow paces.

"Bloody hell. There've been times I didn't know how to look at you. Because you were such a good girl, and in my mind, I'd made you do such wicked, wicked things. I have wanted you ever since I can remember wanting."

"Even with all the women you've had."

"Even with all the women I've had."

She clutched the loosened gown tight to her chest. She couldn't believe any of this.

"But you said it was because of Piers. You wanted me because you were envious of him, and it wasn't really anything to do with me."

"Oh, yes." He returned to stand before her. "That's what I told myself. I told myself a lot of things. I told myself that it just so happened you were my sort." He swept a hungry look down her body. "I was only attracted to you because I'm always attracted to fair-haired, blue-eyed, lushly curved women. That would make sense, wouldn't it?

"It would make perfect sense."

His gaze snapped up to hers. "It was a lie."

"So . . . you're . . . *not* attracted to fair-haired, blue-eyed, lushly curved women?"

"Oh, I am," he said. "I am. And it's because they remind me of you."

Heavens.

Her knees . . . They weren't working anymore. They might not exist anymore.

She reeled backward, and her back met the bed-post.

"Your body"—he closed the distance between them—"is my every raw, lusting, carnal dream. I've spent years wondering what you look like under all that."

"Well . . ." She uncrossed her arms, and the lace gown slipped to the floor. "Wonder no longer."

She wasn't quite naked. Even with her gown and corset in a heap at her feet, she still wore her chemise and petticoats. But the delicate, tissue-thin fabric left little to the imagination.

Rafe didn't say anything. He simply stared at her.

She grasped the ribbon bow at the neckline of her chemise and pulled it loose.

He didn't so much as blink.

Clio's pulse raced. She hadn't come this far just to back down. If he left her here, exposed and rejected, her pride would never survive it.

In a moment of pure madness, she stretched her arms overhead, gripping the bedpost with both hands. The pose bowed her spine and pushed her breasts to what she hoped was an enticing angle.

He showed no signs of being enticed.

Oh, Lord. Perhaps all those confessions of his had merely been lies to soothe her feelings. She'd been a fool to believe he found her irresistible. Here he was, standing within arm's reach, enjoying a view of her half-naked body . . .

Resisting.

Her bravery faded, and her gaze dropped to the floor. She started to let her hands drop, too. She needed to cover herself, find somewhere to hide from this humiliation. Perhaps the closet, or a nice crack in the floor.

"Don't."

With one big hand he caught both of her wrists. He pressed them back in place and held them there, effectively shackling her to the bedpost.

"Don't move."

Well. Now this was more like it.

The sudden heat and forceful nature of the contact, his unabashed stare, the vulnerability of her posture . . . it all made her writhe with excitement.

It wasn't just knowing that Rafe found her body attractive.

It was that she found her body rather attractive, too.

"Look at you," he breathed.

She did. She gazed down at herself, admiring the flushed pink of her skin beneath the thin white shift. The sunlight streaming through the windows was warm, and kind to her fair complexion, painting her with a rosy glow. Her peaked nipples strained and chafed against the fabric. Her gently rounded belly and hips made no excuses for themselves.

This was her body. She had learned to take pleasure in it, even if no man had ever done the same. It was curved and generous and womanly and strong, and it was formed to do more than decorate a drawing room, or transfer wealth from one gentleman to another.

She was made to tempt, labor, inspire, create, sustain.

Despite the way Rafe held her bound in his grasp, a sense of power moved through her. For once, she could revel in her femininity and feel it as something other than a disadvantage to be overcome. A quality to be respected, worshipped. Even feared.

She could do anything in this moment. She felt like a—

"A goddess," he murmured.

Dear Lord. Forget sentences. He was finishing her thoughts now.

"You're sculpted just like a Grecian goddess." His gaze pulled up to catch hers. "And the hell of it is, your body's only the third most attractive thing about you. Right after your clever mind and your lovely heart."

If he meant to admire her heart, he had better do it quickly. Because she suspected the organ was going to give out at any moment. Her "clever mind" was already a bowl of blancmange.

"If you were mine to hold and pleasure, I'd . . ."

She sucked in her breath. "You would what?"

He leaned forward, and his voice was dark. "Take you in my arms, at first. Hold your heart close to mine and try to let that be enough. But it wouldn't be enough. I'd start to want more. I'd want to make *you* want more."

Oh, she already wanted more. Clio reclined against the bedpost to steady herself.

Don't stop. Please, go on.

"I'd take down this lovely hair and let it fall through my fingers. I'd run my hands over your arms, your back. And all your tender, softest parts . . . that's where I'd use my mouth. And then . . ." He bent his head, until his words scalded her ear. "And then I'd slide my hand beneath your shift and touch you. Right where we both want it most."

The room blurred in her vision. A dull, aching pulse began to throb between her thighs.

"Do it," he said, releasing one of her hands. "Do it for me."

She startled, but his free hand went to her waist, holding her still.

"There's no one," he said. "No one will know. No one will see. Do what I can't. Just this once."

Her heart climbed into her throat. She didn't know if she could do that. Not like this. Not in front of him.

His temple pressed to hers. "Christ, Clio. I think I'll die of wanting you. If there's any chance you feel it, too . . . Let me know I'm not alone."

This was madness.

But she did want this. And she never wanted him to feel alone.

With trembling fingers, she twisted her petticoat until she could loosen the fastenings—just a touch—and slide her hand inside. The fabric of her chemise still came between her fingertips and her belly, but it was so thin as to be inconsequential.

As she swept her touch lower, she bit her lip.

"Yes, that's it," he murmured. "Yes. That's where you want it, isn't it? And where I want it, too. You're so lovely there. Lovely and pink and warm."

She nodded.

"And wet. You're so wet for me, aren't you?"

Clio's pulse raced at the crudeness of his words, but she couldn't deny the truth. As she pushed her fingers between her thighs, the linen softened and grew damp.

"Here," he said.

Where his hand covered hers on the bedpost, he drew one fingertip between her second and third fingers, slowly tracing the seam as if he were parting her legs. Or the folds of her sex.

Then his touch settled right in the sensitive crook where they joined.

"Touch yourself here," he whispered, moving his fingertip in tight, steady circles that she felt everywhere. "Just like this."

She was beyond any sense of shame or propriety, and his words had caught her in some sort of trance.

When her fingers slid into just the right place, her breath caught in a startled gasp.

"That's it." He kissed her ear. "That's a good girl."

The words made her smile. For once, she wasn't being a good girl. She was being a wicked, wicked thing, and she loved it.

He loved it, too.

The edge of his restraint seemed to be fraying. He traced the shape of her ear with his tongue, then nibbled on her earlobe. Her senses hummed when he gave a husky groan.

And then his hand—the one that had settled on her waist—began to move. Just a little, at first. His thumb stroked back and forth in a coaxing arc. And then his entire hand began to sweep up and down in a gentle caress. With every pass, his fingertips brushed a bit lower on her hip, and his thumb grazed a fraction closer to the underside of her breast.

Please.

She wanted to encourage him somehow, but she was afraid to say or do anything too bold, for fear he might stop altogether.

There was a border they were fast approaching. A point of no return.

At last—with a muttered oath, he tipped them over the edge. His hand slid upward, cupping her breast. When his thumb found her nipple, she went faint with pleasure and relief.

"Come." His whisper was hot and rough. He ran his tongue down her neck. He lifted and shaped her breast through the softened linen, rolling her nipple under the pad of his thumb. "If it damns my soul, I need to hear you come. And I want it to be for me."

She touched herself, and he touched her, and the bliss gathered and built, until it loomed before her like a devastating wave.

She trembled. "Rafe . . ."

"I'm here. I have you. Just let it happen."

His mouth captured hers, giving her the shelter she needed. When the bliss crashed through her, she moaned and sobbed and sighed it all into his kiss. Where she was safe.

And long after it was over, he kissed her still. So sweetly.

He released her arm from the bedpost, and they held each other close. She sifted her fingers through his hair. He touched her cheek. So lightly, using only the backs of his fingers.

It was the closest she'd ever felt to being treasured.

But the look on his face when he broke their kiss . . . Oh, it was like a dagger to her heart. Guilt etched furrows on his brow, and the green of his eyes was the shade of regret. As if he'd robbed her of something, instead of giving her the most beautiful, sensual experience of her life.

"Rafe, that was—"

"Clio, we can't—"

"Miss Whitmore?" A knock sounded at the door. "Miss Whitmore, did you need help with your gown?"

Anna.

"Drat drat drat," she muttered.

Rafe's choice of words was decidedly less genteel.

"Just a moment," Clio called out. She shimmied, then stepped out of the pool of gown and petticoats at her feet. She took Rafe by the hand. "Quickly. This way."

He resisted. "You can't mean to hide me. I'm too big. I won't fit in the wardrobe or behind the drapes."

"You'll fit here." She found a little notch in the paneled wall and slid it open. "This way. Hurry."

He stepped into the secret room, looking around its single slice of window and kneeling bench. "What is this?"

"It's an oratory. A private chapel for the mistress of the house to withdraw and reflect." She nodded at the other side. "There's a similar door that leads into my sitting room."

"You'd never know it was even here." He tilted his head to admire the ceiling. "This castle truly is something."

"I told you as much." Smiling, she moved to slide the panel shut.

"Wait." He put his hand in the gap, holding the panel open. "So are you, Clio. You're truly something. Never doubt it."

He withdrew his hand, and the door slid shut.

Chapter Fourteen

"We must discuss the ice sculptures," Daphne said later that evening.

"Must we?"

The three Whitmore sisters had gathered in Clio's sitting room to dress for dinner. Just like the times when they were younger. Phoebe sat at the dressing table while Clio brushed out her hair. Daphne lay on her side, draped across Clio's bed. With one hand, she flipped the pages of a ladies' magazine, and with the other she plucked raspberries from a bowl.

Despite Phoebe's trouble in the village and Daphne's insulting trick with the too-small gowns, Clio needed her sisters close this evening. She couldn't explain it except to think that sometimes the devil you knew was easier to face than the devil who'd pressed you to a bedpost and rolled your nipple under his thumb.

"I was thinking perhaps a sculpted pair of famous lovers," Daphne suggested. "What about Romeo and Juliet?"

"That ended badly," Phoebe said. "One poisoned, one died by dagger."

"Cleopatra and Marc Antony?"

"Even worse. One snakebite, one sword."

"Lancelot and Guinevere, then."

"He died a hermit. She became a nun."

Daphne sighed, exasperated. "You ruin everything."

"So I'm beginning to understand." Phoebe handed Clio a hairpin. "But this time, it's not my fault. Forbidden love affairs never turn out well in stories."

Clio held her tongue as she twisted her sister's dark hair into a simple chignon.

Phoebe was right. Nothing good would come of this . . . this whatever it was between her and Rafe. She couldn't precisely call it a love affair. The word love had never been uttered, and they hadn't done anything so irreversible that it couldn't be brushed aside.

But she didn't want to brush it aside.

She wanted to clutch it tight and never let go. The way he'd held her so tenderly . . . The security and exhilaration she felt in his embrace . . . She wanted that. She wanted *more*. She wanted him to be thinking about her just as often as she thought about him.

Which was, to estimate it roughly, with each and every breath.

He had to sign those papers, without delay. He simply *must*. To ease her conscience, if nothing else. Piers might not have treated her with any particular tenderness, and perhaps their engagement was a mere formality—but it had to be wrong to drop your frock for one man while still officially betrothed to another.

"If you want famous lovers, there's always Ulysses and Penelope," Phoebe suggested. "She stayed faithful for twenty years while her husband traveled the world to return to her."

"Swans," Clio blurted out, desperate to change the subject from long-suffering, faithful women. "Aren't these ice sculptures usually swans?"

"Yes, but *everyone* has swans," Daphne said. "They're supposed to be romantic because they mate for life."

In the mirrored reflection, Phoebe arched one slender eyebrow. "So do vultures, wolves, and African termites. I haven't seen any ice sculptures of them."

Clio was about to remark that a termite mound sounded like just the thing, but there was a knock at the bedchamber door.

Anna entered, carrying an envelope. "A message has arrived for you, Miss Whitmore. The bearer is downstairs waiting for your reply."

"At this hour? How mysterious." She broke the seal and opened the letter. "It's an invitation."

And a welcome change of subject. It couldn't have come at a better time.

Clio scanned the paper. "We're invited to a ball. Tomorrow evening."

"Tomorrow evening?" Daphne asked.

"Apparently Lord and Lady Pennington are in residence at their estate near Tunbridge Wells. They apologize for the short notice, but they only just learned we were in Kent." She lowered the paper. "Well?"

"We must accept." Daphne perked with excitement. "I haven't been to nearly enough balls as a married lady."

"Excellent. Then you and Teddy can go. I'll stay home with Phoebe."

"Clio, you must come, too. There will be gossip if you don't."

"There will be gossip if I *do* attend," she said, moving to the escritoire. "That's what I'm keen to avoid."

"Yes, but this time it will be different," Daphne said. "We can tell everyone about the wedding plans. Then they'll know it's really happening this time."

Except that it isn't.

"What about Phoebe?" she asked.

"Let her come, as well. It's only a small country affair. She won't dance, of course."

"I don't wish to go," Phoebe said. "I'd be bored and out of place."

"Yes, but that's why you should come," Daphne said. "So you start learning how to conceal it."

Clio arrowed a glance at her sister. Not that it did much good.

"She's sixteen years old," Daphne said. "She needs some exposure to society."

Even if she expressed it poorly, Clio knew her sister had a point. Sooner or later, Phoebe would have to develop the skill of interacting with people outside their family.

"I don't want to go," Phoebe said, turning on the dressing-table bench. "It would be a miserable ordeal. Don't make me."

"Oh, kitten. Daphne has the right of it. You will

need to start moving in society soon, and a small, friendly ball is a good place to begin." She tapped the envelope. "I won't force you, but I hope you'll choose to attend."

Phoebe considered. "Is Lord Rafe attending? I'll go if he does."

"No," Daphne objected. "He can't. Montague would be fine. But we can't have Rafe. Surely the Penningtons didn't mean to include *him*."

Clio bristled at her sister's words. "The invitation is extended to me and my guests. He's one of my guests."

"Yes, but they didn't know he's here. Otherwise, they wouldn't have invited us at all. Don't suggest it, Clio. You were kind enough to allow him to stay here at the castle. He's Granville's brother; you haven't a choice. But he's not welcome in polite society anymore."

An emotion flared in Clio's breast, hot and volatile. She wanted to gather up Daphne's casual disdain, shape it into a tiny ball, and give it a solid whack with a tennis racket.

It was ridiculous, the idea that a champion prizefighter could possibly need her to defend him. He probably wouldn't care to attend the ball anyhow.

But it shouldn't be up to Daphne—or anyone else—to shut him out.

You're truly something, he told her. *Never doubt it.*

Rafe shouldn't doubt it, either.

"Lord Rafe Brandon," she said, "is always welcome where I'm concerned." Clio checked her hair in the mirror and smoothed the front of her gray silk. "If he wishes to join us, that is."

And with that, she left the room to search out Rafe and ask.

"Still no ring?" Rafe asked the question without breaking stride.

"Still . . . no . . . ring," Bruiser replied. Unlike Rafe, he was breathless. "Can't we slow down a touch?"

"No."

They'd already completed four laps of the castle wall's perimeter. It wasn't nearly enough. Rafe still felt her softness clinging to his fingertips. He still tasted her on his lips. He still heard her soft moans and sighs echoing in his ears.

At this rate, he would be running hard all night. Even then, he'd never run far enough to leave his guilt behind.

What he'd done with Clio this afternoon had been so wrong.

It had also been beautiful, tender, and sublime.

But wrong, nonetheless. And entirely his fault.

Over the years, he'd learned to rein in his impulses, pull his punches. But when she'd let that lacy frock slide down her body, revealing the thinnest linen shift the Devil could weave . . . Inviting— nay, *pleading* for his touch . . .

He shouldn't have given in to the temptation.

Miss Lydia Fairchild had taught him that lesson in his youth. The chestnut-haired daughter of a gentleman farmer, she'd pulled Rafe into the orchard one spring afternoon and drawn his hand beneath her skirts. His first touch of pure woman. He'd been overwhelmed by her warmth, her willingness. The way her hair smelled of apple blossoms.

Most of all, how she'd *wanted* his touch, at a time when he'd felt unwanted everywhere.

After an hour or so of enthusiastic groping, Rafe had managed a weak, guilt-inspired offer to speak with her father. In response, she'd laid her fingers to his cheek and laughed. Her parents had arranged a match with a country squire some twenty years her senior. She only wanted a few thrills with the local hellion first.

She wasn't the last, either. Over the years, women had come to him for all sorts of reasons—pleasure, curiosity, rebellion, escape—but love and marriage weren't among them.

Just as well, he'd told himself. He had too much devilry in him. If he wanted to keep his mind sharp, Rafe needed to be in constant motion. Staying in one place made him restless, prone to rash mistakes. He was incapable of settling down.

But that didn't keep him from envying men who did. And wanting something more than a quick, hard . . .

Well, just wanting something *more*.

When he reached the corner, he paused and jogged in place, waiting for Bruiser to catch up.

"You need to order more gowns," Rafe said. "Better ones. Ones that fit."

His trainer leaned over, clutching his side and making a pained face. "I already did. But it will take a few days."

Damn it, he didn't have a few days.

Rafe boxed the waning afternoon, throwing jab after jab at the sinking sun. As if he could punch the orange disc hard enough to drive it into the sky, and it would stick there—just like the tankard embedded in that plaster wall. Then this day would go on forever, and he wouldn't have to face the promises he'd made.

"There has to be something else," he said. "Something we haven't tried."

"We've been through it all." Bruiser threw out an arm and leaned against the wall, gasping for breath. "Flowers, cakes, ceremony, gowns. There's only one thing I can think of that she's missing."

"What's that?"

"Love."

Rafe cursed.

"You heard her the other night," Bruiser said. "She wants love. And devotion and compromise. Funny, isn't it, how women seem to want those things, when they're saying words like 'Till death do us part.' Now, if Clio—"

"Miss Whitmore." Rafe threw a vicious right hook. "If Miss *Whitmore* believed that Lord Granville loves her, this whole endeavor might be different."

Rafe let his arms drop. "My brother is just like our father. Granvilles are swayed by emotions the same way Alps are rocked by a breeze. How am I supposed to convince her that Piers is in love?"

"I don't know, Rafe. But there's a time-honored method I'm going to submit for your consideration. For thousands of years now, men have used it to great effect. It's called lying."

"I'm bollocks at lying."

"Fortunately, I'm excellent at training." Without warning, Bruiser leapt on Rafe's back. "Yah."

"What the hell are you doing?" Rafe spun in a circle, swatting at his trainer as if he were some kind of gnat. Only more irritating.

"Easy, stallion." Bruiser locked his ankles onto Rafe's hips in piggyback fashion. "Just run like this, will you? I'm spent, and you need more exertion."

Rafe huffed a sigh and started running again. Bruiser was right; he'd tire much faster this way. And if he had any hope of making it through one more night in Twill Castle, he needed to run himself into a stupor.

"Now listen sharp," his trainer said, clinging tight to Rafe's neck as they pounded down the length of the northern wall. "The key to a good lie is embroidery."

"I missed that day at finishing school."

Bruiser dug a heel into his ribs. "Not the needle-and-thread kind. The verbal sort. Embellishments. Particulars. They're what make a lie believable. As they say, the devil is in the details."

Rafe snorted.

"If you want to convince her that Piers is in love, you're going to have tell a good story. One with a time and a place, and plenty of specifics. Now, tell me all about the time you bedded that Parisian opera dancer."

"I never bedded any Parisian opera dancer."

"Exactly my point, you dolt. Make it up."

Rafe tried. He honestly tried. In his imagination, he conjured the fantasy of a dark, mysterious woman, beckoning him toward a bed with beaded scarlet hangings. But his mind kept working a strange alchemy, turning the woman's ebony hair to gold. Her dark, smoky eyes lightened to a familiar, lovely blue. And as for the bed . . . well, the only bed he could picture was a four-post affair with emerald velvet, and row after perfect row of pillows.

Even in his imagination, he just didn't have it in him to bed another woman. Not today.

Probably not for a long, long while.

"This is stupid," he said. "I'm telling you, I can't lie."

"You can. You just need practice. And you're about to get an excellent chance," Bruiser muttered. "Right about . . ."

"Oh, gracious!" someone close—and female—shrieked.

"Now," Bruiser finished.

Rafe pulled up short, chest heaving. Clio's lady's maid—Anna, was it?—stood before them in the center of the path. No doubt wondering why the hell a sweaty, breathless man was running around the castle wall while carrying another grown man on his back.

Her hands fluttered. "I'm so sorry to have interrupted your . . . this."

"There's a reasonable explanation, never fear," Bruiser said. "Lord Rafe had to carry me. I have a condition."

You most certainly do, Rafe thought.

"A condition?" Her eyebrows crinkled together, and Rafe could all but see little cogs turning behind them. "Is it . . ." She lowered her voice. "Is it serious?"

"Sadly, yes. Possibly fatal."

She covered her gasp with both hands. Because, apparently, one hand wouldn't have been dramatic enough. "No. But surely something can be done. What is it?"

"I don't know. I was unconscious when the doctor saw me. Lord Rafe can explain it better." Bruiser nudged him in the ribs. "Go on, then. Tell her the whole story of my malady. In detail. With all the particulars. What did that German doctor call it?"

Rafe gave her a single, unembroidered word. "Syphilis."

The lady's maid turned a pale shade of green. She began backing away in small steps. "I just came to say Miss Whitmore is looking for you, my lord."

With that, she dropped a frantic curtsy and fled.

The moment she was out of sight, Bruiser tweaked his ear. "You bloody jackass."

"What are you complaining about? I lied. She believed me."

"I'll get you for this." He began kicking at Rafe's ribs.

Rafe turned his back to the wall and crushed the man against it.

"My pocket," Bruiser squeaked. "Mind the quizzing glass."

"Fuck the quizzing glass." Rafe let him fall to the ground in a heap. "And to hell with embroidery. I don't need to lie to Clio. She has enough honest reasons to marry Piers. He's a bloody marquess with pots of money, and he's a decent, honorable man. She can't possibly do better."

And Rafe was determined that she would have the best.

"What about you?" Bruiser asked.

"What *about* me?"

Bruiser hauled himself off the ground, clapped the dust from his trousers, and put his hands on Rafe's shoulders. "Your future is on the line here. I can go out and find another fighter, but you are all you've got. And you've fought enough bouts that you know by now, if you're to have any chance at besting Dubose, you have to want it. You have to want it more than you want anything in this world."

Rafe closed his eyes and saw himself on the ground after fighting Dubose. Eyes stinging, head thick. His vision blurred by sweat and blood. The crowd around him chanting and calling as the umpire counted away the last moments of his reign as champion.

Prizefighting had been his life, his salvation. He'd worked too hard, for too long to let that be the way he exited the sport.

"I want to win," he said. "I need to win."

"Then this entire situation with Clio is a distraction. What are we even doing here, Rafe? If you're serious about settling matters, I only see two alternatives. Lie, and tell her Piers is in love with her. Or be honest, and confess that you are."

"What?" Rafe recoiled, as if he'd been dealt a body blow out of nowhere.

In love with Clio?

No. He couldn't be.

He liked Clio. He admired her. And there was no denying that he desired her, to a dangerous degree. His fascination with her had outlasted his interest in just about anything or anyone, save prizefighting.

But nothing could ever come from it. Rafe was just a bit of excitement to her, and his touch could only mean ruin for Clio. He'd made his reputation, and now he had to live with it. Most dangerous of all, she had a way of destroying his hard-earned control.

If he cared for her at all, he would stay far away.

"I don't know where you got such an idea," he told Bruiser. "That's absurd. She's . . . And we. . . ." He gestured uselessly. "I'm not in love with her."

Bruiser rolled his eyes. "You're right. You are bollocks at lying. Let's just go inside."

Chapter Fifteen

In the library a half hour later, Rafe stared longingly at the crystal brandy decanter. He could have used a stiff drink right now. But whatever it was Clio wanted to discuss, he needed to keep his head clear.

"I've been looking all over. There you are."

And there Clio was, standing in the doorway. Muddling his thoughts all over again.

Damnation. Rafe had been counting on having some warning. A bit more time to compose himself before he saw her. As it was, he felt he'd been thrown unawares into a pool of shimmering silk and luminous beauty.

It was swim or drown, and he was breathless. Flailing.

"I . . ."

She'd been so soft and warm in his hands.

Sweet heaven, the taste of her.

"Ahem." Bruiser cleared his throat. Pointedly. He was already standing.

After a moment's lapse, Rafe shot to his feet, too. Christ, was he so far removed from his upbringing that he'd forgotten to stand when a lady entered the room?

Even once he'd risen from the chair, he didn't know what to do with his hands. They kept wanting to reach in her direction.

He crossed his arms and tucked them close. He had to get hold of himself.

He said, "You were looking for me."

"Yes." She gestured with an envelope. "For you both, actually. We've been invited to a ball tomorrow. The Penningtons have an estate near Tunbridge. It's only a few hours' drive. Daphne's keen on attending, and even Phoebe expressed an interest. Will you join us?"

"Jolly good," Bruiser said, in that affected toffish accent. "But of course we shall."

"No." Rafe glanced at him. "We shan't."

"Why not?" Clio asked.

"Nothing good could come of my attending. I don't belong at those things anymore. I never did."

"Why would you say that?" she asked. "Of course you belong."

"Oh, indeed. Everyone wants a brawling prize-fighter at their high-class party."

"Maybe not, but they all want lords. No matter what else you've done in your life, you will always be the son of a marquess. Birth and lineage are everything to the *ton*."

Yes, birth and lineage were everything to the *ton*. And that was precisely the reason Rafe despised them. He would rather be judged on his accomplishments.

"If you come," she said, "I might even forgive you for missing my debut all those years ago."

And then she gave him a smile.

A warm, flirtatious smile, curved like an archer's bow. Its arrow struck home, hitting him square in the heart.

He tried his best to appear unskewered. "You're generous to invite us. But we must decline."

Bruiser tugged on his waistcoat. "Come along, old chap. Upon my word, I don't see why we—"

Rafe threw him a glare. "We. Must. Decline."

"Very well." His trainer lifted his hands. "We must decline."

Clio lowered her gaze and fidgeted with the invitation. "I see. Then if you'll pardon me, I'll go write the response."

As she left the room, her lips thinned to a tight, unbending line.

With a curse, Rafe charged into the corridor, turning just in time to glimpse Clio ducking into the library.

He followed her inside. "We should talk. About earlier. About everything."

"Must it be this moment? I need to write this reply, if you don't mind. The messenger has been waiting for an hour." She sat down at the desk.

"You must understand. I'm not welcome at these things."

"Of course I understand." She sighed, then let the

pen clatter to the blotter. "Actually, I don't understand at all. For eight years, I've reached out to you
with one invitation after another. I don't know how
you can say no one wants you at these things. *I* want
you at these things. I always have."

"What were you hoping, Clio? That I'd come to the
ball, dressed in a black tailcoat and tall, gleaming
boots? Stand at the top of the stairs, be introduced to
the room as Lord Rafe Brandon of Somerset? Search
you out in the crowded room and make my way to
you?" He chuckled. "Ask you for a *dance*?"

She didn't laugh. Or say anything.

Her cheeks flushed pink, and she stared at the
blotter. After a prolonged pause, she dipped the
quill and began to write.

Well, damn.

So that's exactly what she'd been hoping would
happen. And now he'd mocked her for daring to
think it.

He hated to hurt her, but maybe it was for the best.
That little scene she'd imagined was never going to
occur. It *couldn't*.

And she needed to understand that, in no uncertain terms.

"Clio, I'm sorry if you—"

"No, don't. Don't apologize. Why should anything between us change, just because you confessed to desiring me for years, then fondled my
breast? Never mind that it was one of the most passionate, thrilling hours of my life. I suppose it's just
another Thursday to you."

"You know that's not true."

Her head lifted, and her blue eyes burned into

his. "You're right. I do know it's not true. And that makes this hurt all the more."

Curse it. Rafe knew he was making a hash of this. "I just don't belong in that world anymore. But you do, Clio. You should go and enjoy yourself."

"I'll be surrounded by gossip." Her pen scratched across the page. She lowered her voice to a mocking whisper. "There she is, Miss Wait-More. Wonder if she'll manage to bring him up to scratch this time. Care to place a wager on it?"

"It's not going to be like that."

"You're right." She paused in writing. Her demeanor softened. "You're absolutely right. It's not going to be like that. Because by this time tomorrow, I won't be engaged any longer."

Damn. Rafe didn't like the sound of this.

She sealed the envelope with a bit of wax. "I won't ask you to attend the ball. But you must sign those dissolution papers before I leave."

"The week's not over yet," he pointed out. "There's still tonight."

"I can't imagine what you could possibly do in one night that would change my mind." She gave him a wry smile. "If you'll excuse me, the messenger is waiting."

She left the room, sealed reply in hand.

And Rafe started thinking of embroidery.

Dinner was miserable. At least, for half of the people at the table.

Clio was out of sorts and quiet. Rafe was out of sorts and quiet. Phoebe was out of sorts and quiet.

Conveniently, however, the other half of their party seemed entirely oblivious to anyone's distress.

Daphne prattled on about tomorrow night's ball at the Penningtons'. The Esquire, as Clio had taken to calling him in her thoughts, filled any gaps by recounting his "Continental" escapades. And Teddy monopolized the fish course with a lengthy description of his newest pair of bespoke Hessians.

When the meal was over, they all adjourned to the drawing room.

"I'm finalizing the menu for the wedding breakfast," Daphne said. "It's almost finished. How many sauces should we have?"

"Can we speak of something else?" Clio asked, her voice breaking. "Please? I feel like such a neglectful hostess, making you work the whole week. And look at poor Teddy. He's bored out of his mind by all this talk of menus. Why don't we have a game?"

"What kind of game?"

"Any kind of game." She'd agree to chase a greased pig through the corridors if it meant changing the topic from weddings. "We'll play cards or backgammon or something."

"Not cards," Daphne said. "Not with Phoebe. She's impossible to win against."

"That doesn't mean we can't enjoy playing with her," Clio said, anxious for her sister's feelings.

Phoebe turned a page of her book. "I don't wish to play cards."

Mr. Montague spoke up. "If I might make a suggestion . . . What say the ladies to a parlor game?"

"A parlor game?" Clio chanced a look in Rafe's direction. The pained expression on his face was clear. He'd rather eat slugs than play parlor games. "Parlor games sound delightful."

"Oh, I adore parlor games," said Daphne. "They're all so perfectly wicked. If they don't have kissing, there's blindfolded groping, or sitting on one another's lap."

"I was thinking of one particular parlor game. I learned it during my time on the Continent," Montague said.

"A Continental parlor game?" Daphne asked. "This sounds promising. Does it involve groping?"

"No, Lady Cambourne. But I suspect you'll enjoy it anyway." He smiled. "We take turns, and each player makes three statements. Two must be true, and one must be a falsehood. The others have to guess which of the three statements is the lie."

Daphne was quick to cut straws. When they were passed around, Rafe declined. Clio ended up with the shortest.

"But that will be too easy," Daphne complained. "We've known Clio all her life, and she hasn't any secrets."

"Hasn't she?" Reclining in the chair, Montague propped his left boot on his right knee. "I don't know, Lady Cambourne. I have a suspicion Miss Whitmore just might be full of secrets."

Clio said, "As a matter of fact, I am."

At this, Rafe threw her a warning look. Her heartbeat accelerated.

Impossible man. Was he worried she'd announce her plans to break the engagement? Or perhaps he worried that she would confess their passionate embrace?

It would serve him right if she did either one.

But Clio was tired of thinking about Rafe and Piers. For once, she was ready to talk about herself. "Here are my three statements. First, my favorite color is green."

Daphne groaned. "Make it a *little* less obvious."

"Second," Clio forged on, "I am planning to build a brewery here at Twill Castle. And third . . ." She swept a glance around the room. "I have never been kissed."

She folded her hands and waited for their reaction.

The room lapsed into stunned silence. Daphne, Teddy . . . even Phoebe . . . They weren't merely surprised. They all looked positively aghast. Was the idea of a brewery truly that upsetting to them?

Teddy shook his head gravely. "That's . . . well, curse it. I don't know what to say to that. Except that I'm dashed sorry."

"Oh, darling." Daphne rose from her chair and came to sit beside Clio on the divan. She put a hand on Clio's knee. "He's never kissed you? In all these years, not once?"

Clio inhaled slowly. It was a sad comment on her life that her nearest family believed *this* to be the most likely truth.

"I suppose we all knew it wasn't a love match," Daphne said. "But I thought surely you two shared some fondness for each other by now."

"He won't get out of it." Teddy roused himself from his chair. "We won't allow him to cry off, no matter how he tries to weasel his way out of this engagement. After eight years, the man owes you a wedding."

"Wait," Clio said. "You're jumping to conclusions. How do you know the kissing one isn't the falsehood?"

"Because it's obvious," Daphne said. "Everyone knows your favorite color is green. So that's ruled out. And a brewery, really? That can't be true. Of all the outlandish ideas."

"What's so outlandish about it? The estate's resources need to be used, or the local community will suffer. Don't you think I could do it?"

"She could do it," Rafe said.

Clio turned to look at him, surprised. She didn't think he'd been paying attention.

"She could do it," he repeated, leaning one shoulder against the paneled wall. "This region is ideal for beer-making. Miss Whitmore has the funds, the land, the wits. With the right help, she could make a go of it."

"Perhaps she could," Teddy agreed. "But her intended wouldn't approve. Are we to believe the pubs and taverns will all be serving Lady Granville's Ale?" He chuckled. "Your brother wouldn't allow such a thing."

"You're right," Clio said, gathering her courage. "I don't imagine Piers would allow it. But that's just it, you see. I'm not going to ma—"

"You're not going to open a brewery. Of course not. How absurd." Daphne clapped her hands. "Well, that settles Clio's turn. Who is next?"

"Wait," Rafe interjected, in a tone that would not be disobeyed. His eyes flashed. "Clio's turn isn't over. You have it wrong, Lady Cambourne. You have it entirely wrong."

"What makes you say that?"

"Miss Whitmore has indeed been kissed," Rafe said. "I'm certain of it."

"But how can you possibly know?" Daphne asked.

Clio's breath caught. Did she want Rafe to answer that question honestly? Perhaps she did. But even though she'd started this game, the decision was out of her control.

He gestured in anger. "Because I was there."

Damnation.

Rafe hadn't meant to say that. The words had just fired out of him, like a wild, reckless punch he should have checked.

Everyone stared at him. Including Clio, he assumed, but he didn't dare glance her way to confirm it.

"Lord Rafe, are you telling us you witnessed this kiss with your own eyes?" Daphne didn't bother to hide her skepticism.

"No," he replied honestly.

He hadn't witnessed it with his own eyes. What kind of jackass kissed with his eyes open?

He'd witnessed it with his own *lips*.

But telling that truth wouldn't do his cause any favors.

"Then I shall stand by my answer," Daphne said. "Now whose turn is next?"

"Mine," Rafe said.

"Your turn?" Clio asked. "I thought you weren't playing."

"I changed my mind."

"Afraid you'll have to wait for the next round, Brandon," Sir Teddy Cambourne said. "My lady here cut straws and passed them around. That part's been done. You can't have a turn if you don't have a straw."

Rafe threw the man a look. A look with the force of a fist. "Really?"

Cambourne had nothing further to say. Neither did anyone else.

Rafe took the collective silence as his invitation. "First statement. In my original championship bout, I defeated Golding with a hard blow to the liver in the twenty-third round. Second . . ." He settled into a chair. "The last time I spoke with my brother, Piers told me how much he regretted the extended absence imposed by his duties, because . . ."

Just get it out, man.

"Because he was so deeply in love," he finished.

The room was quiet.

Until Daphne dropped a two-word pin into the silence: "With Clio?"

"*Yes*, with Clio."

Rafe rose from his chair again and began to stalk the carpet fringe. He was irritated beyond belief. What was wrong with these people? This shouldn't be difficult for any of them to believe. Yes, his brother was reserved, but surely *they* all loved Clio. She was entirely lovable.

All *too* lovable.

He might have entered into this falsehood half-heartedly, but he was committed to it now.

Committed with everything he had.

"When we last spoke, Piers reminisced about her

come-out ball," he said. "How she wore a gown of pale blue silk with lace at the edges. Pearls studded in her hair. He recalled how lovely she looked, even though she was nervous. He took note of how she greeted every guest with genuine kindness. And he told me that he knew, right then, there was no lady in the room her equal. That he felt like the luckiest of gentlemen, knowing she was promised to be his." He swept a glance around the room. "He loved her then. He loves her still."

Everyone was quiet as he returned to his chair.

"Not bad," Bruiser muttered.

Cambourne smacked his thigh with his gloved palm. "Well, that's a comfort. Isn't it, dumpling?"

"You're assuming that's a truth," Clio said evenly. "We've only heard two statements from Lord Rafe. I'm still waiting on the third."

"The third. Right." He cleared his throat. "I sleep in a lavender nightshirt. An embroidered one."

Bruiser sipped his brandy. "How very literal of you."

Daphne laughed. "Really, it's no use. None of you know how to play this game at all. Your lavender nightshirt is almost as preposterous as Clio's brewery. Do let's play cards after all."

Well, that was that. He seemed to have convinced her family at least, and Rafe didn't know how to feel about it. Relieved, triumphant, disgusted with himself . . . His emotions were some combination of all these.

But *his* feelings were irrelevant. There was only one person in the room whose emotions mattered.

And if Rafe hadn't managed to sway her tonight, there was no hope for him now.

Chapter Sixteen

Clio waited until midnight.

And then she waited a full hour more.

When she heard the footman pass down the corridor on his final patrol of the evening, she sat up in bed.

It was time.

She wrapped her dressing gown over her night-rail and cinched the sash tight. Then she plucked her chatelaine from the dressing table and ventured out into the corridor.

She went slowly. She had to; she hadn't dared bring a candle. And she didn't want to risk waking anyone with her footfalls or rattling keys.

At the end of the hall, she turned and hugged the right side of the corridor, counting the doors until she reached the fourth. After scouting the surface with her fingertips to find the keyhole, she inserted the master key from her chatelaine . . .

Held her breath . . .

And turned it in the lock.

Click.

The door swung inward, soundless on its well-oiled hinges.

She waited in the doorway for a moment, giving her eyes time to adjust. A banked fire glowed in the hearth, coaxing her forward. Clio made her way into the room, then took a stub of beeswax candle from the mantelpiece and crouched to light it with the coals. The single flame painted the room with a weak yellow glow.

She could see the room better now.

She could see _him_ better now.

And good heavens. Wasn't he magnificent.

The bed in this chamber was a large one, but the ranging sprawl of his limbs made it look like a child's bed. All the coverlets had been cast aside. The pillows, too—save one. He slept on his back, draped by a single linen bedsheet. Beneath it, his body was a landscape of sculpted ridges and shadowed glens. With every breath, his chest rose and fell.

She watched, transfixed, until she realized she was breathing in time with him.

Clio left the candle on the mantelpiece and crept toward the side of his bed. She eased herself onto the edge of the mattress, stretching out her legs so that she lay on her side, propped up on one elbow.

With her free hand, she gingerly plucked the edge of the bedsheet and—after waiting one, two, three breaths to make certain he didn't wake—began to tease the linen downward. She worked slowly, carefully . . . knowing the answer she sought would lie beneath.

He stirred in his sleep. Eyes still closed, he rolled onto his side, throwing an arm toward her.

His hand landed on her thigh.

Clio sucked in her breath. She held still, squeezing all her muscles tight. Her heart, however, wouldn't be so easily reined in. It hammered in her chest, so loud she was certain the pounding would wake him.

Oh drat. Oh Lord.

She'd left her room feeling secure in the brilliance of this idea. Suddenly the idea wasn't just an idea, but a reality—an immense, sleeping, sensual giant of a reality—and she wasn't secure at all.

His hand was on her *thigh.*

And *moving.*

Even this afternoon, he hadn't dared to touch her so boldly. His fingers stretched and flexed. His caresses widened to shameless, possessive circles of her hip.

Was it possible she'd entered his dream now?

If so, she couldn't help but wonder what they were doing in there.

His fingers flexed, squeezing her backside. "Clio," he groaned.

Something *good*, it would seem.

With a low moan, he snaked his arm around her waist, and a small contraction of his muscles drew her close. "Clio."

"Yes, Rafe?"

Green eyes snapped open. *"Clio?"*

In a heartbeat, he was on the far side of the bed— as close as he could get to the edge of the mattress without falling off.

Considering the violence of his reaction, Clio tried not to feel affronted. Surely she would have noticed if her face had broken out in leprous sores since dinnertime.

No, that was the look of a man caught out in his lie. Which meant she had him right where she wanted him.

"What the devil are you doing here?" He clutched the bedsheet, holding it level with his neck.

"Isn't it obvious?"

"I hope not."

"I'm here to see the lavender nightshirt."

Oh, his face. Clio wished she were better at sketching, so she might have preserved that astonished look forever.

"The lavender nightshirt," she repeated. "The embroidered one you told us about tonight. You had better be wearing it under that bedsheet. Because I know your story about Piers was pure fabrication, from beginning to end."

"Well, you're wrong." He pushed the bedsheet down to his waist. "See? No lavender nightshirt."

No, no lavender nightshirt.

No nightshirt at all.

He was bared to the hips, every inch of his torso hard and gleaming in the firelight, like a sculpture cast in bronze. She was rocked by the impulse to reach for him, but some ingrained voice of warning held her back—not the voice that warned a girl away from dangerous men but the voice that kept her from reaching for a potato that had fallen in the coals.

He would singe her fingers.

"Then you cheated," she managed to whisper, dragging her gaze back up to his. "You told more than one lie. You rogue. Men have been called out for less."

"What is this? We're dueling now? No one gets called out for parlor games."

"No. They get called out for trifling with a gentlewoman's virtue and ruining her chances at happiness. This is my life at stake. And you lied to me."

The sleep was gone from his expression now. He was awake, and angry. "I said that Piers loves you. Why is that so damned hard to believe?"

"Because *my* lie was so close to the truth. He never even kissed me, Rafe. Not once in eight years of betrothal."

He shook his head in disbelief.

She folded her hands in her lap. "It's true. When you kissed me in the tower a few days ago . . . ? That kiss was my first."

"Your first?" Rafe couldn't believe it.

He sat up in bed. The linen bedsheet pooled about his waist. "That's not possible."

"I assure you, it's true. It's beyond humiliating to admit it, but it's true."

He stared at her, with her delicate profile and her unbound hair falling down her back in golden waves. She was so lovely, he ached. For the first time, he began to question his brother. Could Piers be one of those men who preferred his own sex?

Surely not. Rafe dismissed the idea out of hand. When they were youths, his brother was forever "borrowing" Rafe's best French engravings from his bottom drawer, even though he pretended to know nothing about it when confronted. And there'd been stories of the usual debauched adventures in his university days. Not a lot of stories, but a few.

No, Piers liked women.

Which made Clio's confession all the more baffling to comprehend. How could Piers resist kissing *this* woman?

Rafe had excellent reasons *not* to kiss Clio, and he'd succumbed to temptation—multiple times—despite them.

"I was truly your first?" he asked.

She nodded.

White-hot triumph forked through him like a lightning bolt. Rafe could have run a victory lap around the castle. He hadn't felt this good since winning his first championship bout. He couldn't even be angry with his brother now. Knowing that he was Clio's first kiss, her first touch . . .

It made him want to be her first *everything*.

Not just her first, but her last. Her best.

His hands made fists in the bedsheets. "You need to return to your own chamber."

Instead of leaving, she eased herself farther onto the bed and tucked her crossed legs under her nightrail. Making herself right at home.

To be fair, he supposed she *was* in her own home. Very well. He could be the one to leave. Not just this room, but the castle. If he went to saddle his gelding right now, he could be in Southwark by daybreak.

He nodded at his shirt and trousers, draped over the arm of a chair—just out of reach. "Hand me my clothing, will you?"

She didn't move, except to toy with a lock of her

unbound, golden hair. When she spoke, her tone was husky. "Would you like to hear a bedtime story?"

"Not particularly, no."

Laying a hand to his chest, she pushed him back against the mattress. "You're going to hear one anyway."

Holy God. There was rock-hard, there was hard-as-steel, and then there was the solidity of Rafe's current erection—which so thoroughly surpassed all his previous experience, he suspected it might be of interest to science.

He considered closing his eyes, sticking his fingers in his ears, and chanting Broughton's rules at the top of his voice until either she went away or morning dawned. But one look at the stubborn set of her chin, and he knew it was no use. She was determined enough to wait him out.

She was too accomplished at patience, this woman. And that was his idiot brother's fault.

"Once upon a time," she began, "I imagined myself to be Sleeping Beauty. Promised in my cradle to marry . . . well, not a prince, but something close. I was surrounded by well-meaning relations, showered with gifts. Wealth, good breeding, education. Even a castle."

She hugged her knees and stared at the banked fire. "And right around my seventeenth birthday, I went to sleep. There wasn't any spindle to prick my finger. But I fell asleep just the same, and I stayed that way for eight long years."

Firelight played over her face, caressing her cheek with more tenderness than a brute like Rafe could ever muster.

"All around me, my friends were marrying, traveling, having children, and making their own homes. Not me. I was still asleep in that tower. Still waiting on my prince to come home and kiss me, so I could wake.

"Then one day . . . I decided to give myself a good pinch and wake up. The prince wasn't coming for me. And maybe—just maybe—I didn't need him, anyway. I'd been given so many gifts. An education, a fortune, a castle. Who was to say that simply because I was female, I couldn't make something of those gifts myself?" She looked at Rafe. "Then came *you*."

"I'm no kind of prince."

"No, you're not. You're wild and rebellious and rough-mannered. But you kissed me in a tower. You brought me every flower in the hothouse. You gave me an entire roomful of cake. You swept me off my feet." She rested her chin on her knees and regarded him. "And tonight, you remembered what I wore to my come-out ball when I was seventeen years old. Down to the pearls studded in my hair."

Rafe's pulse stuttered to a halt. His mouth dried. "No. That wasn't me. I told you, that was Piers."

"You're such a terrible liar." Her eyes shot him a lash-fringed accusation. "I thought you didn't come to my debut. But you *were* there. You must have been."

"I was there," he admitted. "But I didn't stay for long. I left almost as soon as I arrived."

"Why?"

"Because I couldn't stand to be there another moment. I've told you how it was. I fancied you then, and you know how I always envied Piers. That night was . . . It was torture. I hated what they'd done to you. The whole purpose of the evening was to wrap you up like the world's shiniest birthday gift and present you to Piers for his approval." He pushed a hand through his hair. "It made me want to hit things. So I went out and found something to hit."

"I don't blame you for leaving." She touched his shoulder. "I wanted to escape, too."

Her words set alarms ringing through his brain, but he was lost for a response. Rendered speechless by the sensation of her fingertips caressing his bare skin. He'd wanted her for so damned long. She was so beautiful. So beautiful, and so here. With him.

With *him*.

The wrong man. The *worst* man.

"Clio . . ." His voice was strangled.

"Hush." She rose onto her knees and closed the distance between them. "Just stop fighting and let something wonderful happen."

And something wonderful did happen.

She tilted her head, leaned forward, and pressed her lips to his.

Sweet heaven.

He'd kissed her several times now, and each kiss had been better than the last. But being kissed *by* Clio? This was new, uncharted territory.

Rafe thought it just might be Paradise.

Her mouth brushed against his, her lips parting wider with each pass. Her tongue teased the corner of his lips, then made a shy sweep between them.

He moaned into her mouth, helpless to resist. Of their own accord, his arms went around her, hauling her close, helping her straddle his thighs.

But her words kept niggling at his brain.

I wanted to escape, too.

With women, Rafe knew he was usually just an

escape. When they came to his bed, women were running from something. Expectations, propriety, boredom, an unhappy marriage . . . sometimes all of the above. That was why he'd cut off any liaisons well before his last fight. He'd outgrown the fun of being some kind of sexual stallion the ladies came to for a wild, reckless ride. The next time he began an *affaire*, he'd told himself, it would be with a woman who wasn't running *from* anything. He wanted a woman who was running *to* him.

He rolled her onto her back and broke their kiss, gazing down at her. Searching her face for reassurance. "Tell me why you're here with me. Why are we doing this?"

She drew a breath to respond—an act that lifted her bosom.

"Never mind," he said, hooking a finger under the lacy neckline of her shift. "Don't answer. I don't want to know."

There weren't so many buttons this time. Only five or so. He didn't count, and he couldn't be bothered to undo them all. As soon as he'd reached the level of her sternum, he slid his fingers underneath one panel, easing it over her shoulder and down her arm . . . exposing the pale, exquisite swell of her breast. One teasing, tempting inch at a time. Then the other.

For a long moment, he couldn't do anything but stare.

"I hope I live up to all those years of fantasies."

She sounded nervous, and he hated himself for making her doubt, for even one moment. An eloquent, sophisticated sort of man would compose an ode to her beauty.

He could only scrape out, "Better. You're so much better."

Fantasies weren't warm. Or soft. They didn't make his head buzz with the scent of violets.

And they weren't here.

He found a tiny freckle on the underside of her left breast, and he treasured it, stroking lightly with his thumb. It let him know this was real.

She shivered when he cupped her with his hand. Good. Then maybe she didn't notice him trembling.

He couldn't help but feel overwhelmed. Her skin was so smooth beneath his fingertips. Softer than petals, milkweed, clouds, dreams. And amid all this dreamy softness, her nipple drew to a tight, tawny knot, just begging for attention.

Who was he to refuse?

He bent his head and drew the peak into his mouth.

"Rafe," she gasped. "Yes."

Yes.

She weaved her fingers into his hair, holding him close, and his cock . . . God, his cock was just where it wanted to be, cradled against her cleft. He nudged her thighs farther apart, settling his hips between them. And then he moved against her in a slow rhythm, mimicking the act of lovemaking as he lifted and suckled her breasts.

She was quiet, but not silent. Her soft, sweet moans of pleasure slid down his back like fingernails, drawing his every nerve to awareness.

Soon she began to move with him, riding the hard ridge of his arousal. The layers of linen shift and bedsheets warmed and glided between them, adding to the friction.

And Holy God, it felt good.

So.

Damned.

Good.

Still, those words wouldn't stop haunting him.

I wanted to escape, too.

He lifted his head. Whatever restraint he'd cultivated over the years—every shred of the discipline that had taken him from hotheaded rebel to champion—he drew on it now.

"I changed my mind," he said. "I want to know. I need to know. Why are you here with me right now?"

"Because I want you. I want this." She arched her neck to press a kiss to his cheek, then his lips. And as she did, she shifted beneath him, rubbing against the full length of his cock.

His mind was wiped blank as a slate.

Objections? What objections? Was there some scruple he was supposed to remember? Some issue of duty or loyalty involved? Unless it lay hidden beneath the curve of her breast, he wasn't likely to remember.

His mind could only hold one thought: Clio wanted him. And what she wanted, she would have. Here. Now. No one else mattered. No one else had ever given a damn about him, anyway.

"Rafe. I've wanted this for so long."

When she whispered his name, something feral took hold of him. Pushing her thighs wider, he lowered his body to hers, needing her soft, abundant heat to cushion his pounding heart. Otherwise, the damned thing just might burst out of his chest.

He pressed his brow to hers. Touched her hair, her lovely cheek.

And then she kissed him with a sweetness that made him want to weep.

One of her legs wrapped around his, smooth and strong. Her fingers laced tight in his hair. She was holding him as though he belonged nowhere else. As though everything in his dark, needing, desperate soul was *hers*.

And maybe that was the truth.

This was everything he'd dreamed about since the age of fifteen. She was so passionate, so responsive to his touch. And as much as he wanted to get inside her and spend all that long-frustrated lust, he wanted what would come afterward even more.

Closeness. Affection. Perhaps even . . .

Oh, devil take it.

Perhaps even love.

"You understand what this means, for us to lie together." He worked a hand between them, gathering the gauzy hem of her shift and hiking it upward. "You do know what will happen."

"Yes."

"Don't be frightened. I'll be careful. I'm going to be so good to you."

The murmured words sounded trite even to his own ears, but Rafe meant every syllable. Few would suspect a man built like a brute to be capable of gentleness. And in the past, women hadn't wanted that from him anyway. But he had a great deal of tenderness he'd been saving. Whole years' worth of it.

Tonight, he was going to lavish it all on her.

"I'm not frightened in the least," she whispered. "But you must let me go, just for a moment."

He licked and nibbled his way up her neck, treasuring each inch. "Not a chance."

Now that he had her in his arms this way, he would never let her go.

"I need to go to my chamber. It will only take a moment. They're in the top drawer."

The top drawer.

If this were another woman, he would have thought she was referring to sheaths. Or a sponge. But he had been her first kiss. She was an innocent. He knew she'd been making strides toward independence, but surely Clio wasn't so modern as *that*.

"What's in the top drawer, love? Surely it can wait." He slid his hand up her leg, and his touch met the silken slope of her inner thigh.

Good God. He was inches from the heart of her. All that sweet, tight heat.

"It can't," she gasped. "It's the papers."

Chapter Seventeen

"The papers," he echoed.

Clio nodded. She was so breathless with excitement, she could scarcely speak. The wicked magic of his tongue had driven her wild. The hard heat and weight of him atop her, so fiercely comforting. So dangerously safe.

Now his hand was on her thigh, and the pad of his thumb was . . .

Oh, so close.

She wriggled beneath him, craving friction. Pressure. Anything. She would have never expected herself to be such a wanton, but Rafe made her feel so cherished. He'd stripped her of any shame.

"Please," she begged. "Just sign them first. Then I'm free, and there won't be any doubts or regrets."

"Right." He withdrew his hand from her shift.

Despite the temporary loss of his caress, Clio rejoiced.

This was finally going to happen. *They* were finally going to happen, she and Rafe. Clio felt as though she'd been waiting for this moment—not for days or years, but all her life.

She twisted to a sitting position, fumbling to button her shift. A giddy laugh escaped her. "It won't take but a moment. I'll be right back."

"Don't bother coming back."

His sharp tone startled her. "What?"

"I'm not signing."

"Why not?"

"Because you don't want this." He gestured at the space between them. "You just know that *I* want this. What you want is to escape."

Clio didn't understand. Just a moment ago, he'd been pressing passionate kisses to her breasts, and now he seemed . . . upset. Almost angry.

Or was he feeling hurt?

"This has been your plan the whole week, hasn't it? It's the reason you let me stay." He turned away from her, reaching to gather his trousers from a nearby chair. "You know my reputation. If I won't sign the papers you put in front of me, surely I'll seduce you. And that would work just as well. I'd have no choice but to sever the engagement."

"No," she hastened to assure him. "No, that wasn't my plan at all. I promise. Rafe, you're misunderstanding."

He stood, hiking his trousers. "This is why you came to me in Southwark. It's why you've let me kiss you, see you, *touch* you . . . You're too timid to confront him yourself, and I make a convenient villain."

"You are not a villain," she said.

"Of course I am. You've followed my career. You know my reputation. I'm the Devil's Own. In your eyes, I'm useful for one thing—destruction. Dissolving your engagement. Ruining you for marriage. Punching holes in tavern walls to sell beer." He threw her an angry glare. "You don't want me. You just want a way out."

Now Clio was growing angry, too.

"I am not timid. Not anymore." Her hands balled in fists. "All my life, I've been raised to believe that I am worthless on my own. I'm nothing but a dutiful gentleman's daughter on her way to becoming an aristocrat's compliant bride. Even at that, I haven't been successful. You have no idea how much bravery it took to even conceive of breaking this engagement."

"Then find the courage to tell Piers yourself," he said. "I won't sign your papers. Not today, not tomorrow. Not ever."

Not ever?

Her stomach lurched. "You can't refuse. You promised me."

"You made promises of your own to Piers."

"I was a *child*."

"You aren't a child any longer." He loomed over her, bracing his hands on the mattress. One hand on either side of her hips. "You're a woman. Twenty-five years old, a lady of property and fortune. You could have broken this engagement at any time. Written him a letter ages ago. But you didn't. You've put your family through this weeklong charade of wedding plans just to spare yourself one uncomfortable conversation."

His accusations poked at her, pushing her toward

a dark, unpleasant corner—but the cage of his arms left her nowhere to hide.

She said, "I just want the chance to make my own choices, define my own life. You must understand. I know you want that, too."

"I know who I am. I'm a prizefighter. I'm not a hired brute. If you want to deal a man a sucker punch after eight years, make a fist and do it yourself."

Clio didn't know a thing about sucker punches. But she knew she couldn't let the conversation end this way.

Concentrate. Anticipate. React.

She shot both hands forward and tickled him in the rib cage. He yelped in surprise. When his arms buckled at the elbow, she grabbed his neck and tackled him onto the bed, turning him flat on his back.

Before he could recover from the shock, she straddled his chest. "You're not getting away from me that easily."

Lord. His rigid abdominal muscles were mortared bricks beneath her sprawled thighs, and his nostrils flared like those of an enraged bull. She had the best of him for this one moment, but he would have no difficulty flipping their positions if he wished.

"We had a bargain," she whispered. "I trusted you. I did everything you asked. I tried on those humiliating gowns. I . . . I bared myself to you, in every way."

His gaze made a bold sweep of her body, then settled on her breasts. "You did, didn't you? You let me put my big, rough hands all over you."

"Yes. And all I've been able to think about is letting you do it again. I want *you*, Rafe." She pounded the flat of her fist on his chest. "How can I make you see? I dream about your touch. I feel a pang in my heart whenever you're near. It only gets worse when you're far away. And I don't . . ."

Her words trailed off. In her mind, she heard her own voice echoing. It was a chorus of one word, over and over: *I . . . I . . . I . . .* With the occasional trill of *Me-me-me*.

Could she be any more selfish? She was here confessing her feelings *about* Rafe, but she wasn't giving a thought to Rafe's emotions at all.

"And I don't love Piers," she continued, feeling a heavy realization fall in place. "But you do."

His chest rose and fell.

"You love him, don't you?"

He didn't say yes. She didn't expect he would. He had too much of the Granville disposition for that.

Instead, he released a gruff sigh and said, "He's my only brother." As if that explained everything.

And it did.

She was a fool not to have seen it earlier. That's what this week was about. Not Rafe's career. Not his convenience.

No matter how much had happened, no matter how he tried to disclaim society, the bonds of blood still meant something to him. Judging by his expression, they meant a great deal.

"Why didn't you just say so?" She gave his chest a playful push. "Men. I have to come into your room, seduce you in your sleep, tackle you to the mattress . . . and only then will you admit to caring for your own brother."

He relented. "I just can't take his bride from him. Not after everything else."

"Everything else?" She moved to the side, releasing his arms. "What else did you take? Even if you've made some bad investment or lost a part of the fortune, I doubt that Piers will blame you."

"If only it were that simple." He struggled up on his elbows. "I took his father, Clio. I was responsible for the marquess's death."

It was clear they needed to talk.

But if Rafe was going to manage this conversation, it needed to happen somewhere less bedlike. And they needed to be wearing more clothes.

By the time he stumbled into the kitchen a quarter hour later, dressed in an open-necked shirt and loose trousers, Clio was waiting for him.

She'd plaited her hair, cinched her dressing gown tight, and laid the counter with candles and a few refreshments. A midnight picnic for two.

Were the circumstances different, it would have been romantic. Tonight, he felt like a condemned man settling down for his last meal.

He surveyed the table. "Cake. And beer."

"Thanks to you, we'll be eating cake for a month or more." She dipped her finger in the icing and tasted it. "This one's gooseberry. The tartness should complement the anise notes in the porter."

The anise notes? In the porter?

"Who taught you all this?"

"I learned on my own. When I first started considering the brewery plan, I asked the cook to order in a firkin of every beer, porter, ale, and stout available. My 'finishing' included instruction on selecting wines. I took to it. It turns out, beer isn't that different." She pulled an inch of reddish brown porter into her glass and held it to her nose. "This one's nice and malty. A hint of cocoa. Here, try."

She handed it to Rafe, and he took a sip. It tasted like porter. Excellent porter, but . . . porter. Malty, to be sure. All porter was malty. Whatever hints of cocoa and notes of anise were in it, they eluded his detection.

"I don't know how you taste those things."

"I think we're all attuned to detail somehow, we Whitmore girls. Phoebe's a marvel with anything mathematic. Daphne could tell you who made a bit of lace, and where and during what season, just by glancing at a three-inch sample." She shrugged and sipped. "I can taste the lavender border that grew next to the hops."

"Daphne and Phoebe don't hide their talents, though."

She filled the rest of the glass. "I'm already the dumpling of the family, *and* I'm the one with a knack for tasting? You can imagine the teasing I'd suffer. From my brother-in-law alone." She slid him his beer. "But we're not here to talk about me."

No, they weren't. Rafe drew up a stool. "It's a long story."

"It's a large cake." She pushed a fork in his direction. "And before we begin, I should like one thing noted. I *knew* you had Secret Pain."

His chest lifted with a humorless chuckle. "After tonight, it won't be so secret anymore."

"Well. At least that's *something* I can claim. None of your other women ever came this far."

She had no idea. No other woman had even come close.

She poked at the cake with her fork, teasing berries out of the filling and popping one into her mouth. As she swallowed, her eyes closed involuntarily.

When she opened them, she caught him staring at her.

"You're doing it again," he said.

"Doing what?" she asked, her mouth still partly full.

"Cake sounds."

"Sorry." She swallowed. "I didn't even notice."

"I noticed. I always noticed. I'm a bastard that way."

"I wish you'd stop saying that." She set down her fork and stacked her arms on the table. "No, I mean this, Rafe. You throw that word about so casually, and I've been wrong not to object before now. I think a great deal of you, and . . . And it hurts to hear you disparaged that way, by anyone."

Sweet girl.

"It fits, though. I always felt fatherless. From boyhood, I was always the odd one out. Piers was cast from my father's mold, and I . . . I just wasn't. I was a miserable student. I didn't excel at their gentlemanly pursuits. I didn't have the right upper-crust friends. I was big and rough, not handsome and refined." He took a draught of his porter. "Piers could sneeze, and the old man would beam with pride. I was always the mistake. Sometimes I wondered if I was even his natural son."

"Of course you were his son. How could you doubt it?"

"Because *he* doubted it. He didn't even want to claim me. I must be the Devil's own boy, he always said."

"Your own father gave you that name?"

He tapped his fork against the table. " 'No son of mine.' I can't count how many times I heard that growing up. He was always after me for one thing or another. 'No son of mine will run with the common boys.' 'No son of mine will be sent down from Eton.' 'No son of mine will engage in fisticuffs.' "

With each sentence, he jabbed deeper into the cake.

"He couldn't understand me. Hell, *I* couldn't understand me. As a boy, I wanted, more than anything, to be the son he could love. To do well in my studies. To make him proud, as Piers did. To cease fighting with everyone. But I never could manage it." He gestured vaguely toward his chest. "I'm too damned restless and impulsive. By now I've learned to check my punches. But I've always had a habit of blurting out words I wish I hadn't."

"Words like, 'Clio, I think I'll die of wanting you'?"

"No. Words like, 'I don't want to be your son, I don't want a penny of your money, and I hope to never see you again.' "

Her fork paused in midair, and she sucked in her breath. "Those words would be more difficult to retract."

"Where my father was concerned? Not merely difficult. Impossible."

"What happened?"

"I asked to purchase a commission in the Army.

My father wouldn't hear of it, with Piers already overseas. He'd decided I should have a living instead. In, of all things, the Church. Perhaps God could save me where he'd failed." He cracked his knuckles. "That notion didn't sit so well with me."

She laughed. "I can imagine it wouldn't."

"I refused. He raged. We argued, worse than ever before."

This is the family legacy. No son of mine will be an aimless wastrel. No son of mine will squander his potential.

That was when Rafe had thrown the wildest, most ill-considered blow of his life.

I don't want to be your son.

"I knew at once," he told Clio. "So did he. As soon as the words were out, I could see it in those cold eyes. I'd crossed a line, and there would be no going back. He told me to leave his house. From that day forward, we were estranged. No inheritance. No home. No family."

"That's a harsh punishment for being youthful and brash."

Rafe shrugged. No more harsh than starvation. After what Clio had endured, he wasn't going to cry to her for sympathy. "I did ask for it. And at the time, I was happy to go. You know how it is. When you've been denied something long enough, you start telling yourself you didn't want it anyway."

She took a healthy bite of cake. "So you left. And turned to prizefighting to support yourself."

"Aye. Best thing that could have happened to me, really. Gave me discipline and a chance to find my own success. And I can't deny it made for delicious revenge. He was such a snob, you know. I took joy in fighting under the name he'd given me, engaged in such vulgar sport for money."

Rafe sipped at his porter. Clio took bites of her cake. She didn't press him for more. Only waited.

"He came to my fights."

She swallowed. "The marquess?"

He nodded.

"I confess, I'm shocked. I visited the late Lord Granville once a fortnight. He never mentioned it."

Rafe cracked his neck. "We never talked, before or after, but he was always there in the crowd somewhere, all tight-faced and stern. Never cheered. Never applauded. He just came to register his disapproval, I suppose."

"Were you pleased to see him?"

He shook his head. "Made me so damned angry. Made me fight harder, too, because I sure as hell wasn't going to lose in front of him. I had this wild idea . . . a hope, I suppose . . . that one day, I'd win and he'd come down from the crowd and shake my hand. Say, 'Well done, Rafe.' That would have been enough. In all my four years as champion, it never happened.

"The day I fought Dubose," he went on, "I spied him there. And for the first time, I thought . . . if winning for four years straight doesn't impress him, what would the old man do if he watched me lose?"

"Are you saying you lost the fight on purpose?"

"No. I can't say that. That would be unfair to Dubose. He was bloody brilliant that day. But the thought of losing got in my head. And any trainer will tell you, once that idea's in your head . . . it's all over but the bleeding. I started making mistakes, slowing down, throwing wild punches that only caught air."

"And you lost."

"Badly."

"Yes. I remember the bruises." She winced. "So? What *did* your father do?"

Rafe took a long swallow of porter, fortifying himself for what came next. "He went home without a word to me. That night, he had a heart attack. You know the rest. Never recovered. Dead within the week."

The words echoed dully in his chest.

"Oh, no." Her voice softened. "Rafe. Surely you don't blame yourself."

"How could I not?" He massaged his temples. "I don't have the faintest notion what was in his heart that night. Was he disgusted? Concerned? Pleased? Whatever emotion he kept so tightly bottled up in there, it finally exploded. And I'd lit the fuse."

"Rafe, listen to me." Her blue eyes drilled into his. "It wasn't your fault. It wasn't. He'd suffered two smaller attacks in the past year. The man wasn't well."

He acknowledged her words, but they did little to ease his guilt. If what she said was the truth, Rafe should have known. He should have been even more careful. If he hadn't antagonized the man, he might have lived to see Piers come home.

"They sent me word he was dying. Asking for his son. I told myself I shouldn't go. That I wasn't the son he wanted. But in the end, I . . ." His voice broke. "I couldn't stay away."

Clio reached forward and took hold of his hand.

He started to pull back, but caught himself. Instead, he squeezed her fingers in silent thanks. If she could be brave enough to make the gesture, he ought to be man enough to accept it.

"So I went to the house. I stood at his bedside. He was half-gone already, it seemed. Weakened, confused. I've seen a great many fighters in a bad way, but I've never seen a man go from indomitable to frail so quickly. He didn't know where he was, or when. He just kept saying, 'my son.' Over and over again, 'my son, fetch my son.' I . . ." Rafe cleared the emotion from his throat. "I told him Piers was in Vienna. He didn't seem to understand."

"Perhaps he *was* asking for you."

"Perhaps he was. Maybe he loved me all along. Perhaps he attended all those fights in hopes I'd come up into the crowd and reach out to *him*." Rafe released her hand. "I only know that afterward, it all seemed so stupid. All those years of being bad in every way I could manage, heaping brimstone on my devilish reputation just to spite him. So much stubborn pride and wasted time."

"It's only wasted time if you don't learn from it."

"You believe that?"

"I have to believe that. Or else I'd weep every time I thought about the past eight years."

He thought on it. "I suppose you're right. I'll never be able to go back and be a better son. But I have a chance—if a dwindling one, after tonight—to do right by Piers. We're never going to be best friends, the two of us. He'll never see his father again, and that's my fault. I can't do anything to bring the old man back, but at least I can—"

"Keep his dog alive," she finished. "And make sure his bride is waiting."

He didn't bother to deny it. "You say Piers doesn't feel any passion for you. Maybe you're right; I can't honestly say. But he and our father were so much alike. I can't set aside the possibility that my brother cares for you, deeply. In some reserved, distant Granville way. So much that losing you could break him."

At heart, Piers and Clio were two of the best, most decent people he knew. If Piers did love her, and if the two of them could be happy together . . . ?

Rafe wanted that for them both.

She rested her head in her hands.

"I know you despise being told to wait. But it's only a few weeks. If you want to break it off, I won't stand in the way. I just can't be the one to deal the blow."

Rafe had one broken heart on his conscience already. That guilt was more than enough.

He said, "You'll never know how he truly feels unless you give him a chance."

"He's had eight years of chances. I worry I'll never have mine."

"This *is* your chance. Don't wait as a favor to me. Do it for yourself. Because it's your decision, and both you and Piers deserve to know that."

"You're right," she said after a pause. "I know you're right. It was selfish of me to ask you to sign those papers. Selfish, and cowardly. I've just been so afraid. How on earth am I supposed hold my own with him? He's a diplomat who's spent the past eight years convincing governments to surrender. I'm terrified that when he comes home, my mother's lessons will overwhelm my intentions, and I'll marry him just to be polite."

"You'll be fine," Rafe said.

She laughed aloud.

"I mean it. All week long, you've had no difficulty arguing with me."

"That's different." She gave him a confessional look. "I've never talked with anyone the way I can with you. You don't agree with any of my ideas, but at least you listen to them and pay me the compliment of arguing back."

He cast a bemused look at his porter. "We've been training you all wrong."

"*Training* me?" Her eyebrow arched. "Like a dog?"

Rafe groaned. Not this again. "Not like a dog, like a fighter. Bruiser had this idea that we should go into wedding planning the same way he'd prepare a prizefighter for a championship bout. Get your head in the ring, boost your confidence. So you could imagine yourself victorious."

"Well, that explains a few things. Like the compliments. And the kisses. And that ridiculous lie about Piers at my debut." She covered her eyes with one hand. "So embarrassing. You only wanted to boost my confidence. And then tonight I—"

"And then tonight you were nearly ruined." He pulled her hand away from her face. "I've always desired you. It's one of the reasons I kept my distance. You're too damned tempting, and it's not in my character to resist."

In response, she pushed a morsel of cake around her plate.

Surely she couldn't doubt him on this. Even if she believed Rafe capable of deceit, she had to have *felt* his lust for her tonight. Every hot, steely inch of it.

On the other hand, considering that she'd received nothing but casual insults and neglect from her family, peers, and intended groom for the past several years . . . to the point of being starved into illness . . . Rafe supposed a little dirty talking and a prod in the soft bits might not be the gesture of confidence she craved.

A lacy white gown probably wasn't the answer, either.

Damn. Rafe had never been any kind of scholar, but this week, he'd truly been an idiot.

I want a challenge, she'd told him. *Something that's mine.*

She was already a fighter. He should have recognized it from the first. She couldn't have survived these past eight years if she didn't have a champion's heart. But she didn't want to win at "Mother's game," any more than Rafe wanted to be world champion of lawn bowls.

She wanted to define her own success.

"So that grand wedding of every girl's dreams," he said, "where you float down the aisle like an angel and prove all the gossips wrong. That isn't the victory you're wanting."

"No. It isn't."

He nodded. "Then finish your cake and porter. And we'll see about toughening you up."

Chapter Eighteen

Clio hadn't the faintest idea what Rafe had in mind. They took lamps in hand and moved to the drawing room, where he cleared the small tables and chairs to make an open space.

"What are we going to do?" she asked.

"I'm going to teach you to throw a punch."

She laughed. "You want me to *punch* your brother?"

"No." He pushed a settee toward the wall.

"Then I don't understand why this is relevant."

"I know you don't. But give it a chance. The time for politeness is over. You need to get meaner, Clio. Understand the power in your body and how to harness it."

"Power?" She lifted her delicate arm for his appraisal. "Do you see any power in this body?"

"Yes, I do."

"You mean the power to draw a man's gaze, perhaps. Apparently that never worked on Piers."

"I mean strength. It's in there, just waiting to be unleashed." Having cleared the last of the furniture, he came to stand before her. His gaze homed in on hers. "Trust me."

Clio wanted to trust him. However, she suspected this entire exercise would only make her look like more of a fool. Her, throwing a punch?

But she had to try. Rafe claimed he wanted to settle his debts with Piers. She knew his yearning went much deeper than that. He needed a family. Lasting connection. And if he was to have any chance at it, Clio couldn't ask him to fight her battles. She needed to learn to take swings of her own.

"Very well. What do I do?"

"First, you need to loosen up."

He took her wrists in his big, roughened hands and shook out her arms as though they were a pair of eels he meant to clobber. She felt ridiculous.

"Good." He released her wrists and circled to stand behind her. His hands moved to bracket her skull. "Now roll your head back and forth a bit. Stretch out your neck."

She did as he guided, looking from side to side, and then to the ceiling and floor. She bounced back and forth, transferring her weight from one foot to the other. "When does the punching start?"

"Patience, patience. Stand with your feet apart, about the breadth of your shoulders. Shoulders down, arms loose. Find your center of balance." His splayed hand settled low on her belly. "Here. You feel it?"

How could she *not* feel it?

If the goal was loosening her up, he'd achieved it.

The warm, possessive weight of his hand on her belly, coupled with the low, rumbling voice in her ear . . .

Oh, he made her feel all sorts of loose.

"I . . . I think I'm ready now."

"Then show me a fist."

She made a fist and held it up. "Here."

He tsked. "No, not like that. You'll break your thumb." He unfolded her fingers and balled them up again, this time placing her thumb on the outside.

Then, molding his arms around hers, he guided her into a fighting stance. Right leg slightly back, both fists up in a posture of defense. The broad, solid heat of his chest worked like an iron, smoothing all the tension from her back.

"The first punch you learn is a jab," he said. "Step forward with your left foot, and push your left fist straight out. Let your body weight propel it forward. Quick and sharp, like a bee sting. Then retract. Like this, see?"

Clio made her joints limp and allowed him to move her through the punching motions as though she were a marionette.

"Then you follow with a right cross." He guided her right fist forward. "Can you feel your torso twisting behind the punch?"

She nodded.

"That's where the force comes from. It's not your arm, it's the rest of you."

When he threw their combined fists forward, she could feel the sheer bulk of him backing the blow. Sheets of muscle bunching and flexing beneath his skin.

With Rafe behind her, she felt as though she could topple mountains. But it was all borrowed strength. He could flick his fingertip and send a man flying, if he wished.

"Now it's your turn." He released her and plucked two firm, upholstered pillows from the divan. He held the cushions in either hand, the flat side presented to Clio at approximately shoulder height. "Have a go."

"You want me to punch the pillow?"

"Why not? You need a target." He lifted the pillows. "And these stupid things need a purpose."

She bit her lip. "They make me feel less alone."

His brow wrinkled. "What's that?"

"The pillows. That's their purpose. The reason why I keep so many of them everywhere. They're soft and warm, and they stay in one place. They make me feel less alone." She sniffed. "I suppose you're right. It is stupid."

Lowering the pillows, he moved toward her. "Clio . . ."

"I'm fine." She stepped back, balling her hands in fists. "I'm ready to punch."

"Fists up," he told her. He held out the pillow on her left. "Try a jab."

Her first few attempts were embarrassing. The first time, she failed to connect with the pillow at all. On her second attempt, her "jab" was more of a nudge.

But Rafe didn't laugh at her attempts. He kept at her, encouraging and teasing by turns, and taking breaks to correct her form. After a few dozen attempts, she threw a punch that seemed to land with something that resembled . . . force.

"There," he said. "Felt good, didn't it?"

"Very good," she said, breathless. But "very" was too polite a word. This was bare-knuckle boxing, after all. "Damned good. Bloody good."

He smiled. "Don't tell Bruiser, or he'll start angling to get you in a ring."

She cocked her head. "There are female prize-fighters? Really?"

"Oh, yes. Very popular with the crowds. Mostly because they often end up bare-breasted."

The shameless devil. She sent a right cross that hit the pillow with a satisfying *oof*. "I'm starting to understand why you like this."

"Then maybe you can understand my true secret now. The one none of those other women wanted to believe."

"What's that?"

"That I don't need to be saved from fighting. Fighting saved me."

Clio lowered her fists and regarded him. She did believe it. The tone of his voice as he explained these simple motions . . . It was imbued not only with authority but something that almost sounded like love.

Prizefighting was more than brute violence or rebellion to him. It was a craft he'd worked years to master. Perhaps even an art.

"Thank you," she said. "For taking time to teach me."

He raised the pillow. "Oh, we're not finished. Do it again."

She did it again. And again. She punched at those

pillows over and over, until she started driving him backward and he circled to keep from being backed against the wall.

"That's right," he said. "That's my girl. Punch back at everything they told you. That you weren't good enough. That you never could be. It's bollocks, all of it. Look how strong you are."

She threw punch after punch, pushing out all the anger and frustration of the last eight years. Until her arms were custard.

"Now"—he threw the pillows aside—"I'm Piers. I'm back from Vienna. Ready to marry you. Give me your worst."

"My worst? I thought you wanted me to give your brother a chance."

"It's the same thing. Give him a chance, but give him hell. If he can't win you over, he doesn't deserve you."

"Er . . . " She was out of breath from all the boxing. "Oh, goodness. Piers, I—"

"No, no. Your posture's gone all wrong." He corrected her with his hands, laying one palm between her shoulder blades and the other on her belly. "Remember, you can do this. You're not seventeen. You're a woman. A strong one."

He released her and took two steps back, pretending to be Piers again. "Now, what is it you have to say?"

"I . . ."

"Eye contact. Look up."

She forced herself to meet his gaze. "I am glad to see you home safe and well, but I don't think we should marry."

"Oh, jolly good." He slung himself into the nearest chair and propped up his feet.

Clio shook herself and laughed. "What are you doing?"

"What you've been claiming Piers will do." He folded his hands beneath his head. "You promised me he'd be nothing but relieved. Overjoyed, even."

She sighed.

"See? When you're honest with yourself, even you know that's not going to be the case." He stood up again. "So he's not going to say 'jolly good.' He's going to say something like . . ." He pitched his voice into an aristocratic baritone. "Of course we're going to marry. It was decided when we were children. We've been engaged for years."

"Yes. But I think it might for the best if . . ."

"No, no." Rafe broke out of his Piers role. "Don't use words like 'think' or 'might.' You've decided."

"I've decided. I've decided to break the engagement."

He narrowed his eyes to a severe stare, in a frighteningly accurate impression of his brother. "You agreed to marry me."

"I was seventeen then. Little more than a child. I didn't understand that I have choices. And now that I do . . . I choose differently."

"Why?"

"Because I don't love you, and you don't love me."

"A deeper affection will come with time," he said. "And no matter how far I've traveled, you were never far from my thoughts. I do care about you."

She swallowed hard. "And I appreciate that. I truly do. But it doesn't change my mind."

"Is there someone else?"

The question caught her unawares. Although she supposed it shouldn't have. It made sense that *Piers* would ask it. But she didn't know what *Rafe* would wish her to say.

"Answer me," he said, forceful and commanding as any marquess. "I demand to know the truth. Is there someone else?"

"Yes. There is someone else. There's me."

His eyes flashed with surprise.

"There's me," she repeated. "I've spent a great deal of time alone these past eight years. I've come to know myself and my own capabilities. I'm resilient. I can withstand a little gossip. Or even a lot of it. I can inherit an estate and devote myself not only to its preservation, but its improvement. Because I've taken all those lessons and accomplishments that were supposed to make me the ideal diplomat's wife—and I've made them my own. At some point, while you were roaming the globe, making treaties and dividing the spoils of war, I quietly declared my own independence. I am the sovereign nation of Clio now. And there will be no terms of surrender."

Rafe was quiet.

"Well?" she asked.

He shrugged, noncommittal.

"Too melodramatic at the end? No good?"

"It wasn't bad."

"Not *bad*?" She grabbed the discarded pillow and bashed his shoulder with it. Repeatedly. "It was brilliant, and you know it."

"Very well, very well." Laughing, he seized one

corner of the cushion and tugged, drawing her close. "It was brilliant."

Clio's heart swelled in her chest. His praise was . . . Well, it was better than cake.

"You're brilliant," he whispered. "If Piers doesn't fall to his knees and beg you to reconsider, he's a damned fool."

Heat and desire built between them, quick as fire taking hold of dry grass. The sensation was so intoxicating. And so very cruel. All her life, she'd been waiting to feel this kind of passion—only to find it with the one man she could never, ever hold.

Discussing how to manage a troubled sister, sitting up all night with a dyspeptic dog, discussing secret pain over late-night cake and beer . . . These were the experiences that proved two people could make a life together.

Now it didn't even matter what they felt for each other. Rafe loved Piers. He wanted the chance to be a good brother, and Clio didn't want to take that away. So whatever this was they shared, the two of them—

Unless she meant to destroy his last chance at family, it could never be more.

"Can't we just pretend to be other people?" she whispered. "For a few hours, at least?"

"I don't want that. You don't, either."

Clio nodded. He was right, she didn't want to pretend they were other people. She wanted to be no one but herself, and she wanted to be with him.

She wanted *Rafe*.

Not because he was dangerous or untamed or wrong but because this felt so *right*.

"You won't be ruined," a familiar voice announced.

Oh, God.

Rafe released her and stepped back. Clio clutched a pillow tight across her chest. But no matter how many feet—or pillows—separated them, they were alone and half-dressed in the middle of the night. No one could fail to see the truth.

No one, that was, except the person who wandered into the room.

In rambled Phoebe, with her dark hair hanging loose about her shoulders and her nose buried in an old copy of *The Times*.

"Phoebe." Clio breathed the name as a sigh of relief. "What a surprise. Lord Rafe and I were just . . ."

"It's the hop yield," her sister interrupted, uninterested in explanations.

"W-what?"

Crops. Her sister was wandering the castle in the dead of night, reading *The Times* and puzzling over hop yields.

Yes, that sounded like Phoebe.

Her sister lowered the newspaper. "Lord Rafe was right. Hops are a fragile crop and a risky investment. But I've found the way you can protect yourself from ruin." She pointed at an article. "Each year, speculators wager hundreds and thousands on the final hop yield. It's in all the papers."

Clio searched her memory. If something appeared in the papers, she would know about it. "Yes, I remember reading the forecasts. I didn't realize wagering was so widespread."

"Damn right it is." Rafe took the paper. "In some

taverns, there's more money bet on hops than on prizefighters. They make charts of every passing rain cloud."

Clio approached to have a look at the paper herself. "But we can't foretell the weather. How would I know what to predict?"

"It doesn't matter," Phoebe said. "You're going to bet against yourself."

"Bet against myself? But why would I . . . ?" As she ran through the outcomes in her mind, Clio was beginning to understand. "So if the farming goes well, we make money on the crop, but if it's a lean year . . ."

"Then you collect on the wager," Phoebe finished. "The earnings are limited, but so are the losses. There's no way you can lose everything."

"Hedging your bets." Rafe scratched his jaw. "That's just mad enough to be genius."

Phoebe shrugged. "I've been called both."

"Well." Clio took her by the arm. "As your oldest sister, I am calling you to bed. We have an important day tomorrow. It's your first proper ball."

Her sister's face was grim. "Oh, yes. The miserable ordeal."

"It won't be so bad. These things can't be avoided forever. Not if you're to have your come-out next season."

"No one's going to court me. Why must I have a come-out at all?"

Clio caught a lock of her sister's hair. "You'll be fine. I'll be there for you. I do know how it is."

"You don't know how it is for *me*." Phoebe's dark

head turned, and the lock of hair slipped from Clio's fingers. "Lord Rafe, you are coming with us tomorrow, aren't you?"

Rafe's eyes were dark as they met Clio's.

Please, she silently begged him. *Please come.*

His presence would soothe Phoebe, and as for Clio . . .

This could be her last chance. *Their* last chance. Once she'd broken her engagement to Piers, she wouldn't have an excuse to invite Rafe to these things. What it could hurt, for the two of them to have one evening to remember?

"You still owe me a dance," she reminded him. "I think it's time to pay the debt."

"It's not a good idea. There's a reason I left your debut ball. I'm out of my element at those things. Restless. And when I grow restless . . . that's when the devil in me rises. People get hurt."

"I rather like the devil in you," she said. "I'll be hurt if you stay away."

In a move that was as awkwardly sweet as it was uncharacteristic, Phoebe reached out and clutched Rafe's forearm. "Please. Do say yes."

He sighed. "I'll sleep on it."

Chapter Nineteen

Rafe didn't sleep at all that night.

And when dawn arrived, he left.

For an hour, maybe two, he kept the horse at a walk. He didn't want to push his mount too hard, and in his current mood, that was all too likely. Step after step, he put distance between himself and Twill Castle.

And Clio.

He knew she'd be disappointed, but he had to go. He didn't trust himself. If he spent one more moment in her presence, with those fair, soft hands reaching out to him—he'd haul her close, ruining her and both their families.

No, this was the perfect time to leave. After he'd done all he could, and before he cocked anything up. He'd made certain his brother would have a chance to win her back, and to be honest, that was probably more than Piers deserved.

After a while, the stretch of road started to look familiar. He wasn't but four or five miles from Queensridge.

And in Queensridge, he could find a fight.

God, that was just what he needed. He'd gone too long without the taste of blood in his mouth and the frenzied roar of a crowd in his ears. He was forgetting who he was.

He could have walked into any hamlet and picked a scuffle with the local loudmouthed blackguard. Every village pub had one. But he wasn't a bully, and he didn't fight amateurs. He needed a proper bout with a skilled opponent.

The Crooked Rook was just the place.

In centuries past, the inn had been a favored haunt of smugglers and highwaymen. Nowadays it mostly catered to a prizefighting crowd. Since prizefights were illegal, they had to be staged well outside Town and could only be publicized on short notice. The broadsheet went out a day in advance, and from there it was a mad race for spectators to reach the designated site.

The Crooked Rook was ideal: close enough to London, not too far from the main road. Only a few hours' journey for most. It had a wide, empty field in the back with plenty of room for a proper ring and spectators. And Salem Jones, the current proprietor, stayed on friendly bribing terms with the local magistrates.

To Rafe, and many others, it had become a surrogate home. If he had entered the place last year—back when he was champion—he would have been met with a rousing cheer from every corner.

Today, when he strode through the doorway just about noontime, his reception was more tepid. Oh, a good many nodded or called in his direction. But the general mood in the place was uncertain. No one quite knew what to make of a vanquished champion.

He cracked his neck. That would change by the time he left this place. It felt like a good day to start a comeback. And a quick glance toward the bar was all he needed to find his first opponent.

Prizefighters fought for different reasons. Some liked the sport. Some liked the money. Some just liked to make men bleed.

Finn O'Malley belonged in the latter category. He'd been champion some dozen years ago, but for the past decade O'Malley had been holding down the leftmost barstool at the Crooked Rook. He only roused himself from that perch for one of two reasons: to go out for a piss or to throw a punch. He'd fight anyone, loser buys the next round.

The man hadn't paid for a pint in years.

Rafe made a path straight for him.

The aging Irishman peered up at him, his eyes dark, wary slits. "Is that Brandon? What do you want?"

"I want a fight. One washed-up champion against another."

O'Malley sneered. "I only fight idjits for pints. I don't fight champions unless there's a purse."

"That can be arranged." Rafe drew his own money from his pocket. He shook a few coins loose and kept them, then dropped the remaining weight on the counter. It landed with a resounding *thunk.* "Hold it for us," he told the barkeep.

A new fire kindled behind O'Malley's eyes. It was a look that told him this wouldn't be easy.

Good. Rafe didn't want it to be easy.

"In the courtyard." O'Malley placed both hands on the counter and levered his weight off the stool. "Give us a minute. After I take m'self out for a piss."

Rafe nodded.

As he stood gathering his thoughts, a tankard of porter appeared on the bar before him.

"From the lady." The barkeep tilted his head toward a hazy corner of the tavern.

Lady? Hah. Only one kind of "lady" frequented this establishment.

Rafe had a glance.

Slender. Dark-haired. Fetching.

Available.

He could see exactly how it would go. First he'd win this fight, then he'd go to her upstairs. He'd start to wash the sweat and blood from his face, but she'd tell him not to bother. When he touched her, she'd shiver—on purpose, because she liked the idea of being scared. His brutishness would excite her.

And from there, it would be just like all his other encounters. Quick and rough and, in the end, unsatisfying.

He lifted his porter, attempting to drown the twinge of guilt. Perhaps that kind of encounter was what he needed. It was time he stopped slavering over a woman—an innocent, betrothed, gently bred _virgin_—he couldn't have.

What did he want with yards of ivory lace and a four-post bed with two dozen pillows? There could be no wedding nights or honeymoons or happily-ever-afters in a bloody storybook castle.

Not for a man like him.

"Rafe Brandon, you dodgy bastard." Salem Jones emerged from the inn's back room. In his arms, he carried a small trunk, which he set down on a nearby table.

Rafe offered his hand in thanks, and Jones used it to draw him into a hug.

"You stayed away too long," he said, patting Rafe on the back.

Jones was a West Indian freedman, born in Jamaica and come to England with a group of abolitionists some twenty years ago. As an eyewitness to slavery with stirring testimony, he'd made his Quaker sponsors pleased indeed.

As a pacifist, however, he'd been a profound disappointment.

Like most prizefighters, Jones had a few good years. Unlike most, he'd parlayed that success into something more lasting—the Crooked Rook.

At those odd hours of the night when he contemplated his life beyond prizefighting, Rafe had thought about offering to buy a stake in the place. Despite what he'd told Clio, he did know his years in fighting were numbered, and he wanted to make something of his future. But it had to be on his own terms. He didn't belong in any sort of office. And he wanted to be more than a tavern curiosity, fighting for pints or slamming tankards into plaster walls.

"I reckon you're here for this." Jones patted the trunk. "The rest are in back. Let the barkeep know where you want them."

Rafe had almost forgotten about the things, to be honest. He'd asked Jones to hold these trunks for him when he moved out of his rooms at the Harrington. He didn't want clutter in the warehouse while he was training.

He opened the trunk, sifting through a stack of linen shirts and wool trousers. He hoped he'd find something more comfortable for a sparring match— but the garments in this trunk were too fine. When he reached the bottom, his hand closed on a small, plain wooden box.

He knew what it contained before he even lifted it into view.

It was the box with Clio's letters.

He laughed to himself. Just when he'd made up his mind to forget her. She'd followed him, even here.

She'd followed him everywhere, hadn't she? No matter how many times he changed his address. Over the years she'd kept sending him these missives—one or two a month, at least. Rafe had stashed them away in this box. He didn't pore over them, but he couldn't bring himself to discard them, either. They just sort of stuck to him, the way sweet things tended to do.

"Well?" O'Malley came back in from his piss. "Are we on?"

"In a bit."

Rafe dropped himself in a chair, ordered another pint of porter, sent a bottle of wine to the "lady" who'd be spending the night alone . . . and then did something he hadn't done willingly in years.

He settled in to read.

Most of the notes were breezy, dashed-off invitations, mixed in with the occasional bit of family news. All of it out of date, and none of it especially momentous.

We're having a dinner party Thursday next. If you have no other plans that night, you'd be most welcome.

Warmest birthday greetings from all of us here at Whitmore House.

I've had a new letter from Piers, and I've taken the liberty of copying the parts that might interest you. We'll be spending August at my uncle's estate in Hertfordshire. If you find yourself passing through, do pay a call.

Nevertheless, Rafe went through letter after letter, note after note, reading every last word she'd penned from salutation to close. By the time he lifted his head and rubbed his bleary eyes, the sky was growing dark.

The notes were so brief on their own, so inconsequential. But when taken together, their weight was crushing.

When he'd walked away from Brandon House, his father had closed the door. The rest of his family and high-class acquaintances had shut their doors, too.

Everyone but Clio.

She'd reached out to him, again and again. Never letting him drift too far away. Ready to welcome him, whenever he might decide to appear.

She couldn't know what that had meant to him.

Probably because he'd never made the effort to tell her.

It was so ironic. As a youth, he'd never felt he belonged. Now the older he grew, the more he could see the Brandon traits he'd inherited. Qualities like ambition, and pride, and the stubborn refusal to admit any feelings until it was too damned late.

He tamped down the futile swell of anger. The past was decided. There could be no changing it.

Nor would there be any changing him.

He couldn't be the man Clio needed. Even if he returned to society, scandal would always follow him. It wasn't merely the gossip. He was formed now, set in his ways—for good or ill. There was too much restlessness in his mind, and his body craved constant action. He wasn't suited to the life of a gentleman, and he didn't want to be. He could never be one of those useless, preening prats like Sir Teddy Cambourne.

Rafe simply didn't know how to do nothing.

Which was why, now that he'd finally read all these missives, he couldn't sit idle another moment. He owed her a debt much larger than a dance. Even if he couldn't be the man she needed, Rafe needed to do *something*.

He stood, gathering the letters and envelopes one by one. When piled, they made a stack as thick as his wrist. Over the years, she must have invited him to hundreds of dinners, parties, balls.

The least he could do was show up to one, and somehow make it worth all the rest.

He rose from the chair, stretching the stiffness

from his arms and legs. It wasn't too late. He had an hour or two of waning daylight. A few suitable items of clothing in this trunk. He couldn't dash off penniless, however.

He went to the bar to retrieve his money. "Sorry, old friend," he told O'Malley. "The bout will have to wait for another day."

Rafe reached for the purse.

"Not so fast." Finn O'Malley's big hand clapped over his. "You want that back, you'll have to fight me for it."

"I don't think Lord Rafe's coming."

Clio had been holding the words back all evening, and now they slipped out. Here, in the quietest nook of the Pennington ballroom, where she and Phoebe had passed the last two hours. Waiting, watching. Punctuating the boredom by straightening the seams of her gloves or rearranging the drape of her rose-colored silk.

Every once in a while, an acquaintance made the pilgrimage to their remote corner to exchange greetings. They asked about Piers and the wedding, and practiced the art of the subtle-yet-unmistakable smirk. She could tell what they all were thinking: Will Granville this time, or won't he?

But it wasn't Piers and his absence that occupied Clio's mind.

More than eight years after her debut ball, she was still waiting—in vain—for Rafe Brandon to claim his dance.

As they watched the ladies and gentlemen pairing up for a dance, Phoebe teased a bit of string from her pocket. "He'll be here."

"It's half past eleven. Perhaps something happened to change his plans."

She'd meant to seek him out earlier that day, make certain he meant to attend. She didn't want Phoebe to be disappointed. But he hadn't come down for breakfast, and then she'd been too busy with her sisters, preparing for the ball. By the time she went searching for him midafternoon, he'd already gone. Bruiser said he probably meant to meet them at the ball, but who could know the truth.

He could be back in that Southwark warehouse by now, carrying on with his life.

Or he could be thrown from his horse, lying injured in a ditch and using his last bits of strength to write her name in his own blood.

She really shouldn't hope for the second scenario, but a horrible, selfish part of her preferred it to the first. He wasn't here, and she couldn't help but feel hurt. It dredged up all those all subtle insults.

You're a good girl, Clio. But that's not good enough.

They were joined by Sir Teddy, who carried two cups of punch, and Daphne, who brought them a delicate scowl. "Phoebe, I can't believe you brought that string."

"I don't go anywhere without string."

"Well, you can't have a ratty bit of twine in a ballroom." She plucked the string from Phoebe's hand and cast it on the floor, where it was immediately trampled. "Tonight, we want people talking about Clio's wedding, not your peculiarities."

"I have more," Phoebe said.

"Peculiarities? Oh, yes. You have no end of those."

"String." She reached into her reticule and brought out another length of twine.

"Give that here." Daphne grabbed for the twine.

This time, Phoebe held tight. "No."

"Leave her be," Clio said. She was not in the mood to tolerate Daphne's mothering.

For that's what all this was. Mothering, as they'd learned it in the Whitmore house. Daphne *thought* she was being caring and protective, in her own strange, misguided way. But she was wrong.

Teddy clucked his tongue. "You're making a scene, kitten."

"I don't care," Phoebe said loudly. "It's mine. You can't have it."

People turned. Stared. Around them, conversations withered and died.

This entire evening was a mistake, and it was all Clio's fault. She should have protected her sister. Phoebe wasn't ready for this. Perhaps she never would be.

"Leave her be," Clio repeated.

"It's for her own good, Clio. She has to break the habit."

"For heaven's sake, why? Let her keep her string, and her peculiarities, too. Let her keep her*self*." She tilted her head toward the crowded, glittering ballroom. "We were brought up to care too much about what others think of us. It changed me. It changed you, too, Daphne. And I'm sad to say, neither of us changed for the better. I refuse to let Phoebe meet the same fate. She's remarkable."

" 'Remarkable' is just the word. Everyone will be remarking."

She turned to Phoebe, tucking the string in her sister's hand. "I'm going to make a promise. To you, and to myself. I'm your sister and now your guardian, and I love you. I will never make you feel you must be someone else, just to please society."

"Don't be naïve, Clio," Daphne said. "You can't brush aside society. You're going to be the wife of a diplomat, and a marchioness."

"No, I won't be. I'm not marrying Piers."

"Oh, dumpling," Teddy said, giving her a nudge in the side. "Don't give up now. I hope you're not listening to what they're saying in the card room."

"Why? What are they saying in the card room?"

Her brother-in-law looked sheepish. "They're wagering, of course. On whether the wedding will take place. Lord Pennington's giving odds of four to one against it."

Ah. That was probably the true reason they'd been invited here tonight. To provide a bit of idle speculation and amusement. A joke.

In that moment, Clio realized something wonderful. She just didn't care.

Perhaps they'd worn her down. Or perhaps five-and-twenty was a magical age where a woman came into her own. For whatever reason, she truly, genuinely did not care one whit.

And then, as though announcing a prize she'd been awarded, the majordomo cleared his throat. "Lord Rafe Brandon."

No one was worried about string now. Not even Phoebe.

Clio knew the man could make a dark, dramatic entrance on horseback. But turn him out in a fitted tailcoat, snowy cravat, and polished boots . . . ?

Good heavens above.

The strong cut of his jaw was pure Brandon, as was the easy air of command. But he brought with him that essential Rafeness, too. The aura of rebellion and danger that made the air prickle and set her heart racing.

Everything about his looks declared he was born for just this setting.

Everything about his expression told Clio he *hated* it.

But he was here anyway.

For her.

He crossed to their corner and bowed to each of them in turn, saving Clio for last. "Miss Whitmore."

She dropped a small curtsy. "Lord Rafe."

"You came," Phoebe said.

"Yes." He gave his cuff an uneasy tug and cast a glance around the crowded ballroom. "Sorry to arrive so late. Miss Whitmore, I suppose all your dances are spoken for."

Clio couldn't help but laugh. "No. All my dances are free."

"How the devil is that possible?"

"I've been sitting out with Phoebe."

The orchestra struck up the first strains of a waltz. Rafe took her by the hand. "Well, you're not sitting out a moment longer."

Wearing a look on his face that blended defiance and unease, he led her to the dance floor and spun her into a waltz.

He was a most capable dancer. It made sense that he would be. Moving with coordination and grace was a part of his trade.

"I confess, I'd lost hope. I didn't think you were coming."

"I wondered, too."

When she could bear to look up at him—and how strange that was, that gazing up at him was what she most wanted to do, and yet it cost her every scrap of courage she could muster—she noticed a faint purple shadow on his left cheekbone. And his full, sensual lips were even fuller than usual on one side.

"You've been hurt. What happened?"

He shrugged. "Hit a bump in the road. So to speak."

"It rather looks as though the bump hit back."

His swollen mouth tugged to one side. "It was nothing I wouldn't have done ten times again to get here tonight. But I can't stay long. I just came to give you the dance I owed. And to say farewell."

"Farewell?"

He swept her into a turn. "I'm returning to London tonight. I assume I can leave Bruiser and Ellingworth at the castle with you."

"Of course, but . . . Why? Piers will be home within a week or two. You'll want to see him, and I . . ." Her chest deflated. "I just don't understand why you have to go so soon."

He drew her close and lowered his voice. "Come along. You're a clever girl, and it doesn't become you to pretend otherwise. You know why I have to leave."

"I don't know at all. We can agree to keep our distance."

"There's agreeing in principle, and then there's nightfall. There's being alone when it's dark and quiet, and knowing you're somewhere beneath the same roof. We can't rely on your insomniac relations to keep saving you. If I spent one more night in that castle . . ."

His gaze swept down her body. She ached everywhere.

"I'd come to you."

I'd come to you.

Those words. They made her heart flip and her knees go weak.

"I'd come to you," he repeated, as if taking a solemn vow. "I wouldn't be able to stay away."

"I could change rooms. I could move to—"

He shook his head. "It wouldn't matter. It wouldn't matter if you locked yourself in the highest, farthest tower. I'd find you. I'd come to your door in the night. And then . . . You know what would happen then."

She couldn't breathe. "What would happen then?"

"You'd answer." He moved closer, until she was faint with his heat and the clean, male scent of him. "You'd let me in, Clio. Wouldn't you? You couldn't turn me away."

She nodded, entranced by the low, dark thrum of his words.

He was right. If he knocked at her door in the middle of the night, she would let him in. And it didn't have anything to do with kindness or generosity. It had to do with yearning and desire. The wild chase of blood through her veins whenever he drew near. The pang of need that answered whenever he looked at her like this.

The power of the emotion in those bold green eyes . . .

If this man were ever to love—truly *love*—a woman could spend her whole life reeling from the force of it.

But he was here to say farewell, and the sharp pain of losing him was enough to make her dizzy.

He slowed them to a stop. "You've gone pale."

Had she? Now that he mentioned it, the ballroom had gone dark at the edges. And her head was still spinning, even though they'd stopped dancing several moments ago.

Her heart was just so full. And pounding. His suit, those words, the waltz . . .

How could any mortal woman bear it?

"Perhaps I just need some air," she said.

Rafe shored her up with an arm about her waist. Then he steered her to the edge of the room, back to the corner where Daphne and Teddy were waiting with Phoebe.

"Lady Cambourne." He nodded. "You should take your sister to the retiring room."

"No." Clio scooped in a shallow breath. "Don't leave me. I'll be fine. It's just all that twirling on an empty stomach. Tight corset laces. You, in that coat."

You, you, you.

He didn't acknowledge the compliment. "Why is your stomach empty? Didn't you eat before the ball?"

"Of course she didn't," Daphne said. "A lady never eats before a ball."

Rafe looked only at Clio. "When's the last time you had a proper meal?"

She hedged. "That's not . . ."

"Answer me."

With reluctance, she admitted, "Breakfast."

He swore under his breath.

"It's a bad habit." A habit Clio knew she needed to break. If she was going to guard Phoebe from damaging expectations, she had to extend the same protection to herself. "All I need is a cup of lemonade or barley water, and I'll be fine."

He pulled her to her feet, lacing her arm through his. "You need proper food. I'm taking you in to supper."

Daphne held them back. "But you can't. Not yet."

"Not *yet*?"

Goodness. Clio had never seen him wear an expression so stern. The furrow in his brow could have crushed walnuts.

But Daphne, being Daphne, shrugged off his obvious anger. "There's an order to these things. Perhaps you've been out of circulation so long, you've forgotten it. But we don't all flock to the buffet like gulls. We go in to supper according to precedence. Beginning with the highest ranked, down to the last."

"Then I can take her in first," Rafe said. "I'm the son of a marquess. No one here outranks me."

Daphne corrected him. "We go by the ladies' rank. And my sister, as unmarried Miss Whitmore, is near the end of the queue."

"She's engaged to marry a lord."

"She's not married to him yet."

Rafe clenched his jaw. "This is bollocks."

Daphne smiled. "This is society."

"At the moment, Lady Cambourne, I don't see a difference between the two." He tightened his arm, drawing Clio close. "We're going in to supper. Precedence be damned."

"Truly, I can wait," Clio murmured.

"But you won't." His deep voice shivered to the soles of her feet. Barely controlled anger radiated from him. "Not tonight. When I'm around, you don't wait out dances. You don't go hungry. And you sure as hell don't come at the end of any line."

Good heavens. It was a struggle not to swoon all over again. But she didn't want this to mean the end of their evening.

"I promise, I can wait. I'm already feeling better."

"That's a good girl," Teddy said. He nudged Rafe in the side. "We do have to permit the ladies their vanities, Brandon. It's like I've told our dumpling again and again. Best to go easy on the supper buffet. Lord Granville already has one heavyweight in the family."

Her brother-in-law chuckled merrily at his own joke.

Clio wanted to disappear.

"That's right," Rafe said, sounding amused. "Lord Granville does."

Thwack.

No one saw the punch coming. Not Clio, not Daphne. Certainly not Teddy, whose head whipped to the side with the force of Rafe's blow.

He blinked. Then he staggered backward and fell, dropping on his arse with a weak, undramatic "oof." A dull thud that seemed to sum up the man's whole existence.

She wanted to cheer.

"Teddy!" Daphne cried. She knelt beside her husband, drawing the handkerchief from his waistcoat pocket and pressing it to his bloodied lip. Then she turned a scathing gaze in Rafe's direction. "What's wrong with you? You're like some kind of animal."

But Rafe wasn't there to hear it.

When Clio searched the crowd for him, he was gone.

Chapter Twenty

Well. That was that.

Rafe's great return to society was over before it had even begun.

A crowd gathered at once. Crowds were always drawn to blood.

From the moment he'd entered the ballroom, they'd all been hoping for a scene like this. Rafe had half expected it, too. This was why he'd told the grooms to keep his gelding saddled.

As he carved through the crush of bodies on his way to the door, whispers and rumors buzzed about him like bees, stinging from all sides.

They knew he didn't belong here.

He knew it, too.

He was an impulsive, reckless devil with no sense of comportment. There was only one reason he had any interest in attending balls or claiming the privilege that accompanied his given title: to pay his debts to Clio. Well, his aristocratic birthright couldn't even get her into the damned supper room. And he couldn't last ten minutes without unleashing his inner brute.

Now the best thing he could do for her was to leave.

A steady rain had started, turning the drives and pathways to mud. He turned up the lapels of his coat and made his way to the stables. He wouldn't get far in weather like this, but he would get somewhere.

"Rafe! Rafe, wait."

He turned. She came dashing to meet him, wet silk clinging to her legs. For that matter, wet silk was clinging to her everywhere.

And of course the silk would be pink. It had to be pink.

He drew her into the stables. "Clio, what are you doing? Go back in the house."

"If you're leaving, I'm leaving with you."

He threw a glance toward the grooms and lowered his voice. "Don't be absurd. It's raining. You'll catch a chill. And for Christ's sake, you still haven't eaten. Go inside at once."

She shook her head. "I'm not going back. There's no going back."

There's no going back.

He didn't know what those words meant to her, but the possibilities both thrilled and horrified him.

He shook off his damp coat and wrapped it around her shoulders, taking the chance to search her expression.

Locks of golden hair were plastered to her face,

and raindrops dappled her cheeks. Her nose was red. But her eyes had never been so clear and determined.

Beautiful, foolish, impossible woman.

"What about Phoebe?"

"I asked her. She would be more upset if I didn't go after you."

"If you want to leave, I can order your carriage driver to . . ."

"I don't want the carriage. Not unless you mean to ride in it, too. Rafe, can't you understand this? I'm not running away from the party. I'm following you."

No, no. Don't say that. Take it back.

He could resist anything but those words.

"Don't do this," he warned. "If you push me right now, I'll do something brash. Something you'd only regret."

She stepped forward. "If you leave these stables without me, I will follow you. On foot. In the rain. Without a cloak. I'll walk all the way to Southwark, if that's what it takes." She blinked away a raindrop caught in her lashes. "So if you're concerned for my health and well-being, Rafe Brandon, you had better—"

Rafe never heard the rest of her impassioned threat. He put his hands on her waist and lifted her onto his gelding.

Then he mounted behind her, circling one arm about her middle and bracketing her hips with his thighs.

As he nudged the horse into a canter, he pulled her roughly to him. Holding her not like a lover, but like a captive. She'd asked for this. Tonight, she was in his keeping, for all the best and worst of what that could mean to them both.

And she was right on one score.

There could be no going back.

Clio was soaked to the skin and shivering in the dark. She had no idea where she was, or where Rafe might be taking her.

And she'd never been happier in her life.

Never mind the cold and the darkness. His body was warm. And her heart had enough joy inside it to blaze like a lantern. She could stay forever like this—tucked against his broad, strong chest and blanketed by his coat as the horse faithfully trudged through the rain and mud.

They stopped at the first inn they came across. Rafe ushered her inside, presenting some tale to the innkeeper about newlyweds and a broken carriage axle.

Clio tried not to make too much of the fact that he'd introduced her as his wife. He was only being protective, no doubt. Trying to deflect suspicion from the appearance of a man and woman traveling alone.

Still . . . When he uttered the phrase, "a room for my wife," she leapt at the chance to nestle close to his side.

Once they'd been shown upstairs, he gave orders to the serving girls.

Well, not only to the serving girls.

"Stay on that side of the room," he directed Clio. "I'm only here until you're settled. Then I'll go down for the night."

"That'll be a blow to your pride, I fear. We're supposed to be newlyweds. They won't think the honeymoon's going well."

He shrugged. "I'll tell them you're timid due to my prodigious size."

She smiled, hugging herself to keep her teeth from chattering. Now that he'd released her, she was so cold. "About earlier. Rafe, I just want to say thank you. That was brilliant. All of it."

"It was stupid. And loutish and impulsive." He pushed his hands through his hair and blew out his breath. "I shouldn't have brought you here. I shouldn't have hit him."

"I'm glad to be here. And I loved that you hit him. That was the best part."

"He's your brother-in-law."

"Yes. But he's insufferable."

He rubbed a hand over his mouth. "I could have hit him harder. I wanted to hit him harder."

"I know."

"Bloody hell. I could have killed him."

The back of her neck prickled. "You'd never do that."

His dark gaze locked with hers. So intent, she felt it from across the room. "You don't know what I'd do for you."

Whomp. Her heart slammed against her rib cage with such strength, she lost her breath.

"Beggin' pardon, sir."

Rafe moved aside as three of the inn's serving girls entered the room. One carried a washtub, and the others held great pitchers of steaming water. Clio and Rafe stood silent as they went about filling the bath. It took them longer than it ought, because all three of them kept stealing glances at Rafe.

Even after they left, he kept his sentinel post by the door. "It wasn't supposed to go this way."

"I imagine it wasn't. You looked magnificent in this." She hugged his finely tailored topcoat around her. "I don't suppose you went to all that trouble just to come serve my brother-in-law a mean right cross."

He made a futile gesture. "We were supposed to dance. A proper dance. One long enough for me to tell you how goddamn beautiful you are in that gown. The way I should have done at your debut, years ago."

Oh, Rafe.

"And then before I left, I was going to pull you aside somewhere quiet and give you . . ."

"What? Then you'd give me what?"

He nodded at her. "Check the pocket."

She slid one hand to the breast pocket of his tailcoat and reached inside. Her fingers closed on a packet of papers.

The papers.

"You didn't."

"I had to. You deserve that much. I—"

"Sir, beggin' pardon again."

The serving girls were back. Once again, Rafe stepped out of the doorway to let them through. They brought yet another pitcher of water for the bath, an armful of towels, and a tray with a pot of tea, bread, and what smelled like rabbit stew.

"Will that be everything, sir?" the eldest tavern girl asked.

He nodded. "Ready a meal for me downstairs, if you would. I'll be down in a trice."

The three of them left, and the moment they disappeared, Clio could hear them giggling and whispering in the corridor.

"Listen, I can't stay and chat. I'd wager we have about three minutes before your reputation is destroyed."

"They don't know who I am."

"They know who *I* am. Or someone will. And it wouldn't be difficult to find out the rest." He shook his head. "You can't imagine. I wouldn't mind it if the whole world knew. I'd like to hang a sign on this door that says 'Ruination in Progress,' and lock the both of us inside."

None of that sounded so terrible to Clio.

"But that's not why I came to the ball tonight," he said. "I wanted—"

With a glance down the corridor, he ducked under the lintel and entered the room. The door remained open.

He lowered his voice. "Clio, I wanted to give you choices. Not take them."

Her fingers curled around the papers. "So you do mean to sign these?"

"I already did."

She looked down at the papers, uncurling them to verify. There it was, his signature on the final page, scrawled bold and unapologetic across the parchment.

"You're no longer engaged, as of half-seven this evening. I wanted to let you know right away. In case it improved your enjoyment of the ball tonight. I owed you more than a waltz. I wanted to you to feel free. Free to dance, to flirt, to tell the gossips to go to the devil." He shook out his arms. "Instead, we're here."

"Yes. We're here."

And Clio wasn't upset about it in the least. Perhaps this wasn't what he'd planned, but to her it was a thousand times better than any waltz.

"Well. For whatever good it does you, you're an independent woman now. Free to go wherever you please and do what you like."

She stood silent for a moment. "In that case . . ."

In calm, measured steps she walked around him and went straight for the entryway.

Then she closed the door and turned the key, locking them both inside.

"I want to spend the night with you."

Chapter Twenty-one

Clio held her breath. For a brief, terrifying moment, nothing happened.

He made no sound. No movement. No reaction at all.

Not even a blink.

And then, in a heartbeat, he had her pressed against the door. Her spine met the wood with a teeth-rattling urgency. His hands slid to her backside, and he lifted her, molding her body to his.

His words were a low growl against her lips. "I was hoping you'd say that."

She slid her hands to his hair, smiling so broadly it was difficult to kiss him back. "I was hoping you'd do this."

He kissed her. Hungrily, at first. Then sweetly. More sweetly than ever before, sipping at her top lip, then the bottom. Teasing her tongue with his. Mur-

muring soft words she couldn't make out, but didn't need to, really. Stroking her cheek with the backs of his fingers and taking all the time he wished. Because now they didn't need to rush. They needn't worry about any interruption.

At last, it was only the two of them.

All too soon, he pulled away. "We should w—"

"No." Panicked, she pressed her fingers over his lips, pursed as they were on the brink of destroying her. "Don't say that word. I'll take any other word beginning with W, but not that one. Writhe, wash, wiggle, whip . . ."

He looked a bit alarmed at that last option.

"It's an example. You know what I mean. The next word out of your mouth had better be anything but 'wait.'"

She removed her fingers.

His thumbs traced soothing circles on her lower back. "Warm. We should warm you up. Get you something to eat."

"Oh. Well, that's fine. And much better than any of my suggestions."

"No doubt. I'll get you a blanket, and then we'll see about peeling off this silk." As he lowered her to the floor, his face went suddenly, direly grave. "You'll have to marry me, you know."

Yes.

She did know.

In that moment, Clio looked inside her heart. It was the clearest glimpse she'd ever had. She saw the entirety of her future. *Their* future. The castle, the brewery. Children. Christmases and Easters and summer rain.

They'd always have rain.

"There's no way around it," he said, backing away and going to the bed. "It might not be what you wanted, but . . . You came after me in the rain, all wet and shivering. And I should have sent you back, but I'm too impulsive for anyone's good. Especially yours."

Oh, drat. He was hurt. She should have just blurted out the word yes, but she hadn't and now he didn't understand. He'd mistaken her pause for reluctance.

He tugged at the blankets. "I'm a fighter. If anything good remained of my reputation, last night I've destroyed it. The only thing I can offer you is the protection of my body."

"Rafe . . ."

"But there's no refusing it now." He paused, pillow in hand, holding it like shield. "You don't have a choice."

"Of course I have choices. When you signed those papers, you gave me all the choices in the world. I'm a new Clio. I'm not doing anything because I have to, and I don't care what people say. I'm certainly not going to marry you simply because you say I must."

His fingers flexed, digging a stranglehold into the pillow.

"For heaven's sake, that poor cushion."

She took the pillow from his hands, and gave it an apologetic plumping before placing at the head of the bed.

"Rafe," she said, "I'm going to marry you because I love you."

He blinked at her, and she realized with a sudden

pang in her heart that he might never have heard these words before. His mother was gone so young. No matter how his father and brother might have felt, they wouldn't be the sort to voice it aloud. And if what he told her was true, about his history with women being shallow and unsatisfying . . .

Clio was likely the first. And the fact that she could give him this gift? Oh, it just filled her heart with joy.

She took one of his hands in both of hers. "I am madly in love with you, Rafe Brandon."

He was quiet for a while.

"Are you feverish?" he asked.

"No."

"Are you certain?"

"Yes." She lifted his hand and pressed the back of it to her brow. "See?"

"I didn't mean about the fever. Are you certain about me?"

Clio supposed she deserved that skepticism. As far as Rafe knew, these feelings were a recent development.

"I'm certain. It's been coming on for some time now. I'm not even sure when it began, but . . . long before this summer. For years now, I've read everything I could find of your career. I cheered your successes; I worried when you were hurt. Why else would I keep reaching out with all those silly invitations and holiday greetings? I'm a nice girl, Rafe, and yes, I was raised to be the model of gentility and good breeding. But even I'm not *that* polite."

She took his hand and kissed it. "I love you. And I understand if it's difficult for you to believe that fully today. But it's just as well. It's a short little phrase. I can repeat it as many times as it takes. You can practice taking it the way you take jabs." She raised her fists the way he'd taught her and boxed his shoulder. "I *love* you. I *love* you. I—"

He caught her in his arms. His eyes were fierce. "Clio, no. You have to stop."

"I won't stop. Not even a heavyweight champion of England is strong enough to make me." Giddy with the power of it, she laced her arms around his neck. "I love you. Take that."

Oh, Rafe intended to take it, all right.

He was going to take it, hold it tight with both hands, and never, ever let go.

"On second thought, never mind the blankets," he said. "I'm going to warm you myself."

"I like that idea."

So did he.

He put his hands on her waist and turned her so that she faced away from him. And then, for the second time that week, he set about the task of unbuttoning and unlacing her.

But it was so much different this time.

This time, she was his.

He'd been waiting a long time to have someone who belonged to him. Someone he could care for, unreservedly. Honestly. With every part of himself, not just the brutish, broken bits.

"Eat something while I do this," he told her. "We can't have you swooning again."

She reached for a roll and broke off a piece. "If you

didn't want to make me swoon," she said with her mouth full, "you should not have been so dashing."

"You've little room to talk, in this gown." He unbuttoned the last of the closures and cleaved the damp silk from her back. "When I first saw you in that ballroom, I thought *I* might faint."

He pushed the gown down to her waist and over her hips, helping her step out of it. Then he set to unlacing her corset and untying the tapes of her petticoats. Wet knots were trickier than dry ones, but he finally managed to work them loose.

She turned to face him, clad in only a damp, tissue-thin linen shift. It clung to her, pasted to her every curve—all but translucent. Holy God. His gaze wandered from her hardened nipples, to the sweet flare of her hips, to the dark amber triangle of shadow guarding her sex.

If he hadn't been jerked back to awareness by her sudden shiver, he could have stood there gawping all night.

"Sorry," he said. He needed to hurry this, or she'd catch a chill. "Why don't you do the rest yourself and climb into bed. I'll take care of myself and join you."

She nodded, and he turned away, dropping into a chair by the fire so he could remove his boots. After those were dispatched, he stood and worked on the rest. In a matter of seconds, he'd stripped off his waistcoat and shirt, then shucked his trousers. Holding his clothing in a ball before him, he turned.

Clio lay nestled in the bed linens, her hair unbound and falling about her shoulders in damp waves. So lovely. She looked like a painting one might find in a Venetian palace.

And this picture of feminine delicacy was staring at him. The way a stray cat might eye joints of meat in the marketplace.

"I . . ." She looked abashed at being caught, but she didn't look away.

He tossed the balled-up clothing aside and spread his hands, as if to say: *Go ahead; look your fill.*

Her gaze flirted with his shoulders and abdomen, but quickly dropped to his most vital parts. Her cheeks turned an entirely new, rather alarming, shade of pink. He didn't even know how to name that shade of pink. It might not have existed in nature until tonight.

"I don't know what I was expecting." She hooked one finger on her teeth, pensive. "You're a large man. Everywhere. It stands to reason that you'd be . . . large . . . there, too."

He scratched the back of his neck, trying not to laugh. He wasn't freakishly big. Just on the larger side. But her unintentional compliments—and that fierce blush creeping up to her hairline—were only making matters worse. He was rapidly growing even larger.

She stretched a hand forward, tentative. "May I . . . ?"

As if he'd say no.

He moved closer to the bed, his cock jutting out before him like the prow of a ship. He was certain he'd never been harder in his life.

She touched him with one fingertip—one single fingertip, skimming him from shaft to tip—and his whole body went up in flames.

She tilted her head. "Are you very sure that this will—"

"Yes."

"All of it?"

"In time." He joined her on the bed, coaxing her to lie back on the mattress. "We'll take it as slow as you like. If you want me to stop, you've only to say the word."

He stretched out next to her, drawing her body close to his chest and enfolding her in his arms. Giving her his heat. He had plenty to spare.

"Warmer?"

She nodded.

As he bent to kiss her pulse, her head rolled to one side, stretching her neck into a pale, graceful curve.

An invitation.

And this was one invitation he would never refuse.

He began at her ear and kissed down her neck, all the way to her collarbone. His hand had drifted to her breast of its own accord. While kneading one, he kissed the other, nuzzling close to her violet-scented skin.

Even if they lived and made love for fifty years— and he fervently hoped they did—Rafe didn't think it would ever cease to astonish him, that she *wanted* this. His big, roughened body rubbing against her soft perfection.

He laid her on her back and kissed his way down her belly, pausing halfway down to prop his chin on her navel and gaze up into her face.

"I'm going to make this good for you," he promised. "Beyond good. I want . . . I want cake sounds. No, scratch that. I want *Rafe* sounds."

She laughed a little. But as he slid a hand up her naked thigh, her laugh became a sigh of pleasure.

"There's my girl. That's a start."

He finished kissing his way down her belly, then dipped his head lower. She startled. He held her hips tight.

"It's all right. If you trust me."

"I trust you."

He didn't take that gift lightly. He stroked her first with his fingers, parting her folds with the pad of his thumb, and pushing just an inch inside. When she gasped and moaned, he took the encouragement.

He nudged her legs apart, wide enough to accommodate his shoulders. And then he sank between her thighs, laying his tongue to the very heart of her. She bucked in surprise at the first contact, but he wouldn't be deterred. He teased her with slow, lapping strokes of his tongue. He loved the taste of her. She was so sweet, with just the right amount of tart.

"Rafe." She touched his shoulder. "*Rafe*, are you sure—"

"It's all right." He spread her wide with his thumbs. "It's perfect. You're perfect."

She cried out in pleasure. Her thighs clamped together, catching his head like two sides of a vise. He wasn't going anywhere now. So he settled into his task, teasing and tasting. Learning her every contour, her every response. Within moments, she was panting for him.

"Yes," she moaned.

He moaned, too. His cock throbbed vainly where it lay trapped against the bedsheets.

When he couldn't wait any longer, Rafe crawled his way up her body. Keeping his weight on his arms, he nestled his hard, aching cock in the cradle of her sex. He made no move to enter her. Not yet. He just rocked his hips back and forth, stroking her where he knew she'd like it the most. Giving them both more heat, more friction.

More teasing, maddening bliss.

"Oh," she sighed. "Oh, Rafe."

He loved this feeling. It wasn't just the joy of pleasuring her—though that was brilliant, in and of itself. It was this heady, superhuman awareness, the intensity of focus that could push him out of his troubled mind and make him feel he could do *any-thing*. In all his life, he'd only ever felt this way when fighting.

Until now. Until her.

As he slid back and forth, he balanced on his arms above her, watching her every reaction. The steady crescendo of her pleasure was like a captivating story. One written in pink brushstrokes across her pale skin.

She was so beautiful.

And ready for him, judging by the slickness gliding between their bodies. It was a damned good thing, because he couldn't wait much longer.

"Please," she whimpered, fisting her hands in the bed linens. "Soon. Please."

He took his cock in hand and positioned himself at her entrance. "Tell me you want this."

"I want this."

Gritting his teeth, he teased them both by slid-ing the tip of his erection in, then out. "Tell me you want *me*."

Her eyes opened and locked with his. "Rafe. I want you. Only you."

He felt like a god as he pushed into her. Omnipotent. Arrogant. Possessing the keys to Paradise.

She was wet, but so tight. What felt nigh-on glorious for him had to be hurting her. He didn't try to sink deep all at once but instead moved forward in gentle, steady thrusts. Still, her expression tightened with every inch he advanced.

He paused. "If you're hurting, tell me to stop."

"Don't stop. I love this. I love you. There's just . . . a great deal of you to love, that's all. Be patient."

Be patient, she said.

But patience was *her* strength, not his. Rafe was approximately as skilled at patience as he was at embroidery. He was already drawing on every available reserve of self-control. He was still only halfway inside her, and wild to bury himself to the hilt.

He reached between them, touching her in just the right place. Those small circles of his thumb were his only motion. He tensed every muscle of his body, determined to hold the rest of him utterly still.

Soon her breathing grew ragged. Her hips began to move, undulating in gentle waves. He held his position through sheer force of will. She worked herself up and down on him, taking him a fraction deeper each time.

Her moans and sighs grew louder, and her back arched off the mattress. It was killing him not to move.

Be patient.

When her climax broke, his control broke, too. He thrust deep, hoping her pleasure would overshadow any pain.

At last. He was at the heart of her. She was holding him tight.

So damned tight. The last pulses of her climax rippled around him. When he slid back, her body gave his cock the tightest, wettest, most purely blissful hug of his life. And no sooner had he withdrawn to the tip than he was plunging back in, eager to feel it again.

He told himself to slow down, be gentler. Perhaps he should withdraw and finish himself with his hand. But he couldn't bring himself to do either. He'd waited too long for her, and he'd exhausted every bit of patience, and all that was left was this raw, relentless need. His looming orgasm was like a jockey on his back, whipping him faster and faster.

In the end, he decided a sprint to the finish would be the kindest way.

"Hold on to me," he said, feeling the tingle at the base of his spine that told him the crisis was close. "Hold me tight, with everything."

She tightened her arms around his shoulders and locked her legs at the small of his back. And when he came inside her, it was heart-stopping. Brainblanking. Bone-melting.

And sweet.

So damned sweet.

In the aftermath, he pressed kisses to her lips, trying to savor every last bit of that sweetness.

He knew it couldn't last.

This was his life, after all. And he knew from twenty-eight years of experience being Rafe Brandon . . .

It didn't matter what promises he made to her, or to himself. When his emotions flared, his good intentions burned to ash. His brother's intended bride somehow became his own. A waltz turned into a fistfight. *Be patient* translated to *Faster, harder, now.*

Someday, he would hurt her. He would follow the wrong impulse, say words he didn't mean. He'd find a way to cock this up in some stupid, irretrievable manner. Rafe felt sickly certain of it.

All the more reason to treasure this closeness now.

He would let her hold him just as long and as tight as she dared.

Chapter Twenty-two

*M*orning brought an ironic realization. One Clio was oddly unprepared to face.

"You do realize what this means." In the early light of dawn, Rafe pulled his shirt over his head and pushed his arms through the sleeves. "Now we actually have to plan a wedding."

"Oh." She paused in buttoning her chemise. "Must we?"

"Unless I dreamed all that?" He shot a meaningful look at the bed. "I'm fairly certain we must."

She gave him a reassuring kiss. "You didn't dream one moment of that."

And neither had she. Their night together had been wonderful, and wonderfully real.

After making love the first time, they'd risen to bathe and take some dinner. Then talked until they fell sleep in each other's arms. But not for long. Twice more in the night, he'd woken her with kisses that quickly became something more. They repeated the cycle as long as the night lasted—making love, falling asleep, then waking to make love again. As though they could make the one night feel like several.

"It's not the idea of marriage I'm balking at," she said. "Just the wedding plans. You've already carried me up the grand staircase in a white lace gown. We've fed each other cake. We've spent our night in the honeymoon suite. Can't we just dispense with all the ceremony? I would be happy to get married in the middle of a field, in a dress I've worn twenty times before, so long as I loved the man I was marrying."

"Simple suits me. I am not going to complain about a lack of bunting."

Smiling to herself, she reached for her stays. "Of course, I would like to have my sisters there. Frustrating as they can sometimes be, my wedding wouldn't be the same without them."

He busied himself with his trouser fastenings and didn't reply.

She cringed, instantly regretting her thoughtless words. Yes, she could have her sisters. When they married, there was no chance Rafe would have his brother in attendance. Piers might never speak to either one of them again.

Rafe was giving up a great deal for her. She wasn't in the habit of believing that she could be worth that, to anyone. He was worth everything to her, too. She vowed to love him so fiercely and so well, he would never feel the deprivation.

As she untangled the tapes of her corset, an idea formed in her mind.

She wet her lips and gathered her nerve. "Remember what you told me the other day? That when we were younger, you couldn't bear to look at me sometimes because in your mind you'd been making me do such wicked things?"

One of his dark eyebrows rose. "I remember."

She let the corset fall to the side, standing before him in her chemise and stockings. "Make me do wicked things."

He regarded her for a moment, as if trying to gauge her sincerity. Or perhaps her courage.

Clio forced her spine straight and held her chin high. "Well . . . ?"

In calm strides, he walked to an armchair and sat down in it. When he spoke, his voice was dark as sin itself. "Take off the shift. Leave the stockings."

Her arousal was instantaneous.

A hot blush pushed to her face as she loosed the same buttons she'd only just done up. He watched her as she disrobed, his bold gaze giving her nowhere to hide.

Even though this had been her idea, she felt strangely shy and exposed. But she suspected that her shyness was part of the fantasy for him, so she didn't try to pretend otherwise.

"Good." His gaze swept her bared body. "Now come undress me."

She approached his chair in soft, catlike steps. With shaky fingers, she gathered the hem of his shirt and began to lift it high, exposing his sculpted masterpiece of a torso.

She was suddenly conscious that this would be different from any of the times they'd made love last night. Namely, there was sunlight now. They could see each other clearly. Rafe was so perfectly chiseled everywhere, it was difficult not to feel self-conscious.

But unless he was a very good actor, he seemed to be enjoying her body, too.

His eyes roamed her every curve. As she pulled the shirt over his head, she allowed her breasts to brush against his cheek. He sucked in his breath on a sharp hiss.

Then she dropped her gaze to the closures of his trousers. They would be difficult, if not impossible, to undo with him sitting in the chair.

"Did you mean to stand?" she asked.

"No."

His meaning rocketed through her.

To remove them, she would have to go down on her knees.

The idea was shocking and wicked. She worked his trousers down, and he lifted his hips just an inch or two to help.

She eased the trousers lower, freeing the hard, eager length of his erection. Pure, unapologetic virility, staring her in straight the face.

Abashed, she dropped her gaze.

"Look," he said. His brusque tone settled low in her belly. "Look what you did."

Her cheeks burned. But Clio had proposed this game. She couldn't disobey now. So she looked.

Had she done this, truly? All of it?

If so, she felt rather proud.

She put both hands on him, claiming as much of his thick, curved length as she could manage. Then she worked her hands up and down. "Am I doing it right?"

"Just right. Now—" His breath caught. "Now use your mouth on me."

The crude command sent an erotic thrill chasing through her.

"How?"

"Start with your tongue."

Bending her head, she gave the tip a tentative lick. "Like that?"

"Yes. Like that. All over."

She swirled her tongue around the plum-colored head, then down the underside of his shaft. He smelled of soap and just-washed skin. She hadn't expected him to be so soft. So soft, and so hard at the same time.

When she licked back up toward the tip, his breath caught. His hand moved to cradle the back of her head.

"Now like this."

He nudged her open mouth over the crown, tangling his hand in her hair to guide her up and down.

Beyond that brief lesson, she didn't need more encouragement. The lewdness of it excited her beyond anything she could have imagined. She worked to take him deeper, then a fraction deeper still—loving the fact that she'd never be able to take him all. Craving the taste of him, savoring the soft groans she pulled from his chest.

"Clio. God."

He tightened his grip in her hair and gently pulled her away. She whimpered, disappointed.

"Stand," he told her. "Spread your legs and straddle my lap."

She did as he asked, working quickly. Her stocking snagged on the chair's upholstery. She didn't care.

"Lift your breasts," he said, sounding impatient now. "Bring them to my mouth."

She held them up for his attention. First one, then the other. Then both at the same time. He moved his head from one side to the other, teasing her nipples with alternating kisses and licks. His mouth fitted over one, and he suckled hard. She felt his growl vibrate all through her.

"Please," she whispered. "I need . . . I want . . ."

"What is it you want, love? Tell me."

"I want you."

His hand caressed her arm. "Then you have me. I'm right here."

"You know what I mean." She wriggled on his lap. "I . . . I want you inside me."

"Like this?" Reaching between them, he slid one finger into her depths. The sensation took her breath away . . . but it wasn't quite enough.

The devil. He knew exactly what she was craving. He was only teasing her.

"More," she panted, working against his hand. Each time her sex brushed his palm, a ripple of bliss moved through her. "I want more."

"Then say it." He drew her close and kissed her ear. "Tell me you want my cock."

She froze. A thrill rocketed through her.

"Go on," he urged, pushing his finger deep. "I can feel how wet you are. You like hearing me say these things. So say them yourself. Tell me you want my cock deep inside you. Hard and fast."

"I . . . I can't say that."

"Why not? It's already been on the tip of your tongue. And it's just a word."

"A wicked word."

"You wanted to do wicked things."

Yes, but she'd expected him to do the talking. When it came to speaking of carnality and desire, he never had any qualms. But Clio had qualms. So many qualms. Great heaps of qualms she'd amassed over a lifetime.

He teased his thumb in devious circles, right where he knew she'd feel it most. His breath caressed her hair. "You're here. With me. It's safe. You can say whatever you feel."

Her whole body ached with need. He had her so excited, she would have done anything.

"I want your cock." Her voice was breathy. "I want it inside me."

He drew his finger from her slickness and took himself in hand, positioning the smooth, broad crown of his erection at her entrance. "This is what you want?"

"Yes."

He put his hands on the arms of the chair. "Then take it."

She sank down on him, a little lower each time, taking his hard fullness into her in delicious increments until her lap rested on his.

"Now look." He turned her head toward the dressing table. "Look what you did."

Their reflection filled the looking glass. His big, bronzed hands gripping her pale flesh. The gentle bounce of her breasts as she rode him in a lazy rhythm. The haze of desire in his expression.

"God, you're beautiful."

His hands sank to her waist, and he guided her into a swifter pace, driving up with his hips to fill her. She slumped forward and buried her face in his neck, surrendering to it all. The feel of his hard length dragging in and out of her, teasing her most sensitive places again and again . . .

The pleasure rose and gathered so swiftly, her climax caught her before she knew it. She went limp in his arms, sobbing faintly with pleasure, trusting him to keep up the rhythm she needed.

And he did.

When the last tremors had subsided, he tightened his arms around her, stroking her hair.

"That didn't go as I planned," she said, when she'd finally recovered her breath. "I was supposed to be giving *you* wicked pleasure."

"Oh, you did. You most certainly did."

He brought her mouth to his, and it was like their first kiss in the tower—a tender, languorous sweetness spread atop a chasm of need.

She marveled at his patience. He was still so big and hard inside her. He had to be desperate for release.

Bending her head, she kissed his neck. She stroked her fingers over his shoulders and through the dark hairs on his chest. He began to move inside her again. Thrusting slowly. Tenderly.

So deeply, she could feel it in her heart.

His arm tightened around her waist, and his thrusts grew harder, more desperate. Until each one wrenched a sob from her and a harsh, guttural sound from him.

Closing his eyes, he let his brow fall against hers. His thrusts redoubled in force. They clashed against one another—cheek against jaw, teeth against chin. Raw, openmouthed kiss against kiss.

Then his hand tightened in her hair, and he broke the kiss, pulling her just a few inches away. He held her so tightly, forbidding her to look anywhere else. She had no choice to but to stare into his eyes.

"Look," he said. "Look what you did."

Those bold green eyes held hunger and yearning and stark, unabashed want.

And something more.

Something that could only be love.

"I know," she said. "I know. It will be all right."

He seemed to swell inside her. One . . . two . . . three final, desperate thrusts. Then with a growl, he shuddered and slumped forward in her arms.

As his breathing slowed, she drew soothing touches up and down his back and murmured soft, crooning words in his ear. It seemed the act left him so spent and vulnerable, he would allow himself to be fawned over—and she took full advantage.

"That was . . ." He released his breath, then seemed to give up on the sentence entirely.

"It was, rather." She looked up at him. "Let's go home."

Chapter Twenty-three

Rafe hired a postchaise to convey Clio home. He rode out on his gelding. He might have shared the coach with her, but he had his reasons for riding alone. For one, he knew she had to be sore from their night of passion. Two hours with her in a small, dark space? He wouldn't be able to keep his hands off her.

Second, he needed the time to think.

There was much to be done. Once he had Clio settled in at the castle, he needed to set things in motion with the solicitors. He would ride to Dover and wait for Piers. It wasn't going to be a seaside holiday, greeting his brother with the news that his bride was no longer his bride. But Rafe didn't want the news to come from anyone else.

In the meantime, there were other hurdles to clear. Such as his reckoning with Sir Teddy Cambourne.

Upon their arrival at Twill Castle, however, it seemed his reckoning would be delayed.

"How surprising," Clio said, after conferring with Anna and changing into a simpler frock. "We've beaten them home. They must have stayed very late at the ball. Or very early."

"Perhaps they didn't want to travel in the rain."

"So long as they're safe and well, that's a lucky stroke." They entered the castle's entrance hall, and she spoke to him in low tones. "As far as everyone at the ball knows, you brought me home to the castle last night. And as far as everyone at the castle knows, we stayed at Pennington Hall. We might not need to explain ourselves to anyone. Not until Piers comes home."

"I'm not waiting for Piers to come home." Rafe explained his intention to go to Dover.

"To Dover?" she asked. "But I'm the one who's going to speak with him. We practiced the other night."

"Things have changed. My signature is on those papers, and he deserves an explanation from me."

"But I spent the whole ride home planning out my speech. And I had the best idea."

She led him down a side corridor and into a room that seemed to be her office. The shelves were lined with household ledgers and books. On the wall were pinned a survey of all the surrounding lands and various architectural sketches.

She said, "Sit in that armchair, if you will. Behind the desk. Be Piers again."

Bemused, he did as she asked. "I'm sitting in the armchair. What now?"

"I have the rough sketches for the oast and the

brewhouse, of course." She reached for a ledger. "I've done the tabulations of what it will cost to convert the local fields to hops. But before we get to those specifics, there's this."

If her intent was to make him understand, she did the worst possible thing. She placed two books on the desk blotter, side by side. One bound in blue; the other in red.

He peered at the titles. His sense of foreboding didn't improve. "Cookery books?"

"Humor me for a moment. You'll see." She opened the first—a faded blue volume—to the listing of contents. "This is my mother's cookery book, purchased when she was first married." Then she opened the second one to the same page. "This is the new edition I received on my eighteenth birthday. If you scan the two side by side, they are much the same—but not identical. Can you find the difference?"

At a glance? Hell, no. And Rafe did not have the patience to go through both lists to find it, either.

"Curry." She jabbed her finger in the center of the page. "And over here, arrack punch. See?"

He drummed his fingers, expecting that there must be some explanation forthcoming.

"There wasn't a single Indian dish in my mother's cookery book. Today, you wouldn't find a collection of recipes without them."

He looked blankly at her.

"Hold that thought. There's more." Next, she pulled out a length of fabric and thrust it at him. "Here."

He turned it over in his hands. A piece of light, patterned cloth. "What am I to do with this?"

"Just look at it. *Think* about it." She bounced on her toes a little bit.

Rafe looked at the fabric. He thought about it. He had no idea what sort of thoughts he was supposed to have about a few flowers and springs printed on cheap cotton.

"It's chintz," she said. "When we were children, it was all the rage to have imported Indian cotton. For curtains, shawls, quilts. Pillows. But now the factories use domestic cotton and print chintz here. None of it is imported anymore."

He frowned. "I'm not right to play Piers in this scenario. He's the world traveler."

"No, no. This is about England. And you're the perfect person." Her eyes sparked with excitement. "Trust me."

Rafe shifted in the armchair, feeling ill at ease. "Can we come to the point?"

"The point is this." She flattened both hands on the top of the desk. "What happens in India doesn't stay in India. It comes home to England and becomes the latest fashion here. This was true for curry, and it was true for chintz, and it's going to be true for beer."

She opened a folio, bringing out her last bit of evidence. A newspaper clipping. Wonderful. More reading.

He stared at the small, printed notice. "So there was a shipwreck."

"It's not the shipwreck that we're concerned with. It's the cargo." She pointed to a specific line. "The ship's bill of lading notes that it was transporting a new kind of pale ale. The manufacturers up north have been brewing it for a few years now, specifically for export to India. The climate there isn't suited for beer-making, and the extra hops in the brew help this ale survive the sea voyage. It's all the rage among Englishmen living there. Piers even mentioned it me in one of his letters."

"But they're already manufacturing it up north."

"Yes. For *export*." She leaned her hip on the desk. "That means this is the ideal time to stake out a share of the home market. As men like Piers return from their travels, they'll be looking for the ale they enjoyed abroad. Then the taste for it will spread. Just as it happened with curry, or chintz. Within a generation, no one will be drinking porter anymore. Pale ale in the India style is going to be the beer of choice. I'm certain of it. This is the brewery's chance."

She ceased talking and took a slow, deep breath.

"Well?" she prodded, after a few moments had passed. "Are you convinced?"

He sat back in the chair and regarded her, admiring. "I think I might be. You should have been a lawyer."

"Oh, I have other, better plans." She smiled. "I'm going to open a brewery. And I hope you'll be my partner."

"You're going to ask Piers to be your business partner?"

"Of course not." She laughed a little. "Rafe, I'm asking *you*."

Her partner? He didn't know what to say.

"I thought you might have some hesitation," she said. "I'm prepared for it, actually." She gave him a mischievous smile. "Prepare to be dazzled."

Dazzled.

"Forget anything I said the other day about punching tankards into walls." She went to the office entryway. "Imagine your name on the door. Right here. Lord Rafe Brandon, Partner in Brandon Brewery."

"Clio . . ."

"No, no. I'm just getting started." She gestured widely around the room. "Imagine, this is *your* office. You'd have papers and ledgers. And a secretary to sit right here." She flew to a smaller desk at the side of the room and sat behind it, posing with a quill. "Shall I take a letter, my lord?"

"A secretary." He leaned back in his chair. "Would she be as pretty as you?"

"*He* would be middle-aged and balding, but very efficient." She rose from the desk, drifting back toward the door. "And people would come to meet with you, all day long. Important people.

"People like . . ." She ducked outside the door, and after a minute returned, wearing an old, borrowed coat and a straw hat. In one hand, she clutched a garden rake. "Farmers."

Again, she went out, then reappeared wearing a cap, holding a pewter mug in one hand and using the other hand to drape a finger-moustache over her top lip.

She made her voice deep. "Or brewers."

Rafe fought the urge to smile. He lost the battle. She was adorable. Ridiculous, and possibly addled in the mind, but adorable.

She disappeared one more time. He waited for her to reappear in the doorway, brandishing another outlandish prop or dressed in costume.

Instead, what appeared in the doorway was Ellingworth. Decked out in a tall hat. And spectacles.

"Even esquires," she said.

Now he couldn't help but laugh.

She emerged from behind the doorjamb to give the bulldog an affectionate rub. "Actually, meetings with esquires are unlikely. Barristers, no. Solicitors, yes."

Solicitors. Bloody hell.

Rafe rubbed his face. He didn't know what to say, other than the truth. "I'm not suited to office work."

"But that's the best part. You wouldn't be here all the time. Once the day's business is concluded, you'd be off to walk the fields, or to consult with the cooper about new casks, or to taste the latest brew. I can promise you all the beer you can drink. And I'll even throw my heart in the bargain." She popped up to sit on the desk before him, her feet dangling. "Well? Aren't you a little bit tempted?"

Tempted?

Rafe had three toes over the threshold of Perdition. The picture she made before him would tempt a saint. But this arrangement she proposed? Managing, record-keeping, correspondence . . .

She swung her legs back and forth. "Well?"

"I mean to provide for you," he said. "Take care of you. But I'm a prizefighter. Not a clerk."

Rafe knew himself too well. He could want to be good at this. He could make her promises and try his damnedest, for a while. But in the end, he would let her down.

"It's out of the question for now. I've got to get back in the ring. As soon as we're married, I'll go back to training and—"

"As soon as we're *married*? As soon as we're married, you're leaving to train for a rematch with Dubose?"

"Of course. If it's the brewery you're concerned about, you should want that, too. No one will want to drink Brandon's Loser Ale. I'll be more help to you when I've won my championship back."

"You'll be more help to me if you have your health." She pressed a hand to her chest. "I love you. I can't bear the thought of losing you."

Love. Damn, he'd been waiting a lifetime to hear that. But every time she spoke the word, his instinct was to dodge it.

"You won't lose me." He rose from his chair, putting his hands on her shoulders. With his thumb, he traced the gentle slope of her collarbone. "I know you're frightened. But I've been doing this for years. There isn't one good reason why . . ."

"Reason one. You could be killed." She counted them off on her fingers. "Two, you could be maimed. Three, you could kill or maim your opponent. Four, you could be arrested, charged with riot and assault, transported to Australia, and never seen again. Those are four excellent reasons, Rafe. Four."

"None of those things is likely to happen."

"But they're all possible. And just because they haven't happened yet doesn't ensure they won't."

He sighed gruffly. "Do you not believe in me?"

"I do believe in you. But I also know Jack Dubose is an opponent unlike the others you've fought. I've followed the sport for years now, remember? I know how he demolished Grady, and I read what he did to Phillips. The sporting papers said that man might never fight again."

"Phillips will fight again." He might not *chew* again, but he'd fight.

"And I saw with my own eyes what Dubose did to you. I can still picture it, Rafe. Every break." She ran a finger down the rugged slope of his nose, then laid a sweet caress to his cheek. "Every bruise."

He caught her hand and squeezed it. "That's why I can't end my career that way. I need to prove to myself—to everyone—that I'm not just a washed-up brawler."

"Then don't be a washed-up brawler. Rafe, you have a great many talents. You could do so much more with your life."

So much *more*?

His hands flexed at his sides. What was *more* than being the bloody best prizefighter in England? Most people would consider that an impressive accomplishment.

"How many people can say they're the best? At anything?" He lowered his voice. "We've been over this. I don't need to be rescued from the sport I love. I thought you understood that. I thought you understood *me*."

She pinched the bridge of her nose and sighed. "Just once. Just once I would like to know how it feels to be worth making plans around. I spent eight years shunted aside for the sake of your brother's career. And now, even after everything we shared last night, I learn that I come second in *your* life, too."

"That's not fair. This isn't about coming first or second or third; this is a part of me. Asking me to give up fighting is like asking me to give up an arm."

"I'd never ask you to give up fighting. I'm only

asking if there's some way to continue in the sport that doesn't mean risking your life in our first few months of marriage." She gestured at the castle walls. "If you don't like the brewery idea, perhaps you could open a school here. A boxing school. Oh, you'd make an excellent teacher."

"Tutoring prigs like Teddy Cambourne, you mean? Oh, that will be fine."

"It wouldn't have to be wealthy gentlemen. Perhaps disadvantaged boys."

He shook his head. "It's a nice idea for someday, once our income is secure. But you said it yourself. There isn't much money in orphans."

And Rafe needed to earn money. More than anything, he wanted to provide for her. Keep her safe and give her the life she deserved. Living on her dowry and the castle's income would be possible, he supposed. But his pride demanded that he contribute, too.

He felt confident he could do that, once he got back in a ring. But in this restrictive little cage of a room? He could only fail.

"I can't . . ." Christ, he'd never tried to explain this to anyone. "I just can't do this sort of thing. And it's not because I don't wish to, or because I'm too lazy to try. I can't concentrate on ledgers and schedules and books. They make me feel like I've stuck my head inside a beehive. My whole life, I've been this way. Eventually, I grow weary of trying and . . . lose interest."

"You lose interest."

He shrugged. "That's the best way I can describe it. Yes."

She bit her lip and regarded him. "Are you worried you'll lose interest in me?"

"That's different. You're different."

"How can you be sure?" she asked.

"How can you even question it?"

The words came out too forcefully. They sounded angry, even to his ears.

His conscience—that living, breathing spirit of a lifetime's accumulated sins—was screaming at him now. Retreat, it said, before he went too far. Said something he didn't mean.

"Fighting is who I am," he said. "If you want a man who'll be happy pushing papers around a desk . . . maybe you *should* marry Piers."

As soon as he heard his own words, he regretted them.

Rafe, you idiot.

She winced. "I can't believe you said that."

He rubbed his face with one hand. He wished he could claim the same surprise. His whole life was a string of rash words and actions he wished he could take back. Last night, those impulses had worked out in ways that pleased her. But he'd known it was only a matter of time before he cocked it up.

There was just too much of the devil in him. He was doomed to push away the people he loved most. He would never be able to hold anything good.

If he lost Clio now, that would be no worse than he deserved.

Hell, as far as she was concerned, it would probably be for the best.

"Listen," he said, "I shouldn't have . . ."

And then—just because it was exactly what Rafe's

life didn't need that moment—Bruiser appeared in the doorway.

"There you two are. I trust the ball was enjoyable. I"—Bruiser clapped his hands together—"have good news."

Rafe doubted it. He made throat-slashing, *shut-it* gestures.

Bruiser, naturally, ignored them.

"First, Miss Whitmore, I'm happy to report the engagement ring has, er . . . reappeared."

"Really?" Clio said. "What interesting timing. We were just discussing the wedding plans. Weren't we, Rafe?"

Damn it.

"And second," Bruiser went on, "your new gowns have arrived from London. They're made expressly for you, and they are magnificent. The dressmakers are waiting in the sitting room."

Rafe shook his head. "She doesn't want to—"

"Oh, but I do." Her cool gaze met Rafe's. "I do, Mr. Montague. I can't wait to try the gowns."

Chapter Twenty-four

$\mathcal{I}$n actuality, being fitted for yet more flouncy gowns was the last thing Clio wanted to do this morning. But she and Rafe needed some space from each other, and this seemed the best way.

After an entire week of telling her she couldn't break an engagement she'd entered into at the age of seventeen . . . They had one argument, and Rafe was calling off *theirs*?

It was a touch alarming, how quickly his mind leapt from the realm of "mild disagreement" to "irreparable rift."

Maybe you should marry Piers.

Of all the things to say.

But she knew he didn't mean it. And she should have known better than to put him on the spot like that, in a setting so far removed from his strengths.

He'd warned her, hadn't he? Ballrooms, drawing

rooms, schoolrooms, offices . . . When he felt ill at ease, something brash would result.

But what she admired in him was that Rafe understood this about himself. He'd found his own ways to not only succeed but flourish. If she wanted to build a life with him, she would need to understand and respect that, too.

She owed him an apology, but she doubted he was ready to hear it yet. To pass the time, she might as well try on a pretty gown.

As she was making her way to the sitting room, she heard the coach pulling into the drive. One by one, her family alighted from the carriage.

Clio rushed to greet them in the entrance hall. "Phoebe. How are you?"

"Exceedingly fatigued." With that, her youngest sister disappeared in the direction of the library.

Well. Clio could stop worrying, she supposed. That was Phoebe as usual.

Daphne and Teddy came in next.

Clio curtsied to her brother-in-law. He jammed his hat down to shade his bruised face, barely acknowledging her with a nod before proceeding upstairs.

Daphne sidled up to explain. "Clio, you had better be grateful. We overstayed our welcome with the Penningtons in the worst way."

"You, overstaying a welcome? How difficult to believe."

"I was determined that we would be the last guests at the ball," she said. "We had to manage the rumors, you know. Teddy was a saint on your behalf. He laughed off the punch as a bit of sport between friends.

We told every person who asked that you swooned and Lord Rafe escorted you home." Her sister regarded her closely. "That *is* what happened, isn't it?"

"More or less."

The events didn't unfold in exactly the order Daphne might assume, and a great deal more had happened besides. But strictly speaking, it was a truthful statement.

"Then good," her sister said, inhaling sharply. "That's that."

Clio didn't fool herself. She knew Daphne and Teddy's scrambling was as much about preserving their own social status as it was to do with hers.

But if the potential for scandal was already managed, there wasn't any need for a hasty elopement. She could have whatever sort of wedding she wished.

All the choices were still hers.

"Now," Daphne said, "unless you mean to make me the worst sort of liar, the wedding had better be spectacular. And soon."

Clio led her sister to the sitting room. "Perhaps it will be. Come with me."

No fewer than six dressmakers and assistants stood waiting to assist her. The room was so spattered in frothy white, it looked like a volcano had erupted. A volcano of meringue.

Clio turned to Daphne and said the words she knew her sister had been longing to hear for years.

"Make me beautiful."

"This is madness."

Rafe had spent enough time in drawing rooms

this week to last him a lifetime. And he certainly had no wish to see Clio fitted in a gown for a wedding that wasn't meant to be theirs.

"Maybe we ought to leave," he said.

He didn't know what the devil was wrong with him, but if he had any decency, he would cease inflicting it on Clio.

"Are you syphilitic?" Bruiser had his ear pressed to the connecting door. "We are not going to leave. Rafe, you don't know what I've been through in the past few days. Just getting the dressmakers here from London was difficult enough. But that ring? Oh, you owe me for that ring."

Rafe didn't know how to argue with that. In truth, he owed Bruiser all manner of debts. It occurred to him that his trainer just might be the one person in his life he'd managed to *not* drive away.

"How long have we been working together?" Rafe asked. "Five years?"

"Six, by my counting."

"And I'm going to assume that you dream about leaving my employ just as often as I contemplate setting you loose."

"Daily, you mean? Oh, certainly."

"So how is it that we've kept this partnership together?"

Bruiser gave him an annoyed look. "By not overthinking it."

Right.

Perhaps there was a seed of truth in his trainer's impatient answer. Rafe should stop overthinking things. He loved Clio. He'd do anything to keep her. Anything. That was God's truth as it lived in his heart, and what he meant to tell her the instant she came through the door.

"She's coming. Stand up."

He knew he was in trouble before she even entered the room. He could hear it in the rhythm of her footsteps. Brisk. Confident. Fierce.

No thunks.

Or clunks.

She felt powerful. Which meant she would be beautiful.

He rose to his feet, found his center of balance, kept his joints loose, and got ready to roll with the punch.

The doors opened.

Holy God. He didn't stand a chance.

She was a knockout.

Bruiser pumped his fist. "Now that's more like it."

Rafe didn't even see the gown. It was white, he assumed. Or eggshell, or ivory. There was probably silk and lace involved. Perhaps a few brilliants or pearls. Really, he couldn't have described the cut or style or fabric to save his neck.

He only saw her.

The gown was like a master-crafted gold setting, and Clio was the jewel allowed to shine.

"Well?" Daphne prompted. "What do you think?"

An excellent question. What *did* he think? His brain had ceased responding.

Words. He should say some words, but he had no words. He was finding it difficult to locate air. All that came out was, "You . . . It's . . . Buh."

"Exquisite."

The suavely articulated pronouncement came

from somewhere behind him, but Rafe recognized the voice at once. He didn't even need to turn. Now that the old marquess was dead, that voice could only belong to one man.

"Piers," Clio breathed.

It was Piers. In the flesh.

Every time Rafe saw him, Piers looked more and more like their father. Tall. Strong, but lean. His dark hair had picked up a few new threads of silver. Squared shoulders like a shelf, with that refined, aristocratic face—unbroken nose and all—as its only ornament.

Ice blue eyes that saw everything and found it all wanting.

"I can't believe you're here," Clio said.

"It's me. I'm back in England for good this time. And this is the best possible welcome home." His gaze alternated between Clio and Rafe. "Seeing you both. The two people I care for most in the world."

Piers crossed the carpet in decisive, very Granville strides, coming face-to-face with Rafe. "About Father."

All the apologies and explanations Rafe had mulled over during the past few months . . . They all fled his brain.

And then his brother pulled him into a hug.

"I'm sorry," he whispered in Rafe's ear. "I'm sorry you had to bury him alone. Damn it. I should have been there, too."

Oh, Jesus.

"This is magical." Bruiser dabbed a tear from his eye. "I couldn't have planned it any better."

Rafe didn't want to hear about Bruiser and

his magic. His emotions were in such turmoil, he thought he might be sick.

It only got worse.

Next, Piers walked the distance to Clio, putting his hands on her shoulders. "Just look at you. Exquisite. Perfect."

And then . . . oh God . . . he kissed her.

Piers kissed "his" bride, right in front of everyone, and there wasn't a damned thing Rafe could do about it. Except inwardly howl and bleed.

"I should have done that years ago," Piers said upon lifting his head. "I wanted to."

"You wanted to?" she asked.

"Yes, of course."

"Then . . . Why the eight bloody years of delay?" It really wasn't Rafe's place to ask, but he couldn't help it.

"It was for your safety." His brother released a heavy sigh. "I owe a thousand apologies to you both. I've lied to you for years now."

"Lied? About what?"

"The nature of my work."

"Were you not a diplomat?" Clio asked.

"Oh, I was working for the Foreign Office. And diplomacy was the larger part of it. But there were other duties, too. Ones I wasn't so free to discuss."

Rafe swore. "You're not saying you're some kind of spy?"

"No. We avoid saying that, generally." He turned back to Clio. "It didn't seem fair to marry you until I'd finished my work. But these damnable wars kept dragging on and . . . What's this?" Piers lifted her hand and peered at it. "You're not wearing your ring."

"Oh, that." Bruiser leapt to explain. "It's being cleaned, my lord."

Piers turned and stared at him. "Who the devil are you?"

Bruiser tugged on his lapels and straightened his spine. "Who do you think I am?"

"An imposing jackass?"

Bruiser lifted the quizzing glass. "What about now?"

"An imposing jackass with a monocle."

Maybe this scene *was* some sort of magic. Rafe had always known there was much he should admire about Piers. But in this moment, he actually liked his brother.

Daphne intervened. "Oh, Lord Granville. Don't be such a tease. You know it's Mr. Montague. We've been working on the wedding preparations all week. Everything's ready. Why, with Clio all dressed . . . the two of you could be married today."

"*Daphne*," Clio said.

Her sister replied through clenched teeth, "Don't argue. It would be a prudent idea, after last night."

"What happened last night?" Piers asked.

Daphne waved a hand. "There was the worst sort of scene at a ball, but Clio was blameless. It was all Lord Rafe's fault."

Piers smiled a little. "The worst scenes are usually Rafe's fault."

Oh, yes. They were.

And Rafe felt another scene coming on now.

His brother had an arm around Clio. Like it belonged there. It was enough to make Rafe taste smoke and smell blood.

Step away from her, he willed. *She's not yours.*

"Piers, we need to talk," Clio said.

"Yes, I think we should. I'm beginning to suspect I never actually left the Continent, and this is all just one elaborate hallucination." Piers cleared his throat and brought out that classic Granville ring of authority. "Will someone tell me, in simple words, just what is going on?"

"I will." Phoebe meandered into the room, holding a book. "Clio's not going to marry you. She's going to live here in this castle and open a brewery."

"Thank you," Piers said. "Now I know I'm going mad."

"She's not yours," Rafe said.

"I beg your pardon?"

Rafe knew he was the one who'd be begging all the pardons. But it had to come out, and he couldn't wait. "You heard me. She's not yours anymore."

His brother's gaze narrowed to an icy beam of interrogation. "What did you do?"

"Only what she asked."

"You bastard. Did you touch her?"

"I—"

"Rafe, don't," Clio said, sounding frantic. "Please."

Her words were a stab to the heart.

Granted, it was a self-inflicted wound. He'd told her all week she should marry Piers. He'd repeated that same stupidity this morning. And now the man himself was back, setting all her insecurities to rest with a worldly air and a hero's mantle. And kisses.

Why would she ever choose Rafe?

If Rafe could choose to *be* any man in this room, he wouldn't choose Rafe.

Clio turned to Piers. "You must understand. Your brother's been so loyal to you. When I had doubts about the wedding, he tried to change my mind. He made every effort to convince me, said such lovely things on your behalf. That's not all he's done. He's managed Oakhaven in your absence. And wait until you see what marvelous care he's taken of . . ."

Her voice trailed off as she glanced about the room, ducking to peer under the furnishings.

"Oh, dear. Has anyone seen the dog?"

Chapter Twenty-five

*E*llingworth! Ellingworth, darling, are you here?"

Clio hurried up and down the garden paths, ducking to peer under every bench and shrub, and pausing at each corner to wipe the rain from her eyes. They'd searched the entire castle already. He had to be outside somewhere.

The mud puddles sucked at her heeled slippers, slowing her down. Eventually, she gave up on them, kicking her shoes off. Her stockings were already wet through.

Slippers clutched in one hand and skirts gathered in the other, she began to race down the row of neatly trimmed hedges and arbors. The longer they went without finding the bulldog, the more her anxiousness increased. Dogs were made to withstand some rain and chill. But a dog this old, already in poor health?

Poor Ellingworth.

Poor Rafe.

It would kill Rafe if something happened to that dog. He'd taken care of the beast so faithfully all these years. Those meticulous diets, all the special veterinary care . . .

But it wouldn't only be the wasted effort, or the disappointment of letting his brother down. Rafe loved that ugly, old dog. Clio knew he did.

And Clio loved Rafe.

She began to run faster. A thorny branch caught the puff of her sleeve, and she yanked free, ripping the fabric.

"Ellingworth! Ellingworth, where are you?"

She stumbled over a rock in the path, wrenching her ankle and nearly sprawling face-first into the mud. She caught herself on hands and knees instead.

"Damn."

She pushed to her feet, wiped her hands on the ruined ivory silk, and trudged on, pushing her panic aside. *Focus, Clio.* Fear wasn't helpful now. She began preparing a list of orders in her mind. The moment they located Ellingworth, she would send one of the drivers for the veterinarian. Direct the housekeeper to prepare hot water, warmed towels. Ask cook for a mince of beef, mixed with raw egg. Did dogs take beef tea? It was good for chilled people, after all.

They had to find that dog. They *would* find that dog.

As she crossed beneath an arbor, she pulled up and stopped. A flash of white caught her eye.

There. On the far side of the garden, low to the

ground. Beneath the bank of apricot-colored roses. Was that . . . ?

Letting her skirts fall into the mud, she swiped aside the rain-matted hair from her brow and blinked into the rain. Her labored breathing made it difficult to concentrate. She struggled to calm herself and look sharp.

"Oh, no."

There was Ellingworth. Huddled beneath a rosebush. Lying on his side.

Unmoving.

Please. Please, God. Don't let him be dead.

Dread gathered like a rain cloud as she rushed toward the bulldog. Ellingworth was on the opposite side of the rosebushes, so she had to race down the length of the aisle and around the other path to reach him.

"Ellingworth, darling. Hang on. I'm coming."

When she rounded the corner, she stopped short.

Rafe.

His dark green coat had blended in with the shrubs, and she hadn't been able to see him from the arbor. But he was there, crouched beside the unmoving bulldog, one of his big, knotty boxer's hands placed to the dog's side.

Rafe didn't raise his head. But Clio sensed he knew she was there.

She swallowed a lump in her throat. As she moved closer, all the urgency was gone from her steps. "Is he . . . ?"

She couldn't even ask the question.

He shook his head no.

Relief flooded her as she covered the remaining distance to Rafe's side. "Oh, thank goodness."

Now that she was closer, she could make out the slight rise and fall of the dog's breathing. Thank heavens.

But even though the dog was alive, all the vigor seemed to have gone out of Rafe. He was so quiet.

"Best not to leave him lying here," she said, trying to sound cheery. "Poor old dear. The ground's so wet and cold. Let's bundle him up and carry him in. Don't worry, we'll have him mended in a trice. I'll send for the veterinarian from the village. The one from London, if you like. There's some excellent beef loin Cook has from the butcher. It was meant for our dinner, but it will be perfect for Ellingworth. We'll mince it finer than—"

Rafe shook his head. "It's no use, Clio."

"Of course it is."

"He's not gone yet. But he's going."

No sooner had he spoken the words than the dog released a faint, wheezing breath.

"No," she protested. "No, he can't be dying."

"It won't be long now. This is the way with dogs." His voice was quiet and emotionless as he stroked the dog's ear. "Just how they are. They know when it's their time. So they slip away and find a quiet place to—"

His voice broke, and Clio's heart broke with it. She pressed a hand to her mouth to stifle her emotion, not wanting to distress dog or man. Nevertheless, her voice wavered as she reached to stroke Ellingworth's paw. "We're here, darling. We're here, just as long as you need us."

Rafe said, "You should go inside. I'll stay with him."

"I'm not leaving either of you."

After rubbing her hands together to warm them, she reached out and placed a gentle touch to Ellingworth's paw. "What a good boy you are. How proud you've done us."

Rafe stood just long enough to remove his coat. As he sat beside her, he moved to drape the coat over her shoulders. A thoughtful gesture, but Clio stayed it with a shake of her head.

She took the coat from his hands and draped it over the dog instead. "He needs it more than I do."

One by one, their party grew.

"Oh, dear." Daphne and Teddy made their way down the path. "Is he . . . ?"

"Soon," Clio said.

"Jesus and all the saints." Bruiser joined them, for once not bothering to hide his broad, common accent. "Not now. How can he do this to us now? Surely there's something to be done."

Phoebe found them next. "He's fourteen," she said, crouching next to Rafe. "The typical life expectancy of a bulldog is no more than twelve years. If you compared his existence to a human life, he would be nearing one hundred years old. So there's really no reason to be surprised. Or, for that matter, to grieve. He had a long life."

Rafe nodded. "I know."

"Just the same, I . . ." Phoebe threw her arms around him in an awkward hug. "I'm sorry about your dog."

Oh, dear. Now Clio was certainly going to cry.

Ellingworth's breathing grew rattling, raspy.

"He's going, isn't he?" Daphne buried her face in her husband's lapel. "I can't look."

"We're here, darling." Clio sniffed back her tears and stroked the dog's wrinkled head. "We're all here with you. Be at peace."

And then the rasping breaths ceased.

All was quiet.

"Here you all are." Piers joined the group. "Is that Ellingworth under the rosebush?"

No one knew what to say. Clio reached for Rafe's hand.

"I tried," Rafe said hoarsely. "I tried my best, but I should have known . . ."

If Piers heard him, he didn't reply. Instead, he knelt and wedged himself between Rafe and Clio, breaking them apart. He knelt at the dog's side and lifted the corner of the coat. "Good old Ellingworth. Did you miss me, old fellow?"

"It's no use," Rafe said. "He's gone."

"No, no. We played this game all the time. He's only hiding. Aren't you, pup?"

Beneath Rafe's coat . . . something moved.

The wheezing canine breaths that had dwindled to nothing . . . resumed again. They began to grow stronger.

The dog's head lifted. He emerged from under the coat and started to lick Piers's hand. His stumpy tail wagged to and fro.

"Cor," Bruiser said. "He's alive. The dog's alive."

Daphne pulled her head from her husband's lapel. "It's a miracle."

And perhaps it was. Ellingworth was like a pup again. Wagging his nonexistent tail, bounding up and sniffing at Piers's hand.

"That's a good boy," Piers chuckled as he scratched

the reviving bulldog behind the ears. "It's fine to see you again. It's been a few years."

"He's glad to see you," Clio said.

"It would seem he's happy I'm home." His eyes caught hers. "Are *you* happy I'm home?"

"I . . ."

Oh, goodness. Piers had always been handsome, worldly, authoritative . . . but whatever he'd been doing in the past eight years, it had taken those qualities and honed them to weapons. The absence of any vulnerabilities in his demeanor was what convinced Clio those weaknesses must be there somewhere beneath the suave control. When he'd kissed her, she'd felt it. He wasn't an arrogant young diplomat anymore—but a man who'd come through trials and confronted his mortality. A man who just might be ready to share those vulnerable parts of himself with another, trusted soul.

"Yes," she said. "I am so glad to see you, Piers. You returned at the perfect moment."

She was glad Piers had come home. She was glad he seemed to want her. She was glad he'd kissed her—just this once, and after all this time. Because now she knew, without any question, that the choices in her heart were *hers.*

"I have papers you need to see," Rafe said. Wearing a grim expression, he rose to his feet. "I'll dash up to get them, and then we'll talk."

"Rafe, wait."

Rafe shook out his arms as he walked back to the castle.

This was so like Piers. It wasn't enough that he'd been their father's favorite son. It wasn't enough that he'd returned from some sort of mysterious, dashing work in the service of the Crown and would probably be decorated with knighthoods and laurels. It wasn't enough that he had the most beautiful bride in all England ready to walk down the aisle with him this very day.

All that would have been impressive, to most men.

No, Piers had to take it one step further.

He brought dogs back from the dead.

It was too bloody much. So predictable.

Rafe entered the castle through a back entrance and began the spiraling journey upstairs.

But someone had followed him.

"Where are you going?" Clio's voice echoed up to him from the bottom of the stairwell.

"To get the dissolution papers. I'll speak with Piers. We'll have this settled today."

"Surely that isn't—"

He cut her off. "It's too late. Don't try to argue. We both know you could be carrying my babe even now. You said it last night. There's no going back."

"You . . ." She caught up to him in a patter of steps. "You think I've changed my mind?"

"I don't fault you." He resumed climbing. "Believe me, it's nothing new. Who wouldn't prefer him to me? My father certainly did. All our tutors and nursemaids adored him. Even the damned dog likes him better."

He heard her give a little laugh. "I thought I wasn't the dog!"

He reached the top of the stairs and turned into

the corridor. "I tried to warn you. I told you you'd regret chasing after me. I told you Piers cared for you—even if he didn't show it."

"It doesn't matter. None of it changes anything."

He flung open the door of her bedchamber. "Where are your things? Your maid already put them away." He strode toward her writing desk. "I imagine she'd put the papers in here."

"Good Lord, Rafe. It's like you're not even hearing me."

She dashed ahead of him, plunking herself on the top of the desk before he could search the drawers.

"Clio, move."

"No."

"Move, or I'll move you."

She caught him by the shirtfront. Her gaze snared his. "Remember your bout with Espinoza?"

What?

The question caught him completely off guard. Yes, he recalled his bout with Espinoza. He recalled every detail of each of his fights. But that was three years ago. What could it possibly have to do with anything?

"I know he nearly went down in the fourth," she said slowly, frowning at her lap in concentration. "But then he recovered. The two of you battled several more rounds. I can't recall quite how you finished him. Wasn't it a facer in the ninth round?"

"It was a blow to the kidneys. In the thirteenth. What of it?"

"Nothing of it." Her gaze came back to his. "I just needed you to calm down so we can talk."

Holy God. She understood him so well. He would

love, bleed, crawl, beg, and die for her—just for that alone. And she thought he would let her go?

The devil he would.

He'd snapped into focus now. Perhaps it was the talk of fighting. Or perhaps it was just her.

She was lovely. A beautiful bride, in her ivory silk. That subtle blush rising on her cheeks.

He braced his hands on the desk, on either side of her. "Downstairs. You looked so . . . I meant to . . . And then he was there. I've spent how many months wishing and waiting for my brother to come home. Hoping to make amends. And when he touched you, I wanted to punch him in the face."

"It's understandable if you're angry with your brother."

"That's the most irritating part. I can't even be angry with him." He made a fist and tapped on the desk. "Just look at him. It wasn't enough that he was a diplomat. He risked his life in service of the Crown. He's probably a goddamned hero. He apologized to *me*. He's always perfect. Always better than me, no matter how much I accomplish." He looked her in the eye. "But he did one thing wrong. He stayed away one day too many, and now it's too late. He can't have you."

"No. He can't. Because I don't *want* him. Rafe, you know I'm in love with you."

He didn't, really. He knew she kept saying so, but it was just so damned difficult to believe. Every time he tried to wrap his mind around it, his heart attempted to make a mad break from his chest.

It didn't make any sense.

She framed his face in her hands, forcing him to

look at her. "Yes, Piers is a good person. Yes, it appears he cared more for me than I believed. Yes, maybe he's even a hero. I'm relieved beyond anything to see him back in England safe, and I'm so glad he came home when he did. Now there won't be any doubt."

"There's no doubt. You're marrying me."

"Of course I am, you ridiculous man." She released a breath. "You say your brother is perfect? Well, apparently I prefer men with flaws. Maybe Piers is one of England's heroes. Rafe, you're mine." Her grip tightened on his shirt, and she pulled him closer. "Do you hear me? You're mine. I'm claiming you, and I won't ever let go."

God. He hadn't known until that moment, but this was what he'd been longing for all his life. Not to claim, but to be claimed. Irrevocably. To feel free to love and be loved, without the looming fear that a few impulsive words could end it all.

"If you want to keep prizefighting, I won't stand in your way. But you'll need a new name in the ring." She gave him a fierce, determined look. "You're Clio's Own now. The Devil himself could come for you, and he'd have to get through me."

It was too much. Too much. He wasn't sure his heart could take it.

"Do you hear me, Rafe? You're mine."

"You're mine." Clio said it again. Because it felt so good, and because his needing, stricken expression couldn't help but touch her heart. "My hero. My love. My future husband, hopefully."

"Your future husband. Definitely." His hands

captured her by the waist. His eyes darkened. "I'm yours, then. And you're mine, as well."

She nodded.

"Let me hear it," he whispered roughly. "Say the words. You're mine."

"I'm yours, Rafe. Always."

It happened so fast. His lips fell on hers, and his arms gathered her in a tight embrace. Their mouths melded in a kiss so fierce, so needing, not even a whisper could have come between them.

Clio ached for his touch. She wanted to feel him everywhere. His hand claimed her breast through her gown. It wasn't enough. She tugged at the restrictive silk, trying to coax it lower. She didn't have any patience for buttons today.

"Don't tear your gown." He slid his hand under the fabric, cupping one of her breasts. When his thumb grazed her peaked nipple, she sighed with pleasure.

"It's already ruined." She ripped away a garden-bedraggled strip of lace just to prove the point. "It doesn't matter. I only wanted to wear it for you."

Something changed in him when she said those words. A wildness took over.

He kissed her neck. Mouthed her breasts. His hands were everywhere at once. And still, she wanted more. At last, here was the intensity she'd been craving. Last night's patience gave way to pure, unfettered wanting, and she reveled in it.

His hands slid downward, hiking the layers and layers of sodden fabric to her waist. He pushed her knees wide and moved between her legs.

"I need you." His voice was dark. His fingers found and traced her most intimate places. "Here. Now."

"Yes."

He thrust a hand between them, working open the closures of his trousers.

She wrapped a leg over his hips, drawing him close. She moved her pelvis, grinding against him in ways that made them both moan.

"I . . ." He cursed. "I'm not certain I can be gentle."

"Then don't be gentle. Just be you."

Still, he hesitated.

"You won't hurt me," she lied.

Her intimate places were stretched and sore from last night, and she wasn't fool enough to think a hard tupping on the desk would make it better.

She wanted this anyway.

Yes, this. The sweet burn of him sliding into her. The exquisite weight of his strong, muscled body anchoring hers. The desire and possessive need in his eyes.

She wanted all of this.

He leaned her all the way back onto the desk, then hooked his arms under her legs, spreading her wide. Viewing the contrast between her pale, stockinged legs and his broad, tanned shoulders excited her.

He thrust deep. "Tell me when it's too much."

"It won't ever be too much." She gripped his arms.

"I love you." He nudged deeper. "I love you. Take that."

Her heart swelled.

With every movement, he pushed her spine against the unyielding mahogany. The firmness of the desk gave her nowhere to hide. She was at his mercy, and she couldn't get enough.

When her climax broke, she cried out. In pain, in

pleasure. She dug her fingernails into his neck. He growled in response, holding her still as he spent inside her.

Afterward, he held her so tenderly. Right against his pounding heart.

"I was so stupid this morning," he whispered. "If you want me to shuffle papers, I'll shuffle papers. If you wanted me to give up fighting, I'd do that. I'd do anything to keep you, Clio. I love you. I wish I had better ways to show it. All I have is this brash, reckless heart. But it's yours."

She looked up at him. "Really?"

"Really."

"Good. I hope your love for me will survive this."

She opened the top drawer of the desk, located the dissolution papers Rafe had signed—and cast them in the fire.

"Clio, no."

He lunged to save them, but he was too late. The papers flared and burned in the grate.

He speared his fingers through his hair. "Why did you do that?"

"Because I'm not going to let you be the villain today. I was stupid this morning, too. And when Piers came home, I realized this is happening so fast. We need a little time, each of us. You need to fight your battles. I need to fight my own. And we owe it to Piers to do this right.

"You are still brothers, despite everything. He needs someone to welcome him home, and it's not going to be me. If we married right away, you'd never be able to mend things with him. But if I break the news and we bide our time . . . Piers will overcome any disappointment he might feel. With any luck, he'll choose another bride."

"He's a man of fortune, rank, and privilege. He can take care of himself. I want to take care of you."

She touched his shoulders. "I know. But how could I claim to love you, then ask you to choose between me and your only brother? You needn't choose at all, if we wait."

"I can't ask you to wait. I know how you detest that word. You've waited eight years."

"I can last a few months more." She stroked his cheek. "It will be different now. This time, I know I'm worth waiting for."

He weaved his hands in her hair and held her close. "You're worth anything. You know that, don't you? I'd swallow nails. I'd walk through fire."

"Oh, that would be too easy. I'm asking you to do something far worse. Go spend time with your brother."

Chapter Twenty-six

"C lio! Clio!" Daphne accosted her in the corridor, breathless and flushed. She placed her hands on Clio's shoulders. "Did I just see Lord Granville *and* Lord Rafe mounted on their horses and riding away?"

Clio's heart pinched at the thought of Rafe leaving. But if he must go, at least he was leaving with his brother. "You probably did," she said. "Yes."

"Well, what are they about? Have they gone to fetch the license?"

"No, they've . . ." She shrugged as they entered the drawing room, joining Sir Teddy and Phoebe. "They've simply gone."

"Gone?" Daphne shook her head, laughing. "But what can you mean?"

Clio squared her shoulders and drew a deep breath. This seemed as good a time as any to announce it.

"I've broken the engagement," she said.

There. The words were out, and they hadn't even been that difficult to pronounce. If she'd managed to hold her own when informing Piers of her decision, she could certainly relay the news to her closest family.

"What?" Teddy's boot hit the floor. "You mean you let him off the hook?"

"I wouldn't phrase it that way, but—"

"That's not fair, dumpling." Her brother-in-law rose from his seat, visibly agitated. "He kept you dangling for eight years. Humiliated you. Squandered the best years of your life. Make the man come up to scratch."

"You're mistaken," Clio said, trying to keep an even temper. "I am the one who broke the engagement. It was my decision. I don't wish to marry him."

"You, breaking off with him?" Teddy chuckled. "It's a nice attempt to save face, but no one's going to believe that tale."

"It's not a *tale*. It's the truth."

But when had these two ever recognized the truth, from Clio's lips?

"Oh, Lord." Daphne sank onto the sofa and released a slight, deflated moan. "Oh, no."

Clio shook her head. For heaven's sake, *Piers* had accepted the news with less melodrama than this.

He'd taken it well, actually. He'd expressed a convincing degree of disappointment, but Clio could tell his pride was taking the deepest wound. His heart wasn't in danger. They were little more than strangers after all these years. She hoped in time they could be friends.

He was a good man. Just not the man for her.

"Can't you try to mend things?" her sister asked. "Perhaps it's not too late. Or . . . Or Teddy can ride after them and demand Lord Granville make good on his promises."

Clio shook her head. "It's over."

"It can't be over," Teddy said. "After all these years, we can't give up. You mustn't let him escape."

"*Escape?*" She laughed. "Should I be locking him in the dungeons?"

"Laugh all you like, but this is always your failing." Her sister clucked her tongue. "You let this drag on far too long, when you should have stood up for yourself years ago. You're too accommodating."

She thought on it. "You're right, Daphne. I am too accommodating."

"I'm so glad you see it."

"That's going to change," Clio said. "Today."

"Oh, yes. Let's go after him. We'll order the carriage this moment. *Teddy.*"

Her sister snapped her fingers, and her husband roused himself from the sofa. Together they hurried into the corridor.

Clio followed. But when they approached the entrance hall, she held back.

"It's your last chance to go first," she told her sister, smiling sweetly. "Once I marry Piers, I will take precedence."

Daphne smiled. "That's the spirit."

She waited until Daphne and Sir Teddy had walked through. And then she ducked into the nearby alcove, reached up with both arms, and pulled the lever.

With a groan and rattle of iron, the portcullis smashed shut.

"It's been lovely having you visit," Clio told her shocked sister and brother-in-law, waving her fingers through the barrier of the iron grate. "Please do come back at Christmas."

"What on earth are you doing, dumpling?" Teddy asked.

"Using my castle for its intended purpose. Protection. And kindly refrain from calling me dumpling. Rafe taught me how to punch, too."

Teddy blinked in alarm.

"First you're letting Lord Granville slip away, and now this?" Daphne asked. "Clio, have you gone raving mad?"

"Perhaps." She shrugged. "Daphne, you are my sister, and I love you. I know you mean well. But you can be astoundingly hurtful at times."

Clio had Phoebe's well-being to consider. She just couldn't be accommodating anymore. Teddy and Daphne were one of those things best taken in small amounts. Like ground cloves. Or smallpox.

"I know that once you leave, I shall miss you," Clio told her sister. "I'm looking forward to missing you."

"You can't do this!" Daphne rattled the gate. "You can't just boot us out."

"Actually, I can. I might still be a spinster. I might never be a lady, or even a wife. You might always be my social superior. But I am mistress of my own castle. On this property, I make the rules. And today, I'm feeling a bit medieval."

Clio waved good-bye to her shocked sister and brother-in-law through the iron grate. "Do have a safe journey. I hope you don't encounter much traffic on the bridge."

That done, she turned to Phoebe. "I don't suppose you're interested in helping me start a brewery?"

"I'm not sure what help I'd be." Phoebe fished a bit of string from her pocket. "But I won eighteen hundred pounds in the card room last night. I want to invest."

"The stewards tell me these fields could be put to better use." Rafe drew his mount to a halt on the southern border of Oakhaven. "How do you feel about barley?"

"I don't know that I possess strong feelings about barley."

"I don't know that you possess strong feelings at all."

Piers gathered his reins and set his jaw. "Actually, I do have a few. None of them especially charitable at the moment."

Rafe walked his gelding in a tense circle. They hadn't been back on Oakhaven land for ten minutes, and already they were back to their old, familiar boyhood conflicts. If Clio hadn't asked him to do this . . .

"Maybe we should have it out, the two of us," Rafe suggested. "Take off our coats, roll up our sleeves. Get it over with."

"I'm not going to fight you. It wouldn't be fair."

"I suppose you're right." Rafe puffed his chest. "I *was* heavyweight champion of England for four years."

"I know how to kill a man with a letter opener and make it look like an accident," his brother said coolly. "I meant it wouldn't be fair to you."

Rafe rolled his eyes. "You're so damned predictable. For as long as I could remember, I lived in your shadow. Always failing. Always envious. Fighting was the one thing I could do better than the perfect, upstanding Piers. But no. You had to go and one-up me on that score, too."

"Of course I did. You weren't the only one with envy."

"Why the devil would you envy me?"

"For a hundred reasons. You did as you pleased. Said what you liked. You had more fun. With considerably more girls. You had that roguish air they all like, and your hair does that thing."

"My hair does a thing?" Rafe made a face. "What thing?"

His brother declined to explain. "I took assignments I wouldn't have chosen otherwise. Dangerous work. Because even though you were a continent away and the truth of what I was doing must be kept secret from everyone, I couldn't help but feel I was still in competition with my little brother. As it turns out, we *were* in competition. In one way, at least. And there, it seems I lost."

So, it would seem he had gathered the truth about Clio. Rafe *had* won that round, hadn't he?

About damn time.

"I don't feel guilty about it," he said. "I'm far from perfect, but I am better at loving that woman than you could ever hope to be. I know her in ways you don't. I need her in ways you'd never understand.

And I'd fight to be with her, to my last breath." He took a deep breath to calm himself. "But she doesn't want us fighting. She wants us to be friends."

"Friends? I don't think we'll ever be friends," Piers said.

"You're right. It would be stupid to try."

Damn. Rafe was doing it again. Speaking words in reckless anger. Words he didn't mean.

He faced down that vague, ill-formed cloud of resentment that had been roaming through his chest ever since he left Twill Castle. It was an anger born of self-loathing and all that wasted time. If only he'd been man enough eight years ago, he could have offered to marry Clio first.

But that would have been a disaster. They would have married too young. He would have had no means of supporting her. Perhaps his father would have given him some kind of living, and Rafe surely would have failed in spectacular fashion. Clio would have been isolated, pregnant by the time she turned eighteen, still suffering under the dangerous strictures her mother had placed on her.

If he had any chance of making her happy, it was only because they'd been forced to wait. In that respect, perhaps he should be grateful to his father, and to Piers.

The time was only wasted if he didn't learn from it.

"I didn't mean what I said just now." Rafe faced his brother. "I'm sorry. We should try."

"To be friends? I don't see how—"

"Just hear me out. I'm no great speechmaker, but I do have things to say every once in a while. If my fighting career has taught me anything, it's that friends are easy to come by. True opponents—the rivals who force you to work harder, think faster, be better than you knew you could be—those are rare. If that's what we are to each other, why change it?"

His brother looked out over the fields. "Perhaps you're right. So we won't be friends. We'll leave it at 'resentfully affectionate lifelong adversaries.'"

Rafe shook his head. Whatever mysterious special duties his brother had been given, Piers was a diplomat at heart. No one else would reach for four lofty words where a simple, single one would do.

"We could call it that," Rafe said, mounting his horse. "*Or* we could just say 'brothers' to save time."

"Very well. Brothers it is."

Chapter Twenty-seven

*E*ight years, four months, and sixteen days after first accepting Lord Piers Brandon's proposal of marriage, Clio paid the man a visit at his new offices in the House of Lords.

"Why, Ellingworth." Upon entering, she greeted the ancient bulldog with a pat. "You're looking fit as a pup."

"Come in," Piers said. "Do have a seat."

Clio settled herself in an armchair and pulled a velvet pouch from her pocket. "This first. I don't want to risk forgetting it." She shook its glittering contents onto his desk blotter.

"I don't need the ring back," Piers said. "You should keep it."

"Keep it?"

Clio glanced at the gold-and-ruby band. And then she glanced at the dog.

"A magnanimous gesture, my lord. But one I couldn't accept."

He began to object.

"I insist." She warded him off with an open hand. "I really . . . truly . . . sincerely . . . could not possibly accept."

"Very well, then." With a shrug, he placed the ring in a locked drawer of his desk and withdrew a sheaf of papers. "I'm sorry I had to ask you to come all the way into London for this."

"It's no trouble. I know you're busy, and I had business in London anyway."

Clio had a look at his office. Papers piled high, volumes of law and parliamentary records stacked neatly for his review. He was throwing himself into his new role with typical Granville dedication and attention to detail. And the mantle of authority became him, she had to admit. Even with the stray thread of silver in his hair, he was more handsome than he'd ever been.

She wondered what sort of woman could possibly challenge his devotion to duty. She wondered what secrets he might tell that woman in the darkest hour of night. But those things weren't Clio's to find out. Not anymore.

They never truly had been.

"I'm not attempting to change your mind. But out of curiosity," he said, "was there something I might have done differently?"

She smiled. "Other than not leaving the country for eight years and never being honest about your purposes?"

"Right. Other than that."

Clio shook her head. "You could only be yourself. And I needed to grow into me. It's all for the best."

The actual signing of the papers was all very amicable.

When it was done, Piers sat back in his chair and regarded her. "So you had business in Town. Is it the brewery?"

She nodded. "We're on our way. The hopfields will go in next spring. Construction on the new oasts is beginning next month. I've just seen the plans from the architect."

She'd decided not to convert the old castle tower after all. The architect had declared the structure sound enough, but Clio just couldn't bring herself to destroy the neighborhood's favored trysting place. Not after she'd made a surveying trip there with the land agent and spied a remarkably fresh addition to the collection of lovers' graffiti.

RB+CW

Right on the wall. Carved in stone.

He must have known she'd see it. She wondered when he'd etched it there. It must have been sometime after Piers's return. It couldn't have been as soon as after their first kiss.

Or could it?

Waiting on Rafe was more difficult than waiting for Piers had ever been. She missed everything about him—his impatience, his gentleness, his strength, his touch, his scent. But these months had not been wasted time. To distract herself, she'd thrown herself into the work, accomplishing more in less time than anyone—including Clio—would have suspected. She hoped Rafe had done the same.

"How is your brother?"

She couldn't resist asking. She hoped the question tripped off her tongue sounding breezy and polite, and not at all imbued with a heart's worth of pent-up emotions.

"Fine," Piers answered. Then he added, "I think."

"You *think*?"

"I haven't seen him for a few weeks. He's been in training again."

"Oh. He has a bout scheduled, then?"

"It would seem so."

A prickle of anticipation ran up her spine. "Is it with Dubose? Is he fighting to regain his championship?"

"I don't know. But I just had a notice the other day . . ." He riffled through a stack of papers on his desk until he found the one he sought. "Ah. Here it is."

Then he held it out to her—a broadsheet, emblazoned with Rafe's likeness.

Lord, just seeing his picture felt like having his big, boxer's fist reach straight into her chest and wring her heart.

Her eyes skipped over the energetic prose of the broadsheet. "Rafe Brandon . . . the Devil's Own . . . the match of his life . . . behind the Crooked Rook in Queensridge . . . the hour of—"

Oh, heavens.

She waved the paper at Piers. "This is happening *today*, ten miles outside London. It's due to begin in just a few hours."

"Is it?"

"Yes," she said. "Why are you here? You're not going to watch him?"

"I . . . hadn't planned on it."

"But you *must*." Clio rose from her chair. "You have to be there."

Ever the proper gentleman, Piers stood when she did. "I don't see why . . ."

"You must go," she repeated firmly. "Piers, he sent this broadsheet to you for a reason. You're his only family. He wants you there." She saw his hat hanging on a hook on the wall, and she jammed it on his head, then grabbed him by the arm and pulled him from the chair. "We're going, the two of us."

"The two of us? Absolutely not. A prizefight is no place for a gentlewoman."

"Neither is a brewery or Parliament, I'm told—and yet I've visited both already this morning. Hurry. We'll make it just in time, but only if we leave now."

"Why are you so set on this?" he asked, frowning. "Why does my scoundrel brother's prizefight matter to you?"

The question hung in the air for a moment.

"Because I love him," she said, breaking the glassy silence with the only words that possessed sufficient blunt force. "And you should come with me because you love him, too."

"How long have you been in love with my brother?"

Piers asked the question while they were rattling down the Old Kent Road, somewhere near Gravesend. As if they were just continuing the conversation they'd paused two hours prior, in his office.

"Since always, I think." She folded her hands. "But I only realized it recently."

His reaction was predictably stoic.

She couldn't fathom how Piers could remain so calm in the face of her revelations. Much less in the face of this traffic. Good heavens, the snarl of carriages and carts waiting at the bridge would have given her brother-in-law an apoplexy.

Even Clio was drumming her fingers on the seat and tapping her toes in her slippers. The autumn day was heating to a simmer, and the warmth didn't improve her patience.

The coach lurched to a sudden halt.

"Why are we stopping? Is there a turnpike?"

"The road is clogged with carriages, all the way to the bend," Piers said, craning his neck. "We must be close."

Clio checked her timepiece. Almost noon.

There wasn't any time to waste.

She reached for the door latch. "Then I'll cover the rest of the distance on foot."

"Clio, wait."

She laughed as she pushed the door open and escaped the confines of the carriage. Of all the futile words to call after her.

Clio, wait.

She wasn't waiting one second longer.

Piers followed her as she raced along the side of the road, clambering over a stile to cut across a field. High, impertinent grasses tangled about her boots and grasped at the hem of her skirt.

When she reached the tavern, she could see the fight had drawn onlookers by the score. Perhaps by the hundreds. They were flocking like linnets toward the grassy meadow behind the inn.

She picked up her skirts and dashed the remaining distance, attempting to pick and weave her way through the crowd. "Excuse me, please. I beg your pardon. Please let me pass."

A man trod on her boot.

She made a fist and cocked it. *"Move."*

The last, inner ring of spectators gave way, and Clio emerged into the center clearing.

There he was.

Rafe.

Standing not thirty feet away. His back was to her, but she'd know those shoulders anywhere.

"Rafe!" She hastened across the meadow. "Rafe, wait!"

He turned, pausing in the act of fixing his cuff. He frowned at her. "Clio. You're early."

Early?

Perhaps she ought to have wondered why he seemed to be expecting her, but she was too busy feeling relieved that she wasn't too late. Evidently the fight wasn't due to start quite yet. He was dressed much too fine for boxing—wearing a blue tailcoat, freshly starched cravat, and a striped silk waistcoat.

And those tall, gleaming boots.

Dear heaven, he looked magnificent.

"What are you doing?" he asked, looking past her toward the road. "Where's my br—"

"I'm not . . ." She pressed a hand to her belly, breathless. "I'm not here to stop you."

"You're not?"

She shook her head. "I won't even watch if you don't want me to."

"You . . . won't."

She shook her head. "But I wanted you to know I'm here. Cheering for you. Believing in you. Most of all, I needed to show you this." She pulled a paper from her pocket and unfolded it, handing it to him. "Go on, have a look."

He peered at it.

"It's for the brewery," she explained. "I've just ordered seven hundred casks with that design. So you'd better win. I should hate to have to change them all now."

He read the inscription aloud. "Champion Pale Ale."

"You're going to beat him, Rafe. I know you will. You're the strongest and bravest man I know, and you have the most heart. You supported my dreams. I believe in yours. Go get your title back."

He was quiet as he stared at the paper.

For interminable moments.

"Could you . . ." She swallowed nervously. "Could you say something? Or do something? Anything, really. I feel quite alone right now."

He brushed aside a stray lock of her hair, and the sensation made her breathless all over again. She'd gone so long without his touch.

"You're not alone. You never will be." Folding the paper, he added, "I think Champion Pale Ale is a fine name indeed. It's only . . . we'll have to ask Jack Dubose to endorse it."

"No, no. *You'll* endorse it. You're going to beat Dubose today."

"That would be difficult, seeing as he's not here."

She didn't understand. "But I saw the broadsheet. It said, 'Witness Rafe Brandon meeting his most formidable opponent yet. The match of his life.' Who else could that be, but Dubose?"

That boyish grin tugged at his lips. "Who indeed?"

Clio was so confused. She stepped back and turned in a circle, for the first time taking a proper survey of the area. The space was wide and open, and she couldn't see Rafe's opponent anywhere. The onlookers appeared to be remarkably well-groomed for a prizefight, and . . .

Goodness. How odd. Was that her cousin Elinor? What on earth could she be doing at a prizefight?

"Where's the ring?" she asked, turning back to him. "There's no ring."

"Oh, there's a ring. I have it right here."

He reached into his breast pocket and pulled out a band of shining gold, balanced between his enormous thumb and forefinger.

A lump formed in Clio's throat as she stared at it. Three lovely, soft green emeralds surrounded by smaller diamonds.

"You said your favorite color is green. I hope that was one of the truths."

"This is for me?"

"It's all for you. The ring. The guests. The broadsheet. Sorry, but I thought you'd suffered through enough of these preparations already. And I didn't have the patience for proper invitations."

Her heart pounded in her chest as she began to understand him. "This isn't a prizefight at all. It's a wedding."

He nodded. "Ours, I hope."

Oh. Oh, this man.

The air went out of her. "I can't believe you did this."

"You did say you wouldn't mind a wedding in the middle of a field. Just so long as you loved the man you were marrying."

And she did love him. She loved him so much, it hurt to breathe.

She cast a glance at Piers, who'd only just caught up. "You *knew*," she accused him. "You knew the whole time. You truly are devious."

The man shrugged. "I did owe you a wedding, after all that."

"Believe me, you don't know the half of his deviousness," Rafe said. "We've been working on this for weeks now. He helped plan everything."

Piers said, "That's the duty of the best man."

The two shared a look of fraternal conspiracy. If Clio hadn't been so overjoyed to see them getting along as brothers, she would have tweaked their ears for torturing her this way.

"But what about prizefighting? The championship?"

"I'm not done with fighting," Rafe said. "But Bruiser's been negotiating with Dubose's second. We might decide we can make more money with an exhibition."

"An exhibition?"

"A series of them, more like. Champion versus champion. They'd be real fights, but legal ones. Conducted in proper arenas. With more rules and gloves, so it's less dangerous."

Clio liked the sound of this. "And would this series of exhibition fights need a sponsor? An up-and-coming brewery, perhaps?"

"It just might." He cocked his head, indicating the nearby inn. "Now, go on. Daphne and Phoebe are inside with your flowers and gown. The wedding breakfast is waiting, too. Bruiser planned it, so brace yourself for the worst. But I did personally arrange for the cake."

"What kind of cake?"

He leaned close and nuzzled her ear. "All the kinds of cake."

She couldn't help but laugh.

"Clio, you are the match of my life. You're the one who challenges me, who meets me blow for blow. Leaves me reeling and wanting more. You push me to be better. I want to spend the rest of my life doing the same for you." He took her hand and slid the ring on her finger. "Marry me. In a field. In front of all these people."

She looked at the ring on her finger, emeralds sparkling in the midday sun. Then she lifted her gaze to his, staring into those bold green eyes, full of fierce, unwavering love.

She put her hand in his. "What are we waiting for?"

Epilogue

Several months later

Could that be him?

From her perch in her sitting room at Twill Castle, Clio leaned close to the glass and stared hard through the window.

A cloud of churning dust appeared at the end of the drive, and as it neared the castle, the cloud transformed into a bay gelding with a dark, enigmatic rider.

It couldn't be anyone else.

As he pulled his mount to a halt in the drive, she louvered the windowpane and waved to him.

He raised a hand in greeting. "I'll just put up my horse."

Goodness, he'd been gone for three whole days, visiting taverns and inns to secure their custom. Did he really mean to keep her waiting a half hour more?

As he started to head for the stables, she called out to him. "For once, let the grooms do it? I have something for you upstairs."

"Well, then." He made a suggestive bow. "As my lady commands."

She bounced on her toes with impatience as his slow footfalls climbed the stairs.

"The room's this way," she called out. "Don't get lost. Follow the sound of my voice."

She was only teasing. After residing several months in the castle, Rafe *did* know his way to the bedchamber. In fact, since their honeymoon, they'd worn a deep path. She would need to replace the corridor carpet soon.

When he reached the doorway, he fell against the doorjamb, as though reeling from the sight of her.

A little smile crooked his lips as he looked her up and down. "Well, this is a fine welcome home."

"I have a surprise for you," she said, pulling him into the antechamber of their suite. "Three surprises, actually."

"My day gets even better."

She led him toward an elegant table for two, laid with the castle's finest china, silver, and crystal.

"Now for the surprises. Here's the first." She whisked away a cloth to reveal an oaken cask, ready to tap. "The first official brewing of Champion Pale Ale. Are you ready to taste it?"

"Hell, yes." His grin widened. "That's brilliant."

"Don't say that yet. It might be terrible. But at least I feel a bit more certain that the second surprise will be tasty." She removed a shining silver dome from its platter, revealing an iced toffee-nut cake. "What's a beer without cake?"

"In this house?" he asked. "A sorry excuse for a beer."

"Indeed."

"You said there was a third surprise," he said.

"There is. But it's best if it waits until we're done with these two."

Sitting down to the table, Clio cut them each a thick slice of cake. Rafe hammered the tap into the cask and pulled two glasses of ale.

"I'm nervous," she confessed, taking hers.

"The color is good." He held it up to the light. "Not cloudy."

There was only one way to judge. She gathered her bravery and lifted her glass. "To Champion Ale."

"To Champion Ale."

Their glasses clinked in a toast. Then they each took a cautious sip.

Followed by pensive silence.

"It's . . . not bad," he said, at length.

She laughed. "It's not grand yet, either. But it's only our first attempt. This needs to cellar a bit longer, and next time we'll tweak the recipe." She sipped the beer again. "Actually, the more I drink, the better it tastes."

"Funny how that works."

When she lifted her beer again, he reached out and stopped her from drinking.

"Wait," he said. "Are you certain it's healthy?"

She frowned into her glass. "It might not be the best ale in England—yet. But I'm fairly sure it's not poisonous."

"No. I mean, healthy for the . . . you know."

She blinked at him. "I truly don't."

"Don't play innocent. The third surprise, remember? I have a suspicion what it might be."

"Do you?"

"Come along, Clio. You've been acting mysterious for the past fortnight."

He rose from his chair and came around to her side of the table, kneeling at her side. His big hands encircled her waist, turning her to face him, and he stroked her cheek.

"I can see the change in you," he said. "You're blushing a new shade of pink. Baby pink."

Oh, goodness. He believed she was—

"Rafe . . ."

"Don't be worried," he said. "I know we said we'd try to wait a year or so, until the exhibitions were over and the brewery was on its feet. But I don't mind that it's happening sooner. In fact, I'm . . ." His green eyes locked with hers. "Clio, I'm so . . ."

He never finished that sentence. But he managed to get across his meaning when he claimed her mouth in a passionate kiss.

He was so happy. Deeply, truly happy.

So was she.

As their lips met, a languid sigh eased from her throat. He tasted of ale, and he smelled of that familiar blend of leather and wintergreen. She'd missed him so much, and he'd come home not a day too late—his scent had almost worn off the shirt she slept in at night. She stroked her fingers through his hair, drawing him closer still.

But much as she was enjoying her husband's attentions, Clio started to feel a bit guilty. There was another little someone in the room who was growing more and more anxious, the longer this interlude went on.

"I knew I'd noticed a change in you," he murmured. His tongue traced a curving path on her neck. "You even taste different. Sweeter."

She barely managed not to giggle. "Rafe."

He worried her earlobe with his teeth. "Mmm."

"I have to tell you something."

"You're with child. I know, love. I know."

"I . . ." She gasped with pleasure as his teeth caught her earlobe. "But I'm not. I'm not with child."

"What?" He head jerked up, and his brow clipped her chin. "You're not?"

"No." She smiled. "I'm with dog."

The look of sheer bewilderment on his face . . . Oh, it was priceless.

Taking pity on him, she rose from her chair and retrieved the basket she'd stashed beneath the bed.

When she lifted the woven lid, out tumbled a puppy.

A bulldog puppy, with a flat black nose and a coat like velvet pile.

"See?" she said. "He's your third surprise. The little fellow is nine weeks old today. Just weaned."

She placed the brown-and-white bundle of wrinkles in his arms.

He looked at it. "A dog."

"Yes."

"There's no baby."

"Not yet. Oh, and now you're disappointed." She put a hand to her temple. "I should never have tried to hide this from you."

"I'm not disappointed. Just . . ." The pup licked and nipped his thumb. "You pulled off a true surprise."

She smiled. "Good."

"Does he have a name?"

"Not yet."

He considered for a while, scratching the pup beneath the ear. "There's Champion, I suppose. But it feels a little obvious."

"I agree. One champion in the house is enough. The right name will come to us."

Within an hour, the pup had fallen asleep on one of Clio's emerald satin pillows. Rafe insisted he was going to find uses for all twenty of the dratted things, eventually.

They sat on the floor, backs propped against the wall, sipping ale and enjoying the bulldog's tiny snores.

Clio tilted her head. "I think we should call him Devil."

"Devil? *This?*" Chuckling, he rumpled the handful full of velvet wrinkles. "Why?"

"Because you're the Devil's Own. And it's clear already—that pup owns you, heart and soul."

He didn't even try to deny it. "Envious?"

"I don't mind sharing. You're so wonderfully big. There's enough of you to go around."

He wasn't only big in body, either—he had the largest, most loyal heart. She knew this man had enough love in him for a wife, a brother, a few sisters-in-law, friends, a puppy, too . . . and then some.

Clio squeezed his hand. "May I ask you something?"

"Anything."

"When you said you wouldn't mind a baby so soon, were you being sincere?"

Rafe set his ale aside and rose to his feet. Then, bending down, he gathered her in his arms, lifted her straight off the floor, and carried her toward the bed. "Let me show you how sincere."

Give in to your Impulses!

These unforgettable stories only take a second to buy and give you hours of reading pleasure!

Go to *www.AvonImpulse.com* and see what we have to offer.

Available wherever e-books are sold.

AVONIMPULSE

IMP 0811